PRAISE FOR
RON FAUST

"Faust's prose is as smooth and bright as a
sunlit mirror."
—*Publishers Weekly*

"Faust's style is laconic, his story engrossing, his
extraordinarily wide variety of characters
richly realized."
—Gregory Mcdonald, award-winning author of *Fletch*

"The kind of stunning writer you want to keep
recommending after you discover him."
—David Morrell, author of *Covenant of the Flame*

"Faust is a Homeric storyteller with an eye for the odd
character and a fine gift for Spartan dialogue."
—*Library Journal*

"Voluble villains, wise friends and fickle ones . . .
Faust writes well . . . charming and violent."
—*Los Angeles Times*

SEA OF BONES

RON FAUST

TURNER

Turner Publishing Company
424 Church Street • Suite 2240 • Nashville, Tennessee 37219
445 Park Avenue • 9th Floor • New York, New York 10022

www.turnerpublishing.com

SEA OF BONES

Cover design: Glen Edelstein
Book design: Glen Edelstein

Library of Congress Cataloging-in-Publication Data

Faust, Ron.
  Sea of bones / Ron Faust.
     pages cm.
  ISBN 978-1-62045-448-0 (pbk.)
  1. Florida--Fiction. 2. Paranormal fiction. I. Title.
PS3556.A98S48 2014
813'.54--dc23
                                              2013025187

Printed in the United States of America
14 15 16 17 18 19 0 9 8 7 6 5 4 3 2 1

For Jim Donovan

SEA OF BONES

PART I

Bones

ONE

This was the second day I had watched the beat-up cabin cruiser search a grid pattern over the area where I had deep-sixed Raven Ahriman's corpse.

I had a good view from the tower of Martina's light-house. The inside platform was forty feet above the reef and an additional five or six feet above the bay waters. From that height I could look out over the bay, above the breakwater, and beyond to the undulating blue Gulf.

I heard a hiss and a soft despairing whimper—Martina, forty feet below in her little studio at the base of the spiral stairway, had fumbled a line, made a false brush stroke, smeared a color. The conical tower amplified her kittenish sounds into a sort of ghostly anguish.

The cabin cruiser had appeared a little before noon on Saturday and searched until dusk. It had returned this morning. I recognized the boat. *Catcher* was thirty-six feet long, old, and poorly maintained: It needed paint, varnish, bronze polish, rust remover, and an engine overhaul—oily smoke emerged from the engine compartment and exhausts. The boat was owned by the Mackey brothers and docked at a marina south of Bell

Harbor. Earl and Kyle Mackey were roughnecks who hustled a chancy living from the sea. They chartered the boat out for diving, deep-sea or line fishing, beer parties, anything that brought in an honest or semihonest dollar. The brothers were known locally as more rascals than crooks; that is, it was understood that they took under-sized lobsters, poached other men's lobster and crab traps, and disobeyed game laws, and if they should dis-cover a jettisoned bale of marijuana floating at sea they wouldn't turn it over to the police. I easily recognized the brothers; they were big, bearded, shaggy-haired men suntanned to a color Martina would describe as burnt umber. I was unable to make a sure identification of the third man. My binoculars were powerful, but the cabin cruiser was never less than two miles offshore.

"What?" Martina said.

"What?" I said.

"Dan?"

I leaned over the railing and looked down. Martina was seated at her drawing board. She wore a black smock, and her face appeared to buoyantly float through a bright cone of light.

"What did you say?" she asked.

"Nothing."

"You said something."

"No."

"Oh. I thought . . ." She leaned over the drawing board.

Poor Martina was hearing voices now. She sweated over her cartoon panels as Michelangelo must have agonized over the Sistine Chapel or Van Gogh over his wheat fields.

The cabin cruiser made a tight turn and took a new line on the north-south grid. I supposed they were trailing an underwater camera. Mostly they just crisscrossed a big patch of water a couple miles out, but three times today they had anchored and one of the brothers had put on diving gear and gone down. It was over a hundred feet deep out there. Bad light, silty bottom, vagrant currents.

"Baby?" Marty called.

"Yes?"

"What the devil have you been doing up there for most of two days?"

"Why?"

"It makes me nervous to have someone lurking overhead."

"I'm thinking," I said.

"Why don't you go into the house to think? Think about the bar exams. You came out here to study, so then study instead of lurking. Barefoot. Barefoot lurking."

Of course Ahriman's flesh had long since been picked clean by fish and crabs in the seven months that had elapsed. He was just bones now, skull here, jawbone over there, pelvic girdle, femurs and fibulas and ribs and scattered vertebrae, all now colonized by various organisms.

I said, "'. . . Of his bones are coral made; Those are pearls that were his eyes; Nothing of him that doth fade, But doth suffer a sea-change Into something new and strange . . .'"

"What?" Martina asked.

"I didn't say anything."

"You did so. You were reciting verses."

"No, Martina. Steady, now."

She was quiet as she determined whether she was annoyed or amused, and then finally she laughed.

Among the scattered bones you'd see an anchor and length of chain, frayed rope, rags, and an aluminum spear shaft. Peter Falconer was out there somewhere, too, dispersed ashes and bone grit, spiritual traces as well if you believed in that sort of thing. Falconer and Ahriman, victim and victimizer now sharing the same dismal accommodations.

Catcher, at the extreme of its northward run, turned and commenced cruising south. She was a dirty, smoking, disreputable boat, but originally expensive, very well made, and she rode the swells with a proud grace. Sunset was an hour away. They would be coming in soon.

I hung the binoculars around my neck and went down the twisting iron stairway to the circular room below, Marty's cluttered studio.

"The barefoot lurker descends," she said.

Martina was working on a Sunday color cartoon panel. I saw Ollie Alligator, Gilbert Possum, Buddy Hare, and the rest of the droll creatures who populated Martina's Edenic marsh and woodland country (deer and cougars and kites and mice and rattlesnakes and raccoons), natural enemies in real life but here united against the Progress People. The PPs were human: land developers, polluters, water thieves, dumpers of toxic waste. In her present series all of the animals, birds, and reptiles were gathering to thwart a developer who proposed to drain a marsh and level a wood in order to construct a gated golf course community named Parvenu Pointe Estates.

"What do you think?" she asked.

"I like it. It has a certain . . . *je ne sais quoi.*"

She smiled. The tip of her tongue was blue and scarlet from absentmindedly licking brush tips. It was a childhood habit that she claimed she could not break. The gooseneck lamp attached to the drawing board silvered her dark hair.

"The raccoon?" she asked.

"The apotheosis of raccoonhood."

Martina had been influenced by the old Walt Kelly comic strip featuring Pogo and other furred and feathered creatures of the Okefenokee Swamp. Influenced but not overwhelmed: She had her own viewpoint and approach, and a highly individual style that caused rude people to suggest she give up silly cartooning and turn to the fine arts.

"Marty," I said. "Don't you think your strip is becoming too overtly political?"

"What's political about putting in a word—and pictures—in favor of the natural world?"

"If you don't know . . ."

"Oh, I know."

"You've been losing an average of two newspapers a month lately."

"I have eighty-six left."

"And you ought to hire an assistant. Here it is the weekend and you're working. You're always working."

"Something you might try to emulate. I don't want or need an assistant. Go away."

I went through a doorway and down the arched masonry tunnel, through another door, and into the blockhouse. This was Martina's home, comfortable enough except for the lack of good outdoor light—there were no ordinary windows, just rows of bronze-rimmed portholes set into the east and west walls. Aside from the enclosed bathroom, it was one fairly big space partitioned by the kitchen counter and tall, painted (by Martina) bamboo screens. My books and papers were spread out on the all-purpose table. They piteously called out to me: *Come; work; duty.*

I scorned their whining appeal, got a can of beer from the refrigerator, went through the heavy front door and outside into steeply angled sunlight. There were a few puffball clouds, a luminous sky the color of a gas flame, and a sun beginning to turn orange as it descended toward the horizon.

The reef was a thick slab of rock maybe eighty yards long and fifty wide, with tumbled piles of quarried blocks at the north and south ends. Late in the nineteenth century the reef and lighthouse had lain outside the small natural harbor; since then, dredging and landfill had extended the promontories, and construction of a large breakwater had isolated the structure inside the bay. The marine light had long ago been removed. Martina had bought the property at a government auction. Bought the lighthouse and bought into years of complicated litigation.

I walked south, wary of ambush by Martina's ill-mannered dog. Cerberus was a mutt composed of diverse body parts: head of this breed, limbs of that, chest of something else. He liked to launch his one hundred and twenty pounds at my back. Then he grinned and slavered and licked my hand.

A powerful tide was beginning to stream out through

the opening in the breakwater. This was a spring tide, when the sun, a new or full moon, and the earth are roughly aligned. Only a very strong swimmer would be able to fight this tidal rip.

I walked to the extreme southern tip of the reef and sat on a rectangular stone block the size of a diesel truck engine. It was possibly the same block that Raven Ahriman had sat on during the morning I'd killed him.

Cerberus, without the usual preliminary mugging, picked his way among the stone blocks and lay down at my feet. He placed his ugly head on his paws and rolled his eyes so that he might gauge my mood.

"Bad dog," I said. "Evil beast. Hellhound."

His tail twitched, and then he yawned, snapping his jaws shut with the finality of a guillotine blade. Martina had named him after the dragon-tailed, three-headed dog that guarded the gates of Hades. He had not so long ago saved my life. It hadn't been intentional.

I got a solitary cigarette and a single wooden match from my breast pocket. At Martina's urging, I had mostly quit smoking six weeks before. I found that I was able to regard myself as a nonsmoker so long as Martina didn't catch me.

You need dirty chemical clouds for a spectacular sunset, serious air pollution. This one was mediocre, a few flamingo pinks, a bloated sun. The channel into Bell Harbor—sixty yards off my position on the reef—was marked by buoys that automatically lighted at dusk, and they came on just as *Catcher* appeared inside the breakwater. She had to muscle her way against the ebbing tide. Her running lights were on and she still flew her diver-down flag.

One Mackey brother, Kyle, sat at the controls on the flying bridge; Earl, I supposed, was below in the cabin. Charles Sinclair, the third man, sat in one of the rear fishing chairs. He held a tall frosted glass in one hand and a cheroot in the other. He wore white duck trousers, a teal-and-white horizontally striped T-shirt, a neck scarf, and the kind of long-billed cap favored by deep-sea fishermen. Charles was a playful guy, and he liked to dress up or dress down to suit the occasion.

He smiled when he saw me. He smiled boyishly, raised his glass in a private toast, drank, and then yelled something that I could not understand above the engine noise.

I cupped a palm to my ear.

He nodded, flicked his cheroot over the side, drained his glass and tossed that overboard too, then lifted an object from his lap and held it aloft.

I raised my binoculars. It was a human skull. The jaw was missing. Charles inserted his hand into the cranium from below. A big skull, white bone and round black eye sockets, a chinless yokel grin. Charles shouted.

I shook my head.

He nodded. Okay, dumb show. His lips moved. He began talking to the skull, which he turned, cocked, so that it appeared to be listening. Ventriloquist and dummy. Now it was the skull that was supposedly speaking. Charles seemed surprised, asked a question, listened, then formed his mouth into an exaggerated circle of shock and maybe moral outrage.

The cabin cruiser was passing up the channel toward town. Charles smiled and waved.

I got up and, with the dog, walked back to the lighthouse. Charles had been Raven Ahriman's one-time

cellmate, criminal partner, and jester, and a formidable
thief and extortionist in his own right.

It was full night when Martina, tired and tousled,
daubed with paint, emerged from the tunnel. In her over-
sized smock she looked like a girl who has awakened
groggy and irritable after a nap.

"What are you cooking?" she asked.

"Marinara sauce. We're having spaghetti with
marinara sauce, salad, and one of your bottles of
bargain-bin wine." I looked at the label, which illustrated a vineyard and an adobe mission church, with
furrowed brown mountains rising in the background.
"An Arizona merlot, vintage—let me see—Thursday."

She smiled and went off to the shower.

I cleared the books and papers off the table. My
examinations for admission to the Florida bar were
scheduled for late July, just two months from now. I was
a recent graduate of a night law school in a dubiously
credited community college, and most of my friends
predicted that I would fail the examinations on my first
try. Conversely, a few non-friends, chiefly lawyers in the
SA's office, hoped that I might pass so that they could
defeat me in court.

After dinner we carried deck chairs out onto the
reef. The dog, tired and sore-pawed from chasing imaginary beasts all day, slumped at Martina's feet with a
self-pitying moan. The tide was still going out. It was
a relatively cool and dry night for Florida in late May,
and the moon-washed sky vibrated with stars. Many
of those apparently solo stars, the astronomers told us,
were actually distant galaxies, great spiraling systems
which contained fifty billion or more stars. Stars,

comets, planets, maybe other worlds. I looked for the Big Dipper, found it, and followed the bowl to Polaris. And there was a constellation of lights behind us, too—Bell Harbor, the sodium vapor lamps that lined the bayside esplanade, traffic lights, house lights, auto lights, and neons that bled improbable colors into the dark.

"All right," Martina said. "What's troubling you?"

"What makes you think I'm troubled?"

"I know you, buddy."

"I'm serene," I said. "Complacent, even."

"You've been fine the last few months, Dan. And now this brooding again. Why won't you ever confide in me?"

I had never found the courage to tell Martina about the day I had killed Raven Ahriman here on the reef (while she slept in the house), and disposed of his body at sea.

"I received notice of another lawsuit last week," she said, as if demonstrating how one confides bad news.

"The town?" I asked. Bell Harbor's mayor, town council, and legal counsel wanted to seize Martina's property under the law of eminent domain. The city intended to take over the lighthouse as a tourist attraction and symbol of the community.

She said, "You remember when that boat crashed into the reef in February. The owner is suing me, saying I maintain a navigational hazard."

"The boaters were drunk, going too fast, and they didn't follow the damned buoys. The reef was properly lighted."

"Even so, they're suing. And my insurance company claims that I'm not covered."

"What does your lawyer say?"

"He says 'settle.' I say I'm going to hire a new lawyer. Who do you recommend?"

"Why don't you talk to Levi Samuelson?"

"The old judge? He's years past it, isn't he?"

"Not at all."

"But he's a criminal defense lawyer. I need a civil lawyer."

"Levi heard plenty of civil cases when he was serving on the bench. See him tomorrow morning. Just walk in; he usually isn't very busy."

"Not busy? That can't be good."

"Just see him, Marty."

We sat quietly for a time, sipping the last of the acidic Arizona merlot.

"I ran into a friend of yours at the market Friday," Martina said. "Rather, he ran into me. I mean, his shopping cart ran into mine. We got to talking."

"Who was he?"

"His name was Charles Sinclair."

"Good old Charlie," I said.

"He claimed he recognized me, though I don't recall ever meeting him."

"What did he have to say?"

"Oh, he said you two had some exciting adventures together. He told me some funny stories."

"No kidding."

"He wants to take us out to dinner Wednesday night."

"What did you say about that?"

"I'm not sure, but I think I accepted. He's a very charming and witty man, isn't he? I liked him."

"Well, Christ," I said. "Imagine that. Good old Charlie."

TWO

"Them shoes is a disgrace."

"Undisgrace them."

Augustine Piñero (most of his customers referred to him as "Piñata") had been a jockey until he grew out of the job. He then became a boxer, a slow bantamweight, not a good thing to be, as the scar tissue around his eyes and his cartilage-free nose attested. His shoe-shine stand was on the ground floor of the Dunwoody Building. He shined shoes, gave horse-race tips with the expectation of being tipped back if his choice won, and, every now and then, unsolicited, he told your fortune. Tom Petrie called him the "addled, pint-sized oracle." His oracular pronouncements were often cryptic, paradoxical, possessing only the meaning your imagination could provide.

"Had a dream, boss," Piñata said on Monday morning while he buffed my disgraceful shoes.

It was a form of extortionate charity; I added a five-dollar bill to his usual fee and tip.

He glanced around, alert for spies who might want to steal my destiny, and whispered: "Both the swan and the swan's reflection are illusions."

"Where do you get this stuff, Augie?"

"I told you, boss. I get these dreams."

I thought about it while riding an elevator up to the fourth floor: *Both the swan and the swan's reflection are illusions.* Maybe Piñata was a sort of idiot savant whose inner voice, in dreams, spoke grammatical, meaningless sentences in an affected accent. Bill Buckley's voice.

Candace was at her usual station behind the front desk. She was tweezing out eyebrow hairs when I came through the door, and she continued attending to that task.

I said, "Both the swan and the swan's reflection are illusions."

"Okay," she said. She cocked the mirror, searching for more renegade hairs.

"Is Mr. Samuelson in his office?" I asked.

"Maybe, if he came to work before me this morning. If not, not."

"I heard you've become engaged, Candace."

She put aside her mirror and tweezers. "God, it was so romantic. Evan proposed during a candlelight dinner." She held up her left hand so that I could admire the diamond for which Evan had mortgaged his future. "The ring was inside the chocolate mousse. Imagine my surprise."

"I can imagine it. Well, I hope you'll be very happy."

"I'm already very happy," she said. "Oh, Mr. Shaw, I'm literally walking on the proverbial air."

There were two offices at the rear of the room; mine, on the left, was furnished with yard-sale and fire-sale and flood-sale bargains. On humid days I believed that I could smell soot and seaweed.

A six-inch-high stack of papers lay on my desk, paralegal work I was doing for a coastal chain of banks: paperwork for liens, foreclosures, automobile repossessions. It was dreary work. I would turn it over to the bank's lawyers, who would then turn it over to the bank along with a bill for five times more than what I was being paid.

I sat down at the desk and dialed the Petrie law offices up on the top floor. The firm had recently installed a new voice mail system that weeded out all but the most desperate callers. I digitally punched out answers to impertinent recorded questions, listened to synthesizer music, was disconnected, and started again. Finally I reached Petrie's secretary.

"He's in a meeting," she said.

"Have him call me." I gave my name.

"What is the nature of your business?"

"Tell him that Charles is back in town, he's been trolling the waters off the lighthouse, and he seems to have found the bird."

She hesitated. Clearly this was not a conventional message. Indicted felons were more lucid. "What," she asked, "is the exact nature of your business?"

I hung up.

Tom Petrie was a first-rate criminal defense lawyer, a champion fencer, an aviator, a sensualist, a devious political operator, and a snob despite his origins, which he himself facetiously described as "seventh-generation inbred hookworm-infested redneck from the south-central Florida swamp and palmetto wastelands." He had commenced climbing early and, in his early forties, was still climbing.

I knocked on the door separating my office from Levi's.

"In," he called.

The old man was standing against the far wall like a spy waiting to be shot.

"No blindfold, Judge?" I asked him.

He lifted a pencil to the crown of his head and drew a line on the wall, stepped away, unspooled a ribbon of tape from a chrome dispenser, then measured the wall line to the floor.

"Ah," he said, reeling in the tape. "Seventy-seven inches. I thought so. I've lost two inches, Daniel, since my college days. Only six five now, alas. I've shrunk two inches since I played basketball."

"With the Spartans," I said.

"The Wolverines. I played center at six seven. That seemed tall back then, but according to today's standards we were a team of dwarves."

I nodded. "Both the swan and the swan's reflection are illusions."

He narrowed his eyes, thought. "Lao-tze?"

"Piñata."

The judge was wearing one of his eighties three-piece Savile Row suits, this one a pin-striped wool worsted, a shirt also tailored in London, with a rep tie, and hand-lasted brogues that had probably been resoled two or three times. Augustine would never get a chance to lay a dirty rag on those shoes. His office was cluttered with the sort of dark, heavy furniture that you saw in English TV dramas recreating the last years of the nineteenth century—Victorian chic.

"I just popped in to tell you that Martina will be

coming to see you this morning. She's going to switch counsel. There's a lot of litigation over the lighthouse."

"My lord," he said. "A client."

"What are you working on now, Judge?"

"I'm writing an appeal asking that the Revolutionary Council overturn the death sentence of King Louis the Sixteenth. In French. My French isn't very good, I'm afraid."

"Tough case," I said.

The old judge had not been very busy since coming out of retirement, passing the Florida bar, and setting up his practice. He spent most of his time in the fantasy defense of those convicted in famous old cases: Nicola Sacco and Bartolomeo Vanzetti, Captain Dreyfus, the Rosenbergs, and Bruno Hauptmann, the kidnapper of the Lindbergh baby.

"Well," I said, "put the king's appeal aside for now. Marty will keep you busy."

"I'm pleased, my boy. Thank you for the reference."

"Remember, with Martina, you're tough, aggressive, and uncompromising."

He smiled. "I am, you know, when acting as advocate. Though not many around here believe that."

"That's because you're a gentleman, Judge. And people don't understand that a gentleman can be a mean son of a bitch."

Levi smiled, pleased by my suggesting that he could be a mean son of a bitch. He started to speak, halted, cocked his head, and listened to the faint chiming that issued from his clothes. He patted his pockets, found the watch in a vest pocket, removed it, and looked at the dial.

"Time for my pills," he said.

* * *

Tom Petrie was shuffling through the stack of papers on my desk when I returned to the office.

"Look at this," he said. "Talk about boilerplate. You might as well work on an assembly line."

"It puts food on the table."

"Sure it does. Roots and bones, Dumpster cabbages." He leaned back in the swivel chair, linked his hands behind his head, and gazed at me. "Been chatting about the good old days with the faux Jew?"

The judge—originally Arnold Elsworth Crowcroft, from Grosse Pointe, Michigan—had changed his name soon after serving in the Korean War. One Private Levi Samuelson, a reluctant draftee, had lost his own life while saving the judge's during a battle with Chinese infantry south of Pyongyang. In a quixotic gesture, after his discharge, Captain Arnold Crowcroft had changed his name to Levi Samuelson and assumed financial responsibility for the dead man's mother and sister. He had changed his name but not his religion.

"The judge," I said, "is trying to save King Louis the Sixteenth from the guillotine."

"The judge has a gift for picking big-time losers."

"The game keeps his mind ticking over."

"Does it?"

"Everyone underestimates the man. He served for years on a Michigan appellate court, as you know."

"Which only proves that he had important political and social connections."

No one had ever heard Tom Petrie express approval

of a judge or prosecutor. They were the enemy. They were the conspirators who fought to execute or imprison his clients.

At first meeting, Tom seemed an ordinary guy, just another mid-level businessman or professional, though less amiable, more cynical than most. He affected a languor which failed to conceal his intelligence and energy. His gaze was cool, his smile conditional, and he spoke with ironic inflections that left an afterburn in your psyche. But he could be charming. He charmed juries, anyway, and women, and there were men who liked him and were fiercely loyal.

"Charles?" he said.

I told him about my observation of the cabin cruiser over the weekend, and Charles's ventriloquist act with a skull that might or might not be Raven Ahriman's.

"Pal, you told me that the bird was down and would stay down."

"I know."

"Someone saw you kill him."

"I doubt that. You remember what that morning was like; we were on the fringe of a goddamned hurricane."

"Did you ever tell Martina about it?"

"No. I told no one. Did you?"

"Of course not."

"Did you tell Leroy?"

"Only that Ahriman was dead and gone."

"Well, Raven's dead, all right, but maybe not altogether gone."

Petrie got up and strolled around the office, looking at the furniture, the worn carpet, the cheap prints hanging on the walls.

"How can people live like this?" he asked.

"I don't live here, Tom."

He nodded, smiling a little, pleased that he had needled me into a response.

"Let's go for a ride," he said.

"To where?"

"We'll go look at some polo ponies."

"You're going to buy polo ponies?"

"I might," he said, meaning he had no such intention.

"Just what is this about?"

"This is about opportunity. Opportunity has come knocking at your burrow. Money, lots of money, travel to exotic foreign climes, association with an elite pack of scoundrels, thugs, and cutpurses, and maybe—who knows, kid?—maybe romance."

"Sounds okay, but I've got to finish all of these legal documents by three."

He sat down behind my desk. "I'll have one of my paralegals take this petty crap off your hands." He punched out his office number on the phone, listened, punched another digit, listened again, and he had just started to speak when the line went dead.

"Jesus," Petrie said. "I can't get through to my own office."

I said, "Both the swan and the swans reflection are illusions."

"Confucius," he said quickly and with his usual certainty.

"Write a note to your paralegal. We'll have Candace run the papers upstairs."

"Can your Candace find the top floor?"

"Sure. She's engaged to one of your lawyers."

"No. Not so. This is cruel. Don't say that. Which lawyer?"

"Evan Hughes."

"I'll fire the half-wit. They can honeymoon in a shelter for the homeless."

On the elevator, he said, "Buddha. It was the Buddha who said that about the swans."

THREE

Petrie had the convertible top down on his Porsche Boxster. We inhaled car exhaust fumes during the ride east through the varied neighborhoods of Bell Harbor, ate diesel smoke in the traffic jam along the tacky commercial strip on Highway 41, continued east, and crossed the Interstate into the scrublands; then, Petrie angled off on a twisty back road where he could play Grand Prix champion. He double-clutched while gearing up and down, used both lanes of the road on his entry into the tight curves, and managed to drive never less than twice the posted speed limit. I smelled hot oil, hot clutch plates, and hot brakes, but the Porsche compensated for Tom's recklessness, forgave him his driving sins.

We entered a sandy flat back country of dusty oaks and palmettos, farm and pastureland, unpainted migrant worker shacks, patches of marsh, and muddy irrigation canals. Herons and cranes stood in the shallow water or on the banks. They looked, Petrie said, like herons and cranes trying to look like lawn ornaments that looked like herons and cranes.

We passed through a crossroads hamlet of half a

dozen frame buildings, and then Petrie turned off on a lane surfaced with crushed seashells. We passed through a giant wood arch in the shape of a horseshoe, and ahead I could see big oaks shawled with Spanish moss, white board fences, and an iron-framed windmill. Horses, trailed by cattle egrets, grazed over spring green pastures.

The yard was a big dirt quadrangle lined around by stables, a barn, a tractor shed, a big frame house, and a gated white wood fence with a sign that directed riders to the bridle paths and show rings. Petrie parked next to a water tank, beneath the creaking windmill. It was hot and quiet away from the sea. Insects out in the brush ticked and whirred and strummed. Overhead, a few vultures with ragged-looking wings carved ellipses into the pastel blue sky. They were ugly black birds that soared like angels. We were only twenty-five miles from Bell Harbor, but it seemed much farther; it was like another country.

"Tell me more about opportunity," I said.

"Opportunity," Petrie replied, "can come disguised as a grand dame or a poxy slut."

"And which is this?"

"I'm not sure. Poxy grand dame, maybe."

The windmill pumped water into a rusty stock tank that leaked from its welded seams. The water was scummed with algae and wriggled with mosquito larvae. There would be a plague of mosquitos here when that generation matured. Four tables were spaced out on the veranda, and a sign above the door read:

PRIVATE
Hunt Club Members Only!

"Do they really hunt foxes out here?" I asked.

"So I've heard."

"And play polo?"

"We'll find out."

I had been only vaguely aware that this place existed. It was sometimes referred to in the society columns or magazine sections of the newspapers. The horsey crowd from Bell Harbor and other coastal cities did what they did in these several hundred acres. I tried to imagine the sounds of bugles and horns, picture riders and their mounts leaping fences, leaping irrigation ditches filled with alligators, dashing through palmetto wastelands with cries of "Tallyho!" and "Hark, the fox!"

A sinewy old black man pushed a wheelbarrow out of one of the stables. He was shirtless, and wore a baseball cap and bib overalls with the pant legs stuffed into knee-high rubber boots. He halted, lowered the barrow, and looked across the yard at us.

Petrie and I got out of the car. The man watched us approach. His posture, the way he held his head, indicated suspicion and perhaps a weary patience: two white men in suits, arriving in an expensive foreign car, and now advancing in confident strides across the dusty yard. He straightened, lifted his chin, let us know that he was a man who would preserve his dignity.

"Good morning," Petrie said.

"Morning."

"Is Walt Bailey around the premises?"

"Gone to the bank. Be back by noon, he say."

The barrow was filled with a mix of straw and horse manure acrawl with sluggish, iridescent flies.

"My name is Thomas Petrie. This is Mr. Daniel Shaw."

"Josh," the man said.

"Do you mind if we look around, Josh?"

"Look around where?"

"I'd like to see the polo ponies."

"Polo ponies," the man repeated, smiling a little.

"And ask you a few questions." Petrie removed a business card from his wallet, wrapped a twenty-dollar bill around it, and gave it to the old man.

Josh returned the twenty without comment, rubbed his fingertips over the raised lettering on the card, then nodded as if an old suspicion had just been confirmed. "Embossed," he said. "Gilt, too, I believe. Thomas Petrie, LL.M."

Petrie ignored this little satire. He stuck the rejected twenty in a pocket. "Just a few questions, if you don't mind."

"Sorry. I ain't allowed to gossip."

"I'm not asking you to gossip."

"I can't talk about the club members or guests. You'd best wait for Mr. Bailey. You'll find your polo ponies over there. They still in they stalls." He pointed across the yard to another stable. That building was two stories high, with a loft above and, on the roof, a dovecote and a bronze wind vane in the shape of a rearing horse.

We were halfway across the yard when Josh called out. "Mr. Petrie? You don't remember me?"

Tom turned, stared back at the old man for a while, then shook his head. "Sorry."

"Tha's all right. Was a long time ago."

We went through a door into a cluttered room that smelled of leather and leather oils and horse sweat.

Saddles of various types were mounted on sawhorses. Folded blankets lay on a tier of wood shelves. And hanging from pegs on the walls were bridles and halters and braided whips, some at least six feet long; in the corner stood a rack of polo mallets.

We entered the stable through a sliding metal door. The long room had twenty stalls but there were only nine horses, most of them brown or brown with white markings, none unusually big or very small. They watched us with what I interpreted as skeptical horse curiosity. One laid back his ears as we passed. The place smelled of straw and hay and the not unpleasant odor of horse manure.

"Do they look like polo ponies to you?" Petrie asked.

"I don't know what polo ponies are supposed to look like."

"They look like ordinary nags to me."

"Do you know horses, Tom?"

"I expected more distinguished animals."

"I wouldn't know."

"A good polo pony has got to be worth a lot of money. I can't imagine Trebuchet leaving these horses behind if they weren't nags."

I declined the bait, refused to ask who this Trebuchet might be.

I followed Petrie up a fixed wooden ladder to a loft half filled with bales of hay. One cat calmly watched us from atop a stack of bales, another frantically scurried out of sight. The alfalfa smelled a little like strong tea. A sliding door on the east wall opened to a wide view of the countryside. There were several pastures enclosed by white board fences, outbuildings—sheds, garages, kennels, a barn—and what was probably the show ring. A slender girl stood in the center of the ring, slowly turning as a gray horse trotted around and around the perimeter. A rope was stretched tautly between them. She held an end of the rope in one hand, a long whip in the other. She wore high boots, jodhpurs, and a white blouse. After watching for a while, I got the illusion that the girl was effortlessly swinging the big animal in circles. In the farthest pasture, two black kids were exercising horses. It seemed to me that they were running the mounts much harder than the owners would appreciate. Beyond, there was a patchy wood of oak and cypresses and palms and a single flowering hibiscus. Everything was green at this time of year, varying shades of green beneath a porcelain sky.

"I think I probably should buy a horse or two," Petrie said. "Join the club. You know, lounge on the veranda with a cool Pimm's cup in my hand, socializing with the kind of people who can afford my fees."

"Tom, just what is this about?"

"In due course."

"Let's talk about Charles, then."

"Nah. Later. Charles is just a little fish."

"A barracuda."

"We'll pull his teeth."

"He might have Ahriman's skull and bones. And maybe the anchor and line, the spear."

"We'll torture and murder Charles, and kill all his friends and relatives."

I was among the few who might recognize that Tom Petrie was in a very good mood today.

"Two horses at least," he said. "In case one throws a shoe." He cocked his head, widened his eyes, and displayed his capped teeth in a bright, false smile.

Petrie hated to disclose information of any sort, even that which possessed no significance. He liked mystery. Secrets. He liked, always, to have an edge, and exclusive knowledge was to his way of thinking a big edge. He hoarded information in the same way a miser hoarded coins. Tom would have to inform me eventually, no doubt in bits and pieces, dribbles of relevance, though it would cause him pain.

Out in the show ring, the gray horse continued to circle the girl trainer as regularly as a plaster merry-go-round pony. Farther out, the two boys had dismounted and were lying on their backs in the grass.

"Did I tell you?" Petrie said. "I'm going to run for governor in oh-six. Are you going to vote for me?"

"Sure. Better the devil you know . . ."

"I won't get through the primaries, of course. But it will look good in my *Who's Who* entry—'Candidate for governor, 2006. Lost due to electoral misconduct.' Let's get out of here."

We went down the ladder, past the horses, and into the tack room, and then outside into bright sunlight. Josh was not in the yard now. A mockingbird, high in an oak, did his best to imitate the mewing of a cat and, as if in response, dogs began barking out at the kennel. A mare and her spindle-legged colt were grazing in a nearby pasture.

"How would you describe this place, Shaw? Rustic? Pastoral?"

"Bucolic," I said.

We watched a chalky cloud moving toward us over the entrance drive. The crunching of tires on seashells sounded like radio static. A pickup truck came in through the gateway and parked in front of the clubhouse. A stocky man bearing a grocery bag got out and kicked the door shut. He wore a sweat-stained cowboy hat, denim shirt, whipcord trousers with slash pockets, and scuffed cowboy boots. He walked with a limp.

We reached the clubhouse stairs at the same time as the man.

"Mr. Bailey?" Petrie said.

"Walt," he replied. He paused on the stairs, ready to take the final step up onto the veranda.

Bailey was around fifty, compactly built, abrupt in manner, with thin sandy hair and skin that had been creased and tanned leathery by the sun.

"I'm Tom Petrie. This is Dan Shaw."

"Yeah?"

"Chester Dalhart phoned you, told you that I would be coming here today."

"Yeah. He did."

"So then—can we talk?"

"No time today. Try tomorrow. No, Wednesday. Wednesday would be better."

"How about Thursday?" I asked.

"Thursday's okay."

"Friday," Petrie said. "Would Friday be more convenient?"

Bailey shifted the grocery bag, took some of its weight on the thigh he had lifted to climb the last step.

"Then," Petrie said, "shall I tell Mr. Dalhart that Walt Bailey has refused to spare us half an hour?"

"Oh, shit," Bailey said. "I'm treated worse than a dog. Sit down out here."

"Bring us a beverage when you return," Petrie said, "if you will be so kind."

"A dog," Bailey said, and he stepped up onto the veranda, opened the screen door with his free hand, unlocked the inner door, and vanished into the dim interior.

Petrie and I sat down at one of the veranda tables. It was very hot now, and quiet except for the click and creak of the windmill. The shadow of its blades, elongated by the sun's angle, slowly revolved over the dirt yard.

"They ought to screen in this porch," Petrie said. "Lots of flies."

"Lots of horses, lots of flies."

"I've had about enough country life for this year."

Bailey returned with a six-pack of beer and a bag of potato chips. He cut the plastic rings with a jackknife, and passed two cans to Petrie, two to me, and kept a pair for himself. Then he removed a pack of cigarettes and a butane lighter from his shirt pocket and slapped them down on the table.

"Go," he said, opening a beer.

"When was the last time you saw Victor Trebuchet?"

Bailey thought, counted back. "A week ago yesterday, Sunday. Eight days."

"Who was with him?"

"His lady."

"Adrienne Debarret?"

"Yeah. And the lord."

"Lord Warfield?"

"Whatever, yeah."

"Anyone else?"

"Mr. and Mrs. Kensington, their kid. The chauffeur."

"What did they do that day? Did they go riding?"

"Miss Debarret and the lord—Lord Warfield—they did."

"Were they good riders?"

"I suppose," he said grudgingly. "Yeah, they could ride."

"And Victor Trebuchet?"

"I saw him go out a few times. He was okay, not at the same level as the other two."

"The Kensingtons?"

"So-so."

"All classy folk, were they?"

"I didn't catch none of them molesting the livestock."

"That's a relief. Did Trebuchet and the man who called himself Lord Warfield ever practice polo? Go out and whack a ball around?"

"No."

"They were polo players, weren't they?"

"So they said."

"Are there many polo clubs in the state?"

"Miami, one in Naples, I think, and a hotshot club down in Palm Beach. Maybe others, I don't know. Trebuchet said they were arranging a match with the Palm Beach club, when the rest of the team arrived from Europe, when some horses cleared quarantine. Listen, you could have asked me these questions over the phone."

"Ah," Petrie said, "but then I wouldn't have horseshit on my shoes and sunshine in my heart. Those nine horses in the barn—polo horses?"

"No. Hell, no! I had the kids take some of them out. I rode one. They're just ordinary saddle horses. You couldn't have used them for polo, not trained for it. That was all part of the scam, wasn't it? Polo! That Trebuchet is something."

Bailey pronounced the name Tree-byo-chet; Petrie, Tray-boo-chay.

"So the horses aren't worth much?"

"A couple, half Arabian, might bring in three or four thousand dollars. The others—maybe eight hundred if you sold them for riding. A lot less if you sold them for dog food."

"Are you going to sell them for dog food?"

"Can't go on feeding and boarding them forever."

"Can horses be traced?"

"Sure. They're all branded, the brands are registered, stock inspectors track the movements. I recognized a few of the brands. Colorado, one from Arizona."

"Did they—Trebuchet, Miss Debarret, Lord Warfield—ever go out on your fox hunts?"

"There hasn't been a hunt since last fall. None while that crowd was around."

"So they left you with nine horses."

"Not me. I'm just the head wrangler, the horse flunky. They left the owners of this establishment with nine horses and maybe two tons of manure. Not to mention feed and boarding bills, vet bills, farrier bills, Hunt Club restaurant bills. The bastards signed for everything except tips. Big cash tips paid out to the employees—grooms, waiters, the chef, exercise kids, old Josh, me. I knew from the beginning they were phonies."

"How did you know that?"

He finished his beer, snapped the tab off another can, and said, "They were really nice people. Not stiff, not snobs, not bossy, and big tippers, like I said. I knew there had to be something wrong." He grinned at us. "Everyone here, the working people, liked them. I liked them. I still like them." He laughed. "That's how I knew."

"Did you ever mention your subtle intuitions to Mr. Dalhart or other members?"

"No point. You can't tell the rich anything. Anyway, everyone here was in love with them, including Dalhart."

"Who signed the bills?"

"Trebuchet, mostly. The others now and then."

"Will you give me some photocopies of the signed bills?"

"Yeah. All right."

Josh, pushing his wheelbarrow, appeared at the far end of the yard. He moved slowly. He would move slowly throughout his eight- or ten-hour shift. You had to pace yourself at that age, in this heat, doing his kind of work. He would have enough energy remaining tonight for a couple of beers, a couple hours of TV.

I opened a can of beer and took one of Bailey's cigarettes.

"Do you know," Petrie said, "if there are any photos of Trebuchet and his gang around?"

"Why would there be?"

"Members and guests out riding, practicing dressage or whatever, jumping horses—you'd think there would be a lot of cameras and camcorders in use here."

"Right. Talk to the members."

"This man known as Lord Warfield—he spoke with a British accent?"

"Yeah."

"Authentic?"

"It sounded Brit to me."

"And Trebuchet?"

"An accent, but I can't tell you what kind, where from. Miss Debarret—French, I guess."

"But the Kensingtons were American?"

"California, they said."

Petrie removed a card from his wallet and placed it on the table. "Phone me," he said, "if you think of anything that might help me find those people."

"Oh, absolutely," Bailey said. "Don't stray far from your telephone."

"A good tip will be worth good money. The right photos or videotapes, very good money."

"How big was the swindle?"

"Swindle," Petrie said. "What swindle?"

Bailey grinned.

"Call me. Come into my office with some pictures and collect your money. Have you ever seen a five-hundred-dollar bill?"

"I probably won't be around here long."

"Quitting?"

"Expect to get fired. A lot of people who think they're smart were very stupid. They were stupid and greedy and they got conned out of a lot of money. My experience—first thing such people do is look around to locate lower-downs who can be blamed, fired, prosecuted."

"In my experience, too," Petrie said. "Do you mind if we wait inside while you photocopy the bills?"

"Follow me, lawyers."

A foyer opened into a big square room that contained twenty or so tables. The carpet was burgundy red with a pattern of gold fleurs-de-lis. There was a bar and lounge in a rear alcove, and a hallway led to the kitchen and office. A stairway ascended to the upstairs rooms. Hunting prints lined the walls; there were small bronze sculptures of horses displayed on wall shelves; and in the corner a trophy case contained inscribed gold cups and ribboned certificates.

"I wonder if the food is good," I said.

"I'm sure they call it cuisine. And no, it probably isn't very good."

Bailey returned down the hallway carrying a sheaf of papers. He limped, favoring his right leg, and turned his shoulders slightly with each step.

Petrie took the papers. "What's upstairs, Walt?"

"A billiard room, card room, and a couple of bedrooms for members too drunk to drive."

"How much does a membership cost?"

"Fifteen thousand dollars initiation fee, annual dues of seventy-five hundred."

"And is the selection committee very selective?"

"They accepted Trebuchet and his gang, didn't they? You could probably get in."

Petrie smiled. "They really ought to fire you."

"I've been fired before."

"I can understand that. How did you get that limp? Fall off a horse?"

"Fell off a roof."

It was past noon when we went outside. Josh was sitting at a picnic table in the shade of a great oak. A lunch bucket and a thermos jug were on the table, and so were three sparrows that nervously strutted about, dancing for crumbs.

Petrie took a beer can from the veranda table and carried it to Josh. "I remember you now," he said.

"Do you? Tha's good. Did I ever thank you, Mr. Petrie?"

"You did. Better than that, you paid me."

Josh smiled. "I always pay, don't always remember to thank."

On the drive back toward the coast, Petrie told me about Josh, who, nearly twenty years before, had been one of his first clients. This was in Bell Harbor, not long after Tom got his lawyer's ticket and set up practice. Josh Pardee worked as a self-employed handyman, doing yard work, some gardening, a little carpentry and a little painting and a little hauling—whatever brought in an honest dollar. His wife, something of a slut, Tom said, became involved with another man. She hired a lawyer and filed for divorce, and the court took away Josh's house and truck. He was out of work for a time except for seasonal jobs picking fruit or hacking down sugar cane. One night, back in Bell Harbor, he got drunk, went to his old house, and drove away in the truck. Josh returned the truck the following morning, but even so was charged with felony theft by the state attorney's office.

"Imagine," Petrie said, "a man who worked hard, no criminal record, not even a driving violation, and then one little mistake, more a prank than a crime, and he's facing five years in the penitentiary."

"How did it turn out?"

"I got him acquitted. The jury was out for less than twenty minutes. That jury was truly pissed off. A little more passion in my summation and they might have turned into a lynch mob—hanged the prosecutor and the snotty judge."

"Keep your eyes on the road," I said.

"So, what's the moral, buddy?"

"The moral is, don't get born poor and black."

"Nah. Wake up. Are you studying to be a lawyer or a social worker? The moral is, criminal defense lawyers are the good guys, beloved by their clients—the acquitted ones—and the only thing that stands between the powerless and injustice. The only thing that stands between the powerful and justice, too, but that's another story."

"Where are we going now?"

"Paradise Key."

"Martina's aunt and uncle live there. I ought to drop by and say hello while we're down there."

"Not on my time," Petrie said.

FOUR

Paradise Key, forty years ago, had generally been known as Stink Banks. It then smelled like rotten eggs and sewage (sulfur and methane gas) and muck and decaying organisms. It hadn't been worthy of a notation on any chart. It just squatted there and stank. Stink Banks had been nothing more than a crescent-shaped, mosquito-infested offshore mud shoal that supported a few acres of tangled brush and sawgrass and stunted mangroves. But beneath the mud lay a submarine limestone ridge two miles long and half a mile wide. That underwater reef could provide support and stability. You could manufacture your paradise there. If, first, you persuaded or coerced or bribed the county politicians to guarantee annexation, which then of course would guarantee a taxpayer-funded bridge from the mainland, guarantee as well sewer and water and electrical conduits, police and fire services, and all the rest.

Then you began to dredge and fill. You drove in some strategically placed pilings; you anchored your mud cay to the limestone reef below. You trucked in a few hundred thousand tons of sand and created a fine beach that extended the length of the seaward side of the island. An obscure federal agency paid for that. You excavated a marina harbor and dredged a channel out to deep water. You hired a landscape architect who proceeded to turn Stink Banks into a benign jungle. He spread a thick rich topsoil over the salt-infused base and began to plant: hibiscus and jacaranda, frangipani, mimosa and lilac, a variety of palms, cypresses, lemon and lime and orange trees, oaks that would eventually grow great cloaks of Spanish moss. And tropical plants, broad-leafed and ferny; day blooming and night blooming shrubs that perfumed the air all year round.

A road is paved down the center of what is now a real island, dividing East Paradise from West Paradise. Shops, conforming to a strict code, line the road: boutiques, gift shops, restaurants, a liquor-wine store, a small meat market, a yacht chandlery, a genteel bookstore, and a gas station that looked like a stucco cottage. They don't look like commercial enterprises. There are no neons; all the signs are small and lettered in a pseudo-Elizabethan script. (But those merchants can spell; there are no Ye Olde Shoppes lining Paradise Lane.)

Before all that, though, lots were sold, architectural plans submitted to the development board, restrictive covenants signed and witnessed. They were big lots, with plenty of space for pools and tennis courts and guest cottages, and teak decks where one might greet the sunset with gin in hand. The developers presold half of the lots, then slowly, one by one, sold most of those remaining as property values appreciated. There were two lots left after forty years, each now priced at $1,750,000.

Petrie drove over the arched bridge, then turned south on Paradise Lane.

"You say Martina's aunt and uncle have a place here," he said. "They've got that kind of money?"

"His was the swing vote on the board of county commissioners forty years ago. The corporation gave him a lot and a piece of the action."

"Phil's corrupt?"

"He was that one time, anyway."

"Often once is enough. And this aunt and uncle raised Martina?"

"After her parents died."

"Of . . . typhoid fever . . . in Africa."

"Cholera. In Turkey."

"I always read her cartoon strip," Petrie said. "I love all those fey, philosophical woodland and marsh creatures—they're cute. But, pal, Ollie Alligator and Buddy Hare would have protested this development. Do you think Martina would have preferred being raised on Stink Banks?"

"Ask her, Tom."

"Maybe we should drop in on the Karrases after all, pay our respects. Phil lives here; he might have been one of the suckers swindled by Trebuchet."

Nearly all of the houses were named: Seabreeze, Leeward Cottage, the Cypresses, Folie à Deux, Equinox. Equinox was located halfway down the island. Martina's aunt and uncle had a place a few hundred yards farther on.

A high cedar fence obscured view of the Equinox property. Petrie got out of the car, sorted through a key ring, unlocked the gates, and pushed them open.

He returned, and we slowly cruised down a seashell drive lined with lilac and bougainvillea and jasmine. The place had the look of a neglected botanical garden. The lawn needed cutting, the hedges and fruit trees were overdue for pruning, and a rainbow carpet of flower petals covered the swimming pool. There was the pool, a marble fountain, a practice putting green, and a gazebo that resembled a miniature pagoda.

It was a big frame house two stories high, with dormer windows and oddly angled gables. Petrie stopped the car beneath the colonnaded porte cochere.

"This is the place Trebuchet leased," Petrie said. "The real estate people gave me the keys."

"What are we looking for?" I asked.

"Why, whatever we find, of course."

There were only nine rooms in the house, but they were all big, with high ceilings and good views of the beach and sea. We passed through the foyer and into a vast space that hummed with echoes of the sea. Oriental carpets were scattered over the tile floor. Most of the furniture was in a style that might be termed backache-modern.

There were unwashed glasses on the mahogany bar at the far end of the room, a leather cup with dice inside, dirty ashtrays, and a bowl of salted cashews. I sat on one of the six stools; Tom moved behind the bar.

"Beer," I said.

He dipped into the cooler and removed two bottles of Guinness Stout.

"Trebuchet," I said. "What nationality is that?"

"He claimed to be French."

"What was the scam?"

"The usual, the quickest and best. A modified Ponzi."

"And you want to find him."

"Him, the lovely Mademoiselle Debarret, the poseur who calls himself Lord Warfield, and others."

"There might be prints on these dirty glasses."

"I hired McNally and Cavaretta. They'll be here soon to dust for prints and do whatever they do."

I sipped my beer and ate cashews while Petrie frisked the bar, looking into all the cabinets and coolers, studying labels with a stern, discriminating air.

"Gads, sir," he said. "Look at that." He placed a bottle of Martell Cordon Bleu cognac on the bar. The brandy had been bottled in 1953. Petrie broke the seal, removed the cork, inhaled the aroma, breathed "Ah," then thrust the bottle beneath my nose.

"Nice," I said. "But none for me."

"I wasn't offering you any. This is my private stock." He replaced the cork. "You're a beer-and-nuts sort of guy, Shaw."

"You're a bootleg-whiskey-and-pork-rinds kind of guy, with pretensions."

He ducked behind the bar again, and a moment later rose with a box of cigars. "Cubanos. Monte Cristos. This is my lucky day."

"How much did Trebuchet take in the scam?" I asked.

"Not all of the precincts have reported. Somewhere between sixteen and twenty million dollars."

"That much? Lots of broken hearts in Paradise."

"In Paradise, in Bell Harbor, up and down the coast."

"And what's your involvement?"

"My friend. Dear constituent. I have been retained to find the villains and recover as much money as possible."

"Who retained you?"

"The swindled investors formed what they like to call a consortium."

"Why did they pick you, Tom?"

"Because in some quarters I'm regarded as a sharp and shady lawyer. They confuse me with my clients."

"The victims aren't going to the cops?"

"They don't want justice or vengeance. They just want their dough."

"So you're going to sue Trebuchet when you find him."

"I know you're trying to provoke me into indiscretions. But this is highly sensitive stuff. There are men whose reputations are on the line. Reputations and fortunes. Identities must be protected. We're operating on a strict need-to-know basis, here. Got it?"

I said, "I'm not working for you. I'm taking the day off while your paralegal does my work."

He removed a cigar from the box, sniffed it from end to end, bit off the tip, and clenched it between his teeth.

I finished my beer and got off the barstool. "Tom, sooner or later we're going to have to talk about Charles and the bones he found."

"Fire in the hole!" He struck a match, held the flame to the cigar, and began puffing clouds of smoke.

There were three upstairs bedrooms, each with its own bath and dressing chamber, but only the largest showed use. There were rumpled lavender sheets on the bed. The walk-in closet was empty except for a pair of women's sandals and a beach towel that smelled faintly of suntan lotion. Nothing in the cabinets or dresser drawers, nothing in the bathroom medicine cabinet except for a jar of petroleum jelly and three condoms. I hadn't expected to find anything. Nor had Tom. Petrie had little hope for my future as a lawyer, but he did believe that I was a good investigator and a discreet coconspirator. I had served twelve years in the Army's Criminal Investigation Division, more time in Florida working for lawyers and the state attorney's office while attending night law school; but Petrie hadn't taken me to the stables this morning or to this house now so that I might play detective—I was being recruited into some probably criminal mischief.

Petrie was still standing at the bar when I returned. He shook the leather cup and rolled the dice. "Find anything?" he asked, glancing at me.

"No."

"Try the big kitchen freezer." He nodded. "Go ahead." The kitchen was bigger than my entire apartment, the chopping block nearly as long as my rowing skiff. Stoves, cabinets, pantry, two refrigerators, an ordinary stand-up freezer, and, in the back of the room, a heavy insulated door that led into the walk-in freezer. I entered. My first impression was eyes, a hundred coldly staring eyes.

There were rows of fish, at least fifty fish, in the freezer, all hanging from hooks that ran along overhead rails. Fish that I couldn't identify, others familiar— snapper, dorado, tarpon, sea bass, barracuda, sailfish, and sharks. Eyes, teeth, spiky fins, stiffly curled tails, and a cold dank sea smell. A seven-foot crocodile hung from a hook at the rear of the freezer. It looked alive: The eyes glowed red-pink with reflected light, and the rough, pebbled skin was moist, as if the reptile had just crawled from the swamp. It appeared to be grinning slyly at the crowd of fish around it.

Petrie was waiting at the bar. He scooped up the dice and dropped them into the leather cup. His cigar fumed in an ashtray.

"Notice?" he said. "None of them had been gutted."

"You wouldn't call Trebuchet and his friends sportsmen."

"And the gator," Tom said. "This will break Martina's heart. I recognized him—it was Ollie Alligator for sure."

"It wasn't an alligator," I said. "It was a crocodile."

"Florida doesn't have crocs. It was Ollie."

"There's a species of New World crocodile. A few are left in Florida, not many."

"Nah. Ollie's dead."

Petrie violently shook the dice and rolled them out on the bar: six deuces; three pairs of snake eyes; triple craps. He hunched over, looking down with the frowning intensity of a shaman who has just glimpsed dire omens in an array of chicken entrails.

"That doesn't count," he said. "I didn't get a clean roll."

McNally and Cavaretta arrived a few minutes later. They were former Bell Harbor cops who had opened a private detective agency after retiring from the police force. Both men carried crime investigation kits. They were in their middle fifties, one—McNally—an overweight bulldog, and the other a lean, grizzled terrier. They were slow-moving, laconic, flat-eyed, and you observed in them the spiritual depletion that afflicts some men who have been cops too long. They were often—behind their backs—referred to as Mutt and Jeff.

"Heard a shotgun blast down the road just now," McNally said.

I explained that many of the residents of Paradise Key used noisemaking devices in their yards to keep birds away.

"They don't like birds?"

"They don't like birds eating all the seeds in their spring gardens."

Petrie briefed them, gave them the house and gate keys, and then picked up the brandy bottle and the box of Cuban cigars.

"Listen," he said, "don't clean out the bar. Just take a couple bottles each. But you can steal anything you find in the walk-in freezer."

FIVE

We drove south along Paradise Lane. The houses were mostly concealed behind fences and jungly vegetation, though now and then you could see a flash of window glass, a patch of ceramic roof tiles, a vine-tangled gazebo, or the rainbow spray from a lawn sprinkler. Signs warned of guard dogs, security patrols, alarm systems, the consequences of trespassing. The inhabitants of Paradise Key lived as though under siege by roaming gangs of brigands, but we saw only Mexican gardeners and black handymen who drove battered pickup trucks.

"Phil Karras's wife?" Petrie said.

"Alice."

"I heard something—she's a zombie?"

"She has advanced Alzheimer's."

"Tough."

The Karras property lay on the west side of Paradise Lane. The gate was open; we did not have to ring for admittance. Petrie turned off on a gravel drive that curved through palms and big ferns. The house was situated on an elevated section of lawn, flush against the sound that divided Paradise Key from the mainland.

It was smaller than most of the houses we'd passed, though large by ordinary standards; a two-story stucco building with a screened veranda, eight-foot carved double doors, and on the upper floor a row of French doors set in bronze frames and opening onto balconies. A great live oak, shrouded with ragged skirts of moss, shaded a flagstoned patio area. Phil Karras sat alone at a table beneath the tree.

Petrie parked the car; we got out and walked across a Bermuda grass lawn. Karras did not turn to look at us. His head was lowered, his shoulders slumped. I supposed he was dozing over the newspaper spread on the table. Beyond the table, gradually becoming visible with the changing angle of our approach, was a bulky tarpaulin. Next to it, partly concealed in the grass, lay a double-barreled shotgun. A chain with an attached collar was secured to an eyebolt screwed into the base of the oak. Petrie and I halted.

"Phil," I said. His eyes were open. "Phil?"

He appeared to be intently reading the sports section of the newspaper. He looked up at me. There was no recognition in that gaze, no light or focus in his eyes.

"What happened here?" I asked.

One of the four chairs had been overturned. There was an insulated coffee pot on the table, a jug of orange juice, cups and saucers, a glass vase of gardenias, and blood spatter. Blood on the white tablecloth, the newspaper, on Karras's white shirt and shorts, on his forehead and mostly bald scalp. Blood soaking through the tarp, too. Alice's feet had not been covered; small feet, chubby with thick veined ankles and untrimmed nails.

"Phil," I said. "You know me. Dan Shaw, Martina's friend."

Petrie moved away, lifted an edge of the tarp for a moment, let it drop.

Shock affects people in various ways. Some become agitated, garrulous; others, like Karras, appear sleepy and apparently indifferent to the awful event that had changed everything.

"Phil, where is Lupe? Where is your wife's nurse? Is she all right?"

Karras carefully folded the sports section in quarters, pressed down the creases, and then let it fall to the flagstones. He looked at me. His expression changed. He became aware. If you didn't know the man you might say he smiled. A stranger might testify in court that he had grinned a few minutes after killing his wife. But there was no mirth in that baring of teeth. It was, rather, a guilty abject cringing, a reflection of horror at his action.

I heard the remote ululation of a siren, no louder than a mosquito's whine at first, but growing louder.

Phillip Karras was a robust man in his sixties, short and stocky, darkly tanned and fit. He reminded me of photos I had seen of the elderly Pablo Picasso, vital and impish, arrogant at times. But Karras was crushed now; there was not much left of him.

"Stand away," Petrie said to me. "He doesn't need a gentle friend, he needs a lawyer."

I left the table area. Karras had once showed me the shotgun that now lay in the grass. He had been proud of it, an old Purdey twenty-gauge that he'd used for hunting doves and quail.

The sirens were louder now. I could distinguish the several tones and pulses; police cars, an ambulance. Some people were watching us from behind a big hedge that separated this property from the neighbors.

"Listen, old man," Petrie said harshly. "You hear those sirens? They'll be here in two minutes. Listen to me! By Christ, they'll take you away and toast you if you don't wake up fast."

I heard a clicking noise overhead; Karras's pet capuchin monkey, Dodo, had slipped his collar and was sitting on a low branch of the sheltering oak. He looked down at me with a sorrowful, inquisitive monkey gaze. The species was named after the Capuchin friars because of the hoodlike halo of hair around their heads. It seemed to me that there was something in Dodo's gaze that corresponded to the look in Phil's eyes—an animal fear and grief.

Petrie was saying, "I want you to talk it out. Do it. Talk right now, quick, to me, but not to the cops, not to the SA, not to your cellmate tonight. I'm your lawyer, bud, at least until you elect to choose other counsel. Regrow your spine quick."

The air sparkled as a flock of parakeets darted low over the lawn, then swooped up and landed in the branches of a tree in the neighboring yard. They were feral birds, pets that had been released or had escaped from captivity, flocked up, and managed to thrive on Paradise Key. The faces behind the hedge—yard workers, a housemaid—somberly watched us.

"You killed her," Petrie said, "because you could no longer bear to see her that way. And you intended to kill yourself, didn't you? The second cartridge was for you. But you couldn't do it. And that's your shame, your horror: You couldn't complete it."

I thought that Petrie was handling it wrong. He was berating the man, assaulting him with what might or might not be the truth.

The sirens were close now, and I expected to see the first of the vehicles turn into the drive, but they went on past, heading down toward the south end of the island.

"Maybe you did the right thing," Petrie said. "It was a way of honoring her. Honoring your life together. I won't let you dirty that now with whining confessions and pleas for understanding and sympathy. Do you hear? Hang yourself in the fucking jail tonight if you can, but don't look to the world for understanding. The world will cheer when they pull the switch at Starkie. Christ, don't spoil the courage and honesty of your action by seeking solace."

The emergency vehicles had reached the dead end at the south side of the key. The sirens gradually became loud again as they turned back. They would not miss the place a second time. I jogged across the lawn and down the driveway. The gates were heavy but well balanced; I closed one door, then the other, hearing the lock click shut, lowered the big wooden latch bar, and then I turned and jogged back to the patio.

"I'll have one of my associates at the county jail when they bring you in," Petrie said. "His name is Hughes. Don't talk to the cops on your ride into Bell Harbor. Don't even comment on the weather, ask the time. They'll try to coax you into talking. Shut up. Here's my card. I'm your lawyer, and my associate is your lawyer. Flash this card every time they ask you a question."

The monkey shifted on his branch, rubbed a hand over his face as if brushing away cobwebs. Now, at last, Phil Karras spoke. "I'll need to change my clothes and wash up."

"Forget it. They'll take you as you are. It's part of the standard humiliation."

"We were drinking coffee," Karras said. He told us that his wife had not been "there" for years. His dog, his monkey, were more "there." Alice was surely going to die soon, in months, weeks, any time. She fell down. She choked on her food. She had to wear diapers. Her nervous system, motor control, was seriously affected. How can a human be erased? Die, sure, but progressively erased? She had no soul remaining. No soul. The disease had stolen everything except the machine, her ravaged body, and now even that was going.

The cars were outside the gates now. Sirens continued to whoop for a moment, faded to growls, and in the ensuing quiet I heard doors slamming and men shouting.

"All those memories," Karras went on, "all those memories and emotions and events, her *life*—erased. Erased, her childhood, her parents, her first marriage and her children, all our years together."

The cops were shouting and kicking the gates.

"Hold on!" I shouted. "I'm coming."

"This morning . . . I was talking about a time soon after our marriage. I knew she couldn't understand anything, but my voice soothed her. And then, my God, I saw it in her eyes. A tiny piece of her brain was still there, a few cells maybe, and I was sure, I *knew*, that she remembered that moment I was talking about. She understood for an instant what had happened to her. It was there in her eyes, then it was gone. But I just couldn't take that instant of . . . cognition."

A sheriff's deputy climbed over the fence and dropped to the ground. He trotted to the gates.

"I went inside and loaded my shotgun. One cartridge for her, one for me. I came up behind her. It was cowardly, but I just couldn't look at her face when I did it."

The gates were open now. An ambulance and three police cars—two local, one from the Sheriff's Department—pulled into the driveway.

"The shotgun double-fired."

Policemen were coming across the lawn toward us.

"It might have been mechanical—the shotgun double-fired. Or maybe I jerked both triggers. I didn't have a shell left for myself."

Deputy Sheriff Zack Parsons, a red-faced, big-bellied man who was often in petty trouble with the sheriff for wearing a nonregulation Stetson and cowboy boots (at least a few times with spurs), shambled toward us, saying in his phlegmy rumble, "Lord, Tom, now the ambulances are chasing you."

"Zack," Petrie said, "treat my client well or I'll strew your guts all over the courtroom floor."

"Wouldn't be the first time. That was real cute—locking the gates."

I said, "We were protecting the integrity of the crime scene."

"Stop there," Zack said to the paramedics. "We got to wait for the coroner and the mobile crime lab."

Half a dozen policemen stood around nearby. I knew a few of them; we exchanged nods.

Zack lifted an edge of the tarpaulin, looked down at the remains of Alice Karras, let the tarp drop. "Christ, man," he said to Karras. "Couldn't you have smothered her with a pillow last night, and saved yourself and us from all the crap that's going to rain down?"

"Don't answer, Phil," Petrie said.

I heard one of the cops say, "She had mad cow disease."

"Bob," Parsons said, "why don't you amble over there and ask those people hiding behind the bushes what they saw and heard. And Harley, Paul, handcuff the gentleman here, put him in the car. Read him his rights. Do it."

Karras stood, half turned, and passively waited while a deputy handcuffed him. He glanced sideways at Petrie for reassurance as he was being led away. Tom nodded and placed a vertical finger over his lips.

"Phil," I said. "Where is the nurse?" I was afraid he might have harmed her.

"Day off," Karras called back.

"What the hell is that?" one of the paramedics said.

"A goddamned monkey," Parsons said. "You never seen a goddamned monkey before?"

Petrie removed a cigar from an inside breast pocket and gave it to Parsons. "I inherited a box of Monte Cristos."

"Thanks. I'll save it for later. Now, Tom, I'll want statements."

"Of course. We'll follow my client to the lockup and give statements there."

"Hold on. Did you see him kill her?"

"You're presuming, after three minutes on the scene, that my client killed his wife?"

"Come on, Tom. Shit. Did he talk? What did he say?"

"Come on, Zack. Shit. You know better than to ask me that."

"How long you been his lawyer?"

"That doesn't concern you."

"How did you happen to arrive here during or just after a murder?"

"You're wasting time."

Deputy Parsons looked at me. "You ain't the perp's lawyer, Shaw. I think maybe we'll take you in for a chat. Keep you a while, as a material witness."

"You're right," Petrie said. "Shaw isn't a lawyer, not yet, but I am, and he works for me. He shares my attorney-client privilege. We'll give you *voluntary* statements at the jail. I'll give you a preview now: We arrived here no more than five minutes before you, and we saw what you're looking at. That is about it."

The mobile crime lab truck pulled into the driveway and eased off onto the grass, and two men got out and began pulling on their sterile coveralls.

Parsons hitched his gunbelt, lifted his shoulders, and said, "What a mess. And look at that—you two have been tramping through the blood evidence."

Petrie showed him one of his thin, mean, happy smiles. "Look again, Zack. We don't wear cowboy boots."

"Go on, get the fuck away from here. And by God, be at the jail when I get there."

I borrowed Tom's cell phone and, on the drive north up Paradise Lane, I dialed my office. Candace answered after eight rings. I persuaded her to put me through to Judge Samuelson's office.

"Levi," I said. "This is Shaw. Is Martina there?"

"Hello, my boy. No, not yet. Soon, though; she made an appointment for one o'clock. Incidentally, thank you for the referral."

It was twelve-twenty now. "Listen, Judge, Martina's uncle just killed his wife."

"My lord!"

"Keep her there in your office. I'll phone back at one or a little after."

"You don't want me to say anything?"

"No, I think it's better if I talk to her."

"Certainly. Yes, that's best."

"Later, then," I said, and I broke the connection.

Petrie turned off onto the bridge that connected Paradise Key to the mainland. The tide was out, and the sound was a smooth expanse of still, muddy water that smelled like spoiled fish.

"Thanks, Tom," I said. "I thought you were handling it all wrong, bullying Phil, but your tactic seemed to bring him back."

"Some clients you brutalize," he said, "and others you romance. Karras might be all right now. He's the kind of guy who's impelled to confess. He might be able to keep his mouth shut now that he's confessed to us."

"Is that important? I mean, Christ, it couldn't be more clear what happened."

"Truth has many faces," Petrie said.

"I thought it was deceit that had many feces."

"That, too."

SIX

We were slowed by the clotted traffic on Highway 54 outside Bell Harbor, an area known as the Death Zone because of the frequent automobile accidents. We passed a three-mile-long strip of fast-food restaurants and gas stations and used-car lots and sex shops and tourist hustles and motels. You could rent a room, fetch a pizza, obtain an erotic massage, buy a handgun, hold up a liquor store, get drunk, get laid, relaid, and parlayed, shoot the punk who cut you off in traffic, and do all of that without putting more than a couple miles on your car's odometer.

Ahead I saw the scrolled neon of the Motel Sans Souci. That was the place where Ahriman and Charles had stayed when they came north to kill us—me, Tom Petrie, and a man named Leroy Karpe. The Sans Souci was a decrepit dinosaur among the newer chain motels, and cheap, a place of peeling stucco and sheet-metal roof patches and a parking lot that sparkled with broken glass. It advertised accommodations by the day, week, month; rooms, kitchenettes, housekeeping units; senior rates, free coffee and doughnuts, cable TV.

"You think . . . ?" Petrie said.

"Sure. He wants to be found."

Petrie turned the Porsche into the asphalt parking lot and halted among a cluster of the old, shock-sprung, smoking Detroit iron favored by that category of the poor that favored big engines and springy rides.

I went into the office and talked to a sour retiree who resentfully informed me that, yes, a Charles Sinclair was registered in Suite 268, second floor corner.

I stepped outside, gesturing to Petrie, and together we went up the warped wooden stairs and down a sagging walkway to the last unit, 268. Moth-eaten curtains were drawn across dirty louvered windows. A MAID SERVICE card hung from the door knob. It would read DO NOT DISTURB on the reverse side. I knocked on the door.

"I was here, this same unit, back in September," Petrie said. "I punched Charles."

"I remember. You told me."

"I gave him twenty-five hundred dollars to get out of town."

"I know, Tom. But he's back."

I was about to knock again when the door opened and Charles, peering through the screened door, smiled out at us.

"I expected you sooner," he said in a tone of mild reproach. "Have you lunched?"

"My old friend," Petrie said. "We plan to sup on your flesh, quench our thirst with your blood."

"If I had known, I would have eaten lots of garlic and marinated myself in Grand Marnier."

We went through the screened door and into a boxy

living room that smelled of mildew and insecticide. The Sans Souci was the sort of place that had to be sprayed monthly for roaches, termites, fire ants, and maybe body lice. But Charles was far superior to his surroundings; he was always princely.

"How friendly of you to call," Charles said. "You're both looking fit."

"And you as well, you jolly scamp," Petrie said.

The TV, sound off, flashed with images of tanks rolling down a dusty street lined by devastated buildings. The "suite" comprised the living room, two bedrooms—doors shut—a dining alcove, and a kitchen behind a plastic curtain. Petrie went off to search for bogeymen.

"What will you have to drink?" Charles asked.

"Nothing, thanks."

A human skull and some bones—a femur, ribs, a few vertebrae—were displayed on top of the dresser. Stubby candles, set in saucers, flanked the skull, and there were plastic flowers, an incense burner, and a photograph of Raven Ahriman taped to the mirror.

Charles, observing my reaction, smiled, then stepped forward to light the four candles and a pellet of incense that smelled like burning weeds.

"There," he said. "Raven is with us."

Charles was still boyish at thirty-one or -two, slender, with pale skin and dark blond hair that he wore in a preppy style, and which always looked full of static electricity. His eyes were that near-violet that some people counterfeited with contact lenses. Long-lashed blue eyes, a candid gaze.

Petrie emerged from a bedroom, halted, and, with his head cocked, stared at the display.

"Hey, nice shrine, Charles," he said. "But isn't it a bit . . ."

"*De trop?*"

"Yeah."

"Honest emotion always appears rather vulgar, don't you think?"

"You've never had an honest emotion in your life."

"Well, I thought it might amuse you."

"Oh, and it does. Doesn't it, Dan?"

I said, "Very campy, Charles. We're amused."

He gave us an aw-shucks smile and shrugged. He would have blushed for us if he were able.

Charles was the prodigal son of a prominent and rich old Boston family that had, quite rightly, disowned and disinherited him soon after his twenty-first birthday. He was an inveterate liar and an incorrigible thief. After his expulsion he had stolen a large part of his family's collection of valuable paintings and art objects, and gone off to Santa Fe to establish himself as a dealer in fine arts. Now and then he sold an authentic painting or sculpture, but mostly he dealt in stolen works and fakes that he commissioned from an accomplished Romanian forger named Carescu. He later branched out into extortion and other crimes and misdemeanors. His luck ran out in California, and he spent two and a half years in San Quentin, where he'd met his future partner, the violent Raven Ahriman. Charles was devious and smart, Raven violent; combined, they were the stuff of nightmares.

Charles was a psychopath and, like many intelligent psychopaths, he could be very charming, even lovable, your best friend until he thought of a way to convert your affection into cash. He was not himself violent, but he could probably watch others kill you without suffering more than mild embarrassment.

Now he said, "You *will* stay to lunch, won't you? You must. I'll warm up the food."

"I'll go with you," Petrie said, "to make sure you don't mistake the Drano for salt."

I waited until they had passed through the plastic curtain into the kitchen, then picked up the telephone, dialed nine to get an outside line, and then punched in the digits of my office number. Candace answered immediately, saying, "I'm sorry, Mr. Shaw, really I am." She switched me to Levi.

"Daniel?" the judge said. "Martina knows."

"How does she know?"

"Candace heard through her network of gossips. She'd heard something about it, and sympathized with Martina when she came in."

"Damn it."

"Martina's in your office now. She wanted to be alone. Keep her grief private. Not have someone watching her at such a moment."

"Get her to the phone, will you, Judge?"

There was a thump when he placed his receiver on the desk, other muffled sounds as he rapped on the door to my office, his muffled voice, and then a twenty-second silence.

"Dan?"

"I'm sorry. I wanted to tell you myself."

"What happened?" She had control of her voice.

"Phil shot her," I said. "He couldn't take the strain anymore."

"Shot Alice?"

"Tom Petrie and I arrived just after it happened. Phil simply cracked."

"How is he?"

"Not good. But a little better than he was when we first saw him. Tom intervened, he talked to Phil, and then he handled the cops when they arrived."

"Where is he now?"

"At the county jail."

"They arrested him?"

"Yes, Martina, of course they did."

"What were you doing there?"

"Tom and I had business on Paradise Key. Afterward we decided to stop in and say hello to Phil."

"And Alice was dead?"

"Yes."

"He killed her?"

"Yes, Martina."

"I've got to go to him. You say he's at the county jail?"

"Yes. Petrie sent a lawyer over there to represent him. Tom and I will be going there soon."

"I've got to go there now."

"Yes. I'll meet you soon. Let me talk to Levi now."

"Daniel?" the judge said.

"Will you go with Martina to the county lockup?" I asked.

"Certainly."

"How is she taking it?"

"Well enough, I suppose."

"Dazed, confused?"

"I would say so."

"All right," I said. "Be sure to go with her, Judge."

"You didn't have to say it twice. You actually didn't have to say it once."

"I'm sorry."

"Do you want me to represent Karras temporarily?"

"Petrie phoned his office. He's sending one of his associates there."

"Very well."

"Keep an eye on Martina, please."

Incense smoke was spreading an acrid haze through the room. It caused instant asthma. I crushed out the fuming pellet, but left the candles burning. The skull leered at the TV screen where a giddy bleached blonde was gesturing toward a flashing weather map. I picked up the skull. It was big, even without the jawbone, though lighter than I expected; and whiter, too, abraded clean by sand and salt water. I tilted it so that I could look into the cranium from below. There were a few grains of sand inside, a patch of mossy substance. The teeth showed the wear you'd expect in a man in his mid-forties. And there were some ugly black fillings in the molars—prison dentistry. I found a hairline fracture on the ridge of bone above the left ear aperture.

Charles paraded back and forth from kitchen to dining alcove, setting the table, bringing in bowls of food, fussing. Petrie came in carrying a bottle of wine. He looked at me. I nodded: It was Raven Ahriman's skull, all right.

In the photograph, Raven Ahriman was leaning back against a ship's railing, grinning, with behind him a tumultuous, foaming sea. The grin was tough, arrogant, a challenge to the world. I derived some satisfaction in comparing the grinning man in the photo with the grinning skull.

Lunch was warmed-over Chinese takeout: sweet and

sour ribs, shrimp in a spicy sauce, rice, bean paste, and cereal bowls full of vegetables.

"This is vile wine, Charles," Petrie said.

"It isn't that good," Charles said, "but it's the best that I can afford at present."

But the food wasn't bad, and I was hungry.

"How is Mirium?" Petrie asked.

Mirium had been Ahriman's wife.

"She's as well as can be expected," Charles said. "She sold Raven's trawler, so she isn't quite destitute."

"And how much of the proceeds from the boat sale did you con her out of?"

"She *loaned* me the money to come here from Guyana to petition you to provide her with financial assistance."

"You think we should establish some sort of trust or pension for the widow and her son?"

"Yes, I do. You burned down her house, you killed her husband. Aren't you both morally and ethically obliged to provide for their futures?"

Petrie laughed. "I love to hear you utter words like 'ethically' and 'morally' in your fancy accent. Say 'integrity' for me. Say 'principles.' Say 'compassionate.'"

Petrie picked up a section of tiny ribs and commenced nibbling at them in a rabbity way.

My turn. "It's amazing that you were able to find some of Raven's bones," I said. "Phenomenal luck. But now you've brought the Mackey brothers into our confidential business."

"I told them nothing."

"Nothing?"

"I told them that I was searching for the remains of my dear old father, who drowned in that vicinity when I was a lad. I had, you know, promised Mother that someday I would recover the remains and arrange a proper, a ceremonial, a respectful interment. Et cetera."

"Not smart," I said. "Those Mackeys have spent a large part of their disreputable lives salvaging things from the sea. They know those bones weren't down very long."

Petrie picked up another strip of ribs and, holding them daintily, resumed nibbling.

"Charles," I said, "how the hell did you know where I deep-sixed Ahriman's corpse?"

"He told me," Charles said, nodding toward Petrie. "The oh-so-brilliant lawyer told me."

Tom slowly lowered the gnawed ribs and stared at Charles. His lips were darkened by sauce and he wore a Hitlerian sauce mustache.

"He told me when he came here in September to threaten me. He said that Raven was dead and now lay on the ocean floor—words to that effect. Well, I knew that Raven had gone out to the lighthouse. That, probably, you had killed him and dumped his body at sea. Where at sea? Not far out. The weather was filthy then, remember? Eureka!"

"You're a bright guy."

"He's a smarmy little turd."

Charles smiled.

Petrie pushed his plate away, wiped his mouth with a paper napkin, and then took a sip of wine which he noisily flushed around his mouth before spitting it back in the glass.

*   *   *

"How much do you want?" Petrie asked.

Charles did not want much; only enough so that he and

Mirium might have sufficient resources to recover from the financial reverses consequent on the burning of the house and the "murder." One hundred thousand dollars cash, plus fifty thousand per year for ten years: six hundred thousand dollars total, not excessive for a lawyer of Petrie's income and reputation. Shaw could contribute according to his lesser income. Call it restitution for our crimes, penance for our sins.

"You called this guy bright?" Petrie said to me. "He has the intellectual powers of a mollusk."

Otherwise, Charles said, he would go to the police. There were witnesses to the recovery of the skull, and no doubt other bones down there, other evidence.

He seemed without guile even as he explained the terms of his blackmail and the result—the "denouement"—if we failed to comply. Charles, by nature, was so lacking in anything resembling guilt or shame that his demands sounded almost reasonable.

"Tell him, Shaw."

"Tom is now going to rebut your claims."

"Go to the police," Petrie said. "They'll be delighted to see you. You're probably wanted in ten states and three countries. And the Mackey boys, that righteous pair, will make reliable witnesses. You've got some bones. What do they demonstrate? A man is dead. Cause of death? No way to determine that. Identification? No chance of an ID if we walk out of here with that skull. Connection between Ahriman, me, and Shaw? Well, yeah, the Peter Falconer affair. The cops know some of that already. But you, Charles, you scabby entrepreneur, you were complicit in those murders down in the Keys. Go to the cops. I'll drive you there now—a sporty last ride before the iron slams shut."

Charles listened politely to Petrie's torrent of legal logic and personal insult. He raised his eyebrows. He smiled boyishly. Now and then he brushed a floppy wing of hair away from his candid blue eyes. A vague air of ill health lent Charles's boyishness a certain pathos. So young, so charming, so tragic . . .

"Ten thousand dollars," he said. "Enough for me to pay my bill here and leave town."

"Jesus," Petrie said, "I'm really disappointed in you, son. I've always had high regard for your laissez-faire larceny, your mythomaniacal lying, your insouciant brand of psychopathy. But you've lost your touch. You reek of doubt. A confidence man who's lost his confidence is just another petty criminal doomed to starvation or spine-warping toil in the prison laundry."

"Five thousand dollars," Charles said. "Two thousand. Don't make me travel by bus."

"But wait," Petrie said. "Inspiration strikes, the Muse whispers. I might, I might just have a job for you. Don't throw up, it isn't anything legitimate. I want you to hang around for a few days. I'll send someone over this afternoon with a little money, enough so you can stay here in roachy poverty or slither out of town. What do you say?"

"The Mackeys know I'm staying in this place. I'm rather afraid of them."

"I'll move you to a different dump."

"I need clothing. Nearly everything I own was lost in the fire."

"You shall be decently shod and attired."

"Very well, then. I am at your service."

Charles dipped his hand into a bowl, removed three fortune cookies, kept one and gave the others to me and Tom.

The cookies were brown-tan, folded like closed flower buds, and had the brittle texture—and probably the taste—of a ceramic material. I cracked mine open with a table knife and unrolled the strip. I read aloud: "'Eastward, your fortune.'"

Petrie read his: "'Rely on your friends.'"

Charles frowned at his strip, and said, "'Both the swan and the swan's reflection are illusions.'"

"That's so true," Petrie said.

Charles provided a paper shopping bag to contain the skull and bones. He did not appear disturbed to see his evidence, the remains of his good friend and mentor, Raven Ahriman, carried out of the motel unit like garbage. He stood on the walkway, looking down, as Petrie backed the Porsche out of its parking slot. His smile was cryptic; his wave was a languid lifting of his right hand, palm out, as if he were swearing an oath.

The traffic had thinned. Petrie accelerated, and ran a traffic light that turned from amber to red as we reached the intersection. Horns blared, a pedestrian leaped back to the curb.

"What's this about a job?" I said.

"I believe in rehabilitation, in salvation. We must do our best to lead errant souls back into the fold. We must forgive, even though we can never forget."

"Tom, you've got the bones, now you dispose of them. It's your turn. Don't expect me to walk off with that shopping bag."

"Not to worry," he said.

SEVEN

I got back to my office at four thirty and immediately went to the safe where I kept a bottle of Scotch. If I didn't lock it away, Candace would now and then come in during my absence and take a nip, which was all right except that she tried to conceal her theft by maintaining the fluid level with water from the bathroom tap. The bottle was inside the safe, along with some documents and the brown paper bag containing Raven Ahriman's skull and bones. Petrie, the son of a bitch, had given me the safe half a year before, and knew the combination; and today he had left the county jail before me. But at least his paralegal had completed my work and delivered it to the bank's lawyers. I packed the skull and bones in a small nylon duffel that I used for an overnight bag.

Usually I stayed in my Bell Harbor apartment during the week, but Martina was upset and preferred to have company, so at sunset we went out to the lighthouse in her little cabin cruiser, *Puck*.

Cerberus waited up on the landing at the top of the steps that lead onto the reef: he was wet from the afternoon shower, his fur was spiky, and he barked furiously to let us know that he was on the job, and then he raced down the steps and shook all of the water out of his fur, misting the air and wetting both of us; afterward, he lowered his head in fake shame.

Martina was silent as she prepared a light meal. I tried to make conversation, but she was distracted, somewhere else in time, and she replied to my small talk mostly in non sequiturs. She did not eat much. Midway through the meal she got up, said, "Sorry," and walked down the cavelike hallway to her studio.

I cleaned the table, washed the plates and utensils, and then went out onto the reef. Cerberus was waiting for me.

"Where's your ball?"

He was a big dumb brute, but he had learned what a ball was, and he raced off to the south end of the reef, ran in circles, found the tooth-gnawed rubber ball, and returned in triumph. I had to wrestle with him before he relaxed his jaws. "You're a dog," I said. "A dawg!" He watched me and the ball with a walleyed canine paranoia. "You're a cat!" I threw the ball toward the far end of the reef, and he galloped away. The game was repeated a dozen times. He was too dim for boredom. Each time I had to fight him for the saliva-slimed ball.

Martina was sitting at the table with a glass of wine when I returned to the lighthouse.

"His saliva," I said, washing my hands at the kitchen sink, "congeals into a sort of jellied slime. It's horrible."

She smiled automatically, then said, "Come on," and led me down the tunnel to her studio. The bright articulated light shone down on a charcoal portrait of her uncle pinned to the drawing board. It was a much younger Karras than the man I had seen this afternoon, at an age before he had lost his hair and become jowly and complacent. There was a crinkle of humor around his eyes, and his mouth appeared ready to smile, or was resisting a smile. His glance had a side- and downward slant. Was he looking down at a child—Martina?—with amusement and affection?

"It's good," I said.

"I wanted to see him as he used to be, not as he was today."

She was ready to talk now. We returned to the block-house and sat together on the wicker settee.

"They let me see him only for a few minutes," she said. "A guard was present. Phil was so frightened, so bewildered, so . . . diminished."

"Shock," I said. "Shock does that. Are they keeping him under a suicide watch?"

"I think so. Yes."

"Did he make a statement to the police?"

"Does it matter?"

"Petrie says it does."

"I don't know. I don't think so. Tom Petrie's associate, Hughes, was there when I arrived. And then you and Tom came."

"I'm sure Hughes and Petrie were able to prevent any kind of interrogation."

"I forgot to thank Tom."

"Of course your uncle can choose his own counsel now, if he wishes. Tom was just reacting to an emergency. He's a criminal defense attorney—he sees cops and he sees a suspect and he automatically goes to work."

"He's very expensive, isn't he?"

"Yes, and very good."

"What a fucking mess," she said.

Martina rarely used profanity: Her vehemence now was for emphasis. This obviously wasn't an ordinary mess. It required extreme language.

We heard Cerberus scratching at the door. Martina got up, went to the door and let the dog in, then returned to the settee.

"The thing is," I said, "if Petrie and I had arrived at the house a few minutes earlier we might have prevented it. Four minutes, five. If . . ."

"A shotgun! Why? Why that way? My God!"

"I know."

"Will they file murder charges?"

"Yes. No doubt."

"First-degree murder?"

"Probably."

"The death penalty?"

"The state attorney's office is very political. There'll be a lot of moral posturing, plenty of sanctimony. You know, the sacredness of human life no matter what."

"Is there any chance, do you think, of a plea bargain? Manslaughter, say, with probation?"

"I don't think so. It will go to trial."

"And?"

"Petrie would say that it's all up to him and the acquired lifetime biases of twelve jurors."

"He's a cynical man. But you like him, don't you?"

"Now and then."

"I don't really blame my uncle for what he did."

"Nor do I. Just the bloody awful way he did it."

Cerberus had found my duffel bag in the corner and was drooling over it. Bones.

"The dorg wants dinner," I said.

"All right, we'll change the subject. And feed the dorg."

The dorg ate several pounds of a gluey gruel, and then the three of us went out onto the reef. A soft warm wind ruffled the water, and the sea was gold-scaled with moonlight and the lights of Bell Harbor across the bay.

"What are you and Petrie up to now?" Martina asked.

"What do you mean?"

"I mean, what kind of trouble are you two chasing now?"

"I'm not sure. It's pretty murky so far."

"Oh, hell. Let's go in and watch TV."

"You don't have TV."

"Then we'll go to bed."

*   *   *

I awakened early and, without disturbing Martina, pulled on swimming shorts and went into the central living area. Cerberus, nose on his paws, waited on his rug near the door. "Devil dog," I whispered. Flattered, he thumped his tail against the floor, got up, and watched me as I collected the duffel, diving mask, fins, and snorkel, and then followed me out onto the reef.

It was a warm, swampy morning, more like July than early June. Light was refracted by the moisture-saturated air, blurring images and doubling the outline of buildings along the town esplanade. A bell buoy at the entrance to the breakwater chimed irregularly in the surging tide, sounding like Morse. I listened, identified a pair of dots, "I"; a pause and then a dot and a dash, "A"; another pause, two dashes, "M"; and then the chiming Morse degenerated into a meaningless alphabetical babble. Cerberus jogged off to hunt for lizards.

I wanted to conceal Ahriman's bones until I had an opportunity to rebury them at sea. There were plenty of hiding places on the reef, niches and angular hollows among the tumbled stone blocks at both the north and south ends; but no place would long remain safe from the dog's snooping. He'd probably drag the bones to the lighthouse door, where he sometimes left tiny lizard carcasses—limp creatures with still a touch of iridescence in their skins—and once he had deposited a bloody seagull that Martina insisted had died of natural causes. She liked to think of Cerberus as nonviolent.

We usually swam at the south end of the island, where a high slab of rock served as a diving platform, and ledges above and beneath the water made egress easy. North, then.

I put on my mask and fins, weighted the duffel with some rocks, tossed it into the water, and then followed it down. The water was cool, sharp with salt, and a little murky from the tidal currents. Beards of moss streamed away from the rock wall. The rock itself was black, though speckled with red and yellow accretions, and bright rings of light were reflected off the sandy bottom fifteen feet below. Panicky small fish flashed silver as they darted away. A red snapper—future menu item—slowly finned off into the fringe of weeds farther out. There were many crevices and pockets in the rock, hiding places for small octopuses and eels, but nothing big enough to hold the duffel until I reached the bottom where an overhanging ledge of reef formed little caves. I jammed the duffel deep into the largest of the recesses, turned, and swam back to the surface.

Cerberus, waiting for me, whined and groveled. The sea was no fit place for man or dog. I had brought along a cigarette and butane lighter, and I smoked it slowly, with guilty pleasure.

Martina was awake, cranky, and brewing coffee when I returned to the lighthouse. I explained that I had an appointment and must hurry: Tee time was at ten sharp.

"Tea time? You're going to have *tea?*"

EIGHT

Tee time had been scheduled for ten o'clock, but the twosome ahead of us arrived late, and at ten fifteen were just getting underway. A paunchy Methuselah with a snake-killing swing chopped a drive that flew seventy-five yards and rolled twenty more. "Bravo!" his partner said. "Right down the middle."

"Jesus," Petrie said.

"They'll probably drop out after five or six holes," Chester Dalhart said. "They usually do. Al will have a coronary event."

We were waiting by the putting green. Mr. Dalhart, a senior partner of Dalhart, Frey, and Saltzman, wore avocado green knickerbockers, a cream silk shirt with green piping, and a cap of the type worn by rioting Irish laborers in old movies. Tom's trousers were chocolate brown, circled by a broad white canvas belt; his shirt was made of some crepelike material that became transparent when wet. Both men lacked credibility.

The other duffer stepped forward to address his ball, wiggled his club and waggled his hind quarters, and then scooped up a drive whose height was double its length.

I said, "H equals L-squared."

"What?" Petrie said.

"Length squared equals height."

Dalhart looked at me.

"Pay no attention to him, Chester," Petrie said. "His mama dropped him on his head when he was a tyke."

Dalhart was a tall, lean man with the kind of profile you saw in old Roman frescos. He had surprisingly small hands and feet, spoke slowly and with precision, and showed a delicacy of manner that was contradicted by his cold gaze and hard mouth. Dalhart ignored me most of the time: I was "he" or "him," and he regarded Petrie with a sort of benevolent disdain. He was a hotshot corporation counsel, while Tom was merely a criminal defense lawyer—an advocate for riffraff.

The old guys were well down the fairway now. They each took a few more hacks, got into their cart, and vanished over a knoll.

Dalhart advanced to reconnoiter the terrain for the exactly right place to insert his tee.

"You really never golfed?" Petrie asked me.

"Half a dozen times, maybe, when I was a kid."

"You could have rented clubs instead of just hanging around."

"I hate the game, though I would dearly love an excuse to wear avocado knickers."

Dalhart divined the proper placement for his tee, inserted it carefully, mounted his ball on top, and then stepped back and stared down the fairway as a cavalry officer might scan the hostile Comanche country ahead. *Nothing moving out there, sir. That's what worries me, son.*

"Chester," Petrie called. "A friendly wager?"

"What's your handicap?"

"Six."

"Mine's four. I'll give you two strokes over eighteen holes for, say, one thousand dollars. Fifty dollars per hole on the side."

"Fine."

The Cold Springs Country Club, south of Bell Harbor, was as flat as the rest of Florida, though bull-dozers had wrinkled the land and excavated bunkers and created the depressions that became ponds. A few of the greens were tricky, but the fairways were fair and the roughs not rough and the hazards not very haz-ardous. It was a vanity course, an easy par 72. Chester Dalhart had suggested that the meeting take place at his golf club: He and Petrie could conduct business amiably, privately, without the usual interruptions, while at the same time enjoying a fine spring day. And, unmentioned, while he billed his clients several hundred dollars per hour.

Dalhart stood over his ball. He fussed a lot, no doubt recalling the admonitory words of his instructor, worrying about grip, foot placement, distance from the ball, the back-swing, club-head speed, all of that; and then he became very still before his swing. It wasn't a bad swing finally, and the ball carried about two hundred yards.

"Pretty shot, Chester," Petrie said.

Tom Petrie did not look like an athlete. He looked as though he had been the kind of snotnosed kid that you put out in right field during pickup baseball games because he couldn't catch a flyball, couldn't run far without falling, closed his eyes when swinging a bat, and cried when you yelled at him. But Tom was strong and quick, and possessed a deadly form of concentration. He hadn't been the snotnosed kid; he had been the boss, the enforcer, and he had exiled boys like the Dalhart kid into right field.

Petrie didn't fuss or fidget: he assumed his stance, paused only an instant, and then hit the ball three hundred yards down the center of the fairway. His swing was economical, fluid, even casual, as if whacking a tiny ball with a long stick was something you did while thinking about something else.

"Excellent strike, Tom," Dalhart said.

I chauffeured the electric cart. We did a lot of waiting while the old guys hacked their way through the first four holes, but then they turned back toward the clubhouse. "Angina," one called ruefully as their cart passed. The match proceeded swiftly then. Both men played well. Petrie won five of the first nine holes, and was three strokes up for the match. They chatted between shots, riding in the cart, though the purpose of their meeting was not mentioned: they talked about golf and golfers; praised each other's good shots while deploring the bad ones; they rated golf courses in the county and beyond; they gossiped about judges and other lawyers, tut-tutting scandalous unprofessional behavior; they criticized the U.S. Supreme Court, Dalhart because it was too liberal, Petrie because it was too conservative; and they told each other dumb jokes, not all of them dirty. I assumed that they were observing some obscure lawyerly protocol. They were getting to know one another, establishing trust or intuiting weakness, maybe even "bonding," as Candace would say.

The clubhouse, a massive stone-and-timber building with a vaulted ceiling and shake-shingle roof, was a bit run down. The money went into the golf course, and over the years the clubhouse had been allowed to settle into a comfortably shabby state, like a rich man's hunting or ski lodge. The members here would sneer at a clubhouse or lodge that looked like the lobby of a four-star hotel. There was a big lounge, a dining room, a pro shop and gift shops, a dance hall with bandstand, and lots of expensive empty space.

We ate lunch on the clubhouse deck. The faded teak planking was pocked by golf spikes, and sunlight leaked through frayed spots in the big awning. The deck overlooked three linked ponds fringed with lily pads, a brook, and a dense grove of trees. From behind the trees we heard the *tock-tock-tock* of a tennis rally. The *tocking* abruptly ceased, and a female voice cried, "Oh, God, lovely shot."

Dalhart and Petrie ordered Dover sole and split a bottle of white Bordeaux, while I had a liter stein of dark German beer and what the menu called *choucroute,* which turned out to be sausages and sauerkraut. The food was good. We praised it. The waiter took away the refuse. It was finally time for business. Chester Dalhart and Thomas Petrie had each taken the other man's measure.

"I hope you didn't lose much money in the Ponzi scheme, Chester," Petrie said.

"What makes you think I was an investor?"

"Were you?"

"That question is out of order."

"Objection noted. The reason I asked—these

big-time confidence men move into a place like Paradise Key and often their first victim is a lawyer highly regarded by the local plutocracy. Now, Christ, I am not suggesting that those lawyers are in any way culpable in the fraud. No sir. But we lawyers are surely as acquisitive, and often as gullible, as your average dope. And a shark like this Trebuchet might very well court a prominent local attorney who has connections to the rich. Court and seduce, so to speak, with a promise of riches. And that hypothetical lawyer, trusted by his clients and associates and friends, could open doors. Open doors, provide introductions, and allay suspicion by his simple participation in the venture. You understand."

Dalhart's expression changed during Petrie's cheerful assault: He looked both hurt and angry. He was a little tired from the nine holes of golf, and now had a full belly and a mind perhaps a bit fuzzy from the wine.

Tom said, "Didn't Trebuchet lease the house next to your place?"

"You're out of line, Petrie."

Petrie smiled. He was feeling mean and enjoying it. "Such a lawyer might be compared to a Judas goat."

"I resent your foul suggestion."

"Then of course I apologize. I intended no personal or professional disrespect."

Dalhart wrapped his hand around a half-full water glass, and for a moment I thought he would throw it in Petrie's face, but he managed to control his anger. Chester Dalhart was not a trial attorney, accustomed to the rude, sometimes nasty, give-and-take of the courtrooms and hallways. He worked on golf courses and on the corporation's motor yacht and in a big office that,

Tom told me, had walls upholstered in calfskin. He did not litigate often. He negotiated in a gentlemanly way with his peers. He spent his time professionally and socially with gentlemen and gentleladies.

"You have a filthy mind," he said.

"Alas," Petrie said.

"Maybe because you spend so much of your life in the company of criminals."

"That's it."

"Robbers, rapists, arsonists, smugglers, murderers . . ."

"I know," Petrie said with fake regret.

"The filth rubs off."

"It does, it does."

"The mind gets dirty, then the hands."

"Not the hands, Chester."

"I think you may be the wrong man for this job."

"If your vanity is the issue, then yes, I am the wrong man. But if you and your fellow investors want to recover at least a part of your money, then I am the right man. You need a dirty mind. You and your squeamish friends can stay clean, pristine even, while me and *my* friends attempt to recoup some of your losses. For a percentage, naturally, and expenses. Or you can turn over your evidence to state and federal prosecutors, and also file a civil suit. That might work out. If you can take the heat, the publicity, the general all-around loss of confidence and trust of the community at large. Your choice, Chester."

Dalhart looked down toward the ponds where half a dozen tame pink flamingos were stalking through the shallow water. No doubt the birds were hunting frogs or small fish, but it looked like they were admiring their reflections.

The female tennis player cried, "Oh, gorgeous shot, Kip!"

Finally Dalhart said, "I suppose we should get out and finish the back nine."

"Right. Do you want to cancel our friendly bet?"

"That tastes like another insult. No. I'd like to increase the wager to five thousand dollars for the eighteen, and raise the per-hole bet to one hundred dollars. If you think you can afford it."

"I'll hold a yard sale," Petrie said.

Dalhart abruptly deflected his anger from Petrie to me. He hooked a thumb in my direction. "Isn't your stooge capable of lucid speech?"

"I don't know." Petrie studied me. "Speak," he said.

"Fuck you both," I said.

Petrie laughed. "He's already a surly bastard, Chester, and he hasn't even taken his bar exams."

They did not discuss golf during the back nine. Not golf, politics, the law, or weather, and there was no genial exchange of bad jokes. They talked about the Ponzi scheme and those unidentified men and women who had perpetrated it. Mostly Dalhart talked and Tom questioned him in a way that reminded me of hostile courtroom cross-examinations. Chester represented a "consortium"—the group of defrauded investors—that wished to recover its money without, if possible, the engagement of the law—local, federal, or international. They wanted their goddamned money back. Petrie had been recommended, never mind by whom, for the job. Never mind asking for the names of any of the investors; none consented to be identified or approached or subjected to questioning: He, Dalhart, was to be our only conduit of information and instruction. Was that clear? The group had, in whole, been swindled of twenty million dollars. Petrie would receive forty percent of all monies recovered. The name of Trebuchet's fake company was Alpha Centauri. Paradise Key investors were given the opportunity to buy a special early stock offering, before shares were made available to the general public, before Alpha Centauri was listed on Wall Street and the Bourse and Japan's stock exchange. The stock was expected to split—two shares for one—soon after it was publicly listed, double again, and probably double again and again after that. You could not lose. It was like deeply investing in Microsoft in the early days. One hundred thousand dollars might turn into ten million, twenty million, fifty million, within a few years. Alpha Centauri was the company of the future. But you had to hurry. The clock was ticking. Men of nerve and foresight would triumph.

It seemed so plausible, Chester Dalhart said, so true, an investment as good as—much better than— gold. The leather-bound prospectus was like the Bible; it struck you like revelation; it compelled faith. Now some of the people involved believed that it was solely the charismatic Victor Trebuchet who had conned them out of their wits and fortunes, but no; actually they had been seduced by numbers. Logarithms, calculus, parameters (a variable or arbitrary constant appearing in a mathematical expression . . .), geometry, mathematical equations as mysterious as ancient runes. Scientific data, elegant diagrams and blueprints, metallurgic reports, charts of thermal tolerances, toss weights and escape velocities, variations in the earth's gravitational field, the frequencies of electromagnetic radiation inside the spectrum and outside—ultraviolet, infrared, X-ray, microwave—and on and on, scientific jargon that seemed to speak with the authority of God. Who was it who said that God was numbers?

Trebuchet and his people had compiled a great amount of material on rocket and satellite technology. No doubt such information was available in scientific and industrial journals, and probably on the Internet as well. But they had gone to considerable effort and expense to bait the trap.

"Do you know how many applications there are for communication satellites?"

"Tell us, Chester," Petrie said.

We were at the thirteenth tee, waiting for a fast twosome—the club pro and a student—to play through. The sky was beginning to cloud up now, but it appeared that rain was still a few hours away.

Dalhart told us that there already were a few companies that were successful in the commercial satellite business. They manufactured or purchased rockets. They established or rented launch facilities. They made satellites, placed them in orbit, and profited on a variety of lease arrangements. There were television and telephone satellites, of course; photo imaging applications (mineral surveying, mapping, gathering weather data, surveillance—spying—for governmental or private agencies), tasks contracted for by universities and research laboratories, and much more, including the eventual launching of civilians into sustained earth orbit.

Chester Dalhart talked like a true believer. He detailed the prospects of Alpha Centauri as if that mythical company really had offered the opportunity of a lifetime. He had been so convinced, so sold, that he still could not wholly believe that it actually had been a swindle. He was like the hypnotized subject who wakes up onstage half convinced that he is a chimpanzee.

The company, Dalhart said, was building its own launch site in Kenya with the cooperation and financial support of the Kenyan government. At least, that was what Trebuchet had told them. The closer one is to the equator, you know, the easier and cheaper it is to put a payload into orbit. The Alpha Centauri site was located a dozen miles north of Mombasa.

"Chester," Petrie said, "this is all very interesting. But what set Alpha Centauri apart from other similar operations? What, specifically, addled the minds of you and your friends?"

Dalhart talked vaguely of several revolutionary scientific "breakthroughs." He was vague because he really didn't understand what he was saying, although he employed the jargon with confidence. One breakthrough concerned the miniaturization of vital electronic components, and an exponential increase in the information storage and multiple function capability of a new generation of microchips developed by AC researchers. One satellite—already off the drawing board and into production—could perform the same variety of tasks previously assigned to a dozen satellites. And all of Alpha Centauri's satellites would be linked, "interactive"; they could "borrow" and "lend" data and function, could, in effect, "crossbreed," and this "hybridization" resulted in something that approached "artificial intelligence." That is, the individual satellites and the controlling "Central Brain System" could *learn,* acquire new knowledge and capacity, and even contrive a self-critical, self-correcting "superego." In addition, the satellites could achieve an extended "reposition mobility" (enabling them to change orbits upon command from the Central Brain System) through a new gaseous diffusion process, a controlled mixing of quiescent solid and liquid chemicals which, through catalytic reaction, created a potent gas propellant. There was no burning in the usual sense; therefore, no oxygen had to be carried aboard the satellites. Not all of the bugs had been eliminated. A new metal alloy was being tested for certain components of the precision valves.

"Stop," Petrie said. "This is a medicine that must be swallowed in small doses. Let's golf."

Petrie took his driver from the golf bag, walked to the tee, then turned and came back.

"Did your gang consult any scientists before investing?"

"We talked to Dr. Lobechevsky."

"Ah." Petrie nodded. "Dr. Lobechevsky."

Dalhart told us that Dr. Vladimir Lobechevsky was formerly second in command of the old Soviet Union's military satellite program.

"Well, sure he was." Petrie returned to the tee.

Dalhart looked at me. "It sounds stupid, doesn't it?"

"I thought parts sounded brilliant."

"I mean, we were stupid. We investors."

"It's a matter of scale," I said. "Two weeks ago I blew fifty dollars on lottery tickets. The odds were one hundred and sixty million to one against."

Dalhart lost concentration, lost his golf swing and

the match. Petrie continued to play well. He didn't need the two-stroke advantage—he won by eight.

"Thank you, Chester," Petrie said as he accepted Dalhart's check. He ignored the contempt with which it was scribbled and ripped from the checkbook. "We must play again sometime."

"I think not," Dalhart said.

"Do you play poker?"

"Only with friends."

"I'll be in touch soon. We have to work out an advance against expenses."

"Fine. But don't phone me at home. Don't come to my house."

Dalhart was still angry, coldly and stiffly furious. I wondered how much of his anger was due to the loss of fifty-eight hundred dollars to a man he despised. It was a lot of money even for someone who hadn't recently been swindled.

On the way back to Bell Harbor, I said, "Do you think Dalhart was in it with Trebuchet?"

"Nah. He was the first investor, the Judas goat, and he opened the corral gates for his fellow goats."

"Where the wolves were waiting."

NINE

Samantha Ridley waved to me from a booth at the rear of Sperino's Restaurant. It was dim back there, and private; you could talk if you didn't mind the parade of waitresses going back and forth through the kitchen's swinging doors. Her hair had been blond the last time I'd seen her, but now was the same rich lustrous red as an Irish setter's coat. Samantha was lean and nervous like a setter, and affectionate, and had a tendency to now and then run away for several days. She looked good as a brunette, blonde, or redhead, and whether or not contact lenses changed the color of her eyes to green or blue. They were green now, which suited her red hair and the deeply sincere gaze she usually affected.

"How have you been, lover?" she asked as I sat down.

"Well enough. And you?"

"Bitchy. Will your fiancée mind you having dinner with an old flame?"

"She isn't my fiancée yet, officially, and she won't mind as long as I tell her that you've lost your looks."

"But I haven't, have I?"

"No."

"It's strange to be back here."

"You're with the Gainesville paper now, aren't you?"

"I was, but now I'm working for *The Miami Times*."

"Big time."

"More money and more prestige and more pressure, but it's essentially the same *merde*."

Samantha had formerly been a reporter for the *Bell Harbor Record*. She'd earned an M.A. in history from Duke University and had more or less stumbled into journalism when she had been unable to get a job teaching at the college level. John Coyle, the owner of the *Record* (described as "crusty" by his friends, a "weasel" by his enemies) preferred to hire graduates in the liberal arts, students of history, English, philosophy, languages. He said that you could teach any reasonably intelligent person the fundamentals of journalism in a few weeks, but it required years to fill the brains of journalism majors, who generally couldn't write anyway.

The waitress arrived and Samantha, without consulting me, ordered veal piccata for both of us. I had a glass of wine, and she asked for bourbon on the rocks with a splash. It was not her first drink.

"Thanks for coming," she said.

"I'm glad to see you again, Samantha."

"Are you really?"

"Of course."

"I'm here to dig into the swindle."

"What swindle is that?"

"Duh. 'What swindle is that.' I've heard that Tom Petrie is peripherally involved. And I heard that you and Petrie are like this"—she held up her hand with the index and second fingers crossed—"these days. So don't what-swindle-is-that me, lover."

The waitress arrived with our drinks, blessed us with a saintly smile, and went away.

Samantha said, "I phoned Petrie's office every half hour today, all day, and my calls weren't returned."

"We were golfing."

"You, golfing?"

"Tom was."

"And you were his caddy? Look, I called your office, too, and a creature called Candy told me that you and Petrie were at the Cold Springs Country Club on business. Who was with you?"

"That hardly concerns you, Sam."

"Was it Chester Dalhart by any chance?"

"No."

"I can get the name. One name leads to another."

"To what point?"

"Rumors have drifted down to Miami and as far north as Atlanta. My nose tells me there's a good story here. My editor agrees. So there are rumors, whispers, gossip, allegations. I want to sort it all out. Will you help me?"

"No."

"Off the record, babe."

"You once told me to leave the room if a reporter ever says 'off the record.'"

"No, I never said that."

"And you advised me to run until my lungs hemorrhage if a reporter ever uses the word 'truth,' as in seeking the truth, only want to tell the truth, and so on."

"Okay. But Dan, this is *me*. I wouldn't burn you."

"How much do you know?" I asked her.

"Not much yet. Rumors of a huge Ponzi scheme that bilked a lot of the local movers and shakers. The Hunt Club, the Cold Springs Country Club, Paradise Key. Does that name mean anything to you?"

"No."

"You lie. Christ, you've become an Establishment lackey."

The waitress returned to ask us if everything was all right.

"What everything?" Samantha asked her. "Nothing has occurred. Bring us two more drinks"—she paused to glance at the waitress's name tag—"Lucinda."

When she was gone, Samantha leaned over the table. "Rockets," she said. "Satellites. Orbiting riches. What do you know about those things? Know about Victor Trebuchet's elite European polo team?" She laughed. "Not very subtle, that. I guess the crooks didn't have to be. Greed, they say, like lust, makes men extremely stupid."

"I can only speak to the lust part."

"Me, too. Dan, was the pompous Chester Dalhart one of the suckers?"

"You're barking up the wrong tree."

"Ah," she said, "you like my hair this color."

"I like you, Samantha."

"We had good times, didn't we?"

"Yes."

"Do you still sail? Still have your boat?"

"Yes, but I haven't got out much recently."

"You were mixed up in that Falconer mess, weren't you? The Mosquito Keys, all of that."

"Which story are you working on?"

"Trebuchet. Strange name. I looked it up. A tre-buchet was one of those medieval siege machines. You know, those massive timber structures that hurled boulders against castle walls."

"Really? Interesting, but . . ."

She smiled fondly at me. "I do miss you sometimes, Dan. Late at night. When the moon is full, and I've got an itch—you're my fantasy guy."

"Talk about subtlety. Give me credit for half a brain."

"Sorry. I've developed a habit of condescending to people, even friends. Nasty. But listen, I've encountered a lot of secrecy around here, guilty silence. What is this really all about? I'll find out, whether or not you help me."

The waitress brought our food, sauced veal on a bed of rice, and two salads.

"A bottle of red wine," Samantha told her. "Not Chianti. Nothing wrapped in straw."

"Starving," Samantha said, and she began sawing at her tough slab of veal. "Sorry to hear about your future uncle-in-law's dotty wife. Jesus, a shotgun. Why didn't he put a pillow over her face years ago?"

"Others have suggested the same thing. We have a lot of potential pillow murderers around."

We ate in silence for a time, and I said, "Why do print journalists pick out such mediocre restaurants? This tastes like one of those TV dinners they call 'gourmet.' I'm sure television people know where and how to eat."

"Don't kid yourself. TV people aren't really people at all, they're simulacra. They talk gibberish without a teleprompter. They eat soup with their hands when no one is watching."

The waitress returned with a bottle of wine, uncorked, and two glasses. "Is everything all right?" she asked. Samantha stared at her for a moment, then said, "Peachy keen, Lucinda."

"There's no need to give her a hard time," I said after the waitress was gone.

"I know. I'm sorry. I'm a bitch. She's probably supporting five kids and a drunkard husband. It's hell out there, lover. And often hell in here, too," she said, tapping her heart. She slyly glanced at me from beneath her brows to see if I was impressed, and then tossed her head and laughed. "But didn't we have fun, lover?"

After dinner, we walked down rain-wet streets to the boulevard, waited for the light to change, and crossed over to a rocky patch of beach. The bay and lighthouse were aglow with buttery moonlight.

"It looks like a minaret," Samantha said. "She lives out there, doesn't she? Your darling."

"Yes."

"I want to meet her."

"All right."

"I like her cartoon strip. She's tough."

"Martina's gentle, really."

"Oh, yeah, but I'm sure that beneath the sweet pudding there is a tough and determined woman. I think I'd like her, and yet I'm jealous. I can't help thinking that any man I've loved is still mine—I own them somehow. They took away a piece of me and left a piece behind. Kiss me, dimwit."

I embraced her, and at first we kissed in a casual way, but then were pressed against each other and the kiss went on much too long and too intensely.

"It's still there," she said when we parted.

"Some of it."

"Why did you leave me?"

"*You* left *me*, Samantha."

She laughed. "Damn," she said, "I'm lost without a research department and a fact checker."

"I'll walk you to your hotel."

Nighthawks swirled around a streetlight, snatching up insects, and somewhere a drunk was loudly saying, "I can drive, don't tell me I can't drive."

She took my hand. I liked Samantha. She was honest, no matter how hard she tried to appear false, cynical, jaded. She enjoyed her work and was good at it. But I had always thought that chance had sent her in the wrong direction, that she really should have been an academic, teaching history at some picturesque little college, living in a white house with green lawn all around, and married to a guy who smoked a pipe and parted his hair in the center and employed words like "dichotomy" and "accidie" and "subtext."

We paused on the hotel's steps. "Thanks for the dinner," I said.

"You are going to help me, aren't you?"

"What makes you think I'm involved?"

"You are involved, aren't you, and you're going to help me."

"We might be able to negotiate a limited exchange of information."

"How limited?"

"You can hardly expect me to become your spy."

"Nor me your spy."

"I'll phone you."

"Wait. This Lord Warfield who was a part of the scam? There really is a Lord Warfield. He lives in Suffolk County, England, and he's the ninth earl in the line. I looked it up in the stud books."

"Stud books?"

"*Debrett's Peerage.* That lists all of the British nobility, their ancestry, and so forth. The German equivalent is the *Almanach de Gotha.* There's also the Domesday Book, compiled by William after the Conquest, but you won't find Warfield in that."

"What made you think of looking up that stuff?"

"I was a history major, remember. Anyway, it's a lead."

"Not a good one. This guy wouldn't use his actual name and title. He was an impostor."

"It's a *lead*," she said. "Your turn."

"Sam, I've agreed to confidentiality."

"Right."

"It would be unethical . . ."

"Absolutely."

"The principals are desperate to avoid publicity."

"Sure they are. But you and I both know they're going to get plenty of publicity, no matter what."

"I can't help you at the moment. You seem to know a lot more than I do. I'll call you."

"Here's another freebie," she said. "Five years ago there was a bigtime swindle in California that was in some ways similar to the one here. Rancho Santa Fe— the place, you know, where the Heavens Gate cult committed mass suicide in order to secure passage to a spaceship. Ever been there?"

"The spaceship?"

"Don't be cute. Rancho Santa Fe is a very wealthy

and insular community. Five years ago a confidence man by the name of Anton Arbaleste arrived in town and a few months later departed with four million dollars and some valuable paintings."

"The same guy, you think?"

"An arbalest, like a trebuchet, was a medieval siege weapon, a huge crossbow."

"Don't tell me; you were a history major."

"Plus a big newspaper's computer files are filled with all kinds of information, going back years, and all nicely indexed. There is also the Internet, and police files—if you have a friend with a badge."

"And people think I'm a good investigator."

"I was never one of them."

"Good night, Samantha."

"Sure you won't come up to my room?"

"I'd like to, you know that, but no."

"Good for you. I hate cheats."

TEN

In the third grade I had a sometime friend named Donald Bullock, a chunky kid who periodically found my presence in the schoolroom and schoolyard unendurable. Usually we were pals, but I knew, when I saw him making ugly faces at me while in class, that after school we would once again meet on the field of honor. Leroy Karpe was like that today, although he was not deliberately making faces: Eight months ago he had been beaten half to death by Raven Ahriman, and the surgeons had not been able to put his face back together quite right; it was lopsided now, askew, and one eye appeared a bit lower than the other.

Tom Petrie said, "During the summer of 1848, a man named William Thompson conned a lot of people out of their valuable gold watches."

Petrie's law offices occupied half of the Dunwoody Building's top floor. At the rear there was a conference room with a long glass-and-chrome table, molded plastic chairs mounted on helices of steel that looked and acted like stiff springs, a green slate chalkboard, a huge chrome coffee pot that reflected a warped view of the room and its occupants, and paintings of the sort that Martina called "high kitsch."

Tom stood at the head of the table. "Thompson was a well-dressed, well-spoken man, and he approached other well-dressed, well-spoken men on the streets in a familiar way. The victim might assume that he had met Thompson, but could not then recall the time or occasion."

There were five of us seated at the table: me; Leroy Karpe with his basilisk stares; the two ex-cops, McNally and Cavaretta; and Charles Sinclair. Charles was relaxed and amiable, as usual, and he faked a profound interest in what Petrie was telling us.

"So," Tom continued, "after a short chat, Thompson would ask the man if he trusted him. 'Do you have confidence in me?' were his words. More often than not, the mark would say, 'Yes. Of course.' Thompson would then ask the man to give him his gold watch to hold for twenty-four hours—to demonstrate his confidence. And that was the origin of the phrase 'confidence man.'"

We were a sartorial potpourri. Leroy wore his standard parole outfit: faded jeans, scuffed work boots, a blue denim work shirt with *Leroy* sewn in above the breast pocket, and a baseball cap with *Leroy's Flying School* printed over the bill. Charles was nifty-casual in tan slacks, tasseled loafers, and a Harris tweed sport jacket worn over a gunmetal gray shirt open at the throat. The rest of us wore suits: Petrie wore a tailored prosperous-lawyer three-piece; I was in my modest paralegal cotton-polyester blend; and McNally and Cavaretta wore old-timer cop suits, shiny at the elbows and knees, with one-and-one-half-inch cuffs, and ties that had seen a lot of burgers and fries pass by.

"And so there you have it," Petrie concluded. "The predatory smart profiting from the abysmally stupid."

"It's not quite that simple," Charles said. "People very much want to believe. In love, God, human solidarity, themselves, money . . . The will to believe is a blind spot, personally and societally. In many ways, Tom, it's easier to con an intelligent man than a stupid one. You merely allow him to believe."

Petrie watched him. Charles could disagree in a tone and manner that made it seem that he was in complete agreement. We listened carefully to Charles for that reason, and because he was the only one of us who had made a career by cheating people out of their money and self-respect.

"You say to them, this truly is a holy relic, a splinter of the True Cross. You say, yes, I can surely put you in contact with the spirit of your deceased loved one. Yes, here is a map of where Captain Kidd buried his treasure. Yes, this priceless Rembrandt painting was discovered in a dusty attic in Duluth. Yes, this investment will make you richer than Midas. They need to believe. Sometimes it's so easy there's no sport in it."

McNally and Cavaretta regarded Charles with sour amusement, virulent contempt. Many cops respect violent criminals more than slick, shifty hustlers like Charles, especially when the hustler is gay.

"That's all very well, Charles," Petrie said. "But we aren't dealing with one of your starry-eyed believers now. Trebuchet is an accomplished con man, probably the best around. He took the people along this coast in just a few months of magic. Our job is to con the ace con man."

"That may be easier than you think. This Trebuchet is very arrogant now, careless, in love with himself and his successful scam. I know the type. I *am* the type. He thinks he's the biggest shark in the sea. He's always thinking about eating you, never about himself being eaten. So, you see, while he's nibbling at you, you're devouring him."

"Well, shit," Leroy Karpe said. Leroy was a practical man from the rural backwoods, most comfortable when flying or working on airplane engines. He had been a helicopter pilot during the first Gulf War, and afterward got into trouble flying drugs into South Florida. Petrie had managed to get him out of jail, had the case dismissed, and now they were partners in a small air charter service based at the Bell Harbor airport. I did not get along well with Leroy; I found him pigheaded; he saw me—as he saw most people—as unnecessarily complicated. Leroy went directly from A to C.

"McNally," Petrie said. "What did you two find at the house?"

Mutt consulted his notes. "It was stripped of personal possessions. They were thorough. They went to a lot of work wiping away fingerprints. But you can't wipe all the prints in a nine-room house, the garage, lawn furniture, chrome pool ladders, gate handles. We got some good latents. We even got latents off a frozen fish. A guy we know is going to do us a favor and run the prints through the computers. Maybe, Tom, we should give him a gift."

"Do it. Send me the bill."

"He mentioned he could use a new outboard for his boat."

"Get it. What else?"

"We're trying to get hold of the house phone records. And our same friend is going to see what he can pick up from the State Department—the passport office. Visas, entries and exits, all that. When we get an ID."

"Okay."

"We talked to the postman who delivered mail to the house. Letters, packages. What he saw, what he remembers. But he's concerned. It's illegal for post office employees to disclose that kind of info."

"Maybe a gift?" Petrie asked.

"A gift would be nice," McNally said.

"Nobody can hide these days," Cavaretta said. "There's always a paper trail, an electronic trail, a trail. We'll identify and locate the son of a bitch pretty soon."

"Charles?" Petrie said.

"I have my antennae out."

"So do all the other roaches," McNally said.

"Shaw?"

"I have an ear cocked," I said. "I have a finger testing the wind."

Petrie showed his disgust with a prolonged mouth-fart. "Have I assembled a team of mopes, of clowns?"

"Tom," I said, "it's too soon to expect much. We just got started."

"Leroy?" Petrie said.

"Hey, fuck this," Leroy said, rising from the table. "I got a charter flight to Charlotte in thirty-two minutes." He used several seconds of that thirty-two minutes to give each of us a crazy stare, and then he stalked out of the room.

Everyone seemed relieved to have Leroy gone. We were quiet for a while, until Cavaretta said, "All the doughnuts been eaten."

"Well, Christ," Petrie said. "I guess that indicates that this meeting is over. Almost over."

He inserted a videocassette into the television VCR: The screen fluttered with light and shadow, then settled into a clear picture of a teenaged girl posing with a big chestnut horse. She wore an English riding outfit, and her helmet barely reached the animal's withers. She stroked and hugged and kissed her horse with an affection that resembled sexual delirium. The microphone picked up background sounds, voices, a car engine, a horse neighing, and a woman—the girl's mother?—said, "You aren't looking at the camcorder, dear. Cynthia?" A man and a woman were crossing at a diagonal in the background. They became aware of the camera, hesitated an instant, and went on. You noticed the woman first, a brunette of classic Mediterranean beauty and the self-conscious grace of one who has always been admired. The man was a fitting escort; they belonged together. They were equally attractive, equally poised. He was tall and well built, with sculpted features, dark hair worn a little longer than the fashion, hooked black eyebrows, and a wide, mobile mouth that appeared to tense for a smile that didn't come. What interested me were his eyes: they were alert, nervously scanning the yard, seeing and evaluating. They were like the eyes of a combat veteran as he moved into enemy territory. He said something; the woman smiled. They were an unreal pair. They were separated from other people not just by their looks and aloof air, but, it seemed to me, by a cool, mocking, fuck-you-all arrogance. They passed out of the frame, and the teenaged girl stood alone, worshipping her horse.

Petrie showed the segment three times, then switched off the TV. "Trebuchet," he said. "And the sexy Mademoiselle Debarret. Sig 'em."

"They look like brother and sister," Charles said.

"What I think," McNally said, rising from the table, "I think the female suspects image will haunt my slack loins tonight. My wife may profit."

When the three of them had left the room, I said, "Did you get that tape from Bailey?"

"Yeah. He brought it in yesterday."

"How is he doing?"

"He was fired. No severance. I gave him fifteen hundred for the tape. He's going to Wyoming."

"Josh?"

"Old Josh is still pushing around a ton of horseshit per shift. I offered him a job here as night janitor, night watchman, night whatever. He said maybe."

"Tom, I know I'm reading too much into ten seconds of videotape, but this Trebuchet—there's something creepy about him."

"Well, we know, don't we, that he isn't an exemplary citizen."

"I want to fly to England tomorrow and interview Lord Warfield."

Petrie closed one eye and with the other sighted down an imaginary gun barrel. "Talk."

I told him all that I had learned from Samantha, though I didn't mention her name.

He said, "It wasn't the real Lord Warfield who blessed the locals with his presence. It was, it had to be, a phony."

"Probably."

"But . . ."

"I'd like to check it out."

"Keep your expense accounts scrupulously. Collect receipts. Chester Dalhart will not pay for your hookers or theater tickets."

We paused a moment at the door.

"Leroy's face is a mess, lumpy and scarred," I said. "And it's getting *worse*."

"The surgeon isn't finished."

"Tom, listen to me. Don't allow Karpe to become involved in this. He's totally unpredictable."

"Leroy?" Petrie said. "Are you talking about our Leroy? Why, damn your eyes, Leroy is as reliable as the day is long."

"Sulfur and saltpeter together are inert," I said. "But add charcoal to the mix and you've got gunpowder."

"That's an ambitious metaphor, and I am unable to extract a meaning."

"Leroy will blow up your plan, whatever it is."

"Ah, that. But I have no plan yet."

"You lie."

"I'll stipulate that I lie. But I'll also state that I stay awake nights, wondering what the fuck we think we're doing."

PART II
Inquiry

ELEVEN

It was about sixty miles from London to Tenwells in Suffolk County. That was not quite far enough to escape the suburban sprawl of southern England, but the core of the old market town remained relatively authentic. I rented a room at the Red Stag, an inn in the Tudor style that, according to a bronze plaque above the door, dated from 1558. It was built of age-blackened timbers and thick plaster, with low ceilings and wood plank floors, and the small windowpanes were made of the crude bubbly glass of that time.

After registering, I went into the public house and ordered a pint of ale. Everything there was old and worn: the tables and chairs, the benches, the bar behind which an aproned man worked on a newspaper's crossword puzzle. I was thirsty after my long flight from Miami and the drive from London, and I quickly ordered a second pint. I drank it, wondering if perhaps Shakespeare and The King's Men, his theater company, had stayed here during one of their flights from London during plague years. I imagined Will and the gang sitting near the fireplace, swilling ale and rudely flirting with the barmaids and disputing gambling debts. I recalled reading that the water had been so bad in those days, so deadly with microbial nastiness, that the people drank cheap ale, quarts and quarts of ale, each day. The prosperous drank wine as well. Water was only for washing, though probably people back then didn't like getting wet often. Exciting times, with everyone smelly and drunk and horny and quick to take offense.

The barman drifted toward me. He was about forty, with meaty red ears, a long jaw, and eyes the color of pewter.

"Another, sir?" he asked.

"Yes, thanks." I was already a bit drunk from the two quick ales on an empty stomach.

The barman drew the ale, let the foam settle to a thin line, and placed it on the bar. He remained there, willing to talk if I wanted to talk, pleased to go away if I wanted to be alone. There was no one else in the room.

"I'm here to see Lord Warfield, if he'll consent to a visit. Is he an accessible man?"

"He's never been inaccessible, though he's very old now, and not well."

"Old?"

"Oh, yes. In his eighties, and quite brittle."

"Will you have a drink with me?"

"Yes, sir, thank you." He drew half a pint of bitter from the tap, raised his glass, said, "Cheers," and we drank.

"Is there a young Lord Warfield? I mean, a sort of Lord Warfield in waiting?"

"He has a grandnephew on whom the estate is entailed. Alfred will eventually—soon, we fear—become the tenth earl."

"Fear?"

"Fear, sir, in the sense that we shall lose the present earl. We're all rather fond of the old boy."

"Is it okay to smoke?"

He produced an ashtray from behind the bar. He accepted the cigarette I offered; we lit up and smoked in silence for a time.

I said, "I represent a conservation organization that disperses funds worldwide. The World Preservationist Fund. We do all we can to save patches of the natural environment. We know that Lord Warfield is determined to preserve his property in its present state, free from encroachment, development, pollution, change. We'd like to help him—his estate—to protect the animal and bird life, keep the woods and hedged fields, the wetlands . . ." The ale was strong; I lost my train of thought.

". . . in a pristine condition," he finished my sentence. "A very commendable goal, sir."

"I'll determine if Lord Warfield's property qualifies under the terms of our charter. If so, and if we can agree on certain provisions, we'll give him a generous grant."

"Aye, save the birdies," the barman said.

"The birdies, the badgers, the hedgehogs, the ferrets, the foxes, the fishies in the brookie . . ."

He smiled, and acknowledged with a nod that I was not quite the stiff he'd supposed.

"Well, sir," he said, "as I mentioned, Lord Warfield is old, and ill, they say, but I have no doubt he'll consent to see you in such a noble cause. It's clear to me, sir, that your motives are beyond reproach, and your fund's financial resources are being put to good use."

He was, in the English phrase, sending me up.

"Another pint?" he asked.

"No. I've had enough."

"Will you be having dinner with us tonight? Roast lamb is the special."

"Sounds good. Mark me down."

"Fine. Eight o'clock?"

"The sum," I said, "that we have in mind for Lord Warfield's estate is small, at most one hundred thousand dollars—roughly sixty thousand pounds. But perhaps it will help."

I signed my tab, including a generous tip, and as I was leaving the room he called, "If you wish, I could ring up the estate and perhaps arrange to have Lord Warfield's secretary join you for dinner."

"That would be fine. Thank you."

"I'll reserve a table by the fireplace for you and Miss Turnbull. Eight o'clock. *Bon appetit.* And may I say, sir, that you are well spoken for an American."

My room was not much more than barely comfortable. Bed with a quilted down comforter, writing desk, night table, coffin-size closet, a ceiling that slanted down from the hallway side to the windows (with panes like Coke bottle bottoms) framed in iron. The bathroom was down the hall. Ambience did not come cheap; you paid for the historical associations.

I went downstairs at ten to eight and ordered a glass of wine from the new bartender, a plump, cheery woman who addressed me as "Mr. Shaw." The bar was crowded, and through a doorway I could see people moving around in the dining room.

At eight sharp a tall, attractive woman came through

the front door, glanced around, and proceeded directly toward me.

"Mr. Shaw?" she asked.

"Yes."

"I'm Cassy Turnbull."

"Cassy as in Cassandra?"

"Cassy as in Cassiopeia, the constellation. My father was an astronomer."

"May I call you Cassiopeia?"

"You may call me Casserole if you order me a drink fast."

"What would you like?"

"Are you on an expense account?"

"Yes."

"Something expensive then. They have a precious bottle of forty-year-old Scotch here."

"Go for it, Cassiopeia."

"You're nice," she said, and she ordered a double of the rare scotch straight up.

Cassy Turnbull had multicolored hair. She was a natural blonde, but a long winter of rare, weak sunlight had allowed it to darken, and so now there were layers and threads of color—wheat blond, dull blond, various shades of brown, and near black at the center part. It would be a glorious leonine mane in July when thoroughly bleached by the sun.

"You're Lord Warfield's secretary, then."

"Actually, no. You might say that I am the secretary to the secretary. Penny is the secretary—and the heir to the estate. Alfred Pennington. It's complicated. And you're the good gray American who has dropped out of the sky to bless us with bushels of money."

"Gray? Really?"

"A figure of speech. You're not gray at all. You're instead rather bronze. You must live in a warm climate. Florida?"

The bar was crowded, but not so packed that she had to stand as close to me as she did, nearly touching. She was a tall woman made even taller by her high-heeled shoes, and we stood eye-to-eye, navel-to-navel. I smelled her hair and skin and the whiskey on her warm breath.

I said, "I think our table is ready."

"Let's go in, and you'll tell me all about your gift. I'm capable of believing almost anything."

I bumped my forehead on the lintel above the entrance to the dining room, and she said, "Oh, dear, I'm so sorry," as if it were her fault that people were short in 1558.

The dining room was small: there were only ten tables, one banquet-size and the rest—except for a pair of two-tops flanking the fireplace—set for four or six. A small fire burned on the hearth. There were racks of iron tools, pokers and rakes and little shovels, and other curious implements that looked like instruments of torture.

She gazed at me over the rim of her glass when we were seated. "We tried to reach your organization—what is it?—The World Preservationist Fund. We could find no such entity in the United States."

"That's because we're registered in Switzerland. Geneva."

"Yes, naturally."

The waiter came for our orders. We both selected

the night's special, roast lamb with roasted potatoes and peas. She asked if she might order the wine, I agreed, and she asked for a 1963 Château Margaux at three hundred pounds for the bottle.

"Is that all right?" she asked with a smile, folding the wine list and passing it to the waiter.

"Well," I said. "Roast lamb . . . If we had ordered a pizza, then . . ."

Still smiling, she reached out to touch my hand. "You're sweet and generous to Cassiopeia, aren't you, my bronze visitor from across the water." Her words and her gaze were taunting, but at the same time she remained provocative, sexually inviting. She flirted until the food arrived at our table and then she tired of the game and turned down the voltage of her witchy sexuality. She devolved from *femme fatale* to *femme ordinaire* between the soup and entrée. Cassiopeia ate like a dragon, and afterward ordered helpings of what she and the waiter called *gâteau* but which to me looked like chocolate cake. We had coffee then, and snifters of cognac that cost Chester Dalhart thirty-five dollars a glass.

She smoked. Others in the room were smoking, and so I accepted one of her cigarettes and lit it.

She gazed at me through the bluish haze. "I enjoyed dinner enormously," she said.

"Good. Then it was worth an overdraft or two."

"On my way here, I thought, oh, God, I'm going to spend an evening in the company of a horribly sincere Yank do-gooder. But you turned out different from what I expected."

"Did I?"

"You're a Yank, all right, but neither sincere nor a do-gooder."

"Thanks, I guess."

"You're an American cop, right? FBI?"

"No. FBI agents really are gray and sincere."

"It didn't take me long—say twenty seconds—to determine that you are a phony."

"Fast work."

"I've had too much to drink. Am I behaving eccentrically?"

"You are."

"Good."

"Two nights ago I had dinner with a woman who's at least as eccentric as you. It seems that more and more women are going in that direction."

"Yes, we become more eccentric while you men become more gray and stuffy and conformist. It's a necessary counterbalancing."

"I suppose you don't want to hear about the World Preservationist Fund and details of the grant."

"God, no. I will say, though, that proposing to charitably grant a large sum of money is a good ruse. Do you use it often?"

"First time."

"Keep it in your bag of dirty tricks."

"Do you know a man named Trebuchet?" I asked.

"Odd name, that."

"I didn't come here to cause Lord Warfield or Pennington or you trouble."

"Don't, then."

"But I will cause trouble if I don't get the information I need."

"Now you *have* become gray and sincere. How dreary."

"Trebuchet is the one I'm after."

"I'm tired, I'm stuffed, I'm bored. You'll walk me to my car, won't you?"

Her Nissan was parked two blocks away from the inn. We passed an elderly couple, a woman walking her dog, another pair, and, on the corner beneath a streetlamp, a constable who nodded to Cassy and touched his cap.

I waited on the sidewalk while she jingled through a key ring.

"Do you have transportation?" she asked.

"I rented a car at Gatwick."

She found the right key and opened the door. "Do you know the way to the house?"

"I have a map."

"Well, then." She started to get into the car, then halted with one foot inside and the other on the pavement. "You will have two choices tomorrow. You can decide to be very cruel, ruin several lives, or . . ." She slipped into the car, rolled down the driver's side window, and started the engine.

I stepped off the curb. I wanted to tell her that I was not a policeman, not a man seeking vengeance, not here to cause trouble for her and her friends. "Cassiopeia, I don't—"

"It's *Cassy*, for Christ's sake!" she said, and she shifted the car into reverse, backed out of the parking slot, and then, burning rubber, drove much too fast down the narrow street.

She had forgotten to turn on the car lights, and the constable on the corner shouted at her. The tail lights came on, the brake lights flashed, and she turned left at the cross street.

"Evening, sir," the constable said as I passed. "You put Miss Turnbull into a perfect fury, I'd say."

TWELVE

An earl, according to my hasty research, was a British peer who ranked above a marquis and below a viscount. (Baron and baronet were lowest on the scale; duke was the highest, excluding royals.) An ancestor of the present Lord Warfield, a man who had served as a privateer with Sir Francis Drake, had been elevated to the peerage by Queen Elizabeth I in 1588 and, with his share of loot pirated from the Spanish gold fleet, had purchased two thousand acres of land in Suffolk and built his house, Heatherhill. In time the two thousand acres had been reduced to six hundred; fields and woodlands had been sold to raise money, and less than half of the remaining acres were now in anything like the original state.

The house was twelve miles out of Tenwells, on a narrow county road that wound through hedged fields and patches of woods and crossroad hamlets that had once been a part of the estate. The house was at the end of a looping driveway, perched on the only visible rise of ground high enough to be called a hill. The house was not as grand as I'd expected. The center building was four stories high, constructed of a rose-hued stone that

119

was mostly concealed behind spring green creepers of ivy, with vertical rows of recessed windows and a gray slate roof that sprouted brick chimneys that sprouted ceramic pipes. Two additional buildings, built in different architectural styles, flanked the main house. And there were outbuildings: garages, a couple of cottages, stables, what probably was once the kennels. A brook angled in from the northeast, paused to fill a circular pond, then exited—now muddy—and snaked down toward the road. There was a marble fountain, empty and cracked, and a few pieces of marble statuary whose classical poses looked absurd in this light, this time—heroes abandoned by a retreating Roman army.

An old man, on his knees and hunched over in a flower bed, was attacking the soil with a trowel. From a distance it looked like murder.

Cassy Turnbull was waiting for me at the entrance. She appeared almost demure today in a blue pantsuit, with her wild mane of hair tamed by pins and clips.

I parked the car on the grass next to the fountain, got out, and crossed the flagstone drive.

"Good morning," I said.

"I was hoping you wouldn't come," she said. "But here you are."

"Here I am."

I followed her through the big door into a bare foyer, then through another door into a big rectangular room with high, raftered ceilings and great fireplaces at the north and south ends. You could spit-roast an ox in either of those fireplaces. There was not much furniture. The carpets were faded and threadbare. A big shield high on the east wall displayed the family's armorial bearings. Pale geometric shapes on the walls indicated where paintings had once hung. Cassy waited while I looked around the room.

"All of the good paintings and nearly all of the valuable antiques have been sold to pay taxes," she said, her voice echoing in the mostly empty space. "There isn't much left to see. Just land. Land for an ugly housing development or maybe a fucking golf course."

I followed her across the big room and down a short corridor, and then through a series of rooms, all of them bare, and then into a final room, which was furnished as an office. There was a desk with carved legs and an intricate marquetry top, wooden filing cabinets, a computer station, a refectory table, a mismatched collection of chairs and settees, and lamps that looked as though they had long ago been converted from gas to electricity. The lamps were burning despite the bright sunlight that poured in through tall mullioned windows. The refectory table held a coffee urn, cups and saucers, cream and sugar, butter and jars of fruit preserves, and a silver platter heaped with brioches.

"Help yourself," she said. "I'll fetch Penny."

I poured a cup of coffee, spooned marmalade over a brioche, and walked to the window. The man I had noticed earlier was scooping weeds and algae out of the pond. He wielded a long pole with a wire basket mounted on the end. He was an old man, unsteady, and barely had the strength to compensate for the leverage exerted by the end-weighted pole. I watched him, concerned that he might slip on the muddy bank and fall in.

Cassy returned with a man she introduced as Alfred Pennington. His handshake was firm and brief, his half smile without tension. He was about thirty-five, with lank dark hair and blue eyes and a wide mouth that had creased commas at each end. He wore a navy blue blazer, gray flannel slacks, and a diagonally striped tie that probably was associated with some school or club or regiment. Brits could glance at that tie and fairly accurately determine his background and education and place on the social scale.

"I see you have coffee," Pennington said. "Care for a bit of brandy in it?"

"No, thanks, this is fine."

"Cassy tells me you're a policeman of some sort."

"No, a lawyer." Almost a lawyer.

"Cassy guessed wrong. Didn't you, darling?"

"A lawyer is worse."

"I don't think so," Pennington said.

His face had a faint amber tint, as if he suffered from jaundice; but it was just what remained of a fading Florida suntan.

Cassy moved to the refectory table and began filling a silver serving tray with an insulated carafe of coffee, a cup and saucer, and a brioche smeared with raspberry jam.

"Look," Pennington said. "We must talk. But now why don't you go along with Cassy and meet Henry. I told him that an American chum would be visiting today. You won't say anything about Florida, will you?"

"No."

Cassy picked up the tray. "Lead on, lawyer," she said to me.

I preceded her through the series of rooms, opening and closing doors, and when we reached the big room

I saw a white-haired man sitting on one of the few remaining chairs. He was old, and gaunt, but sat erectly. His thinness exaggerated the size of his hands, feet, ears, and nose; though lanky, he had a gnomish look. "I hurt my back again, Cassy," he said as we approached.

"You know you shouldn't be straining yourself as you do."

"I just can't sit all day, you know."

"Well, you'll be sitting or lying down for a week now."

He was the gardener, the pond cleaner.

Cassy placed the serving tray on a side table, straightened, and said, "This is Lord Warfield. Henry, Daniel Shaw."

"How d'you do?" he asked, offering his knuckly, age-freckled hand.

"I'm pleased to meet you, Lord Warfield," I said.

"You're Penny's friend. Were you at Cambridge with him?"

"No."

"I'll go get the wheelchair," Cassy said, and she crossed the room and passed through a doorway.

"American, are you?" Lord Warfield said. "Good for you. I never shared the prevailing sentiment about Americans. I served with some fine American officers in the war. The big war, that is, the one with two Roman numbers at the end. Were you one of that wild lot Penny ran with a few years back?"

"No, sir," I said.

"Penny sowed his wild oats. My God, did he! But he's settled down since, and a good thing, too. Soon, poor chap, he's going to be encumbered with this place and the taxes and the bloody peerage. Titles aren't worth the breath needed to pronounce them these days. Just as well, I suppose."

Cassy pushed a wheelchair through the doorway and advanced toward us.

"Cassy," Lord Warfield said, "perhaps you'll help me to eat. I don't like to move much with this blasted back of mine."

"Of course I'll help you," she said, and she gave me a look.

I said, "I'm glad to have met you, sir. And I hope your back heals soon."

"Thank you. It's just one of those damned spasms. Don't mention my back to Penny. I'm not in the mood for reproaches."

Pennington was seated behind the desk now, leaning back in a swivel chair and smoking a cigarette.

"Lord Warfield hurt his back," I said.

He nodded. "He's eighty-three, and still insists on mucking around in the garden or pond." He leaned forward, smashed his cigarette out in an ashtray, and looked at me.

"What is it you want?" he asked.

"I want to hear about it. All of it. Trebuchet and the others, details of the Ponzi scheme."

"Right. But you haven't yet issued any threats."

"The threats are implicit."

He smiled. "The most effective threats usually are."

"How much was your share of the swindle?"

"If you don't mind," he said, "we'll wait for Cassy before proceeding."

We waited in silence for a few minutes, and then

Cassy came into the room, went to one of the settees, and sat down.

"He's still in the chair, Penny," she said. "There's too much pain when he moves. You'll have to help him to bed, carry him, I imagine."

"Best to leave him in the chair for now," he said. "Until the muscles relax a bit."

"That's what he said."

"I am about to tell Mr. Shaw about our friend."

"Your friend," she said.

"All right," Pennington said. "I met him four years ago. He was going under the name Anlace then."

I said, "He's also used the name Caliburn."

"Has he? Caliburn, you know, was the true, the original name of King Arthur's sword in legend. Excaliber. Obviously he chooses the names of weapons for his noms de guerre—Caliburn, Trebuchet, Anlace. An anlace is a medieval dagger. We had a fine one here, used it for a letter opener, but it vanished."

"It was sold at auction," Cassy said. "Along with nearly everything else. Your chum Anlace bought the Dürer engraving, Penny, remember?"

"Now I do." To me he said, "He collects art. He bought a small Constable landscape at a London gallery when I knew him as Anlace. Paid quite a lot. And he obtained some art objects in Florida from one of the investors. I doubt he paid—probably exchanged some worthless stock for the items."

"Did he pay for the Dürer engraving?"

He looked at Cassy.

"Yes," she said. "He paid by having the money wired to the auction house from a bank in the Caribbean."

"Do you remember the name of his bank?"

"I can look it up."

"Please do."

Pennington said, "I met Anlace—Trebuchet—at a London casino called Club Nexus four years ago. He was a rather mysterious figure. He just sort of materialized out of the fog and later vanished back into it. A charming man, as you'd expect. Clever, witty, good manners, very well dressed. An elegant man, you might say, though not a fop, not in the slightest epicene. He was liked by both men and women. His openness was deceptive. He always maintained a certain reserve. It wasn't just the vagueness of his background, or even doubt of his true nationality. He claimed to be French, and carried a French passport, but people were dubious. He spoke English well, with the sort of accent that one can't quite place. French, Italian, Spanish . . . No one guessed that he was an American."

"And he is American?"

"Oh, yes. I found that out in Florida. A Europeanized American, an expatriate."

"And he's a gambler?"

"Yes, as I was then. I was drinking a lot. Drinking, experimenting with drugs, and gambling. I gambled away all of my money. The money I'd earned and the money left to me by my father. The Club Nexus extended me credit. They knew, of course, that I would inherit this property, and probably sooner rather than later. I owed them some sixty thousand pounds when they finally cut off my credit. Now, it isn't like the movies. The Club people weren't going to break my legs or kill me and throw me into the Thames. They could afford to wait. But I was not merely destitute, I was so deeply in debt that it appeared certain that the Club people would try to seize the entire estate when I actually did inherit."

"Enter Anlace," I said.

"Enter the devil," Cassy said.

"He bought my chits, my signed notes—you call them markers in America, I believe. It was, he said, an act of friendship, of sympathy. He would hold the paper as long as necessary. He would not charge interest. I would be under no pressure, there'd be no danger of losing the estate. He said he was very rich, and sixty thousand pounds was an amount of little consequence. Not long afterward he disappeared from London, from England. Until last winter when he telephoned."

I said, "And he suggested that you pay off the debt by joining him in a business venture in Florida."

Pennington nodded.

"You were instructed to pose as Lord Warfield."

"Well, yes, but you know, it really wasn't that much of an imposture. I will inherit the peerage one of these days."

"You, as Lord Warfield, a British earl, were very useful in impressing potential investors. You gave them confidence. Didn't anyone from Florida make inquiries here?"

"Yes," Cassy said. "A man by the name of Dalhart wrote to us here, and later he phoned. I confirmed the lie."

I turned to Pennington. "You knew that what you were doing was illegal. That Trebuchet was a crook."

"Oh, yes. I knew within a day of arriving at Paradise

Key. It was a fantastic scheme. Of course I knew it was fraudulent, but I wanted to recover those notes of debt, save this place from being cut into a thousand parcels. The ends justified the means. There isn't much I can say in my defense. Just this: I never tried to persuade people to invest; I never stated that I myself was an investor; I was a passive participant in all of it."

"And," I said, "you never received your markers."

He smiled faintly. "How did you know?"

"I know a little about the criminal mind."

"When I left Florida, he said that the notes were kept in a safety deposit box in a London bank, and an associate of his would meet me at the airport and give me the papers. No associate, no papers. I telephoned the house on Paradise Key, but by then, of course, he was gone."

"I assume that you don't feel kindly toward the man."

"You may very well assume that."

"Maybe you can help me, Pennington."

"And maybe you can help me."

"And maybe," Cassy said, "you both can help me. I told Emma to prepare a lunch and serve it in the back garden. Penny, why don't you look in on Henry, and then meet us outside."

There was a courtyard behind the house; a grid of gravel walks divided the space into geometrical shapes and traced a way through flower beds and shrubbery. The day had turned warm, with a balmy southwest breeze and a filmy haze that filtered sunlight in a way peculiar to the British Isles.

Cassy and I sat at a table that had been set up on a terrace of pink flagstones. Arranged on the table were three place settings; two loaves of bread, one dark and the other white; a bowl of fruit; a tureen of soup warming over a glass flame; and a platter of cheeses—Stilton, Gruyère, and Camembert. A bottle of red wine was on the table; a bottle of white cooled in a silver ice bucket.

Cassy sat quietly, her hands folded on her lap, gazing out beyond the garden wall to the fields and, beyond, at a far rise of land, a wood that looked mystical in the misty light.

"It's pleasant here," I said.

"Yes."

"The garden looks well maintained."

She told me that gardeners and handymen from the village were hired on a daily or weekly basis. The estate still employed some longtime staff—the housekeeper, the cook, a cleaning woman, a chambermaid—all of them getting on in age now, too old, really, to work so hard. Money was needed to provide for their pensions. Money was needed for so many things.

"Are you and Pennington old friends?" I said.

"Is that a crude way of asking me if we're lovers?"

"A polite way, I thought."

"Well, we are lovers. Have been, are now, and shall continue to be until we're married in the autumn." She laughed. "And maybe afterward, too."

"British titles and honors are a mystery to me. Will Penny become Lord Pennington when he inherits?"

"No. He'll change his name—that's explicitly stated in the entailment. He'll become Lord Warfield."

"And, when you marry, you'll become Lady Warfield?"

"Anachronistic, isn't it? Ancient forms and irrelevancies."

"Did you go to Florida?"

"I stayed behind to run things here and look after Henry, though I did visit Paradise Key for a weekend. I was paraded around and introduced to the silly flock of sheep and the herdsmen who were fleecing them. I hated it. It was all greed and pretense and snobbery. I begged Penny to return to England with me, but he was desperate to eliminate his debt. So here we are, Penny, me, and you. And what exactly do you intend to do?"

"The people I'm working for want to recover as much of their money as possible. They—we—aren't interested in prosecution or scandals."

"That's a relief, if true."

"It is true."

Pennington emerged from the back door and strolled down the walk toward us.

"His back is still in spasm," he said, "he's still in his chair. He may petrify there."

"Oh, dear," Cassy said.

Pennington sat down at the table. "I gave him a shot of muscle relaxant. Mrs. Harris is with him now."

"Penny, Mr. Shaw says that he and his employers have no intention of prosecuting you or disclosing your part in the swindle."

"That's wonderful, if true."

"It's true," I said. "And if I'm able to recover your markers, I'll send them to you."

"That's damned decent of you."

"I want you to tell me all about Florida, everything you know about the swindled and the swindlers. The complete operation."

"Then let me begin by saying that I believe I know where you can find him."

"Find Trebuchet?"

"It's likely that he'll now be going under the name Anton Arbaleste. An arbalest, you might know, was a medieval weapon, like the trebuchet."

"Where is he?"

"I lived as his guest in Paradise Key for almost three weeks. I snooped. I read his post when I could, read his e-mail, rifled his desk drawers, eavesdropped on his phone conversations. Not honorable. Not the actions of an English gentleman, but there it is. I was hoping to find my debt notes and, foiling that, learn all I could about the man who owned my future. During my stay in Florida he was trying to secure a summer lease of property in Italy, in a village called Castelnuovo on the coast south of Sorrento. He used the name Anton Arbaleste in these negotiations. There were difficulties, a question of availability, money. I can't tell you if he ultimately did lease the property, but the negotiations were far along when I returned to England. He was quite determined to secure the lease. He might well be there now, basking in the Mediterranean sun, counting his loot, laughing at all who trusted him."

"Open the wine, Penny," Cassy said. "We're hungry."

We talked through lunch and for ninety minutes afterward. Cassy remembered the name of Trebuchet's bank: The People's Commercial Bank and Trust of Nassau, the Bahamas. I thanked them, expressed my hope that Lord Warfield's back would soon heal, and said that I would not bother them further.

"One more thing." Pennington hesitated. "This man—Caliburn-Anlace-Trebuchet-Arbaleste—I think he might be very dangerous. Something I sensed rather than saw."

"He's a reptile, actually," Cassy said.

They walked me to the car. Pennington shook my hand, Cassy briefly kissed my cheek, whispering thanks, and they remained there watching as I coasted down the long drive to the county road.

THIRTEEN

It was midnight Florida time when I telephoned Petrie at his home. I could hear voices and jazz in the background, and hear a dog whose staccato barking lasted throughout our conversation.

"I'm in Rome," I said.

"Oh, good. Thanks for telling me."

"I'm catching a flight to Naples."

"Where?"

"Naples."

"I can't—for Christ's sake, keep it down for a second."

"Naples, then south to a town called Castelnuovo."

"Castle what?"

"Castelnuovo."

"Who does that dog belong to?"

"I don't know, Tom."

"Eileen, can't you shut up that beast, for Christ's sake!" Then to me he said, "The mutt's dumber than Cerberus. You're going where?"

"Trebuchet—now Arbaleste—has a place on or near the Amalfi Coast. He may be there now."

"What are you going to do when you find him?"

133

"Improvise."

"Listen, pal, don't blow it. We've got to sneak up on this bastard. Infiltrate, skin him, then exfiltrate." Tom liked military jargon; he saw himself as a great strategist.

"I may ask you to wire me money. A lot of money."

"I swear, I'm going to kill that fucking animal!"

"Tom, why don't you take this call in another room?"

"Because it's going to be short."

"You were right about Dalhart," I said. "He was the Judas goat. He was conned first, and he brought the others in."

"Of course I was right. I thought it was stipulated that I'm always right. How do you know where Trebuchet is?"

"Long story."

"Think you're hot stuff, don't you? But we found the name the guy was christened with."

"I'll bet you fifty dollars his true name is the name of an ancient weapon."

"You owe me fifty. The name on his birth certificate is Halbert, Jean, capital J-e-a-n, not J-o-h-n, Halbert."

"Halbert *is* the name of an old weapon. It's a spear with a battle-ax attached."

"That's Halber*d* with a 'd.'"

"Tom, I think Halberd is an acceptable or alternate spelling."

The dog continued barking; people continued to laugh and talk; there was a momentary cessation of music, and then I heard the beginning of a Miles Davis piece, one that had been recorded during his shrieking, atonal period.

"Who put the Miles on?" Petrie shouted. "Take him off!"

"Tom, who are these people?"

"What?"

"I'll phone you tomorrow."

"I sent Mutt and Jeff up to the Hudson Valley to learn what they can about Halbert's misspent youth."

"He's an American."

"I *know* he's American."

"Who are those people?"

"Lawyers and spouses. I met them at a symposium tonight. The speaker told us that cross-examination—the best way of discerning truth—stems directly from the Socratic dialectic. Two thousand five hundred years ago Socrates was cross-examining people in the marketplace."

"No wonder they killed him," I said.

"What?"

"You owe me fifty dollars."

"No I don't. A halber*t* is a lady's corset. Eileen, I really will kill that fucking dog, and you too, if he pisses on my Persian carpet."

"You're drunk."

"Tell me something I don't know."

Miles was shrieking, the dog was barking, Petrie's guests sounded like a lynch mob in the background.

"I'll call you tomorrow," I said.

"Who spilled wine on Chippendale? Goddamn it, who spilled the wine?"

I hung up the telephone.

FOURTEEN

Sorrento is situated at the end of a little peninsula that juts out into the Mediterranean. The Isle of Capri lies several miles offshore. North is the Bay of Naples; south, the Gulf of Salerno. The Amalfi drive runs east to Salerno. That route, famous for its beauty and the spectacular cliffside road, has been featured in many films. Vertigo, a moments inattention, a crazed Italian driver, can send you over the cliff and into the sea.

Castelnuovo is tucked in a valley half a mile east of the Mediterranean. Narrow cobblestone streets zigzag up the hillside to the plateau above. The buildings, big, with whitewashed walls and terra-cotta tile roofs, are perched precariously on the steep grade and appear to defy gravity. Someday, I thought, an earthquake might send all of them tumbling down to the valley floor. You needed strong legs to hike around that town, and reliable brakes on your car.

I had lunch in a café, a vermouth in a dim bar; I visited a few real estate offices, and I chatted with some kids in one of the tiny plazas. Anton Arbaleste was well known in Castelnuovo. He had spent the last three summers there. He was, apparently, a flamboyant character. This year he had taken one of the villas at the highest and steepest section of cliffs, known as "The Leap" because several men and women had, long ago, committed suicide there. Real estate agents referred me to Signorina Polozzi. She had an exclusive listing on the property that interested me.

Signorina Polozzi was a well-dressed woman in her forties, with crisp hair and artful makeup—a maquillage that made me wonder what she looked like beneath the mask. She existed within an aura of lavender scent and feminine efficiency. She spoke English very well: her sentences were ordered, impeccably punctuated, and her diction precise. I found myself trying and failing to match her formal eloquence.

I told her that I wished to secure a rental for the summer, something grand and special, perhaps one of the clifftop houses I had noticed during my tour of the area.

She hesitated. I did not, to her experienced eye, look like the sort of man who could afford one of those special rentals. I hadn't shaved; my suit was rumpled, my shirt collar dirty; and I wore no jewelry except for a $15.95 Timex glow-in-the-dark watch. Yet she did not want to offend me.

"Perhaps I could show you some other properties first," she said. "So that you may have a choice. I have a lovely cottage near the port and beach."

"How much is the rental on a clifftop house?"

"I have only one remaining now." She did some quick arithmatical calculations on a notepad, converting lire into dollars, and said, "Forty-two thousand dollars per month for three months—June, July, and August—paid in advance."

"So reasonable," I said. "My employer will be pleased."

"That amount includes the salary of the gardener and servants."

"I'm sure my employer will want to install his own staff."

"That is quite all right, but the gardener and house-keeper are employed all year round, and must be paid even if they do not work."

"Of course. Will you show me the house now?"

She remained skeptical. One hundred and twenty-six thousand dollars up front. No doubt Anita Polozzi had wasted a lot of time escorting casual lookers around properties in the region. Lookers were the curse of the profession. An acquaintance of mine in Bell Harbor, a top-end real estate agent, complained bitterly of the people—mostly elderly couples—who enjoyed passing an idle day touring grand houses. He suspected that most of them lived in mobile home parks. Looking, pretending to be potential buyers, was a form of entertainment.

I said, "I can probably have the one hundred and twenty-six thousand dollars wired here before the banks close."

We tacked back and forth up the switchbacks in Signorina Polozzi's Fiat. She used first and second gears all the way. A final thirty-degree slope brought us up onto a plateau that was level but narrow, and cooled by a brisk sea breeze.

Two of the three villas perched on the lip of the highest and steepest section of the cliff were owned by an industrialist from Milan, a manufacturer of heavy earth-moving equipment. The houses were usually kept available for various branches of his family or for loan to important clients; but the places were seldom used and so this year the owner had decided to lease them for the summer season. A Mr. Arbaleste, she told me, now occupied one of the villas; the other, next door, was presently available, although there had been several serious inquiries.

An eight-foot-high wooden fence sealed off the rear end of the property. She unlocked the gate, and we passed through into a yard that contained a swimming pool, a hot tub placed beneath a canvas awning, flower gardens, and olive and fig trees. It was rather cramped, everything arranged in less than a quarter acre, but it seemed a lush oasis relative to the old stone village below.

It was essentially a new house in an old, reinforced shell—gray stone and mortar, three stories high, with tall leaded windows, iron-grilled balconies on the upper floors, and a steeply pitched tile roof that had a neon orange glow in the afternoon sunlight. The house's exterior conformed to the local style, but the interior had been radically altered: walls and sections of ceiling had been removed, reducing the number of rooms while increasing the dimensions of those that remained; most of the downstairs front wall had been eliminated and replaced by glass, with sliding glass doors that looked out onto a big terrace and the sea beyond. There were six bedrooms on the top floors, nine if you included servants' garrets; two bedrooms at the rear of the ground floor, a modern kitchen, pantry, laundry room, a servants' refuge; and forward, a single great room that had an undersea aspect because of the tile floor—aqua tiles scrawled with white glyphs. Light pouring in through the glass front wall was reflected off the tiles and shimmered blue and green over white stuccoed walls. The ceiling was high, the rafters peeled and lacquered logs. Furniture was summery in design, color, and fabrics, new or nearly new beach-house stuff, but nothing special. There was plenty of it, yet the room looked only partly furnished because of the empty spaces.

"I think this place will do," I said.

Anita Polozzi, with some enthusiasm now, began pointing out various features: the house was, naturally, equipped with central air conditioning; the view was unparalleled along the entire coast; included in the lease price was a berth for one's yacht at the village marina; because of the height and sea breezes, there was never a problem with mosquitos—one could remove most of the glass wall and, in effect, turn the great room into a part of the terrace, live outdoors, so to speak.

We went out onto the terrace. It was made of Carrara marble, Polozzi said, the marble of Michelangelo, and was certainly big enough to entertain a large group of party guests.

I stood for a while at the rib-high marble wall. The view was stunning. I felt a touch of vertigo; my knees went weak. There was, Polozzi told me, a thousand-foot drop down the nearly vertical cliff face to the beach. Below and a couple miles to my left lay the little beach resort and marina. I felt immersed in blue. There was a multitude of blues—the blue Mediterranean and blue sky, shading from cobalt to a pale pastel, and even the few clouds were blue-tinted with reflections.

To my right, on the other side of a ravine of the sort that mountaineers call a couloir, was a boxy house that appeared derelict, run-down. Anita told me that it was owned by a Neapolitan family that usually occupied it only in August.

On the other side, to my left, separated by a few yards of stony soil, was a big house similar to the one I proposed renting, although the other had more glass, more curves, a certain lightness in the details. A short footpath linked the two buildings. There were gates in each of the terrace walls. An iron spear fence ran along the cliff's edge. Things had been arranged so that family and guests of the Milan industrialist could pass from house to house without difficulty.

"That house?" I asked.

"Leased by Signore Arbaleste."

"It's close. I could toss a pebble onto his terrace."

"Signore Arbaleste is a refined and distinguished gentleman. You need not worry about loud ruffians and such."

"I'm glad to hear it."

"I do not believe that you could do better than to secure this villa for the summer."

"I believe you are right. Has Arbaleste taken possession of that house yet?"

"Yes. He is present with a small group."

"I think," I said, "that my employer will be pleased."

"I'm sure of it." She paused to delicately phrase her question. "Perhaps I am familiar with the name of the gentleman?"

"It's likely. But for now . . . He values his anonymity. Men of his stature and wealth must always be aware of security considerations."

"Of course. Certainly."

"And among his guests will be Hollywood actors and actresses, famous figures from the worlds of art and politics and finance. You can understand why they would insist upon privacy."

"Indeed," she said. And then, "I hope you don't doubt my discretion."

"Not at all. You would recognize my employer's name, Signorina Polozzi. In fact, you will know his name soon, and meet the man as well."

"Ah," she said.

"With your permission, I'll mention you to him when he arrives. I'm sure he'll want to meet you."

"I would like that," she said shyly.

"He isn't a remote man personally, despite the necessity for a somewhat reclusive way of life."

"I understand."

I thought that maybe I had gone too far in my little satire, but Anita Polozzi seemed intrigued by word of my mysterious and powerful employer. She was one of those persons who, living on the periphery of wealth and celebrity, acquainted with some of the individuals through her business, liked to think of herself as an insider, a player. Information—even a lack of information—was an important element in the pretense. I figured that Arbaleste would hear gossip about his new neighbor before the sun set.

I said, "Now I must get to a telephone and arrange to have the money wired to a local bank."

She smiled and touched my hand. "Welcome to Castelnuovo, Mr. Shaw."

*   *   *

It was nine A.M. Florida time—three P.M. in Castelnuovo—when I reached Petrie at his office. I explained the situation to him.

"What do you think?" I asked.

"We might as well go for it."

"Can you persuade Chester Dalhart to release one hundred and twenty-six thousand dollars for a three-month house rental?"

"I won't tell him anything. He'll authorize the expenditure pronto or I'll call the whole thing off. Nice place, is it?"

"Very nice. Gorgeous view. *La dolce vita.*"

"Pool?"

"*Si.*"

"Tennis court?"

"No, but Arbaleste has one."

"Have you seen him?"

"Not yet."

"You know," Petrie said, "this is a bizarre notion when viewed soberly and with the sun shining."

"I know. Bizarre."

"*La dolce vita,* huh?"

"The sweet life, you bet."

"I'm tired. Are you tired?"

"I'm tired."

"We work too hard. We all need a holiday. Be at the bank in half an hour to collect the money."

"Okay."

"If the money doesn't come in today, it's a no go, come home."

"All right."

"The sweet life, huh? We deserve no less."

The money was at the bank when I arrived. A manager asked me to submit to fingerprinting, but I refused, and he then accepted my passport and driver's license as ID.

I took a bank draft to Anita Polozzi, signed the lease, and received the keys, three pages of instructions regarding the maintenance of the property, rules and regulations, and a listing of the services available in the area—medical, governmental, fire and police, electrical and plumbing. She was pleased. We shook hands. She reminded me that I had promised to introduce her to my employer. We shook hands again at the door to her office. "*Buona sera.*"

I stopped at a shop and bought bread, cheese, and a bottle of wine. It was dusk when I reached the house, night by the time I finished my meal. I watched from the terrace as the stars ignited singly and in clusters. The sea had turned indigo; ruffled lines of surf broke on the offshore rocks and rolled up on the beach below. Lights burned in the Arbaleste house, and I heard music, but no one appeared.

FIFTEEN

I slept in an upstairs bedroom that smelled of moth-balls. I opened all of the windows and the French doors leading out onto a balcony, and several times during the night awakened to awareness of a warm breeze that smelled tartly of the sea. And I heard faint music too, Chopin and Mozart. Both the breeze and the music lasted until dawn.

At sunrise I went down the stairs and out onto the terrace. There was a chill in the air now. Rows of herring-bone clouds were moving in from the northwest. The surf was high. A small-craft warning flew from a mast at the marina. I had forgotten to buy coffee or juice at the village, and so I ate a chunk of bread and finished the wine—fruit juice, after all—while watching a vast crescent of sunlight move west over the sea.

I was about to return to the house when a man came out onto the next-door terrace. Arbaleste, naked except for what the French call a *cache-sexe,* filmy briefs hardly bigger than a jockstrap. He moved lightly to the terrace wall. I estimated his height at six feet, his weight to be around one hundred and eighty pounds.

He appeared to be in superb physical condition. He was not bulky, not a weight lifter, but rather he had the musculature of a gymnast or competition swimmer. He radiated health and self-assurance. He was the man in the videotape, but no image can instill life, establish a presence, approximate the reality.

I knew I should speak, let him know that I was present, but he abruptly placed his palms on the top of the wall and swiftly, easily, lifted to a handstand. For an instant I feared that he intended to vault into space, but he lifted to the vertical and remained there. Even at this distance the muscles on his arms, shoulders, and torso were sharply defined. I could detect no trembling, no strain—it looked effortless. You would have to be close to appreciate the difficulty. He remained inverted, erect, for maybe twenty seconds, staring down at the rocks and beach far below; and then, without haste, still tensely poised, he changed the angle of his body, altered his center of gravity, slowly lifted one palm off the wall top and continued with a one-handed stand. It lasted. I could see the strain distort his face. Finally, he lowered himself to safety. Then he half turned and saw me.

"Sorry," I said. "I was going to call out, but I didn't want to startle you."

He smiled. He shook his hands, loose-wristed, as if flicking electrical charges off his fingertips.

"It's a long way down," I said.

"Everyone says a thousand feet, but it's really only about eight hundred."

His accent was difficult to place, a mix of American and British English, with another accent—maybe French—beneath.

"Do you do that often?" I asked.

"Every morning since I've been here."

"Why?"

"Why not?"

"No, really, why?"

"To remind myself how beautiful, how fragile, life is. And to greet the new day with courage."

"You make it look easy and safe. But if you do that every morning all summer, the odds turn against you."

"No. The odds remain exactly the same every morning. The risk is actually small, for me. It's something I know I can do. I don't think of failure. It isn't the body that fails usually, it's the mind. Always the mind—the will."

"And there's luck."

"By definition, luck isn't something that can be controlled. Are you going to be my neighbor for the summer?"

"My name is Dan Shaw."

"Anton Arbaleste. So you've taken the house?"

"My employer has leased the place for the season."

"I hope your employer is a tolerant sort. We here are probably not as disciplined as he might wish."

"Arbaleste—isn't that the name of a medieval siege device?"

"Yes."

"Odd name."

"Is it? Most surnames stem from the names of places, occupations, or objects. Lincoln, Churchill—church hill, you know—Montfort, Croft. Or Archer, Miller, Carter, Carpenter. Or things, Stone, Forest, Arbaleste. Perhaps I had an ancestor who designed siege engines."

It was pedantry, but lighthearted, maybe a little mocking, mocking me or himself or us both.

A woman strolled out onto the terrace. She was nude, and I expected her to retreat when she saw me, but without hesitation she proceeded to Arbaleste's side.

"Anton," she said, "come back to bed."

She was in her mid-twenties, about five four, with a narrow waist and rounded hips and full breasts. Voluptuous was a word that came to mind. She had a fully mature body but the face of a beautiful adolescent. Her smoky dark hair was tousled; her mouth pouty; she looked sleepy and irritable.

Charles had thought they looked like brother and sister, but that wasn't so. It was just that both were dark, dark hair and olive skin, and both were extraordinarily good looking.

"Antonia," Arbaleste said, "this is Dan Shaw, our new neighbor. Shaw—Antonia di Benedetto."

"Hi," she said.

"Hello."

She had been Adrienne Debarret in Florida.

She took Arbaleste's hand. "Anton, really . . ."

I tried not to stare. I looked at her, turned toward the sea, looked back. She was beautiful, sulky, and indifferent to my gaze, my admiration.

"Shaw," Arbaleste said, "why don't you come over for breakfast?"

"Thanks. But I've got to get to Naples and catch a plane."

"Another time, then."

"Yes."

"We have all summer. Do you play tennis?"

"Yes."

"Well?"

"Fairly well, I think."

"Sail?"

"Yes. I've got a little sloop at home."

"There you are," he said, as if he had just proved a disputed theorem.

"Good-bye for now, then," I said. "Good-bye, Miss di Benedetto."

"Bye-bye," she said.

I crossed the terrace, opened the sliding door, and, before entering the house, turned to look back at them. They stood together, Adam and Eve, no shame in the Garden, watching me and smiling. I amused them. They were amused in a friendly way.

I thought about them while I packed my few things, closed all the windows, and set the door locks. I found that I liked Arbaleste. That wasn't a surprise: Being likable was his stock in trade. Like me, trust me. He was relaxed, amiable, transparent, it seemed. Here I am, Anton Arbaleste, come over for breakfast and a chat. We'll sail together, we'll play tennis, we'll have an amusing summer. But that handstand on the terrace wall—repeated every morning—indicated that he was far more complex than he liked to appear.

SIXTEEN

Dodo wore his leather collar, with the chain secured to a ring bolt screwed into the base of the big oak. There was just enough slack in the chain so that he could climb to the lower branches (stray dogs were a danger), but he remained on the ground, watching the nearby people with his old man's monkey gaze. He looked sad and wise, as if he alone might be able to solve the riddle of the swans. Now and then someone tossed him a leftover piece of breakfast fruit, a slice of banana or peach or an orange section, which he sniffed and then either ate or rejected. I wondered what criteria he used in determining quality.

"Ponzi," Petrie said.

Martina and her uncle sat at the patio table. They talked quietly, heads close, urgency apparent in their postures and gestures. Phil wore an electronic monitoring device around his left ankle that looked like a cheap rubber-and-plastic wristwatch. We gave them privacy. Petrie and I stood out near the deep end of the swimming pool; Judge Samuelson, informal by his standards in a blazer and beige trousers, no tie, was strolling across the lawn with the Younts and the Singers, couples in bright senior-citizen plumage, who had come to welcome Phil Karras home. Other friends had been invited but, by not appearing, had expressed either moral compunction or social cowardice.

"Charles Ponzi," Petrie said. "The 1920s."

Tom was giving me one of his spontaneous lectures. He flexed his knees, selected his words with care, and occasionally glanced at me slantwise to ensure that I still listened.

Iridescent blue dragonflies flitted over the lawn; some doubled up in flight for aerial romance.

A Mercedes pulled through the gates into the driveway. The windows were tinted and so I could not clearly see the occupants. The car halted, remained in place for a while with the engine running, and then backed down the driveway and outside to Paradise Lane road.

"Charles probably didn't invent the Ponzi—the pyramid scheme—but he refined it, made it work better than anyone else. Money from the second lines of investors is used to pay the first line, and then both lines recruit more investors. It spreads from the top down, like a pyramid, and when you reach the crucial moment, critical mass, you get out with a big bundle of money."

The silver Mercedes returned. This time it pulled well into the driveway and parked behind Petrie's Porsche. I saw movement behind the tinted windows, and then a couple got out and started across the lawn toward the table where Karras and Martina sat. The man used a cane; the woman carried a bowl covered with foil—potato salad, maybe, a side dish. Their smiles, their cheery calls of greeting, lacked conviction; they were like bad actors in an amateur theatrical production. *ENTER: Elderly couple with friendly smiles and eager calls.* They had reluctantly decided to break bread with their old friend, the wife-murderer.

"You see small-time Ponzi scams all the time," Petrie said, "on the Internet, in the office, at the shop, at the club. Relatively small hustles, but the principle is the same. Your first- and second-line investors are your best salesmen. They do your work."

It was two o'clock, and a man was firing up a gas barbecue grill next to the gazebo while another man, also sent out by the caterers, had set up a compact bar beneath a canvas tent with the sides rolled up.

"I would have told the story in greater detail," Petrie said, "except that I am always aware of your limited attention span."

"Me, too," I said.

"P.T. Barnum: 'There's a sucker born every minute.' H.L. Mencken: 'No one ever went broke underestimating the intelligence of the American public.'"

"*Caveat emptor*," I said. "Let the buyer beware."

Phil Karras had regained self-control since I had last seen him, but he was not the same man, would never be the same. His personality had shattered at the instant he had killed his wife, and now he was trying to put the pieces together by imitating what he had once been. He faked the knowing smile, the gruffness, the swagger, but it didn't work; he still had the aspect of a man half paralyzed by dread.

"Let's get a drink," I said.

Petrie had made some recent purchases: a pigskin cigar case, a gold cigar-tip cutter, and a slim gold lighter, and now he ritually employed them. When the Monte Cristo cigar was burning satisfactorily, he tilted back his head and smiled at the sky.

"Charles Ponzi went to jail," he said.

Karras had been released from jail the previous afternoon on a bail bond that used his property for security. He was not considered a flight risk since he was a lifetime resident of the state and county, a man of some political influence, and a well-known and respected citizen. Still, it had been a remarkably fast arraignment, hearing, and release. Petrie explained that the judge was eager to go on holiday to the Grenadines. And, surprisingly, the prosecutor from the SA's office, Nestor Naranjo, had not vigorously opposed bail. "The fact," Petrie said, "that I was a major contributor to Judge Pickering's reelection campaign had nothing to do with it."

We walked across the lawn to the tent. Tom asked for a Scotch; I had the bartender mix me a margarita and pour it into a salted old-fashioned glass.

Up on the gazebo platform, Judge Samuelson was patiently listening to a woman gush on about her dog, a Lhasa apso of impeccable Tibetan blood, out of the Dalai Lama's own kennel, descendant of a long line of champions, a dog that was not merely intelligent but possessed extrasensory perception. Her husband nodded from time to time. The other couple, the Singers, seemed to have achieved a form of suspended animation. The clairvoyant dog was named Nostradamus. Judge Samuelson was an unfailingly courteous man. I hoped to be present someday when a bore finally cracked his psyche open and exposed the monster.

"Tom," I said, "I want to talk to you."

"Pal, we *have* been talking."

"Come on."

A black Lexus pulled into the driveway and stopped, and three men in golf clothes got out. No wives. One, still wearing a golf glove, carried a putter. They clowned, yelled, overly casual, which just reminded us all that Phil Karras had recently placed the muzzles of a twenty-gauge shotgun at the base of his wife's head and pulled the triggers.

We carried our drinks across the lawn, close to the hedge and cedar fence which separated this property from the neighbor's. The view was further screened by a cluster of palms. A hammock was stretched between two of the trees and lawn furniture was scattered in the deep shade. I sat on a canvas deck chair; Petrie stretched out on a padded chaise lounge.

"I've been thinking," I said. "It isn't going to work."

"Stop thinking."

"This Arbaleste is smart."

"So am I. You? I have doubts."

"He spent several months in this area. He might have seen us, heard of us. Remember, there was a media frenzy over the Falconer business, and we were in the center of it."

"He didn't arrive here until most of that had died down. Anyway, he spent his time here on Paradise Key and at the Hunt Club and the golf course, and out fishing with the sheep."

"I used my real name in Italy. I had to, in order to receive the money you wired."

"Relax."

"All right, then."

"If we fail, we fail."

"Okay, but a considerable sum of money has already been spent."

"Not so much, really. Maybe five thousand dollars for each member of the consortium."

"Who's going to play the role of our mysterious billionaire?"

"Who do you recommend?"

"Not you."

"Why not me?"

"Not you, not me, not Leroy Karpe, for Christ's sake. Not Mutt or Jeff. Not Charles."

"Charles might make a fine gay wastrel, son or grandson of our billionaire."

"Who is?"

"Let me see," Petrie said. He puffed on his cigar for a time, blew a wobbly smoke ring, and said, "What about the judge?"

"Judge Samuelson? You want to bring him into this?"

"He's an imposing man in many respects."

"Forget it."

"An imposing man from an excellent background. Patrician. Intelligent, learned, patrician, with courtly manners. Tall. A bit of a fool at times, but quite tall."

"He would never do it."

"Why not?"

"He's an honest man. What we're planning to do is illegal, and maybe dangerous."

"He might view it as an adventure. Some excitement in his old age. A chance, finally, to be a rogue."

"No."

"He's a widower. His kids are grown and live far away. He's financially secure. He's bored. I think he'd love to play the part."

"No way. I know him. The judge is very serious about things like integrity and decency and honor."

"Yeah? What if I told you that I've talked to him and he's agreed to come in."

"I'd say you were lying."

"He's coming in *pro bono publico,* so to speak. He won't accept any money. But he's our reclusive tycoon."

"It's a bad idea, Tom. You can't ask Levi to risk his freedom and reputation on a crazy scheme like this."

I looked over the sweep of lawn. Judge Samuelson had managed to execute a jailbreak, escape the gazebo and the boring couples, and was now sitting at the patio table with Phil Karras.

I said, "What did Mutt and Jeff find out about Halbert-Arbaleste?"

"They're still in New York, digging."

"How much did Phil lose in the Ponzi scheme?"

"He doesn't want to talk about it. But he will. He damned sure will."

Martina, smiling, walked toward us. She had removed her shoes. Her hair was pinned back and she wore a print sundress with a short skirt and a belt that accented her narrow waist. She was lovely, and I fell in love with her all over again.

"We need a couple of women in our Italian household," Petrie said. "Do you think . . . ?"

"No. Never."

"Hello, Martina," Petrie said.

She stepped into the shade and blinked. "A pair of lazy slugs," she said.

"We're not crazy thugs," I said.

"I said *slugs*."

"No," Petrie said, "the daisy bugs aren't a problem."

"God," Martina said. "Isn't this an awful lawn party?"

"More like a wake," I said.

"A sparsely attended wake," Petrie said.

SEVENTEEN

The three golfers, already drunk from clubhouse rounds, had a few more drinks and then loudly, with much shaking of hands and soft shoulder punches—"Hang in there, Phil."—left Karras and left the grounds.

There were steaks and chicken breasts, potato salad and cole slaw, baked beans, and asparagus with a hollandaise sauce. We did not eat as a group. Martina and I carried our plates to the shade of a catalpa and sat on the grass. I had a steak; Martina, a vegetarian except for seafood, had only side dishes.

"I'm going to stay with my uncle for a few days," she said.

"Good idea."

"There's no one else. Will you go to the lighthouse and feed Cerberus?"

"I'll stay there nights until you return."

"Just for a few days."

"What about your cartoon strip?"

"I'm a bit ahead. And I can work on ideas here, do sketches."

"I'll bring you whatever materials you need."

"His eyes," she said. "He's so frightened."

"Are you okay, Martina?"

She shrugged with one shoulder, tried a smile. "I guess."

"Phil couldn't have better legal counsel."

"I know." She pushed away her plate of food. "What were you doing in Europe?"

"Working on something with Tom."

"You and Petrie . . . I cringe when you two get together. You're like a pair of delinquent boys—Huck and Tom—trapped in adult bodies."

Most of the guests left within an hour after eating. Those of us who remained gathered at the patio table for coffee: Karras, Martina, Petrie, Judge Samuelson, and I. The ghost of Alice Karras lay a few yards away, a phantom shape beneath a phantom bloody tarp.

It was twilight, and two wire screen cages, mounted on top of steel poles, began incinerating insects. Moths, flies, mosquitos, flying beetles, all sizzled and flashed bluish white when they touched the electrified screens. Dodo had climbed onto Martina's lap and fallen asleep in her arms. She was disgusted by the nearly continuous bug executions, and soon asked me to turn off the electrical feed.

"What?" her uncle said. "We'll be eaten alive."

"Dan?"

I found the switch on the nearest of the poles and turned off the juice.

"A couple of weeks ago," Judge Samuelson said, "I found an enormous scorpion in my yard. It was a pale, glossy yellow, and as big as a saucer. It looked like a big crab."

"You didn't kill it, did you?" Martina asked.

"I'm afraid I did, my dear. I crushed it with a rock. But I slept poorly that night. Why had I done it? It was causing no harm. It was no doubt mildly venomous, but surely no danger to humans. But I was revolted by the creature and destroyed it. Another weight added to my already burdened conscience."

We were silent. None of us believed that Levi had a very burdened conscience.

Petrie removed a cigar from between his teeth. "Martina, Judge—will you excuse us? Phil, Dan, and I must have a talk."

Karras led us through the house and out onto the seafront deck. The tide was out and the flats had a sour, swampy smell. A string of colored lights—channel marker buoys—curved out into the breezy twilight. We sat in comfortable wicker chairs.

"Tell us about the Ponzi scam," Petrie said.

Anton Arbaleste (then Victor Trebuchet) had arrived in Paradise Key in late November. With him was his wife or fiancée (it was never quite clear), Adrienne Debarret, a beautiful actress who, according to talk, had appeared in several French art films. They moved into the Equinox house; leased it, with an option to buy. They pretty much stayed to themselves in the early days. Both were reserved, though not unfriendly; if you met them at the marina or golf club, they would chat, maybe have a drink with you if you issued an invitation; but they made no effort to insinuate themselves into the community. They aroused a great deal of curiosity. Both were young and very good looking, charismatic, you might say, with charming smiles and exquisite manners.

You knew immediately that they were foreigners. Both spoke with slight accents and were indefinably European in their tastes and attitudes. Sophisticated. Cosmopolitan, and obviously well educated, though they didn't show off. They were not joiners—at least not at first.

Trebuchet kept a thirty-eight-foot Bertram, rigged for deep-sea fishing, at the marina, and he also claimed to be an ocean sailor. Once, in conversation with Jordan Stoddard, he mentioned, in the self-deprecating way he had, that he had nearly lost his yacht, his crew, and himself during the famous English Fastnet Race.

Later, in early January, Trebuchet joined the Hunt Club, and soon afterward nine or ten polo ponies arrived by truck. He didn't volunteer information, but if you asked he would tell you that he was captain of a polo team based in France and he hoped to arrange some matches in this hemisphere—Palm Beach, Miami, Mexico City. Other team members would be coming to the States in early summer.

Trebuchet and the lovely Adrienne politely refused several dinner party invitations. That, of course, made them all the more interesting. There was an air of power about this Victor Trebuchet. He was a man you wanted to know, to be seen with. The residents of Paradise Key began to feel excluded, an unfamiliar experience; they were usually the ones who played the social game of inclusion or exclusion, acceptance or rejection.

There were rumors, most of them originating with the gossipy servants who had been hired through a local employment bureau: Trebuchet placed many phone calls to European capitals, and talked French or

Italian; a housemaid reported that he once had a long conversation with a person whom he addressed as "Mr. President," and afterward on a notepad she had seen doodles such as a curliqued "GWB," and a drawing that might have been a phallus or maybe a missile, and meaningless scribbles, and the figure $165,000,000.

Petrie and I exchanged a glance. This Paradise Key crowd were champions of gullibility.

Trebuchet did form one early friendship, with Chester Dalhart, whose property adjoined Equinox; and Adrienne Debarret became close to Chesters wife, Margot. The couples played doubles on the Dalhart court; went out together for dinner once or twice a week; and in February cruised down to Port Charlotte in Trebuchet's boat. In early March Dalhart bought a new Mercedes for his wife, paying cash according to gossip. Chester was clearly earning a lot of money above the income from his law firm, and no one doubted that this prosperity was linked to his friendship with Victor Trebuchet. They were pals, and pals shared special insider knowledge and profitable investment opportunities; pals launched you into the flow, the river, the torrent of dollars, francs, yen, and marks. You went to sleep well-to-do and woke up rich. And pals shared pals, didn't they? Chester managed to persuade Trebuchet to include some of his friends and clients in the bonanza; a half dozen at first, men who earned substantial profits in a short period. Word spread; friends of friends appeared and pleaded for admittance to the select group. By the end, when the pyramid collapsed and Trebuchet vanished, there were thirty-three investors in the scam.

"You were one of the late bunch?" Petrie asked.

"Yes."

"How much did you lose?"

"A lot."

"How much?"

"That's none of your business."

"Get a new lawyer."

"Christ," Karras said.

We waited while Phil decided whether or not he wanted a new lawyer.

"Three hundred and seventy-five thousand dollars," he said.

"Cashed in your stocks and bonds and emptied your bank accounts."

"I was going to mortgage the house," Karras said, "but the whole thing collapsed before the bank came through."

"Lucky you. But some of the early investors made money, didn't they? At first."

"They made a lot of money, a lot. Their original investments tripled, quadrupled, in just a few weeks. But they put most of it back into the pot, reinvested. Buy a car or boat, buy the wife a diamond, and then give the rest back to Trebuchet."

"Sure. The big early returns gave them confidence, stimulated their greed. Word spread fast. You can get rich fast and easy if you get on the good side of Victor Trebuchet. At least the Ponzi scheme ended before you could give away your house."

"There was money everywhere. It was raining down."

"It was circulating. It was being recycled. Peter's money went to pay Paul, John's money paid Peter,

James's money paid John . . . And nearly all was returned to Trebuchet for reinvestment. Did you ever receive a payoff?"

"No," Karras said.

"You got in too late. Did anyone quit while he was ahead?"

"I don't know. I didn't know all the investors."

"I doubt it. No one could leave the table. More, more, more, everyone wanted more. And it was just beginning, wasn't it? Mr. Trebuchet had the key to the global economic vault."

"It looked foolproof."

"It was foolproof. Not a fool saw through it. And it was all about—what?—communications satellites."

"Satellites and rockets, launching facilities, a complete package."

"Pseudoscientific humbug."

"No. They showed us real drawings and blueprints, thick bound sheafs that showed the design details of missiles and satellites. Specs and functions, materials, orbiting data, fuel expenditures. Photographs and plans of the launching facility they were building in Kenya. We had full access to the science."

"And how much did you or any of the others understand about that complicated technical stuff? What do you know about missiles and satellites, communications technology, the physics and engineering involved? You trusted. You trusted Trebuchet. You trusted in stacks of technical drawings and fake financial statements and a fake leather-bound prospectus. You trusted Lord Warfield." Tom laughed. He slapped his own cheek, probably a little harder than he intended. "Sure, what acquisitive social-climbing American wouldn't trust an English lord, a goddamned *earl*, a pillar of the aristocratic British establishment. You trusted Kensington, the California whiz kid from the Silicon Valley, inventor of a miraculous new computer chip. Jesus."

"We trusted the Russian, too."

"Yeah. Lobechevsky. Tell me about him."

Dr. Lobechevsky, Karras told us, was Alpha Centauri's chief scientific advisor, a Russian physicist who had, for most of his career, occupied a high position in the Soviet government's satellite research program. After the dissolution of the Soviet Union, he had taught physics at Moscow University for five years, and then left to form a consulting firm which provided advice and information to both governmental and private organizations. Lobechevsky had flown from Russia to Florida in late March, stayed with Trebuchet at Equinox for three days, and provided scientific briefings to some of the newer investors.

"Well," Petrie said. "Jesus." He tapped at his front teeth with a fingernail, *tick-tick-tick,* then dropped his hand and expelled a breath. "This Trebuchet-Arbaleste is thorough, a lot more thorough, maybe, than he has to be. Did anyone run background checks on these people? Trebuchet, his girlfriend, Lord Warfield, the whiz kid, this Lobechevsky? *Any* of them?"

"We left that to Chester," Karras said. "He was head of a law firm. He checked them out. We assumed that he checked them out."

"Chester, sure. That Chester—he was conned out of his mind, he was in love."

"It could have worked," Phil said. "We came so close to the jackpot."

"Did you?"

It seemed that the effects of a really good con lingered, remained in the mind like a prophetic dream or the mournful attachment to a lost first love. Karras was like Chester Dalhart in this. Arbaleste could probably walk into Paradise Key tomorrow and take the rest of their money.

Petrie abruptly got to his feet. "I'm going."

"Aren't we going to talk about the case?"

"Later. Anyway, Phil, there isn't a hell of a lot to talk about. There aren't many fuzzy areas in your case. You'll have to take the stand. We'll go through your testimony well in advance."

"I was going to suggest that we ask the court for a change of venue."

"Were you?" Petrie pretended to consider. "Change of venue. Move your trial out of the county where you've lived your entire life, established a reputation and much good will, acquired many friends and sympathetic acquaintances—and move to a county where the people have never heard of you or your late wife and her tragic illness. Strangers, I mean. A totally impartial jury. Yes, Phil, you might have something there."

Petrie paused in the doorway. "And Phil, don't hesitate to make further suggestions."

Karras, staring out at the sea and star-flecked darkness, said, "He's a rough son of a bitch."

"He is that," I agreed.

"Sarcastic bastard."

"That's Tom."

"I don't like the way he talks to me."

"Few do. But I think he was, in part, testing you."

"Why? For what?"

"He wants to know how you'll respond to hostile questioning at the trial."

"But we didn't even talk about the case."

"He's testing your reactions, your temper, your candor, your emotional makeup."

"I hired a lawyer, not a goddamned psychologist."

"Are you likely to elicit sympathy when you testify about Alice and your actions? Or will you seem remote, cold, hard? Tom wants to know. Can the prosecutor goad you into a display of temper? There's no contesting the evidence. It will all come down to your testimony."

"I still don't understand why he wasted all tonight on Trebuchet and Alpha Centauri."

"Maybe because those facts might influence a jury."

"How?"

"You lost a great deal of money not long before you decided to end Alice's suffering."

"So?"

"People might wonder if there's a connection."

"What? What connection? Christ!"

"They'll wonder if your losses depressed you. Did your reduced financial circumstances make it more difficult to afford the considerable medical expenses of caring for Alice?"

"That's not fair. Goddamn it, Dan, it's not fair!"

"Was Alice's life insured?"

"Of course it was. Both our lives were insured on an old policy—eighteen, twenty years old."

"What's the payoff?"

"None of your business."

"Phil . . ."

"A quarter million dollars. But the insurance company would never pay it, not when I killed her."

"Probably not."

"Who would believe I killed her for insurance money?"

"People will believe anything." Including, I thought, wholly implausible get-rich-quick schemes that involved missiles and satellites, scientific geniuses, an English lord, and nine polo ponies.

"It's not too late to fire Petrie," he said.

"No."

"Though he did get me out on bail."

"Yes, and fast."

"What do you say?"

"Think it over. But don't let vanity make the decision. You're interested in results, not your counsel's affection."

We sat in silence for a time, and when Phil spoke his voice had changed.

"Did you ever wish you could go back in time? I daydream. I wish I'm out there that morning, with the shotgun, but I haven't fired it yet. I cock just one hammer. And I do it. But there's still a cartridge in the other chamber. And I have a second chance to do it right."

I stood up. "Come on, let's join Martina and the judge."

"You go. I'd like to be alone for a while."

"You won't . . ."

"No. Too late now. It wouldn't make sense now, for some reason."

"Was the cookout your idea?"

"No, Martina's."

That was good: To have Phil himself throw a party not long after the killing and a day after getting out of jail might very well sour a jury's mood.

Dodo still slept in Martina's arms. The judge was smoking one of Petrie's Cuban cigars with a smug, contemplative air. A yellow citronella candle the size of a palm stump burned on the table, perfuming the night with a lemony scent and casting just enough light to set hands and faces aglow in the darkness. The monkey, mostly in shadow, looked like a monstrous, mutant baby, ape spawn.

I sat down at the table. The island seemed to be asleep now, although it was not yet ten o'clock.

"Everything settled?" Martina asked.

"Not hardly."

"We have been discussing Plutarch's *Lives*," Levi murmured. "What say you?"

"How many lives did he have?"

The judge exhaled a cloud of smoke that glowed in the candlelight. The monkey sneezed.

"Judge . . ."

"Sorry, my dear." He tossed the fuming cigar out onto the lawn.

I said, "Martina, Phil said that he wanted to be alone. But maybe you ought to be with him."

"Is he all right?"

"I think your company will lift his spirits."

"Actually," the judge said, "it's time I go." He stood up. "Thank you, Martina. It was a fine repast."

I said, "Martina, do you want me to stay?"

"No. It's all right."

The judge picked up his still-burning cigar from the grass as we walked toward the cars.

"Levi," I said, "Petrie tells me that you're joining his crazy scheme."

"Not exactly. I told him that I was intrigued. But I want to hear more."

"What we are going to do is at best borderline illegal."

We reached the cars. Levi paused with his hand on the hood of his old Caddy. "It is never too late," he said, "to commence a life of crime."

I turned: The candle still burned on the patio table, but Martina and the monkey were gone.

EIGHTEEN

I awakened at eight, brewed a pot of coffee, and carried a mug outside. Kyle and Earl Mackey were playing catch on the level section of reef in front of the lighthouse. Cerberus, tongue hanging out, foaming at the mouth, was chasing the baseball back and forth. The dog was not discouraged by his lack of success. He chased seagulls with the same stout heart.

The Mackey brothers ignored me. They both wore dirty sneakers without socks, ragged-hemmed shorts, and gray sweatshirts with the sleeves cut off at the shoulder seams. Kyle was left-handed. Both wore small gloves that appeared to date from the Ty Cobb era, and the baseball was scuffed and filthy. They were big guys, a few inches over six feet, beer-bellied, and probably weighing more than two-fifty. Ponytails, five-day beards, small lashless eyes.

I lit a cigarette, sipped my coffee, and watched them. At last Kyle made a bad throw; the baseball sailed over his brother's head and bounced down toward the end of the reef. Cerberus shot off after it. The game of catch had ended. It was now the dog's baseball, and he preferred to play alone.

"You two throw like girls," I said.

They glanced at me, looked down to where the dog was savaging their baseball, looked at me again. I assumed that their boat was tied up behind *Puck* at the dock.

"Girls," I repeated. "But they probably didn't have a baseball program at reform school."

Kyle grinned and started toward me. Earl followed. Kyle was the dominant brother. They looked alike, though they weren't twins, and both had the same slouching scuff-heeled walk.

"Got a beer?" Kyle said.

"No."

"Then I'll have coffee."

"No, you won't."

Kyle sat down on one of the deck chairs; Earl halted a few yards away, his head forward and his arms bowed, looking at me as a nightclub bouncer might study a potentially violent customer.

"Where's Charlie?" Kyle said. "He ain't at the motel."

"Charles is at the bottom of the sea where he belongs."

"Buried another one, huh?"

"I may have to bury two more."

"Whew," Kyle said. "Tough guy. Here's a tough guy, Earl."

"Tough," Earl said.

"Toss your brother a peanut, Kyle."

"That's some watchdog you got there, Shaw," Kyle said.

"He watches people come and he watches people go."

Kyle nodded and grinned. "Bad thing if someone killed that mutt and nailed him to the door."

"You do it, Kyle. It's your turn."

"Where are the bones we found?"

"I made soup. What do you guys want?"

"A loan. We need to get our boat engines over-hauled. That's three thousand dollars, at least. Plus we need a new prop shaft—the old one's bent."

"Tell Earl to relax," I said.

"Relax, Earl."

"You want me to cosign for you at the bank?"

"Shithead," Earl said.

"We don't got the bones anymore," Kyle said. "But we found anchor and chain and a spear."

"Take them to the sherf," I said, pronouncing "sheriff" as the Mackey brothers did. "See if the sherf will loan you some money."

Earl had not changed his bearlike stance throughout the conversation. He remained ready for action.

"You think we're real dumb, don't you?" Kyle said.

"I think what I'm going to do," I said, "is contact every law enforcement agency around here, city, county, state, maybe even the feds, and tell them that you and your unfortunate brother trespassed here and threatened me and my dog. Do you know why I'll do that? So they'll have a record of my complaint. So that if you ever come out here again, and I shoot you, they'll figure it was self-defense. I'll *try* not to kill you, some birdshot in the four Mackey knees should be enough, and then do you know what will happen? *You* will be prosecuted. Because I am a decent, kindly, law-abiding citizen, and you two have spent your lives, since age seven or eight, in trouble with the law. As for bones—you have no bones. As for anchor and chain and spear—take them to a pawnshop."

Kyle slowly rose from the deck chair. I waited, thinking that maybe I had gone too far with my scorn. The Mackey boys did not consider consequences; they might beat me half to death and only later concern themselves with jail time. Earl was waiting for Kyle to select a course of action.

Kyle nodded, then said, "I want our baseball."

"You don't want that baseball. It's punctured now and soaked with dog saliva. Buy yourself a new baseball. Send me the bill."

Kyle surprised me by grinning. "We ain't finished yet."

"I know we ain't."

I walked with them across the reef and down the concrete steps to the dock. They boarded the *Catcher*. Kyle went up onto the flying bridge to start the engines; Earl glared at me from the deck well.

When they were gone, I went aboard *Puck* to look around. They had stolen a six-pack of beer from the icebox, but nothing else had been disturbed.

PART III
Castelnuovo

NINETEEN

It was raining in Rome, raining in Naples, but by the time I reached Castelnuovo a south-westerly wind had opened long lateral rips in the cloud cover, exposing blue-green sky and slanted pillars of sunlight. I ate lunch in the village, soup and a sandwich, and by the time I finished, the sky was mostly clear and the sun hot. Everything gleamed wetly. Twists of vapor rose from the narrow cobblestone streets.

The cliffs were less steep at the south end of the village, and steps hewn from the rock led down to the beach, a duster of waterfront buildings—shops, terraced café, a ship's chandlery—and a marina that was protected by a natural promontory on the south and an angled stone breakwater to the north. I walked out onto the dock. It was early in the season and there were not many yachts berthed at the piers or anchored in the harbor. Those I saw were split equally between sail and power. Most had the names of Italian ports lettered on the stems, but there were also yachts from Marseilles, Piraeus, and Barcelona. A separate dock area sheltered the local fishing boats, and a few more boats had been hauled up onto the sand for the defouling of the hulls.

I walked north. There were few bathers on the beach after the rain. The sand was pale yellow, wind- and wave-ribbed, and there were some offshore rocks that might provide fair snorkeling. The good beach, the good swimming, ended beneath the nearly vertical section of cliffs. There, most of the sand had been washed away and the ground was covered by shingle—layers of water-smoothed stones that clacked and chattered when the waves broke over them.

Looking up, I could see the terrace walls of the villas on top. Arbaleste had said that it was an eight-hundred-foot drop from the lip of the cliff to the beach. How long would it take to fall that distance? Four seconds, five? The rock face was steep, though not smooth; a skilled rock climber might not find it a challenge. But the view, from the top looking down or the bottom looking up, gave me a touch of vertigo.

I continued walking. The shingle gave way to more sandy beach a hundred yards on, and the angle of the cliffs decreased until I found another flight of stairs that tacked up to the plateau. I became lost in the maze of lanes and alleys and cul-de-sacs and then, by luck, arrived at the rear of the house. The gate was locked. I rang the bell a few times, and when no one responded, I climbed over the fence and walked past the swimming pool and shrubbery to the rear steps. The door opened before I could knock.

"You're late," McNally said.

"Late for what?"

"Late from Florida. We expected you two days ago."

He swung the door wide and I entered the rear foyer. He wore a summery tourist outfit of matching shorts and shirt in a bright floral pattern, but the effect was ruined by his black street shoes and black socks. He looked like a cop on holiday.

I followed him through the downstairs rooms. He and Cavaretta had arrived a week ago and arranged to have workers in to prepare the house; there had been some cleaning, painting, and polishing; the utilities had been connected and telephones installed; and I noticed that the wet bar had been fully stocked.

"Any problems?" I asked.

"The problem of boredom. Solved by gin."

Through the glass doors I saw Cavaretta sitting on the terrace at a table beneath a cocked umbrella. His torso and back were matted with black hair, and at first glance he resembled some furry animal, a bear or ape. Beyond him the sea and sky fused into an almost seamless blue horizon.

"Want a drink?" McNally asked.

"Sure."

"What?"

"Gin."

McNally went toward the bar, and I slid open the door and went out onto the balcony.

"You're late," Cavaretta said.

I sat at the table. "Have you seen Mr. A.?"

"Just the first day. He and the lady left next morning."

"Is there anyone in the house now?"

"Just servants, and a hard-looking guy in a silk suit."

McNally came out onto the terrace carrying a tray that held a bottle of Bombay gin, a bowl of ice, a saucer of lime wedges, three bottles of tonic, and three glasses. He set the tray down, went back into the house, and a moment later returned carrying a platter of crackers spread with cheese and thinly sliced smoked ham.

"Isn't he a dear?" Cavaretta said.

"It's only what you deserve, hon." McNally sat down.

"This has been a domestic week," Cavaretta said. "My head is spinning. My heart beats oh so fast. I ask: Is this what I've been waiting for my whole life? And he can cook. He cooks better than my wife."

"A forest fire cooks better than your wife."

We made our drinks. I took a cigarette from a package on the able.

"Did Arbaleste ask a lot of questions when you saw him?"

"None, actually," Cavaretta said.

"What was his attitude?"

"He was civil."

"More than civil," McNally said. "Almost friendly."

"But I think he made us for cops."

"That's all right," I said. "It's no surprise if body-guards are ex-cops."

"And my God, the woman!" Cavaretta said.

"The woman, Antonia di Benedetto," McNally said.

"Slinking around in her thong bikini."

"Slinking! And you can't stand up, she'll know."

"She'll know that one has been erotically stimulated."

"I threw away my Viagra. Don't need it anymore."

They were amusing themselves with their comical Mutt and Jeff routine: Mutt and Jeff lacking a miscreant to persecute with their wit. Just a couple of bored, cynical cops passing time. They had been partners for twenty years; they had spent what must have seemed like infinity sitting in police cars or shabby offices or interrogation rooms. I enjoyed the joking now, but I hoped that I wouldn't have to endure it for an entire summer.

*   *   *

Charles arrived late that afternoon in a taxi that he had hired at the small airport out in the valley. There were six pieces of luggage, including two big leather portfolios. He cheerily came into the house and commanded McNally and Cavaretta to fetch his things and pay the taxi driver. They looked at me: Do we really have to take orders from this gay sociopath? I nodded. They were security, bodyguards, but as there were no servants yet in the house it became their task to collect the bags. The people next door were surely observing us. Charles, in Tom Petrie's scenario, was playing the role of the spoiled aesthete, the wastrel grandson of our mysterious millionaire. Typecasting.

McNally and Cavaretta sullenly left the big room. They were ex-cops who had taken plenty of rude orders in their careers, but obeying a man like Charles was particularly galling.

"Tell them," Charles said, "that they are to wear suits from now on. Its absurd—employees lounging around in gaudy beach wear."

"You tell them," I said.

Charles's dark blond hair was charmingly tousled, and his candid blue eyes projected a gaze of innocence, almost a virginal purity. He wore an expensive-looking tan suit, a beige shirt with a neck scarf, and hand-lasted loafers that were creased with wear.

I said, "Not long ago you were cohabiting with roaches, and here you are wearing a suit that probably cost a few thousand dollars, and traveling with six pieces of matched luggage."

"Tides rise," he said, "and tides fall. Like my outfit?"

"It's glorious. But the suit and shoes don't look new."

"Of course they don't. It's gauche to be seen in new clothes. It's . . . suburban."

The suit, he told me, was by Armani, the shoes, Ferragamo, and the scarf, Hermès. He had bought an entire wardrobe from charity resale shops in the Palm Beach and Naples areas, and purchased the nicely scuffed Vuitton luggage there as well.

"I feel myself again," Charles said. "Being badly dressed is more embarrassing than walking around naked."

He went off to explore the house, upstairs and down, and when he'd finished prowling, he announced that he had selected a downstairs bedroom, one that looked out over the rear garden and was equipped with a private bath and an alcove that would serve as a dressing room.

My own bedroom was one of the attic garrets at the front left of the house. It was formerly a servant's room, small, with a low ceiling and furniture that was barely functional, but there were windows that cranked open to receive the cool ocean breezes. I had chosen the room because it exposed a view of a triangle of the Arbaleste terrace.

McNally and Cavaretta, in two trips, carried the six pieces of luggage to the center of the tile floor. They stood together, blankly staring at Charles.

"Take them to the rear left bedroom, please," Charles said.

McNally lifted his chin. "The gentleman said, 'Take them to the rear left bedroom, please.'"

"I declare," Cavaretta said. "He did say that, didn't he?"

"He did. Master Charles, he did say that."

Charles watched them, smiling, and then in a gentle voice he said, "Mr. McNally, Mr. Cavaretta. Consider: In our drama, you both occupy subordinate positions here. You aren't servants, but neither are you members of the household. There are social gradations. Mr. Shaw, as personal secretary to the boss, does not carry luggage. Mr. Petrie, as the boss's lawyer, is not expected to carry luggage. But you two, when there isn't a servant at hand, *do* carry luggage. Wait, don't interrupt. That's a thing you never do—interrupt. You dress properly. You are deferential without being servile. You obey promptly, whether or not there are people observing. Make it a habit. You address me and others of position as 'sir'—women as 'ma'am'—whether or not people are listening. Make proper behavior reflexive. Play your parts at all times, and play them well. If you can't do that much, you are useless here. Worse than useless— you'll ruin everything."

McNally and Cavaretta listened to this speech with a sort of puzzled wonder, almost admiration, as you might listen and admire a talkative parrot or comical ventriloquist's dummy.

"Is he real?" McNally asked.

"If he is, we're not," Cavaretta replied.

"Sneer at me when this is over," Charles said. "Sneer, mock, ridicule, beat me up if that will restore your dignity. But for now, please pick up my things and carry them to the bedroom I've selected."

"You punk," McNally said.

"How do you think the punk would do in a place like Raiford?" Cavaretta said.

"I can tell you. I would get by. I spent two and a half years at San Quentin. I got by."

"I'll bet you were everybody's sweetie."

"Enough," I said. "You don't have to like the situation. But there will be people watching us constantly. The servants start work tomorrow. Play your parts offstage and on. Make it automatic. Beat up Charles when this is over. I'll pitch in. Now take the luggage to the room, and then go somewhere for a drink and a talk. Decide if you want to drop out."

They wanted to remain united, act as a team, not make a mistake that would earn the other's scorn; and so for a moment neither was able to move, and then McNally said, "Oh, shit," and he picked up two of the bags and walked toward the rear of the house. Cavaretta followed with two more pieces.

*　　*　　*

Charles spent the rest of the afternoon hanging the two oil paintings and seven drawings that he had brought in the portfolios. He did not allow me to help him, nor did he solicit my opinion. He was very fussy about placement, juxtapositions, separation, the colors and objects in the room that might enhance or detract from the individual works. He needed three hours to do what would have taken me twenty minutes, and when he finished there was a large blank area in the center of the display.

"Lovely," he said.

For years—before turning to extortion—Charles had been an art dealer specializing in stolen and forged works. Now, hanging on the south wall, were two small oil paintings, a landscape signed André Derain, a seaside view by van Dongen; two drawings by Picasso, one signed Matisse, an Odilon Redon, a Daumier pastel drawing on creased and age-yellowed paper, a Raoul Dufy, and a Toulouse-Lautrec whore. Some of the drawings looked hastily done, unfinished; that is, they had probably been preliminary sketches. Martina, with increasing impatience, had been trying to teach me to understand and appreciate modern and. I was only halfway there, though I did like the two small canvases and a few of the more finished drawings.

"Are they good forgeries?" I asked.

"Excellent. Except two are not forgeries. Guess which?"

"The Picasso scribbles?"

"No. There is no point in owning authentic late Picasso drawings when they're so easy to fake. No, the little Derain is genuine, and so is the Daumier cartoon."

"Yours?"

"Borrowed, along with the others."

"Were the fakes done by your Romanian forger?"

"How do you know about Carescu?"

"We thoroughly investigated you during the Falconer business."

"Ah."

"Will these forgeries pass?"

"With faked provenance, certainly. Roman Carescu is a very talented man. And versatile—he can do a fourteenth-century Old Master or a nineteenth-century modernist with equal facility. The man uses paper or canvas from the period, grinds his own pigments, applies crackling and patina—he does it beautifully from the beginning to the end. Not like so many of the untalented hacks forging today. You wouldn't believe how sloppy they are. One clown, until he was finally caught, used acrylic paint—acrylic house paints, for God's sake!—on paintings that were supposed to have been done *before* acrylics. And his fakes sold for enormous sums of money. Really, Shaw, some collectors are far too stupid to pity. All you can do is hope they don't have a coronary before the check clears."

"I'd like to meet this Carescu."

"Would you? Perhaps you shall."

"Is he still living in Avignon?"

"No. He was expelled from France. The French knew what he was doing, though they couldn't prove anything. No, he's living in Naples now, which is wonderfully convenient."

"He's the guy who provided you with most of your forgeries when you were an art dealer?"

"All of my forgeries. He's the best. At this moment there are Carescu forgeries in many of the world's best museums and private collections."

"Care for a drink?" I asked.

"Tonic and a slice of lime, no ice," he said. He caught my look and shrugged. "Petrie made me promise not to drink or take drugs until we've finished our business here."

"A noble sacrifice."

I walked over to the bar, got a beer for myself, poured tonic in a glass and inserted a wedge of lime, and returned.

Charles often was good company. It was easy to like him. His was the kind of carelessness that is called insouciance. He was casual, usually good-humored, and gently ironic, and he loved to chat and gossip and tell stories which, in the end, made him look foolish. Still, one had to remember that he was a career criminal, a man who not only lacked a moral compass but who would have difficulty grasping the concept.

I said, "If this Carescu is so talented, why doesn't he do his own work?"

"It's one of those petty tragedies. Roman's own work is hopelessly banal. He's inspired only when he forges."

TWENTY

With the impetus of some modest bribes, I managed to have a private telephone and a fax machine installed in my garret that afternoon, and the next morning a locksmith came to fit a new set of locks. McNally referred to my attic room as the C and C (Command and Control) Center, or the RRB (Rapid Response Bunker).

Petrie sent me half a dozen faxes each day, none of them important, some canceling previous faxes. He had an imminent court date, and he and the judge would not be arriving in Castelnuovo for at least a week. But he had already prepared "bios" for each of us: two or three single-spaced pages that sketched in our false identities, names, backgrounds, and duties, and advised us that we were expected to "intelligently improvise" within the limits of the biographies. We were not—NOT-—to comment on certain matters until the "master scenario" had been distributed. Our mysterious millionaire was to remain mysterious. The lack of a master scenario convinced me that Petrie had not been lying when he told me that he hadn't yet devised a plan. He rationalized that by saying that we were all involved in an "improvisational drama," and our course of action would, in part, be determined by the actions and behavior of our target, Anton Arbaleste. "Let the subject weave the rope and tie the knot with which we hang him."

*   *   *

It rained hard one night, and lightning illuminated the wave-frothed sea. I got up at a little after midnight to close the windows; got up again to open them a few hours later. In the morning I awakened to the sound of voices speaking French: Charles, Arbaleste, and Antonia di Benedetto. All three were fluent in the language. I could pick out a phrase here and there, but the essence of their conversation was lost to me. It was quiet now; the wind had died, and it sounded as though they were stationed just outside my window. Charles talked for a time. His accent sounded flawless to my ear. Charles had many gifts, even more faults. He spoke, the others laughed, and he went on with what must have been one of his many amusing anecdotes. Charles the droll raconteur.

I had slept late; it was almost nine o'clock. I got out of bed and went to the side window. Below and to my left I could see a triangle of the Arbaleste terrace. I saw Charles, lounging easily in a deck chair, and a diagonal slice of the patio table, but Arbaleste and the woman were invisible except when a hand reached out for a coffee cup or croissant or a cigarette fuming in an ashtray. A man's hand, a woman's. Beyond them, the sea shone a metallic blue-gray streaked with whitecaps and glittering with sunlight.

Charles talked, Antonia laughed, and then Arbaleste said something that made all three laugh. They were pals. They had connected. They had that relaxed, complicit (and exclusionary) air of people whose minds are tuned to the same frequency. They shared viewpoints, assumptions, a sense of humor, cultural references, certain values. It was as though they had known each other for many years.

*   *   *

One afternoon I was dozing on a chaise longue on the terrace when I sensed something, heard something. I opened my eyes. An osprey, a fish clutched in its talons, had landed on the terrace wall. He cocked his head to the right, to the left, then tore a chunk of flesh from the fish and gulped it down. He had the fierce yellow eyes of the raptor, and the hooked beak that can cut as cleanly as a scalpel. The osprey finished eating the fish, fluffed his feathers, and then sailed off into a dimensionless sky.

McNally rushed out onto the terrace. He carried a small automatic pistol, a purse or back-pocket gun. "Shit!" he said. "Did you see that? A fish eagle."

"You'd shoot him?" I asked.

"Sure. What else do you do with them?"

"You harm that bird, McNally, and we're going to fight."

"Your girl's cartoon propaganda has made you soft in the head, Shaw," he said, and he went back into the house.

*   *   *

I phoned Martina every night at ten—four in the afternoon her time—and we chatted for ten or fifteen minutes. She was still saying at her uncle's. Cerberus was with her, and she told me that the dog and monkey had finally reached a shaky sort of detente, and each could now tolerate the presence of the other, though the dog remained the more anxious of the two.

"How is Phil doing?" I asked.

"Oh, he's moody, withdrawn, but not so bad as before."

"Is anyone staying at the lighthouse?"

"No. It's locked up."

"And your work?"

"Fine. I set up a little studio in one of the bedrooms."

"Good."

"How long are you going to be over there?"

"I'm not sure, Martina. For a while yet."

"Is Castelnuovo a pretty place?"

"Very. You'd love it."

"I've never been to Italy."

"Maybe we can go together this fall."

"Why fall? Why can't I come over sooner?"

"Great idea," I lied. "Maybe we can work something out."

"Just what are you doing over there?"

"I'll explain it all later."

"That's what you always say. But there's never an explanation."

"How is the weather in Florida? Getting hot?"

She laughed. "The weather! Is that your idea of an adroit change of subject?"

"It used to be."

"Listen, do you know anyone by the name of Mackey?"

"The name sounds familiar. Why?"

"You asked me to pick up your mail, read it, and let you know if anything important comes up. Well, this Mackey, Kyle Mackey, of an entity called Search and Seizure—can you believe that?—sent you a bill for five thousand dollars. For services rendered. Services spelled s-u-r-v-a-c-e-s."

"I remember now," I said. "It's a joke."

"God, you're a terrible liar. What kind of lawyer are you going to be if you can't learn to lie convincingly?"

"I'm getting better," I said.

"No, dear, you're not."

*   *   *

McNally and Cavaretta had not been able to learn much about Arbaleste in their brief investigation. They said they needed more time. They had gathered information about his early years, to the age of seventeen, but it was difficult for Americans to conduct a thorough investigation in Europe. So many countries, so many different police agencies, so many bureaucracies. Two European detectives had been hired, one Swiss and the other French, to learn what they could about the man. The Swiss had filed one sketchy report; the Frenchman had not yet responded. An Italian detective might also be retained.

While reading the report on Arbaleste's American years, I mentally edited the dozen pages of bloated cop prose and shaky speculation down to the essentials.

Jean Halbert (Anton Arbaleste) had been born in the United States and was therefore an American citizen, but both his father and mother were Swiss nationals. His father, Claude Halbert, was from a French-speaking canton; his mother, Maria Halbert (née Petrillo), had been born and raised in Locarno, on the Swiss-Italian border. Both, like many Swiss, were multilingual, speaking French, Italian, English, and some German.

Claude Halbert died of pancreatic cancer in 1983, six months after returning to Europe; Maria, after living twelve years in Locarno, retired to Fontana in Italy, on the shore of Lake Como, where she now owned a large villa, a small hotel and restaurant, and several rental properties. Her wealth was attributed to the generosity of her son, a distinguished and clearly important man who visited Maria two or three times each year. Jean was a man who valued his privacy and was not well known in the community, although no one had anything unfavorable to say about him.

As a young man, Claude Halbert, Jean's father, had worked as an assistant chef in several good restaurants, first in Lausanne, then in Geneva. Maria, after rigorous training in the Swiss way, entered the hotel business and soon became a valued employee. They met in 1965 while both worked for the Hotel Edelweiss in the ski resort of Saint Moritz. Claude was then head chef of the hotel's three-star restaurant; Maria, the *concierge d'hotel*. They married within a year.

Maria was three months pregnant when the couple received an offer to work in America. Mr. Brian Chadwick, a frequent guest of the hotel, needed a chef for his estate in the Hudson Valley of New York. He entertained often, received many guests, and was eager to hire a first-rate European chef. And he offered Maria a position as housekeeper; she would oversee the day-to-day functioning of the household, and was given considerable responsibility and authority. His offer was very liberal. Claude and Maria calculated that they would only have to work seven or eight years before saving enough to open their own small hotel and restaurant in Switzerland.

Brian Chadwick's great-grandfather, John, had earned his fortune in railroads and oil during the late nineteenth century. He was one of those predatory capitalists known at the time as robber barons. He built an estate on a stretch of the Hudson favored by many of the rich of that period. Land holdings were large, the houses enormous, locally known as mansions—the Mills Mansion, the Vanderbilt Mansion, the Chadwick Mansion. The family also owned a sixteen-room "cottage" at Newport, a house in New York, an apartment in Paris, and a house in Palm Beach, Florida.

Brian Chadwick was certainly not as rich as his great grandfather and other male predecessors; a lot of the family fortune had gone to taxes, tax-exempt foundations, and trusts, and there had been some bad investments. Still, he was very rich and he lived the life of a rich man from another era. He studied law, obtained a degree from Yale, and passed the New York Bar, but he never practiced his profession. He, with hired lawyers and accountants, managed the family fortune and properties. And he traveled, sailed, skied, played polo, collected art, bred and raced his stable of horses. He was "old money," and unlike most of his old-money friends and relatives, he felt no guilt about his inherited wealth and rapacious ancestors.

He did not make a show of living simply and working hard. He was never tempted to enter public service or dabble in politics. He did not want to be an ambassador or serve on prestigious Washington committees. He hated Washington.

The Halberts worked for Brian Chadwick for seventeen years. After the first few years they ceased planning for their small hotel and restaurant in Switzerland. The dream faded. They watched it fade without regret. They were content. It was a good life. In many ways they lived like the very rich, spending summers in Newport or Paris, winters in Palm Beach or Saint Moritz. And they were regarded more as members of the household than employees. The family and their staff—never called servants by the Chadwicks—lived together in a sort of anarchist semidemocracy.

Jean Halbert was raised with the Chadwick children as an equal. They played and quarreled and studied and schemed together. They ran wild in the summers. Louis Chadwick was sixteen months older than Jean, Catherine the same age; Phyllis, three years younger, was the weepy trail-along brat.

Catherine Chadwick became pregnant by Jean when they both were seventeen (at the same time that Claude Halbert was dying of cancer). They defiantly announced to the two families, the Chadwicks and Halberts, that they were deeply in love, intended to have the baby, and wished to marry immediately. Catherine was sent away to stay with relatives at an undisclosed location. Jean much later learned that she had delivered the baby, his son, but that it had immediately been put up for adoption.

It was, everyone agreed, an impossible situation. The Halberts resigned their positions and returned to Europe. Brian Chadwick quietly paid for all of Claude's medical expenses, and he also provided a large sum of money as reward for their long years of service. The pensions were generous.

Claude died six months later in his home village. Maria moved back to Locarno, where she bought a small house and went to work as concierge for a good hotel. There was sufficient money; Maria had her salary, her savings, her pension, and Brian Chadwick continued paying Claude's pension benefits years after his death. Jean attended school first in Locarno, then in Zurich, and at twenty, without obtaining a degree, he moved to Paris. He wanted to become an artist.

* * *

Soon after dawn each morning I descended the cliffs by the north stairway and strolled the three miles down the beach to the resort and marina. Usually, at that early hour, the fishing boats had come in and were unloading their catches. The air around them swarmed with greedy seagulls. A sleepy waiter brought me a cup of cappuccino and a breakfast pastry. I ate, smoked a cigarette, tried a few Italian phrases with the waiter, and then returned north along the beach. But one morning, before walking back to the house, I went out onto the pier to look over Arbaleste's sailboat. Name, *Avanti*, home port, Castelnuovo. She was a cutter-rigged thirty-eight-footer with beautiful lines. You could sail around the world on that boat.

TWENTY-ONE

Charles had assembled a motoring costume comprised of white jeans, a light canvas jacket, a beret, aviator-style sunglasses, and a white silk scarf that trailed gloriously in the windstream. The red Ferrari scared him a little, and the dangerous crash-gallery road scared both of us, but we made it into Naples all right, and Charles maneuvered the car through a maze of back streets to a district of tenements and warehouses. He gave some street kids a handful of lire to watch the Ferrari.

I followed him through an arch that opened into a big rectangular courtyard. Laundry was strung out on a cat's-cradle of clothesline, and some boys were noisily disassembling a bicycle. There was a rack of bicycles, a few parked motor scooters, and a Fiat that looked a dubious squeeze through the archway to the street. The courtyard collected and amplified the sounds of voices: babies crying, cats mewing, and music ranging from rock to old ballads to grand opera. There were four stories linked together by flights of stairs, and wooden walkways that afforded access to the apartments.

Roman Carescu lived on the top floor in a surprisingly quiet and spacious apartment; there were five or six nicely furnished rooms in addition to his studio. I saw nothing bohemian about this forger. He was about sixty, white-haired, and grave in manner, and he wore a three-piece suit with a tie, a gold watch chain looped over his vest, and a Masonic ring and lapel pin.

A buxom Italian woman some twenty years younger than Carescu brought us small glasses of a clear cherry liqueur and offered us Turkish cigarettes from an enameled box. Charles called Carescu "*Maître.*" He and the Master chatted in French as we sipped the liqueur and smoked. When the hospitality ritual was completed, we walked single-file down a hallway and into the studio.

It was a big cubical room with a dirty skylight high above. At first glance it appeared to contain a mad clutter, but after a while I began to sense patterns, an order within the chaos. There were rolls of canvas; bins full of stretcher bars and frame sections; half a dozen tall easels; tubes and jars of paint; cigar boxes full of charcoal sticks and pastel crayons; pestles and mortars for grinding pigments; three long tables, one of which held drying sheets of handmade paper; an old printing press where Carescu could hand-roll prints one at a time; and everywhere paintings and drawings, propped on the easels, layered against the walls, stacked in honeycombs of boxes.

I knew that Charles was eager to study a particular forgery, a Degas, but he did not attempt to rush the *cher maître,* he patiently studied Carescu's recent work, praised some items, frowned at others, and did not protest when still more canvases were produced for examination.

Charles had told me that the artists own work was banal, without interest, but they looked good to my untrained eye. Most were still lifes, portraits, and fleshy female nudes. The drawing was sure, the colors harmonious, the objects and people realistically portrayed. I saw that Carescu was a fine draftsman and obviously technically proficient. I admired the paintings and drawings while never receiving that electrical jolt of wonder that great art often inspires. Maybe that's what Charles meant by banal.

Finally, flattered and reassured, Carescu removed the cloth from a painting with a bullfighter's flourish. It was a fairly large painting, thirty-six inches by forty-four, wider than long, signed *Degas* in the lower right-hand corner, and beneath that, 1873. Carescu called it "Nuit des Créoles"—"Creole Night"—although the title did not appear anywhere on the canvas. Charles pointed at the signature. "That," he said, "is what makes this a forgery. Unsigned, it is a perfectly legal work." And he said that the word "Creole" had different meanings in different places, but in this context it meant a person descended from the original French settlers of Louisiana.

It was a street scene done of the old French Quarter of New Orleans. It looked more like twilight than night, though the oil lamps were burning and light glowed behind curtained windows. There were a number of figures on a street which narrowed with perspective. A sign above the planked walk said *Café Absinthe*. The men wore dark suits, black or dark gray, with matching top hats, and most carried walking sticks. The women wore dresses with full skirts, ruffled blouses beneath short jackets, and wide-brimmed hats—some with flowers and decorative ribbons—at a tilt. The women were dressed more colorfully than the men, but the reds and blues and canary yellows were muted by the failing light. Clearly, these rather stiff, formal people were taking their evening stroll, some in pairs, arms linked, others solitary. There were eleven major figures, six men and four women, and a Negro boy in livery who trailed one of the couples, but you could see others, diminished by perspective, far down the street. Street lamps burned mistily in the blue twilight. It was a very hot night, I knew that; but I couldn't say how I knew.

"What do you think?" Charles asked me.

"It's beautiful," I said. And it was.

"People will say it belongs to Degas's naturalistic period, but there's a new touch in it, something that points the way to his later work."

He told me that the linen, stretcher bars, frame, and handmade nails dated from the early 1870s. The pigments were authentic, what Degas would have used. Sometimes a forger would buy an old painting of the relevant period, remove the paint, and do his work on that surface. But some time ago Carescu had obtained a roll of old French linen, a precious find, and he used it for this and other paintings.

Charles and Carescu discussed the painting in rapid French. I could not understand much of what they were saying except, at times, it concerned money. They haggled. Both men knew that a deal was imminent; it was just a matter of setting a mutually acceptable price, but it appeared that they enjoyed the process. They shook hands.

Carescu then pulled a rope that evidently rang a bell in another part of the apartment, and a few minutes later the woman came into the studio bearing a tray that contained three more little glasses of liqueur and the enameled cigarette box. We again ritually smoked and sipped the cherry liqueur. Everyone was happy. Carescu gave Charles the gift of a forged Raoul Dufy drawing. We shook hands all around in the studio, shook hands again at the door, and then Charles and I descended the flights of stairs to the courtyard.

Charles told me something about Edgar Degas and the forged painting during the drive back to Castelnuovo.

Degas, born in 1834, had been trained in the classical methods, and his early oil paintings reveal that background in their composition and colors, and often in subject matter. Years later in his career he developed his own modernist style, concentrating more on pastels than oils, and he began creating the work for which he is best known today, the ballerinas and nudes, the theater and circus and racetrack scenes.

In 1872 Degas, with two of his brothers, traveled from Paris to New Orleans to visit a third brother, an uncle, and other relatives. (His mother had been born there.) He remained in the city for less than a year. Only one great painting stems from that period, "The Cotton Market in New Orleans," although in a letter to Manet he mentioned a painting then in progress which pleased him very much. He referred to it as "Creole Night." A few preliminary sketches for that painting survived, but the painting itself apparently had been lost, abandoned, or destroyed. The rough charcoal sketches and the description in his letter gave a general idea of how the street scene, if completed, might have looked.

Roman Carescu also had been classically trained, in Bucharest and Paris, and he had mastered the materials and techniques that present-day art students neglected. He ground his own pigments, prepared his medium, and applied paints in layer after layer, in successive glazes, which gave the work a luminous quality that couldn't be achieved in any other way.

He had needed only a couple of months to complete his forgery of "Creole Night," and then put it aside for three years. Oil paint takes a long time to thoroughly dry. And then he had aged and "abused" the painting. It had to look as though it had been neglected during its lost years. Carescu had added crackling to a part of the surface, carefully applied soot and dust, damaged the signature area, and applied a varnish that no artist would have used but which could be removed without ruining the paint. Carescu had first damaged and then restored the painting. Traces of coal soot and varnish and mold would be detected by a scientific analysis. After all, it was a one-hundred-and-thirty-year-old painting, wasn't it?

"So," Charles said. "A great painting. A great lost Degas."

"A forgery," I said.

"Nevertheless, a great painting."

"And where has it been for one hundred and thirty years?

"Why, until recently it was stored in the attic of an old house in Jefferson Parish, Louisiana, unappreciated and unrecognized by a descendant of a Degas relative on the maternal side. It was purchased by a sharp-eyed collector at a garage sale."

"Aren't we lucky?" I said. "How much can you sell it for?"

"Oh, my. It's an important work, valuable not only because it's a gorgeous lost Degas, but because it was painted in America—American collectors and museums will go crazy to possess it."

"How much?"

"In auction? With worldwide bidding? Fifteen million dollars? No, more than that. Twenty million? Thirty? It might well bring thirty million if the world economy picks up."

"Charles, it's a forgery."

"Well, as a forgery it's worth what I paid for it—seventy-five thousand dollars. But look here, for all practical purposes it's a Degas. We've established a convincing provenance. Roman can forge documents, too: letters, sales receipts, family records. But you're looking at this wrong, Shaw. It's a superb Degas oil painting. Please stop insisting that it wasn't painted by Degas. It's a Degas painted by Roman Carescu, who was possessed by Degas's soul and spirit while he worked."

"Where did you get seventy-five thousand dollars?"

"I haven't got it yet."

"What are you going to do with the painting?"

"Sell it to Arbaleste for millions, of course."

"What if he isn't interested in it?"

"Don't be silly. Arbaleste is a collector. He has a fortune in art objects stored in a Zurich bank vault. Collectors *must* acquire, *must* possess, *must* capture. It's a disease."

"You missed the turn into Castelnuovo," I said.

"Our magnificent painting will drive him mad."

TWENTY-TWO

Are you using the speaker phone?" I asked Petrie.

"No. What you hear are the echoes in my head."

"Are you going to be delayed much longer?"

"The case will go to the jury tomorrow."

"How does it look?"

"Not good. Sitting in that courtroom is like going back five hundred years. The judge and the prosecutors should be forced to wear the robes of the Inquisition. Ten of the jurors are decent, earnest, responsible, bloodthirsty citizens. But the other two, luckily, are insane. Don't talk to me about justice in America, pal. This is Florida."

"So what is your client going to get?"

"Get? I think he's going to get a mistrial."

"If so, Tom, it might take the judge days to declare one."

"I know. What's happening there?"

"Very little."

"Getting chummy with Arbaleste?"

"I've hardly seen him. We've just talked terrace-to-terrace a few times. We might go sailing. And I'm playing tennis with him tomorrow morning."

"Well, that's something."

"Yeah, but what?"

"Has he questioned you or the others much?"

"Not at all. He's not interested."

"That's his modus operandi, isn't it?"

"Is it?"

"Sure. He plays hard to get."

"We're playing hard to get, too, Tom."

"Things will start to move when Levi and I get there."

"Why don't you send Levi over now?"

"I can't send him alone. I've got to stay close to him or he'll mess things up."

"What things? Where's the master scenario?"

"It's in my head."

"Along with echoes, evidently."

"Are the others behaving?"

"Mutt and Jeff are sullen, rebellious. Charles is Charles. He's playing the spendthrift gay blade to perfection. I think he's got a boyfriend in the village. They go off to Naples every night in the red Ferrari Charles leased. Did you authorize that?"

"The boyfriend, no, the Ferrari, yes."

"Charles took me to meet a Romanian forger. He seems to have bought a painting for seventy-five thousand dollars. Did you authorize that?"

"Shaw, did you phone me because you're lonely? If so, I'm sorry to tell you that I'm very busy. Not as busy as you with your sailing and tennis and Romanians, but still busy. I've got to finish writing my summation tonight. I've got to be in court in the morning. I have to continue coaching Judge Samuelson in the ways of deception and larceny. I've got to find Leroy—he flew a charter to Knoxville two days ago and hasn't come back. Maybe he crashed. Maybe my luck is turning at last. I'm busy. I've got to meet with Chester Dalhart again soon, and coax and threaten him to give us more money. I'm *busy*."

"Well, then," I said, "why did you phone me?" And I quickly hung up.

* * *

A report came in from the French detective who had been hired by Mutt and Jeff.

In Paris, Jean Halbert was accepted by the prestigious art academy, École Ingres, where he remained for two years. His application to attend a third year was denied. It was unfortunate, he was told, most unfortunate, but Monsieur Halbert's passion for art was not accompanied by an equivalent talent. He had made little progress during his two years as a student; not much more progress could be envisioned in the future. He might make a living as an illustrator or as one of the incendiary fakes who now populate the art world, but he never would produce work of merit.

The record did not resume until eight years later, when Jean Halbert was expelled from Poland. He left with his share of a small fortune that he, a Polish father named Pulaski, and Pulaski's thirteen-year-old daughter, Liza, swindled from the gullible of a dozen countries. There was a period when charter airline flights were arriving daily in Poland, filled with pilgrims eager to visit the place where Liza had miraculously been visited by the Virgin Mary.

According to the story, Liza, a simple—retarded—peasant girl, afflicted by skin ulcers and dying of tuberculosis, had been praying to the Virgin in a forest clearing on her father's small farm. She had prayed only that Mary might reveal to her the reason for her many afflictions. It was a bright, cloudless day, yet the sky was immediately rent by a savage bolt of lightning which virtually exploded a great oak tree. When the holy smoke cleared, Liza saw the Virgin appear in the clearing. Her image was physical and yet somehow ethereal, too—a heavenly hologram. The Virgin, in a voice as liquid-sweet as honey, told the girl that she had been purified by her suffering and faith, and that her afflictions would be rescinded. And then the Virgin herself vanished, but her portrait remained carved in the lightning-split oak. Also left behind were the Virgin's footprints (small, perfectly formed feet) and her blue-dyed wool sash.

A "scientist" without degrees or affiliations declared that the cloth had been carbon-dated to the time of Christ. The footprints and sash were covered by a glass case to preserve both from the weather and yet allow them to be viewed by the faithful.

And the faithful came, Poles at first, then some Germans, Serbs, and Americans. Word quickly spread and soon Pulaski's little farm buzzed with the babble of a dozen languages. Pilgrims, many of them crippled, ill, dying, came in the hopes of a miracle like Liza's. They paid for the privilege of viewing the Virgin's footprints and sash and touching her beautiful image lightning-carved into the oak tree's heartwood.

The now quite intelligent Liza, for a fee, spoke to the gathered pilgrims. She told them of her many afflictions, her despair, the lightning strike out of a clear blue sky and the ghostly appearance of the Holy Mother. She announced that her ulcers had vanished, her mind had cleared, and her tuberculosis had been cured at the moment of hearing the Virgin's comforting words. The pilgrims were eager to pay to hear about such wonders. They could listen to the words of one who had actually *seen* Mary; they could see Mary's footprints and wool sash; they could touch the lightning-engraved image of Mary.

Trinkets were sold on the grounds: medallions with a portrait of the Virgin on one side, Liza on the other; cheap blue wool sashes; photographs of the footprints and wood sculpture; rosaries and crosses and holy oils. You could buy food, too. It was like a carnival or country fair.

A defrocked priest consecrated the holy earth of Pulaski's farm. More "scientists" testified to the authenticity of the sash and footprints (footprints certified to be those of a female Semite of the first century). Many pilgrims claimed to have been miraculously cured.

The Polish government and the Catholic Church combined to shut down the fraud after five weeks. Halbert was expelled; Liza and her father were fined, but criminal charges were dropped. Even today people frequently appear at the farm (no longer owned by Pulaski) to visit the miraculous tree and the patch of earth where the Virgin's footprints and sash were found by the poor, afflicted little Liza.

According to a report filed by the police officers who escorted Halbert to the border, he stated that he indeed felt uneasy about swindling such people—the desperate, the yearning, the stupid. In the future, he said, it would be the top dogs, the rich and powerful, the proud, who would pay his bills.

*   *   *

Leroy Karpe arrived late in the week with a flight bag and a bad attitude. The cosmetic surgeon had been at work again and there were new pink scars on his face, one of which was still laced with stitches. Each operation, McNally said, made him look a little less like Leroy and a little more like Dr. Frankenstein's creation.

Leroy dropped his flight bag in the center of the big room, looked around, and addressed his first words to Charles.

"You don't got socks, asshole?"

Charles was wearing moccasin-style deck shoes without socks. He smiled at Leroy. "This is a seaside resort. One does not wear socks in daylight hours in summer wherever one can smell the sea."

"One is going to get smacked," Leroy said.

He soon teamed up with McNally and Cavaretta in sullen rebellion: the three of them lounged around the house most of the day, complaining about the heat and the food and the futility of Tom Petrie's scheme. They didn't use the swimming pool; they rarely went to the village; they drank and moped.

During a phone conversation with Petrie, I said, "Get them out of here."

"No can do."

"The mood is poisonous."

"They're bodyguards. Rich men in Italy need heavy security. Kidnapping for ransom is always an issue."

"Arbaleste doesn't have bodyguards."

"Who's that mean-looking Italian you mentioned?"

"He's a mean-looking manservant."

"Believe me, Arbaleste will be impressed by our security precautions."

"No, he won't. When are you and the judge coming over?"

"Next week. Tuesday, maybe. Wednesday."

"I'll probably kill the three of them by that time."

"Well, that's all right," he said. "If that's how you truly feel."

TWENTY-THREE

There wasn't a swimming pool in Arbaleste's yard; most of the space was taken up by the tennis court, with just enough room left over for a patch of garden, a couple of lemon trees, and a vine-covered latticed arbor where three or four could sit at a table in the shade. The court was the standard European red clay, today freshly lined with chalk, and the net had been winched tight.

"You like clay?" Arbaleste asked me.

I removed the cover from my racket. "It's a little slow to suit my game," I said.

"Good," he said. He didn't smile.

It was early, a little after eight, still cool, and the sea breeze was not brisk enough to affect the flight of a tennis ball. A perfect morning for tennis. I wanted to beat Arbaleste. He, naturally, wanted to beat me. But the occasion seemed more significant than an ordinary tennis match; I sensed in him a personal antipathy.

We warmed up from the baseline, hitting down the center for a while and then going for the corners, testing each other. He could either slice his backhand or come over the top; his forehand was hit with heavy topspin, looping shots that bounced high in my backcourt. He was very quick and accurate, but he didn't hit with much power considering his size and the timing of his strokes. He learned that I had a tendency to spray the ball on my backhand; that I had difficulty with high-bouncing balls, but that I could rip both forehands and backhands if I had time to set up.

We then spent a few minutes practicing volleys and overheads. Arbaleste, like a lot of clay court players, was not comfortable at the net; he was tentative, defensive, his footwork often a bit awkward. He'd obviously prefer to involve his opponent in long rallies from the baseline where his quickness, physical fitness, and precision were most effective.

While warming up our serving I found that Arbaleste, again, did not hit with the power I expected, and I figured that he was willing to sacrifice power for accuracy and "stuff"—he hit a slice that angled away from my forehand, and a twisting, high-hopping kick serve that I knew would cause me trouble during the match.

It was a long warm-up, and we both were sweating afterward. We met at the bench, toweled off, and drank some water.

"We'll change balls after every six games," he said. He was a rich man.

"Fine," I said.

Close up, Arbaleste looked older than his thirty-eight years. He had translucent skin and the sort of heavy beard that impels a fastidious man to shave two or three times a day. Crow's-feet at the corners of his eyes, scarlike lines bracketing his mouth. His eyes, slightly protuberant, brown flecked with gold, were clear with health but opaque in the sense of concealing thoughts and emotions. And his voice, low and well modulated, gave nothing away. With Arbaleste, as with a good film actor, you found yourself piecing together a character from the subtlest of expressions and inflections. He was a con man; he was what you needed him to be.

He had not revealed his full game during the warm-up. I soon learned that he could hit with power when he chose; a hard flat forehand that he usually ripped crosscourt; and a big flat serve that he aimed directly at me. He sliced his serve to my forehand side; used the kick serve on my backhand return; and went straight at me with the flat serve. But he still relied mostly on his baseline game. He was crafty and, what you'd expect from a gymnast, very agile. Time after time he managed to return shots that I had thought were clean winners. Playing Arbaleste was like playing a machine. He never tired, rarely made unforced errors, never let up; he just kept hitting the ball with his compact precision strokes, and he easily won the first set 6-2.

We rested at opposite ends of the bench. He had brought a jug of orange juice and we sipped that as we talked.

"I was worried about you," he said.

I looked at him.

"A lot of people say they can play tennis when they can't. One shows up at the court and finds a beginner on the other side of the net. A morning is lost. But you can play."

"That's a dubious remark, considering the first set."

I was still breathing hard; Arbaleste, after toweling off, looked as cool and rested as when he'd arrived this morning.

He said, "Do you live in a climate where you can play year round?"

"Yes. Southern California—San Diego."

"A good city."

"You know San Diego?"

"I've been there."

I thought of Rancho Santa Fe where he had swindled people out of millions.

"I spent some time in Florida, too," he said.

"Where?"

"Paradise Key. Heard of it?"

I shook my head.

"Bell Harbor?"

"I've heard about Bell Harbor."

I changed tactics for the second set. I could not beat him from the baseline; could not beat him with my usual serve-and-volley game on the slow clay surface. I stopped overhitting my ground strokes. On my serve, I sacrificed some power for accuracy. I made him play on that section of the court where he was most vulnerable, from his service line forward to the net. He could not employ his perfect, mechanical strokes there. When I could, I chipped the ball short, short and low over the net, and made him come in. I forced him to try volleys, half volleys—hit the ball off his shoetops—and then I put it away. We played much of the second set ten or fifteen feet apart, facing each other over the net, hitting dinks and drop shots and lobs and sharply angled reflex volleys. I won the second set 6-3.

We again went to the bench for a rest and a cup of orange juice. We both were red-faced and sweating now.

"I didn't expect you to change your game," Arbaleste said. "Very smart. Usually you big hitters just want to hit big. You'd rather hit hard than win."

"That's often true," I said. "We get our satisfaction whacking the fuzz off the ball."

"It's ugly."

"Sometimes."

"It's unaesthetic. I myself would rather lose than play without style."

"That's a very French remark."

"Why not? I am very French."

"Shall we play another set?"

"If you're not too tired. Does your employer play tennis?"

"Geriatric doubles, occasionally."

"He's old?"

"Yes."

"I look forward to meeting him. An American?"

"You'll probably recognize the name. Arnold Elsworth." Levi was conducting his part of the masquerade under his original first two given names.

Arbaleste thought, shook his head.

"There was a lot of publicity fifteen years ago. Mr. Elsworth got caught in a net with a lot of other big fish. Insider trading."

"What hypocrisy. All of the world's economic and governmental business is conducted through inside information of one kind or another."

"True, but every now and then there's a political convulsion, and a purge. Mr. Elsworth spent a year and a half in a federal penitentiary. He was humiliated, still is. We never mention it."

"Nor shall I, of course. Does anyone else in Mr. Elsworth's group play tennis?"

"Thomas Peters, Mr. Elsworth's lawyer, plays well."

"Ah, he's good?"

"Good enough to beat me most of the time."

"Well, then, I shall have to beat you before beating him."

Arbaleste won the third set, but it was very close, 7-6 (9-7 in the tiebreaker). He did not change his game, and there was not much improvement in his net play; but by sheer determination and acrobatic effort he managed to hit just enough winning shots to take the match. He simply refused to lose. I also refused to lose, but I lost anyway.

Antonia di Benedetto joined us for breakfast in the trellised arbor. It was cool and shady there, and smelled of the vine leaves. There were iced bowls of fruit, plums and peaches and several kinds of melon, toast, jam, and a pot of coffee. Antonia wore a white dress, but was barefoot, without makeup, and she looked as though she had yet to comb her hair this summer.

"I'm Antonia," she said to me.

"We've met," I said.

"Oh?"

"I'm not likely to forget the first time I saw you."

She remembered, laughed, and said, "Who won the tennis?"

"Anton," I said.

"Anton always wins at everything. Always. I wish someone would beat him just once."

"I can't lose," Arbaleste told her. "When I begin losing, you'll go away."

"Maybe I *will* go away," she said. "You are cruelly inattentive, Anton. Maybe I'll have an affair this summer. Perhaps with this gentleman, Mr. . . . ?"

"Dan," I said.

"Would you mind, Anton, if I had an affair?"

"Not if it made you happy. I would mind very much if an affair made you unhappy."

"There, you see, Dan? He will not mind if we have an affair this summer. It will be your duty to make me happy, very happy, so Anton doesn't challenge you to a duel."

She had a lovely voice, soft and low and a little husky, charmingly accented. European women did not speak with that slurred quacking that afflicted so many American women.

"Are you available?" she asked me.

"My fiancée doesn't think so."

"Oh, good, you are engaged. I'll take you away from her now and return you at the end of summer. But you must not fall too deeply in love with me. It wouldn't do to have you following me around like a lost dog after our affair has ended. I hate that."

TWENTY-FOUR

The next morning Leroy Karpe and I drove into Naples, caught a flight to Milan, and at the Milan airport rented a car for a drive into the lake country. It was a bright clear day and the Alps were cleanly incised into a powder blue sky. There was still a lot of snow on the peaks, and snow-choked ravines radiated down toward the valley. The trees and fields were varying shades of green, wildflowers grew alongside the road, and we passed stone farmhouses and terraced hills and little towns with cobbled streets and ancient churches.

"Pretty country, isn't it?" I said.

Leroy shrugged. He wasn't much interested in scenic beauty. His aesthetic sense was tuned toward the mechanical: things with pistons, precision instruments, finely calibrated devices, technological marvels. A placid lake set among pines was just water; an aircraft engine or an automatic pistol was a revelation of God.

Leroy had changed only in degree since his terrible beating. He hadn't been cowed. He was the same man, only more so: a distilled Leroy, Leroy reduced to his essence. That wasn't necessarily a good thing. More Leroy was too much Leroy.

I said, "The Etruscans lived around here."

"What are they?"

"I'm not sure, Leroy, but I like the name—Etruscans."

He shot me an angled, scornful look.

Lake Como was shaped like an inverted Y, with the city of Como at the tip of the left fork, Lecco, the right. We went into Como and ate a light lunch at a trattoria, and then walked through parts of the medieval old city and on to the Piazza del Duomo. The streets were packed with tourists trekking from shop to shop, stopping traffic while they took photographs, entering and leaving the church, and comparing the scene with the prose in their guidebooks. I had looked over a guidebook before leaving Castelnuovo, and now I pointed out to an obviously bored Leroy the marble Broletto—town hall—which had been built in 1215, the tower of the Commune, and the Duomo itself.

"Yeah, yeah, yeah," Leroy said. "Let's go."

We drove north toward the village of Fontana. Sometimes, topping a hill or rounding a corner, the Swiss Alps rose up and filled the windshield. There were glacier-rounded hills, rectangles of cultivated land, patches of pine forest, grand villas perched above the lake, and villages clustered around gray stone churches. The scenic drive put Leroy to sleep.

Fontana was a lakeside town, small but touristy, with modest hotels and marina piers and, in the central plaza, bronze equestrian statues of forgotten heroes.

The Hotel Suisse, owned by Arbaleste's mother, was located a quarter mile beyond the town. It looked old.

Constructed of mortared stone and blackened timbers, it had a steep, shingled roof, many chimneys, and many gables, with dormer windows on the second floor and a front veranda that extended the width of the building. The parking area was in the rear. I saw no swimming pool or tennis courts. My guidebook stated that the Hotel Suisse was a small—twenty-two rooms—establishment favored by those who appreciated a quiet old-world ambiance. Comfortable rooms. Good restaurant. Fine wine cellar. Excellent service. Chiefly patronized by the elderly. Three and one half stars out of a possible five.

"Wake up, Leroy. We're here."

He lifted his head and gazed around. "Okay. But why are we here? You never told me."

"We're here on a fishing expedition."

"I like to fish," he said.

We were assigned rooms on the second floor. Both were big and comfortable, and each had windows that looked down over flower gardens to the lake.

Leroy left immediately to go fishing. He rented a skiff and tackle, and spent all afternoon and a part of the evening on the lake. It was twilight when he returned with sunburned face and arms, and a sour mood. Scowling, he entered my room without first knocking.

"Catch anything?" I asked.

"There's no fish in there. It's a dead lake."

"No, it isn't."

"There's nothing alive in that lake."

"Leroy, they have lake fish on the menu here."

"Sure. But from what lake?" he said, with a knowing paranoid stare.

"Change clothes. We'll go down to dinner."

"No fish, but I did scout out Arbaleste's house. It's only a few hundred yards north of here, stuck back in some trees. It's been closed up. You could get inside pretty easy."

"How did you find out where his house is?"

"I asked some Italians. Said he was a friend of mine."

"Christ. That wasn't smart." Not, I thought, with his face, manner, and accent; no witness would ever have difficulty in identifying Leroy Karpe.

"I'm going in tonight," he said.

"No, you aren't. Are you crazy?"

"I'm going in. No telling what I'll find."

The dining room was paneled in dark wood, and had heavy chairs and tables covered with white linen cloths; the silverware was actual sterling, the glassware crystal. The clientele, as the guidebook warned, was mostly old people. Most of the men were dressed in tuxes; the women wore long gowns.

"How many you figure'll die before they reach dessert?" Leroy said.

A tall woman, well dressed and wearing a lot of jewelry, stopped at each table and chatted briefly with the guests. I heard her speaking Italian, German, French, and English. Anton Arbaleste's mother. She was about sixty, with golden hair that certainly could not be natural, brown eyes very much like her son's eyes, and a regal bearing.

Leroy talked about fishing. He was an avid fisherman. He had fished, he told me, in nine states, two Canadian provinces, and three Latin American countries. He had caught many fish. Small fish and big fish. But he had never been skunked until today, while wasting his time fishing on a dead lake.

Leroy was a laconic man, but now and then he abruptly became loquacious, rambling on in a throaty drawl that Tom Petrie called flour-sack-curtain hillbilly, and then his monologues were stupefying. (There were, according to Petrie, burlap-bag-curtain hillbillies and flour-sack-curtain hillbillies—the flour-sack clans were on their way to voting Republican.)

Madame Halbert paused at our table, introduced herself, and engaged us in small talk in nearly accentless English. She welcomed us to her hotel, mentioned various amenities, suggested local sights worth visiting, and recommended the freshly caught fish for dinner.

"How long's the lake been dead?" Leroy asked.

"Dead? The lake?" she said. "Why . . ."

Leroy's scarred, lopsided face split into a skeptical grin.

To me, she said, "If you need anything, please see our concierge."

"Did you see them diamonds?" Leroy said after she had gone.

"I saw them."

Later, while we were waiting for the check, he said, "I'm going in soon. Coming?"

"No," I said, but I knew that I would have to go with him if he insisted on breaking into Arbaleste's house. You had to watch Leroy. You had to be there to provide the superego he so obviously lacked. He had torched at least one house.

*   *   *

Arbaleste's chalet looked like the sort of place you'd see at a ski resort or high in the Swiss Alps. It was stone-and-timber construction with steep overhanging roof eaves, and was, as Leroy had said, set among a cluster of trees. It was dark and quiet. All of the window drapes were drawn. We didn't find any evidence of an alarm system.

We didn't have to break any locks or windows: Leroy had fashioned some picks from pieces of stiff wire, a fingernail file, and a fork with three of the four tines bent back. He needed less than ten minutes to open the several front door locks. Picking locks was a talent I hadn't known Leroy possessed. He might have learned the craft in jail.

The chalet, rustic-looking on the outside, was modern and comfortable within. Beyond the foyer there was a living room with a high, beamed ceiling and a huge stone fireplace. Leroy flashed his light around: a bar, a piano, fat furniture in grays and browns, throw rugs on the polished hardwood floor, plenty of open space. The house was dusty and had a closed-up smell. We moved on. There was a narrow dining room that could sit eight without cramping, a big kitchen, and a pair of bedrooms with a bathroom between. Everything seemed ordinary; the ordinary house of a prosperous but ordinary man.

We went up the stairway. Four large rooms there: a study; a bedroom overlooking the lake; a compact gymnasium with parallel bars and a vaulting horse and exercise machines and a tightwire stretched ten feet above the floor. Here is where Arbaleste carved his body, honed his nerves. And there was a cubical room that had been arranged as a gallery (and maybe as a sort of shrine to Arbaleste's memory of himself). Paintings and drawings were spaced around the four walls. The electrical power had not been disconnected. I flicked a wall switch and a dozen scattered fluorescent tubes flickered, brightened. Leroy went off into the study.

All of the drawings and paintings had been signed: *Jean Halbert*. This was the work Arbaleste had done in Paris as a young student. There were charcoal sketches, pastels, portrait studies, drawings from plaster casts and live models, copies of other artists' work, and eight original oil paintings, all of them small. I was no judge but they looked good to me, a couple of them very good. I wondered what Charles or Carescu would say about the work. Banal?

Leroy had gone through the file cabinets and was now rifling desk drawers. I checked the drapes to make sure no light seeped out.

"We'd better get out of here," I said.

He snatched open another drawer.

"Put everything back in its place. Come on, Leroy. This is stupid."

He halted, looked at me. "There's a safe behind that bookshelf. It's a joke safe. I can open it."

"How?"

"All I need is a hammer and a chisel."

"What would you expect to find?"

"Money, maybe jewelry. A coin or stamp collection—you never know."

"Jesus, Leroy, we aren't here to burglarize the place. Let's clean up here and go."

"I found this." He leaned behind the desk, straightened, and held out a leather portfolio.

"What is it?"

"Peek."

Inside, expertly matted, were a dozen black-and-white eight-by-ten photographs of Arbaleste engaging in sexual acts with Antonia di Benedetto. They were naked on a bed covered by black satin sheets. The prints were not the usual porn: These resembled studio portraits, soft-focused, so beautifully composed and lighted that the sexual content seemed almost irrelevant. Light and dark, planes and angles, nearly abstract forms. It was sex idealized, sex as art. Antonia was lovely; Arbaleste, a demon satyr. They had been frozen by the camera, stopped in time, and the sexual acts had been abstracted. It seemed sure that the photographs had been taken by a good professional photographer.

"Where did you find them?"

"In a file cabinet."

"Put them back."

"I'm keeping them."

"These are private, Leroy. *Private.* They don't concern us. Put them back."

"I'm keeping them," Leroy said, and there was no doubt, judging by his stance and expression, that he was keeping them.

*   *   *

We checked out of the hotel at noon the next day, and were in Castelnuovo by early evening.

"Enjoy your little holiday?" Petrie asked me.

226

"No."

"Wasted trip?"

"I had hoped to stay there a couple more days, but when we broke into the house . . ."

He showed his teeth. "Great pictures," he said. "Art photos, no doubt about that. And little Antonia . . ."

"Did you get them away from Leroy?"

"Yeah. I burned them."

"Tom, send Leroy home, get him out of here."

"Look at it this way: He didn't torch the house, did he? That's something."

"Get rid of him."

"That Antonia. Who would have guessed she was so sexy?"

"We all guessed, Tom."

TWENTY-FIVE

Late one afternoon I was swimming laps in the back-yard pool when I heard a pounding at the gate and a woman's angry calls. I went up the ladder, crossed the tiled pool apron and a strip of lawn, unlocked the gate, and swung it open.

"Christ," I said. "Not you."

Samantha grinned maliciously. "Me," she said.

She was flushed and sweaty, and carried over her shoulders one of those big nylon duffels that can be converted to a backpack. She wore hiking shoes, a sweat-soaked cotton blouse, and knee-length khaki shorts.

"Don't they have any fucking taxis in this town?" she asked.

"I'll phone for one. You can be on a train to Naples in an hour."

"Get out of my way, lover," she said, and she pushed past me into the yard.

I followed her to poolside and watched as she slipped off her pack, sat down on a deck chair, and began unlacing her shoes.

She said, "Why don't you get one of those European swimming briefs that reveal a man's endowments?"

"I don't want to scare the horses."

She stripped to her bra and panties, gave me a mischievous, angled look, and then dove into the pool. It was a clean, almost splashless dive. She knifed down to the bottom, turned, and swam underwater to the deep end. She grabbed the lowest rung of the ladder and remained submerged while issuing pearl-like bubbles that rose in a string and burst on the surface. Samantha remained down for at least half a minute, and when she finally came up she was smiling, and her hair, darkened to maroon, was slicked back like a seal's fur.

She climbed the ladder. "That was lovely," she said. Her bra and panties were translucent. "Where is everybody?"

"You can't stay here, Sam."

"Where's Petrie? He'll let me stay."

"Petrie would wring your neck."

"Come on, baby. I won't get in the way, I promise."

"Are you here on assignment from the Miami newspaper?

"No. I quit my job."

"You're lying."

"I'm lying. I was fired."

"Why?"

"I was, ah, deeply involved with the subject of a story eighteen months ago. The paper found out. They wouldn't believe me when I told them that the relationship didn't affect the way I wrote the story."

"Who are you working for now?"

"I'm freelancing."

"Jesus, Sam, you've got to go. You'll blow the whole thing."

"And what, precisely, is the whole thing?"

There was half a glass of lemonade and a package of cigarettes on the table. She drank the lemonade, took one of the cigarettes, lit it, and said, "I've gone back to smoking. Stress."

"Put your clothes on."

"Can't I stay, baby, please? I won't snoop, I won't ask a lot of questions, I won't give anything away, I'll just play a household bimbo for the duration. Honest. I think I can sell this story to *Vanity Fair*, but later, when it's all over."

"Who knows you're here and why you're here?"

"No one. I swear."

"Then how did you find us?"

"Ah, that. I don't want to get her in trouble."

"Candace."

She nodded. "I tricked her."

"Well, Christ," I said. "You can stay tonight, but you'll have to go tomorrow."

She puffed on her cigarette, exhaled, and, looking at me through the smoke, said, "When Lyndon Johnson was president, some of his advisors wanted him to fire J. Edgar Hoover as head of the FBI. Johnson said no. He said, 'I'd rather have him inside the tent pissing out, than outside the tent pissing in.'" She smiled. "The point being—"

"I get the point."

She put on her shorts and blouse and, carrying her shoes (I picked up the heavy duffel), followed me through the house, past stone-faced servants (see no evil), and up three flights of stairs to the attic. I put her into one of the garrets, a room even smaller than my own and with only one window, and so hot in the afternoon that you could bake bread in the cabinet.

"Wow," Sam said. "The Black Hole of Calcutta."

"There's a bathroom next door," I said. "I'm in the luxury garret at the end of the hall. Be there in half an hour. I want to talk to you, Samantha."

"Don't you think," she said, "that summer—sunshine and heat and humidity—is awfully sensual?"

"Awfully."

I telephoned *The Miami Times* and talked to a man on the city desk who transferred my call to the personnel department, now called, according to the fashion, the Human Resources Department. A genderless voice there told me that Ms. Samantha Ridley was no longer in the employ of the newspaper. The voice refused to confirm or deny that Ms. Ridley's employment had been terminated by the company. There were laws that protected Ms. Ridley's privacy. Any additional inquiries must be in writing and directed to Jason Freeberger, Head of the Human Resources Department.

Poor Sam—no longer a human resource.

A few minutes after my call, Samantha knocked on the door, entered, and sat on the edge of my bed. Her feet were still bare, but she now wore a summer print dress that was not too badly wrinkled.

"Did you phone the paper?" she asked.

"Who?"

"*The Miami Times.*"

"No."

She grinned. "I was listening outside the door."

"You're a pain in the ass, Sam."

"Come on," she said soothingly, "don't be angry. I'll be good, I promise. Just tell me who to be and how to act and what to say."

"I guess you'll be my fiancée."

"Then we'll have to sleep together, won't we? For verisimilitude."

"You'll need a ring."

"Got one." She rummaged through a straw purse, and found a wad of tissue which she opened to reveal a diamond ring. "Carat and a half. Pretty, isn't it? I broke off an engagement eighteen months ago—the same guy who got me fired from the paper—and he told me to keep the ring. 'Keep the fucking ring' were his exact words."

"Are you hungry?"

She slipped the ring on her finger. "Starved."

"I know a place where, with luck, you'll be served toxic prawns."

She smiled. "I can't die now, not now when we're finally engaged."

TWENTY-SIX

The women were beautiful and they knew it, five bright suns around which we orbited: Antonia di Benedetto, Cassy Turnbull, Samantha Ridley, and two young actresses from an Italian production company currently filming in Ravello. The women illuminated the night. They wore colorful evening dresses while the men were dressed in drab tuxedos, black or white jackets, black ties, and black lace shoes that pinched the feet. There appeared to be no competition among the women; each was a sovereign beauty, sure of her power and tolerant of the others. In fact, they seemed bound in some vague alliance, a quiet female conspiracy. That's what Tom Petrie thought. He said they were tacitly united in a conspiracy to raise the sexual temperature to an intolerable degree.

"I'm burning up," he said. "I'm turning to ash."

"It's a hot night," I said.

"Prosaic is a word that was coined to describe you, Shaw."

We were standing on Arbaleste's terrace, leaning on the marble wall and looking out at the moon-washed, surf-spumed sea. We could hear the spaced crack and hiss of the waves breaking on the beach eight hundred feet below. At high tide the surf rolled all the way in to the base of the cliff.

"Why do you smell like decaying fruit?" Petrie asked.

"Samantha put my jacket in a drawer with some lemons and melon slices to get rid of the smell of mothballs."

"Don't mention that harpy's name to me."

Petrie wore an immaculate white Palm Beach jacket. My jacket, older and surely cheaper, had a faint yellowish tinge in daylight, but looked white enough at night. And it no longer smelled of mothballs.

"Samantha!" he said. "Jesus, you brought a viper into the nest."

A couple at the far end of the terrace—the Italian film director and one of the actresses—broke out in laughter, and for a moment I thought they were laughing at Petrie's words, but when I turned I saw that they were absorbed in their own conversation. There were just the four of us on the terrace; the rest of the twenty guests were inside the house. Our terrace next door was vacant; Petrie had commanded the others, McNally and Cavaretta, Leroy Karpe, to stay out of sight. "No one," he told them, "wants to look over and see gawking plebeians."

It was hot inside Arbaleste's house even though all of the sliding glass doors had been opened to the sea breeze. Behind us, someone was playing old romantic ballads on the baby grand piano. Charles, probably. Charles was always surprising you with another dilettantish accomplishment. A woman who didn't know all the words was trying to sing along to "My Funny Valentine." Samantha.

"Had a chance to talk to Pennington?" Petrie asked me.

"Lord Warfield. No, but we exchanged significant glances."

"Why is he here?"

"To impress us."

"Are we impressed?"

"Maybe a little. He's legitimately Lord Warfield now. The old man died. A bad back put him in bed and he developed pneumonia."

Petrie finished his drink and threw the ice over the terrace wall. "Once more into the breach, dear friends," he said, and he turned and walked into the house.

Far up the coast people began launching fireworks into the night sky, rockets that burst into fountains of colored light: parachute flares, star bursts, glowing balls that burned out before the dull concussions reached me. The film director and the young actress crossed to the other side of the terrace so that they could better see the display.

Pennington moved next to me. "Is this some holiday event?"

"I don't know, my lord," I said.

Arbaleste had introduced him and Cassy to me earlier in the evening; we had of course behaved as though it were our first meeting.

"Did Arbaleste again promise to return your debt notes?" I asked him.

"He gave them to me this morning. They were all there. I burned them."

"Good."

"He had an improbable story about how they had been lost for years, and only recently found in a safety deposit box."

"Just what is he up to?"

"I have no idea. What are *you* up to?"

"I have no idea. How long are you staying?"

"He invited us to stay for the summer, if we wished, but we'll probably return home in a few days."

"If you learn anything . . ."

One by one a dozen rockets were launched, and one by one they exploded into varicolored showers of light. You could see a haze of illuminated smoke in the blooming and shrinking light.

"Sorry to hear about your great-uncle," I said.

"Thanks. His last words were, 'Follow me, lads,' and then he died."

"Referring to . . . ?"

"The war, I suppose."

More rockets, more geysers of color, more distance-delayed detonations. The other Italian actress appeared on the terrace, watched the fireworks for a moment, and then returned to the house.

"Listen, Shaw," Pennington said. "Do you trust this Charles fellow?"

"*I* don't, no. Why?"

"He and Arbaleste seem awfully chummy, going off for private chats, and looking smug when they reappear."

Cassy emerged from the house and inserted herself between us, saying, "What are you brutes cooking up?"

The skirt of her blue dress was short, showing off her long, long legs. I was reminded of how tall she was, my own height when she wore high heels, and her lion's mane of hair had been bleached by the sun.

"Cassiopeia," I said, "can you identify your namesake constellation?"

"Certainly. It's there." She pointed at a section of the sky. "It's W-shaped, you see? Near Camolepardalis and Cepheus."

"Yes, I see it," I said, though I discerned no identifiable shape among the brilliant array of stars.

Cassy laughed. "Liar," she said.

Three rockets simultaneously arced high into the northern sky, hesitated an instant at their apexes, began to fall, and then individually burst into green, red, and white, the colors of the Italian flag. A moment later we heard a crackling like popcorn cooking, followed by three muted detonations. The film producer and actress applauded.

"I do like your fiancée," Cassy said. "But she doesn't sing very well, does she?"

"No. And I don't have the nerve to tell Samantha that."

"Come along, Penny," she said. "I want you to meet the star of the movie, Vitorio. I *think* he's offered me a part in the film. You know Italian—find out if I have to sleep with him to get the part."

"It's more likely that I'll have to sleep with Vitorio for you to get the part."

Cassy patted my arm. "Be careful, duck. That Arbaleste is a nasty piece of work."

I smoked half a cigarette, flicked it into the abyss, and reluctantly returned to the house. It was hot. The party had proceeded as such parties tend to do; most of the guests were high now, louder and less inhibited, and there was some determined flirting taking place. I observed that the women were drinking champagne. Women liked champagne, or the idea of champagne, and the graceful way you could pose with a flute glass. The men drank hard liquor—Scotch, bourbon, brandy—from squat glasses, and they nervously rattled the ice as they talked. The room smelled of cut flowers and expensive perfumes.

The big front room in Arbaleste's house had about the same dimensions as ours, though it had been arranged differently and contained the sort of spare, angular furniture that you saw in museums of modern art. There were Persian rugs, pots that might have been Etruscan, Venetian glass vases, a damask tapestry, and half a dozen oil paintings, one a small, flowery Renoir that Charles had assured me was authentic.

Charles was still sitting at the white baby grand piano, paging through some sheets of music, but his vocalist, Samantha, had wandered away and was now being hit on by the Italian film producer. He didn't look like a film producer; he was slim and young and had lots of hair. He impressed me, with his shiny black Italian silk suit and slicked-back hair, as a youthful road-show Dracula. He raised a pale hand with his fingers splayed, then dramatically clenched it into a fist. Samantha, her back against a wall, looked at me over the producer's shoulder and raised her eyebrows. She smiled, too, I guessed, but I couldn't see the smile.

Charles was the only man in the place not wearing a black or white tuxedo jacket; his was charcoal gray, with a white carnation in the lapel buttonhole, and he had a stringy sort of tie and a ruffled shirt that looked like white lettuce.

I approached and dropped a ten-thousand-lire note on the piano lid. "Play 'Misty' for me," I said.

He smiled, tucked the banknote in his breast pocket, and began playing "Moonglow."

Judge Samuelson and Anton Arbaleste walked together the length of the room and outside to the terrace. The judge, at six foot five, was nearly a head taller. His walk was stately, his posture erect. He had a noble head and the profile of an aged warrior. Petrie saw the judge as foolish; I knew him as a gentle and enormously considerate man, but not without a sharp wit—he could play the clown or make you seem clownish. But this was another Levi tonight. *Judge* Samuelson. The Superior Court judge, the Appeals Court judge. He might have been wearing his judicial robes as he strolled across the room with authority and dignity. This Levi could send you to jail for life, deny your appeal, though not without sympathy.

Anton Arbaleste held his own. He, too, was an imposing man. The judge did not intimidate him. Clearly, he regarded himself as Levi's equal. At least his equal. They were like a pair of tribal chieftains going off to settle affairs for the rest of us.

Lord Warfield and Cassy were half encircled by a group of film people. They spoke to Penny while looking at Cassy, whose boredom was a provocation. She smiled insincerely. She stood with her weight on one leg, hip out, long arms and legs and freckled breasts—a severe challenge to the Italian libido.

Silvia, the younger of the two Italian actresses—a twenty-year-old with luminous dark eyes and a pixie mouth—bumped into me while backing away from the bar. She tottered on her high heels, spilling wine, and I grabbed her upper arm to prevent her from falling.

"*Mi scusi!*" she cried.

I released her. "*Ha prenotato una camera tranquilla per una notte.*"

She laughed, said, "*Addio,*" and moved off into the crowd.

I had killed time by memorizing mostly useless phrases from a guidebook: This one meant, "I have reserved a tranquil room for one night."

Antonia, looking glum, was standing alone in a corner. I got a glass of champagne from the bartender and carried it to her.

She shook her head. "No, thank you. I'm already dizzy from wine."

"*Il prezzo comprende la prima colazione?*" I asked. Does the price include breakfast?

Antonia gave me a puzzled look, and then laughed. It was easy to make these Italian girls laugh.

"Anton and Antonia," I said. "That sounds like a circus knife-throwing act."

She laughed again, then said, "Please don't make me laugh. I really do think I'm going to be sick."

"You need fresh air."

"Yes."

We crossed the big room and went down a hallway and out the back door. The clay tennis court was the color of blood in the moonlight. We sat together on a stone bench. The air smelled of night-blooming flowers and chlorine from the pool in the next-door yard and, faintly, an odor of gunpowder carried downwind from the fireworks display earlier tonight.

"A nice party," I said.

"Yes."

"The movie people seem pleasant."

"But they are making an unpleasant film, I think. Very dark. The title is *Necropolis*. You know that word?"

"*City of the Dead*. I've heard that you were in a few movies. Is that true?"

"Two movies, in France. Small parts. Really nothing. A man stopped me on the street one day and asked me if I wanted to be in a movie. I said, 'Okay.' So I was. Then another. They were bad movies, and it was very boring."

"How did you meet Anton?"

"That is how I met Anton. He saw me in the second movie—I played a student—and came to Paris to meet me. We met. He took me away. Here I am."

"It sounds as though he's a romantic man."

"He is, yes. He conceals it well."

"Do you feel better now?"

"A little. I drank the wine too fast."

"Where are you from, Antonia?"

"Siena."

"Do you have family there?"

"Of course. Did you think I was an orphan?"

"Is your family wealthy? Are you?"

"What rude questions!"

"I'm sorry."

"I'm not rich, but Anton is. Rich enough for the two of us."

"How old are you?"

"How old do you think I am?"

"Twenty-eight?"

"No. Do I look twenty-eight? I'm twenty-six."

"And what do you want from life?"

"Everything. But especially to be young. I think maybe I will kill myself on my thirtieth birthday."

"No, you won't."

"No, I won't, of course not."

"Do you think you and Anton will marry?"

"No more questions."

She did not inquire about me or any of my friends, not then or later. Antonia never expressed interest in other people. I doubted that even Arbaleste was fully real to her except when present. She was a lovely and intelligent woman, always good company, but there was a childlike self-centeredness about her that excluded others. You served as a sort of mirror; she perceived herself as reflected by you. She animated you, brought you to life in her consciousness, then folded you up and put you away. Narcissistic, solipsistic—such words obscured rather than illuminated her personality. I liked her. Everyone liked Antonia.

Now she removed her shoes and strolled a few yards away. Her dark blue dress blended into the night; her face and arms reflected moonlight with a ghostly radiance.

"The grass is wet," she said.

"Don't step on a worm," I said.

She laughed. "There are no worms in Italy."

"There aren't?"

"Well, maybe there are. A few. But none would dare crawl under my foot."

"Do you feel better now?"

"Yes. Let's return to the party."

The party, fueled by alcohol and drugs and sexual tension, was louder now, and somewhat confused.

More guests had arrived while Antonia and I were in the backyard. Arbaleste had come in from the terrace. He stood alone, framed in the doorway, watching as Antonia and I entered the room. I could not read his expression. She kissed my cheek (maybe a tactic in her campaign to make Arbaleste jealous), and then walked over to him. He took her two hands in his, looked down at her, said something.

I was surprised to see Leroy Karpe standing at the bar. The scar tissue and the asymmetry of his features were less obvious in this lighting, but he still looked pugnacious, ready for someone to challenge his presence at the party. Apparently he had taken one of Charles's jackets, a midnight blue double-breasted blazer with silver buttons and flap pockets. No tie, jogging shoes and cuffless chinos.

"Beautiful woman, Antonia. Sexy."

I turned.

"But, pal," Petrie said, "we don't want to muddy the waters, do we? Stir up a conflict?"

"She was sick. I escorted her outside for some fresh air."

"Sure. Gallant of you. But don't provoke the man, Bunky. We have business with Arbaleste, which won't be improved by making him mad. Right?"

"What's Leroy doing here?"

"Causing a general anxiety, it looks like."

"Are you going to tell him to spread anxiety elsewhere?"

"No. Remember, cool it with Antonia. Right? And now I'm going to make the acquaintance of that little actress, Silvia. A harmless flirtation. Or not so harmless if I get lucky."

"She's too young for you, Tom."

"Of course she is."

"I don't think she knows English."

"I'll speak to her with my soul."

"Whisper, 'A quanti chilometri c'è una stazione di benzina?'"

"Which means?"

"'How many kilometers to a gas station?'"

Petrie bared his teeth in a parody of a smile. "I'll try it," he said, and he abruptly pivoted and walked away. Samantha, arms folded, was leaning on the piano. She and Charles were no doubt discussing songs, tempos, keys. Charles tried a few tinkly notes. Samantha nodded. Sam had borrowed my credit card to buy a new dress and matching shoes. The dress was rose-red, cut low in front, with a tight bodice and a flared, pleated skirt. Now Charles played a short introduction and Sam began singing "Something Cool."

Judge Samuelson was standing alone on the terrace, looking down at surf foaming around the jagged offshore rocks. The air around us hummed with reverberations.

"Come sta, Judge?" I said.

"Oh, hello, Daniel."

"Spectacular view, isn't it?"

"Scary. Does Arbaleste really do handstands on this wall?"

"Every morning, he says. I've seen him do it twice."

"Why would a man do such a thing?"

"He likes the risk, the adrenal rush. Self-control is very important to the man. The handstands are an exercise in discipline."

"A queer duck, this Arbaleste. Queer wolf, rather."

"How do you read him, Levi?"

The judge considered. "He reminds me of some

politicians I have known. Most dangerous when most amiable."

"Yes. Well, *buona notte,* Judge."

"You're leaving so early?"

"Yes."

"It's rather a nice party."

"As parties go," I said, "and so go I."

There was no one in our villa. The servants were usually dismissed in the late afternoon, and I supposed that Mutt and Jeff had gone down into the village. The Degas forgery now dominated the room. It had been delivered this morning and hung with neurotic care by Charles on the wall containing the other paintings and drawings. "Creole Night" seemed to glow with an interior light, softly illuminating the old New Orleans street and the bourgeois *promeneurs.*

I went up to my attic garret, undressed, and lay down on the bed. It was very hot. No breeze came through the windows, and the electric fan on the dresser merely shoved hot muggy air around the little room. I lay sweating on the damp bedsheet, listening to music and snatches of conversation from Arbaleste's place.

I was awakened by Samantha's voice. "You forgot to lock your door."

"No, I didn't."

Enough light filtered in through the windows so that I could watch her undress.

"God, it's hot in here," she said, stepping out of her panties. "We'll be all sticky and gooey with salty sweat. Tactile stuff. I like that."

She stood a few feet away from the bed, teasing a little, posing for me.

"Come on," I said.

"Do you love me?"

"By God I do!"

She laughed. "What a liar! Okay, Shaw, you're in business," and she crawled onto the bed and covered me with her warm body.

TWENTY-SEVEN

The judge and I were drinking coffee at the bar when Arbaleste came over the next morning. Samantha was sunbathing on the terrace, and we heard him say something to her, her murmured reply, and then he was framed in the open doorway. He wore his tennis outfit.

"Come in, Anton," the judge called.

The Degas forgery stopped him three paces into the room. The painting had an impact almost like a physical blow. He recovered, advanced a few paces, and halted.

"Nice little Derain," he said. But he was not much interested in the Derain or the other paintings and drawings.

"Tom is upstairs getting ready," I said. "He'll be down soon."

"Will you have a cup of coffee, Anton?" the judge said.

Arbaleste shook his head and moved closer to the painting. His posture was poised, tense. If you caught him looking at you in the way he looked at the painting you might expect an assault.

"What is this?" He sounded angry.

"We have espresso, some wonderful Italian pastries," the judge said.

I said, "It's a Degas."

"I *know* it's a Degas." He moved again, a bit to one side, a couple of steps back, trying to find the exactly right distance and angle from which to study the painting.

"It was a fine party, Anton," the judge said.

"Thank you."

"Tom's hungover," I said. "But he usually plays well when hungover. He's an adrenal guy and hangovers calm him a little."

"Dated 1873," Arbaleste said. "New Orleans? This is a Degas New Orleans painting?"

"I believe so," the judge replied.

"It can't be."

"I'm sure it is, Anton."

"I've never heard of it."

"Well, I'm told it is rather obscure."

"Obscure! Where did you get it?"

"Talk to my grandson, will you, Anton? Charles makes my acquisitions and arranges for the resales. I'm not rich enough to be a collector, you see, nor do I have the passion. A painting, a sculpture, an antiquity of some sort—Charles is obsessed with those things. But they all rather puzzle me."

"What is the provenance?"

"You must talk to Charles, Anton, really."

"Has it been authenticated?"

"Charles must know," the judge said vaguely. "I'm art-blind as some are tone-deaf."

"Where is Charles?"

"Naples," I said.

"How long have you owned this painting?"

The judge turned to me. "Dan?"

"About nine months," I said.

"This is incredible. Is the painting for sale?"

"It will be, in time," the judge said. "As I mentioned, I'm not a collector, not rich enough to hang tens of millions of dollars on my walls. But Charles likes to keep his discoveries around for a time, live with them. And some do appreciate considerably in just a couple of years."

It was as though Arbaleste was caught in a kind of magnetic field; he tried to pull free, but could not; he moved away, returned, drifted sideways, was impelled forward again. His lack of self-control surprised me. He was normally a cool, disciplined man, a criminal with enough nerve to defy the law and cheat other men out of millions; and yet this painting—this forgery—had made him weak.

"May I ask . . . may I ask how much you paid for it?"

"Really, Anton," the judge said in regretful tones, "I'm afraid you're a little out of line there."

"Yes, you're right. Please. I've been very rude. It's just . . . Please accept my apology."

"Oh, no need to apologize. I understand, Anton. Art drives some people a bit mad. Art, women, God, money, gambling—we're all crazy each in our own way."

With a last, yearning look at the painting—like the glance of a jealous man leaving his love in the company of rivals—Arbaleste crossed the room and sat with us at the bar.

"And what makes you crazy, Shaw?" he asked.

"Evil-tasting envelope glue. Hair stuck to a bar of soap. Stepping in dog shit."

"And Petrie?" Arbaleste asked.

"I'm just plain crazy," Petrie said. He was descending the stairs, and had heard the last part of our conversation. He wore tennis whites with the Nike insignia on both shirt and shorts. "Crazy for the sake of crazy. Born crazy and growing crazier by the day. Worms-in-my-brain crazy."

"Tom," I said, "did you forget your tennis racket?" He halted at the base of the stairs. "Shit," he said, and he turned and climbed back up toward his second-floor room.

"And what is your crazed passion?" Arbaleste asked the judge.

"Oh, I'm too old now for passions. I've even lost most of my vices, though I still occasionally enjoy a glass of good brandy and a poker game."

* * *

On the second floor of Arbaleste's house there was a room about forty feet long and fifteen feet wide. It was furnished as a study, with a big slab-marble desk, two long tables, a computer station, file cabinets, and a wooden bin divided in sections. Spread over the tables were stacks of blueprints, mechanical drawings, spec sheets, designs of missile and satellite components, and photographs showing construction work at the mythical launch site in Kenya. It was all in casual disarray, work interrupted.

A round, felt-covered poker table was sited at the opposite end of the room. There were six of us: Arbaleste and the Italian film director, the judge, Petrie, Charles, and me. The curtains were drawn. A beverage cart and snack table were nearby. No women allowed: Samantha and Antonia were amusing themselves downstairs.

"Draw poker or five-card stud," Arbaleste said. "Table stakes, no limit. Is that acceptable?"

"Deal the cards," Petrie said.

"Twenty-five-dollar ante. Ante up, gentlemen."

"Deal," Petrie said.

Tom had given the judge, Charles, and me ten thousand dollars each; he had more. When I questioned the propriety of gambling with the consortium's money, he'd said, "It's four against two. If we can't at least break even I'll swan-dive over the cliff."

The first dozen hands were a testing, an evaluation of the opponents, a calculated waiting. The early run of hands was mediocre, the stakes small. I felt confident. Like most men I thought I was a good poker player. Consistent losses hadn't been able to teach me otherwise. The game gradually settled into a pattern. After an hour I had a fair idea of the caliber of the other players. Charles, like the film director, was impulsive, with a tendency to stay in too many pots. Petrie, I knew from past poker games, was good, though not half as good as he thought he was. Judge Samuelson was cautious, and he only bet when he had the cards, and then his bets weren't commensurate to the power of his hands. He didn't chase out those players hoping for a lucky draw, and he lost a big pot early because of that.

Arbaleste was a puzzle. I had expected a daring, imaginative gambler, the kind of man who did handstands over an abyss, but he played like a timid bookkeeper. He threw in his poor hands. He checked on his doubtful hands. He raised when his hands were very good. He played by the book. He played like a man who has memorized all the odds and combinations, and has measured them against the amount of money to be won or lost. It was boring poker, mechanical. And he didn't bluff. He didn't bluff until ninety minutes into the game, and then he stole a twelve-thousand-dollar pot. A third of that money was mine. I had tossed in a pair of jacks in five-card draw. He smiled and turned over his cards: nothing, ten high. He wanted us to know he had stolen a pot. And then, a few hands later, he wasn't bluffing when I thought he was bluffing, and I was down to a few hundred dollars worth of chips.

"Sap," Petrie said to me.

Arbaleste and Petrie were ahead when we took a break. I figured that by the rime the game ended they would be playing heads-up. The judge was about even; the film director and Charles were down to a few thousand dollars each. But none of the three was good enough to stay long with Petrie and Arbaleste.

We stretched, made drinks, lit cigarettes or cigars.

"Anton," the judge said, "if you don't mind my asking . . . What are all those intriguing documents at the other end of the room?"

"Just paper," Arbaleste replied. "Related to a business I've invested in. It's exciting to me, but it would bore you to sleep."

"I'm not easily bored. Maybe later you'll tell me a little about it?"

"If you wish."

I gave Charles my last few hundred dollars' worth of chips, said goodnight to all of them, and went downstairs to the big room.

Samantha and Antonia were sitting together on a sofa, sharing gossip and a bottle of champagne. They seemed to have become friends.

"You lost," Samantha said to me.

"I'm afraid so."

"You gambled away your patrimony."

"I did it for you, honey."

I squeezed between them on the sofa, placed my right arm around Samantha's shoulders, my left around Antonia. The scents of their hair and skin and perfumes made me a little dizzy.

"All right," I said, "here's the drill."

"The what?" Antonia asked.

"The plan. We'll go to one of the bedrooms, strip raw naked, get into bed, and vigorously sin."

Antonia smiled. "I want to hear more."

"Forget it," Samantha said.

"In that case, let's go down into the village for a bite to eat and a couple of drinks."

We returned from the village after midnight. Antonia kissed Samantha's cheek, kissed me, said good night, and went next door.

"A nightcap?" I asked Sam.

"No."

"Bed?"

"Antonia's telling people that you and she are having an affair."

"I wish she wouldn't do that. Do you believe her?"

"No. She's just trying to make Anton jealous."

"Why me?"

"Who else? Charles? The ancient judge? Mutt or Jeff? Leroy? Tom Petrie?"

"Why not Petrie?"

"Not her type."

"No, Arbaleste is her type. Do you think he believes that were having an affair?"

"I don't know. No one will know until the moment he kills you." She grinned.

"A few days ago he said he wouldn't mind if Antonia had an affair as long as it made her happy."

"These sophisticated Europeans . . ."

"Arbaleste is an American."

"Is he? Tell me more."

"No."

She made a face. Samantha looked sexy in a tired, disheveled way. "I'll sleep in my own bed tonight," she said firmly, resentfully, as if last night I had dragged her to my cobwebby garret and cruelly ravished her.

I watched her climb the stairs. She moved in a hippy style that let me know that she was aware of being watched. Watched, desired, and prepared to say hell, no.

Charles and the judge came in at one thirty. Charles had lost his entire ten thousand dollars; Levi had cashed in his chips while he had a few thousand left. The film director had also lost, they said, and now Petrie and Arbaleste were playing heads-up. The two men seemed evenly matched; the game would probably last into daylight hours. But half an hour later Tom came in from the terrace. He was in a sour mood. He had lost badly to Arbaleste in tennis and now in a duel at the poker table. He hated to lose. More than most men he hated to lose, and he took it personally.

"He cheated," he said. "But I can't prove it."

"The luck of the cards, Tom," the judge said.

"Luck, my ass. They were his decks, weren't they? The last hour he played like he knew every card in my hand."

"A good poker player," the judge said, "an exceptional poker player, does seem to know what the other players are holding. Especially after a few hours of study."

"You know that, do you, Levi?"

"He beat us, Tom."

"Did he now?"

"He concealed how very good he was. That's legitimate in poker, I think."

"You think that, do you, Levi?"

The judge smiled.

"Well, Christ, Tom," I said, "think of how much you've learned in the last few days. You learned not to play tennis with him. You learned not to play poker with him. Tomorrow might bring other revelations."

Petrie showed me his evil so-the-worms-are-turning smile.

"So then," the judge said. "How much did we lose altogether?"

"Somewhere around seventy thousand dollars."

"Well, surely," the judge said, frowning in doubt, signaling a forthcoming lie, "surely if we succeed in recovering a substantial part of the swindled money, the poker losses are a legitimate expense."

"I'll get that son of a bitch," Petrie said. "Hear me? I *will* get that arrogant son of a bitch."

Charles, the judge, and I went off to our rooms. Petrie remained behind at the bar, seething with rage, maybe a little desperate, as he calculated exactly how he was going to get that arrogant son of a bitch.

TWENTY-EIGHT

I did not always feel guilty about my casual summer dalliance with Samantha. I thought of it that way: the word "dalliance" made our affair seem less serious than words like "unfaithful" or "disloyal" would. Samantha and I were not in love. We were old friends, ex-lovers, and our revived physical expression of affection seemed harmless enough. No harm, no foul. It was easy to rationalize it until I thought of Martina or spoke to her on the phone.

"How is Phil doing?" I asked when she called me one morning.

"Oh, I don't know. He seems very eccentric at times."

"Depressed?"

"Silent for long periods, then talkative, cranky, accusing. He throws tantrums."

"Well, remember that the thing happened just recently. The shock was terrific, especially for a man his age."

Phil Karras's shotgun killing of his wife had become known between us as the "thing" or the "event" or the "incident." We needed the euphemisms. We could hardly refer to the killing as "that time when Phil blew out Alice's brains."

"He hates the confinement," Martina continued. "He wants to golf, go fishing, go out to a restaurant. He hates the electronic monitoring device he wears around his ankle. He hates what he calls 'house arrest.'"

"It *is* house arrest, Marty. He's damned lucky that Petrie was able to get him out of the county jail until trial."

"I know. But Uncle has just been devastated by what happened."

"Of course he has."

"I don't like to burden you with these troubles."

"You aren't. How are you doing? Are you working?"

"You have to work when you're responsible for getting out cartoon art on deadline."

"Have you been to the lighthouse?"

"No."

"Listen, keep your chin up."

"Oh, I'm all right. Really. It's just something that one has to get through."

"And the devil dog?"

"Try playing croquet with Cerberus around. He thinks the game is to steal the ball and run with it. We have to chain him, and then the monkey teases him. And he digs holes in the lawn. Just holes for the sake of holes. No higher purpose."

"Beat him with a rolled newspaper for me. Any more dumb pranks played by the Mackey boys?"

"Two more bills from that ridiculously named Search and Seizure company, signed by Kyle Mackey."

"Dopes. I'll straighten it out."

"And how is Italy?" she asked.

"I'd rather be there with you."

"And I'd rather be *there* with you. Have you met any of those famously charming and sexy Italian girls?"

"I've met a few plump Italian women who have mustaches and Roman noses."

"Dan, I do want to go there soon."

"We'll try to figure something out."

"I'm working hard, and soon I'll be a week or two ahead on the strip. Why can't I join you there?"

"You can, you will. But we're in the middle of a very complicated business. Heading into the vortex. But later, toward the end of summer . . ."

"Just what the devil are you and Petrie and Judge Samuelson doing over there? Why is it such a secret? You have too many secrets, Dan, and I don't like that. What kind of relationship is this when you consistently refuse to confide in me?"

"That isn't fair."

"It is fair, it's true, you don't trust me. And therefore I'm beginning to distrust you."

"This has been a very bad time for you," I said, "what with Alice and Phil. Things look darker than they are."

"And you condescend to me. Like now."

"Marty, what can I say? I want you over here." (But not to Castelnuovo, I thought.)

"When?"

"As soon as possible. Late July or early August. We'll go where you like, do what you like. Florence, Rome, Venice . . ."

After a long silence, Martina said, "My uncle told me that this shady business in Italy concerns Victor Trebuchet."

"Phil's right about that."

"He lost a great deal of money to Trebuchet. Others did too. Are you trying to get it back?"

"We are working along those lines."

"I want to be there. I want to help."

"Martina . . ."

"Have you got a woman over there, Dan?" she asked, either in a sudden stab of intuition or a careless shot in the dark.

"Not yet," I said lightly, "but I'm still interviewing candidates."

"Shall I call you again tomorrow?"

"Yes, or I'll phone you."

"Good-bye, then," she said, and she hung up before I could say the same.

"You are a rat," Samantha Ridley said.

Samantha was lying on my bed, naked except for a sheet twisted around her lower legs. Her hair was tangled, her cheeks were flushed, and her mouth was swollen and pouty. We had just finished making love when the phone rang.

"How can you lie to her like that?" she said.

"No sermons," I said. "Not from you."

"Don't you feel bad?"

"Right now? You bet I feel bad."

"How bad?"

"Very bad."

"Well, it's all right, then, as long as you feel bad."

"Tomorrow I'm going to stop lying in word and deed."

She laughed. "Not me! I'm not giving up deceit."

"Martina is an extraordinary woman."

"Sure, baby, come here and tell me about it."

TWENTY-NINE

Things changed after the party. In a way, the two villas combined; we all crossed back and forth from terrace to terrace, house to house, and there was that kind of informality which seems natural in summer—sandy bare feet, sunburned skin, more food and alcohol consumed than was healthy in the sultry heat, a sexual tension. Some of us spent the morning hours on the beach or by the swimming pool. Antonia, Samantha, Cassy, and the two Italian actresses, when they were around, usually sunbathed topless. They rarely changed out of their swimming suits until sunset.

Petrie sent McNally, Cavaretta, and Karpe back to the States. "You three," he told them, "are like ants at a picnic, body lice in the marital bed. Go." They did not protest. They were glad to leave the villa, Castelnuovo, Italy, Europe, and the many persons they regarded as "fags and phonies."

There were many guests at Arbaleste's house during the summer. People dropped in, stayed a day or several days, moved on to Nice or Saint-Tropez or San Sebastián. Members of the film company, which was now shooting a final two weeks at Pompeii, were there on nights and weekends. And there were visitors from Rome and London and Paris; local (summer) rich; artists and writers and musicians whose names were vaguely familiar; a famous soccer player from Germany; a high-fashion model from Milan; a Saudi prince; an alleged Mafia don; an Argentinian three-goal polo player; members of the minor nobility; opera singers.

The Russian physicist, Vladimir Lobechevsky, arrived in early August. Ostensibly, he was just taking a brief holiday, but we knew that he had been summoned to help sell the Alpha Centauri stock. He was younger than I had expected, maybe forty-five; tall, with blondish hair and those icy eyes—a little green, a little blue, a little white—that seem transparent. It was hard to look into those eyes; you half expected to see the optic nerve, the retinas, the brain behind. But he was a genial man. He spoke English well. Everyone spoke English, and the Europeans two or three other languages in addition.

The judge and Petrie spent time with Arbaleste and the Russian in the upstairs study, listening to what was still a very soft sell on the Alpha Centauri stock. There were no more poker games.

Arbaleste was enchanted by the Degas forgery. I believed that he often came over to the house simply so that he could see it again. He was infatuated by the painting; when near it, he showed the melancholy of a rejected lover. He had many questions about the painting, and Charles lied, lied again, told more lies, and repeatedly said that the Degas was not for sale—not for a couple of years, at least. Then? Well, maybe then he might listen to Arbaleste's offer, though it was likely that more money could be earned at an open auction.

I was not much involved in the master scenario, if there was such a thing, and no longer cared for the game. The opening moves and countermoves were tedious. I spent time on the beach, in the port and village cafés, playing tennis, going out to Pompeii to watch the filming, taking women for long high-speed rides in the Ferrari.

"You're having a midlife crisis," Samantha told me.

We were naked in my bed. I took a pellet of melting ice from the glass on the bedside table, and placed it in her navel.

"I'm too young to have a midlife crisis," I said.

She put the ice in her mouth, crunched it between her teeth, and said, "You're cheating on your girl."

"I don't think about that."

"You're turning into an oily sort of guy, Shaw. Hedonist, seducer, café habitué. You're becoming a Mediterranean roué."

＊　　＊　　＊

I was summoned to a meeting in the judge's suite of rooms at the rear of the house. Petrie and Charles were there, Tom pacing, Charles sprawled bonelessly in a chair. Through the rear window I could see Samantha, Cassy, and Antonia sunbathing topless by the pool.

"What have you learned from Warfield?" Petrie asked me.

"Nothing. Arbaleste doesn't confide."

"What about your bedmate?"

"My fiancée, according to the imaginary master scenario. Samantha seems to have forgotten her journalistic coup for now."

"I guess that's something."

I said, "I'm surprised that Arbaleste is eager to foul his own nest."

"How so?" the judge asked. He was in pajamas, slippers, and a dressing robe, and his uncombed white hair bristled like crabgrass.

"Arbaleste lives in Italy. His mother lives in Italy. He's spent three summers in Castelnuovo and the real estate agent says he's hoping to buy the villa. It doesn't make sense for him to run his Ponzi racket here."

"But it isn't a Ponzi this time. No pyramiding. We're the only marks. It's a one-time scam in Italy."

"Even so."

"Anton's risk is small," Judge Samuelson said. "Alpha Centauri, according to my inquiries, seems a positively labyrinthine corporation. And it *is* a corporation, chartered in South Africa, buried inside half a dozen other shell corporations scattered over three continents. Nearly impenetrable. The U.S. Justice Department would be able to untangle the snarl, but it would take time to investigate, more time to come to trial, and even then . . . And this is Italy. No, Arbaleste is safe here."

"Anyway," Charles said, "we're not going to buy his stock. We're going to trade the Degas forgery for stock."

"Ah," I said. "Now it all makes sense."

"*Per favore*," Petrie said. "None of your cheap sarcasm. It's your own fault if you're ignorant of what's going on. We've kept our eyes on the target. We've been working while you've been acquiring a glorious suntan, squiring around the ladies, sporting around in the Ferrari, generally behaving like a playboy. And when did you start wearing sunglasses indoors?"

"When I started having hangovers," I said. Then, "I do understand now. We swap a worthless painting for worthless stock."

"Is he stupid?" Charles asked.

"Why, yes," Petrie said. "And you're a little slow yourself not to have noticed sooner."

I said, "How much is Arbaleste willing to pay for the forgery?

"It hasn't come to a price yet," Charles said. "We haven't even said we will sell it. But we can try for, say, fifteen million."

"All right. Let's say we sell the painting for fifteen million dollars. Charles, you've told us that if it actually were a Degas, it might be worth twenty-five to thirty million on the open market. Right? And if the forgery is virtually beyond detection, near-perfect, and the provenance is convincing— then what stops Arbaleste from selling the thing for twenty-five or thirty million? The swindled investors recover a big part of their money, but then Arbaleste profits by millions."

"Good point," Charles said.

"Then address the goddamned good point."

"We burn the painting."

"I see."

"We burn it metaphorically. I have photographs of the painting and copies of all the documentary provenance, et cetera. Say that I anonymously send the materials to various art journals in America and Europe, and expose the fraud. Another scandal in the art world, oh my! And the painting becomes worthless, and Arbaleste duped, a fool. He might even be prosecuted."

"And Carescu?"

"There will be some, a few, who recognize Carescu's hand. Can they prove he's the forger? I don't think so."

"All right," I said.

"But it's really a pity. A lost Degas found, then lost again. A great painting."

"You keep looking at your watch," Petrie said to me.

"It stopped a few days ago. I look at it to see if it started again."

"Do you have an appointment?"

"I'm taking Silvia to lunch."

"Go home," Petrie said. "Take the next plane."

"Nope," I said. "I'm having a lot of fun. I've never been a Mediterranean roué before."

"Think about it, Dan," Judge Samuelson said. "It might really be best if you returned home. Martina could use your help at this time, and Phil, too. It's all straightforward here now. We'll succeed or fail within the next two weeks."

I stood up. "Toss me the car keys, Charles."

"You didn't return them. They're probably in the ignition."

"You'll need me," I said, "after everything has been fucked up." All three of them smiled tolerantly.

*   *   *

Petrie flew to the States for several days; he had a pre-
trial hearing that he didn't trust to his associates.

It rained for three days. On the first day two workmen
came into the house, crated the Degas forgery, took it
outside, and loaded it into a van. Charles and Arbaleste
followed them in the Ferrari. It was raining when they
left and raining two days later when they returned. The
same men carried the painting into the house, uncrated
it, and, with Charles bossily supervising, hung it in its
old place.

Charles concealed his jubilation until we were alone,
and then, laughing, he removed some sheets of film
from an envelope and gave them to me. They looked
like X-rays, indistinct and confusing, but I could discern
the ghost of the Degas painting, and another ghost that
Charles told me was a partial underpainting.

"Roman Carescu is indisputably a genius," he said.
"I had no idea he'd done that."

"Done what, exactly?"

"Look here, and here, and there. You see? The old
rogue made some charcoal sketches on the canvas,
painting a little on it—and then he painted over it, as if
his start was unsatisfactory."

"And that makes the painting appear authentic?"

"It certainly helps."

"Where did you and Arbaleste go?"

"Naples. Anton took us to see an art expert whom
he'd invited down from Rome. The man—Pietro
Pontello—took the painting to a laboratory and had
some tests run. X-rays, ultraviolet and infrared pictures,
and he removed flakes of paint for chemical analysis.
And he even took a few shreds of canvas for possible

carbon dating. He was very thorough. I could hardly restrain my laughter. So solemn, so professorial."

"And?"

"Oh, it will pass. Pontello was convinced of the authenticity by the painting alone. He looked at it for ten minutes and was convinced. The tests are merely confirmation of what he already believes. He will simply refuse to believe evidence contrary to his prejudices. Pontello desperately wants to be known as the man who authenticated a great lost painting. It will help him professionally, greatly enhance his reputation."

"So we're home free."

"I wouldn't go that far," Charles said.

THIRTY

Five of us sat at the poker table in Arbaleste's upstairs study, but we were not playing cards. We were gambling in a different sort of game. The judge and Charles sat side-by-side, putative grandfather and grandson; Petrie was present as our lawyer, and I as the judge's personal secretary. Four to one; Arbaleste was alone.

"Are you sure you shouldn't have your lawyer present?" the judge asked.

"That isn't necessary. We can draw up a contract that protects us both. This is not a complicated business."

"Very well. But, Anton, I must say that I am stretched very thin at the moment. I lost a great deal of money in the collapse of the tech stocks and the Internet fiasco. The Silicon Valley economy has been devastated, and so have my investments there. I took a beating in the Asian markets. I can invest, say, three million dollars in the Alpha Centauri enterprise."

"Too bad," Arbaleste said. "You'll never see another opportunity like this."

"I dare not risk more at this time."

"Do you wish to investigate further?"

"No, I'm satisfied that it is, as you say, a rare opportunity. That's why I'm committing three million dollars. I wish I could offer more. Many years ago, Anton, I had a chance to invest substantially in Microsoft. I declined, and that decision has haunted me ever since. Perhaps in a few months I'll be in a position to procure more Alpha Centauri stock."

"It will, naturally, be a splendid investment in a few months, but not as good as today."

"I'm sorry to hear it."

"If, sir, you could find a way to buy the entire stock offering, together we would virtually control the corporation. Our combined holdings, with the cooperation of a few investors I know well, would form a block that can't be outvoted. And as I told you, it's almost certain that the stock will soon be split and doubled."

The negotiations reminded me of a chess game, as boring as chess if you didn't know or play the game yourself. I was not sorry that I had missed all of the previous meetings; the presentation of materials, the tedious details, the techno-scientific lectures by Lobechevsky, the sparring and bargaining, the stilted legal-business jargon, the hype and puffery and fakery. This was the final session.

There was a long silence as we waited for Arbaleste to present his offer. The game was over if he consented to accept the judge's three-million-dollar tender.

Finally, he said, "All right. Consider this. We'll exchange the Degas painting for the entire stock offering."

"What?" Charles said. "No. Never! That's my painting."

"Charles," the judge said softly, indulgently, "it really is my painting, you know. I purchased it."

"I'll take the Degas," Arbaleste said, "in return for the stock. That's eleven and one-half million dollars. I'll buy the stock myself and transfer it to you in exchange for the painting."

"Outrageous!" Charles said. "The painting is worth twice that."

"We can buy other paintings," the judge said. "Many paintings from the return on our investment."

"Go to hell!"

"Charles . . ."

"Go to hell, you stupid old man, you fool!"

I thought Charles was going to cry. His eyes teared, his cheeks had turned scarlet, his hands trembled. He was a fine actor, our Charles, in the emotional soap opera tradition. He started to speak, failed, then abruptly jumped up and hurried from the room.

"I'm sorry about that, Anton," the judge said. "I'm afraid the boy has been rather spoiled."

"I understand and sympathize with his disappointment. It is a great painting. Well, then, what do you think?"

"I'm told the painting is worth considerably more than your offer. A figure of, say, eighteen million might tempt me."

"I daresay that my consultant and I know a little more about art than your grandson."

"Then perhaps *I* ought to hire an expert."

"The painting, you know, is not in pristine condition."

"True, but it's one hundred and thirty years old."

"Poorly cared for during many of those years. It requires a meticulous restoration, and that can be expensive."

"Fifteen million," the judge said.

"I am sorry, my friend. I've thought about this carefully. My offer remains the same, the painting to be exchanged for stock presently valued at eleven million, five hundred thousand dollars."

Of course, none of us asked Arbaleste why he himself didn't purchase the entire stock offering.

The judge smiled. "I had to try. Done. It's a deal, Anton."

"Hold on," Petrie said. "You can't just exchange an expensive painting for stock. Bartering at this scale will fuck up your taxes big-time and forever. There must be two transactions. Two. You sell the painting for X-amount—eleven-five. And you buy the stock for an equal amount. Money is exchanged. I don't care if the time between exchanges is twenty-four hours, it's got to be done that way."

"He's a lawyer," the judge said apologetically to Arbaleste. "One pays lawyers to be cranky."

"Sir," Petrie said, "I won't resign if you insist on this barter. I'll remain your counsel if you wish. But I'll ask you to give me a signed statement acknowledging that you've proceeded contrary to my advice. I don't want to spend the rest of my life talking to the IRS and the SEC and the federal prosecutors."

The judge frowned, hesitated. "Anton, I'm afraid . . ."

"It's quite all right," Arbaleste said. "I agree that there should be a record of an exchange of money. I believe we can conclude our transaction within a few days. I'll expect a sales receipt for the painting, of course; and you'll require evidence of the stock transfer and confirmation of all terms and requirements. You'll automatically be appointed to the Alpha Centauri board. Congratulations. You've made a wise decision."

He extended his hand over the table. The judge, smiling, shook it.

Arbaleste would have eleven and one-half million dollars wire-transferred to the judge's numbered bank account in the Cayman Islands (an account set up by Petrie a month ago). That money, according to the agreement, would then, within forty-eight hours, be wire-transferred to the Alpha Centauri account in Capetown, South Africa. That way, Arbaleste would have possession of the painting and the eleven and one-half million dollars. It was a measure of the man's contempt for us, for all marks, that he should think it would be so easy. But the money he sent to the Cayman Islands account would immediately be transferred to another account that Petrie had established in Panama. We would have the money, Arbaleste would be the owner of a virtually worthless forgery.

"I'm having refreshments sent up," Arbaleste said. "We can have a drink and something to eat before proceeding with the details."

I stood. "You won't need me anymore," I said.

"I can't see that we ever needed you," Petrie said.

Samantha and I drove down to Ravello in the Ferrari. We had a lunch date. The restaurant was perched on a steep hillside, and had a dining room in the central courtyard and another on a terrace overlooking the sea. We sat at a table on the terrace, beneath a tree that smelled like cinnamon and which had colored ribbons tied to the branches. In theory, the fluttering ribbons scared birds away, so they would not squirt mute on your plate.

"Forty minutes ago," I said, "I was in a meeting listening to people talk about millions. Dreary stuff, business, even very crooked business. But it looks as though it'll be concluded in a couple of days."

"It's going to work, then?"

"I think so."

When the waitress arrived we ordered grilled fish, rice, and artichokes, to be served with a bottle of wine.

"Tell me something, Sam. Do you find Anton Arbaleste physically attractive?"

"Why do you ask?"

"I just wondered. Women seem to like him."

"Yes, I would say I find him attractive. Yes, the fact is, I'm in love with the son of a bitch."

I smiled at her.

"I'm not kidding. But he hardly knows I'm alive. It hurts. He's got eyes only for that airhead Antonia."

"Why do you sleep with me if you're in love with him?"

"I don't know. Solace? Boy, I'm an emotional wreck again. Love has never been kind to me. It's bad enough when two persons suffer, but when love is unrequited . . ."

"The man is a criminal."

"Listen, why do you sleep with me if you're in love with your Martina?"

I ignored that. "Sam, don't expect me to take your infatuation seriously."

"It's genuine. Too genuine. I've never felt like this."

"Just what do you see in the guy?"

"Love is blind, huh?"

"What are you going to do?"

"What can I do? Zero."

"Sam, you won't . . ."

"Tell him? No. I hope you fleece the bastard."

"You'll be deeply in love with someone else in a month."

"Sometimes I cry at night. Don't you hear me?"

"No."

"Hard-sleeper Shaw, immune to the sounds of a lady's distress."

"Poor Samantha, Cupid's favorite target."

The fish was good, and after lunch we went to the center of town and strolled around the old streets. Samantha bought a brooch that was represented as ivory, but later turned out to be plastic. Charles tested it with a heated straight pin.

"Just my luck," Samantha said.

THIRTY-ONE

The next morning I got up early and walked along the beach to the little seaside resort. It was still cool at six thirty, clear and blue, but you could smell and taste the heat that would follow in a few hours. The tide had receded, leaving the wet sand littered with debris—plastic cola bottles and Styrofoam cartons, a canvas espadrille, seaweed and pieces of fishnet and hollow crab shells.

I went up onto the restaurant's wooden deck, sat at a rail-side table, ordered my usual cappuccino and brioche, and then lit a cigarette. The fishing boats were gone at this hour and so were most of the scavenger gulls. It was too early for sunbathers, but resort attendants were setting up umbrellas and small changing tents on the raked beach south of the docks.

I saw Arbaleste out on the yacht pier. He was working on his boat, *Avanti*. He wore shorts and a wide-brimmed straw hat. A mat of black hair formed a T on his tanned chest. Arbaleste was a lean and muscular man, and he moved well. I had observed his dancerlike grace before, and thought it self-conscious, an affectation, but he was alone now, thought himself unwatched, and yet he moved in the same fluid way. Maybe, I thought, he'd been an awkward boy and had disciplined himself so that finally grace became habitual.

I was drinking my second cup of coffee when he walked down the pier, crossed the beach, and mounted the steps to the restaurant deck.

"Anton," I called.

He turned, hesitated briefly, and then approached.

"Join me," I said.

"Thank you. I shall." He pulled out a chair, removed his straw hat, and dropped it to the floor. He had put on a denim shirt which he wore with only the bottom few buttons closed.

"I saw you working on *Avanti*. She's a beautiful boat."

"Thank you," he said, and then after a brief pause, "But I really shouldn't thank you, should I? You were praising my boat, not me."

"I was praising your taste and knowledge regarding boats."

"It's odd, isn't it, how we do that? Praise a man for his acquisitions—boats, cars, houses—rather than praising the artists and craftsmen who created them."

"I see what you mean."

Sweat had soaked through the armpits and chest of his shirt. I noticed a peppery smell, unusual but not unpleasant, and his skin had a bronzy look in the shade.

"May I?" he said, gesturing toward my pack of cigarettes.

"Of course."

He shook a cigarette out of the package, tapped the end on the table, and lit it with my lighter.

"I've never seen you smoke cigarettes," I said.

"I used to smoke them. I quit many years ago. Now and then I smoke a cigarette."

"To test yourself?"

"Maybe that."

Arbaleste looked directly into your eyes as he talked, and he rarely blinked. I wondered if he had trained himself to avoid blinking, to stare, when in the presence of enemies. I had no doubt that he regarded me, nearly everyone, as—perhaps not enemies exactly, but as potential threats to his freedom and way of life. Arbaleste was an outlaw, after all.

The waiter arrived, addressed Arbaleste with deference, and took his order for a bottle of mineral water and a fruit plate.

"What is your game?" he asked me.

"What do you mean?"

"Everyone has a game. What is yours?"

"I don't understand."

"I'll change my terms. Everyone has a strategy for coping with life. Most people are unaware that they have strategies, but they do; and over time their behavior exposes distinct patterns, repetitions, designs. They become predictable. What is called personality or character is just the manifestation of a particular strategy, as steam is a manifestation of boiling water."

"But the word 'strategy' implies conscious selection."

"That's why I first used the word 'game.'"

"Are we talking psychology?"

"Not really," he said, and then: "Some, a very few, succeed in choosing their own strategies instead of having them imposed by the outside world. They choose them, or revise those strategies that fail."

"I don't think that life is any sort of game."

"Well, it is, finally. You live and then you die. In between you play the game, well or badly. And I asked: What is your game?"

"I don't know. I must be one of the unaware."

"The game of blindman's bluff."

"If you say so."

Once again I was confronted with Arbaleste's queer pedantry. He had selected a topic and proceeded to lecture me. But it seemed to me that the precision of his words was not matched by a precision of thought.

"Has it never occurred to you to elect a strategy? Choose yourself, in the existentialist phrase. Elect yourself."

"No."

"It seems to me, Shaw, that you are a complacent man. No offense intended."

"No offense taken—I don't think. And complacency is bad?"

"It's neither good nor bad. We aren't talking in moral or spiritual terms. It's a weakness of strategy."

"And if complacency is just my nature?"

"It isn't your nature. It's just a flawed tactic in your overall strategy, learned—selected—when you were very young, probably in response to some event or provocation."

"Well, I'm not really complacent, Anton," I said. "But if I were, how would the tactic of complacency help me in the game?"

"It wouldn't."

"You seem rather complacent, yourself. No offense meant."

"We blame our natures for too much. They are less dominating than we suppose. A physically frail boy can lift weights, exercise, strengthen his body, and in that way become the opposite of what he was—strong. It's the same in more abstract things. One can make himself, define himself, authenticate himself, in opposition to what he was, and become new."

"Are we talking existentialism?"

"Perhaps."

"You should write a self-help book, Anton."

He smiled at my sarcasm.

"Strategies and Tactics for the Game of Life."

The fruit platter and mineral water arrived, and I told the waiter to bring me the check for both of our meals.

I curiously watched as he commenced eating fruit with a knife and fork. He ate in the European style, fork in left hand, tines down, knife in right hand.

He had, of course, been talking about himself more than me. Arbaleste saw himself as a self-invented man, and perhaps he was. He had rigorously trained in gymnastics and the piano and tennis and sailing and art and social forms and crime. He was not a "natural." It seemed to me that he was a man who had tamed an inner chaos, inner doubt, and had fanatically willed a new self. Jean Halbert had consciously created Anton Arbaleste. But of course the chaos remained, quiescent now.

"Have you ever killed a man?" he asked me.

"Yes."

"War?"

"No."

"Murder?"

"Self-defense."

"I killed a man when I was a student in Paris. I was twenty-two years old. I was inspired by André Gide. Have you read Gide?"

"No."

"He wrote about the *acte gratuit,* the meaningless action that, in its very lack of meaning, can provide a sort of personal liberation. Gide has a man gratuitously shove another man, a stranger, off a moving train. He has killed. And in ways that neither Gide nor I can explain, the killer has been altered and the world changed. I killed a stranger in Paris, with a knife, on a dark street, for no reason at all except the expectation of surpassing myself by executing the greatest of crimes, of sins."

"Did you stab him in the back?"

"No, it was face-to-face."

He finished eating, crossed his knife and fork on the empty plate, and gazed levelly at me.

"Do you like Antonia?" he asked.

"Certainly. Everyone likes Antonia."

He nodded. "Antonia appears strong, whole, but she isn't. She is beautiful and fragile like fine porcelain or china. She can easily be broken."

"She hasn't devised an effective strategy?" I asked.

"Don't trifle with her. Or me."

He believed the gossip—started by Antonia—that she and I were having a sneak affair. For days I had considered telling Arbaleste that it wasn't true, just gossip, but this was not the time. To inform him now would be interpreted as weakness on my part, fear. He would think that he had intimidated me with his threatening words and gaze and the story of his *acte gratuit* on a dark Paris street. I chose stubbornness. To hell with Anton Arbaleste; let him believe the rumors.

The waiter arrived with the check. I dropped some Euros on the tray and, when he had gone, I turned back to Arbaleste.

"Your murder in Paris," I said. "Did it liberate you?"

"Only in the sense that it was much easier to kill the next time."

"Another *acte gratuit*?"

"An *acte necessaire*."

I pushed back my chair and stood up. "Damn," I said, "I do love to sit around and listen to war stories."

"Ciao, Daniel."

"Ciao, Anton," I said, and I crossed the deck and went down the stairs into hot sunlight.

Judge Samuelson was sitting at an umbrellaed table on the villa's terrace when I returned. There was a pitcher of orange juice on the table. I poured a glass.

"Levi," I said. "I think that Anton Arbaleste subtly threatened my life twenty minutes ago."

"Well, as long as it was subtle . . ."

THIRTY-TWO

Saturday morning was perfect, dear and bright and blue, with a cooling northerly breeze that swept away the humidity and stagnant air. Arbaleste used the diesel engine to take *Avanti* out of the harbor, and then we raised sail. Penny had done some sailing; Petrie, too; and I owned a twenty-five-foot sloop, and so the three of us served as crew. There was not much to do after the sails had been raised and trimmed. The breeze was light, partly impeded by the peninsula, and we made only three or four knots in the early going. There were other boats scattered over the sea, sail and motor yachts, a couple of fishing boats returning late to port, and the ferry that ran out to Capri.

Avanti was thirty-eight feet on deck, and now a bit crowded with eight of us: Arbaleste and Antonia, Penny and Cassy, Charles, Samantha, Petrie, and me. The women were in bikinis. I prowled the boat, above and below deck. She was a beautiful yacht, Italian-made, fiberglass with a teak deck and teak rails and trim, and all the best in fittings and electronics. I was not an envious man, but I envied Arbaleste his yacht. He lived well, this crook, with his yacht and properties and art collection and millions. His appreciation of fine foods and wines, music and literature, his dogs and horses if somewhere he had dogs and horses, his manners, his tennis game, his gymnastic skill, his woman. But I envied him only his yacht.

The breeze picked up when we were well clear of land. Arbaleste changed course to the southwest. Our speed increased to about six knots. The transparent swells were three or four feet high. The sky remained an immaculate azure. No clouds, not even a vapor trail. We could see Capri to the north. Sicily was a hundred-plus miles to the south; and far to the west, the big island of Sardinia, and north of it, across the Strait of Bonifacio, was Corsica.

Penny was standing up in the bow pulpit. I carefully picked my way past sunbathing females.

I said, "How much longer are you staying?"

"We fly back to England tomorrow."

"Good. It's time."

"You've reached the crux? The trap baited, the rat tempted?"

"The rat's in the trap, I think."

He lowered his voice to a near whisper so that Cassy and Samantha, sprawled prone on the deck a few feet behind us, could not hear. "Are you really having an affair with Antonia?"

"No."

"Too bad. My condolences."

There was a pronounced feeling of motion up on the prow, both forward and vertical, and a sense of the power exerted by the sails driving several tons of boat through the water. The bows lifted, hesitated a moment on the crests, then peeled off glassy waves as they punched down into the troughs. I felt cool spray on my face, and tiny rainbows briefly appeared in the airborne mist.

"I'll let you know how all of this turns out," I said. "You might be in for a small percentage."

"That isn't necessary, Shaw. I've done nothing, really. My debt to Arbaleste has been eliminated, and that's enough."

"Is that an island ahead?"

"Where?"

"Ahead and a little to port."

"I believe it is. A reef, anyway."

It was far away and seemed to appear and vanish and then reappear as we watched. The island was dark gray, a color not much different than the blue-gray of the sea at that distance, and a large part of it lay below the horizon line.

I said, "He's heading directly toward it."

"That explains the picnic stuff aboard."

Over the next half hour the island swelled up out of the sea, bare and rocky, with the base ringed white by surf. It lay on the diagonal, northwest to southeast, divided by a central lengthwise ridge; on the highest point there was a rust red lighthouse.

"I don't see any way in," Penny said.

"There might be shelter on the other side."

We prepared to attend to the sails. Arbaleste would have to steer the boat south and then west, and probably north afterward, in order to come in on the lee side of the island.

He was an able helmsman. He knew it and wanted all of us to know it. He did not use the engine, but under full sail guided the boat in through a tricky passage among fanged rocks and into a small C-shaped cove. I would not have tried the entry, but I was not familiar with these waters, had never looked at the charts, knew nothing of the depths and currents and local tides. Still, it was an impressive bit of seamanship. Arbaleste was a man who liked to do difficult things well.

Penny put out the anchor while Petrie and I lowered and furled the sails. Arbaleste removed the dinghy from the cabin top. The women went below to collect the picnic supplies.

On the left side of the cove, at the end of a curving arm of rock rubble, was an arch, an inverted stone U that was like the arches you saw in desert country. Over the eons, currents and tides had eaten through the center of an enormous slab of stone and left this standing monument. The top was at least sixty feet above the water.

I judged the island to be about five hundred feet long, half that in width, with a ridge that, at the summit, reached one hundred and fifty feet. The island, a solid-looking stone mass at a distance, was strewn with boulders, broken by ravines and fissures and scree slopes, and spattered with white bird guano. On shore a sign printed in Italian, English, and German warned that no boats were permitted to land at this bird sanctuary during the bird breeding season. The penalties were severe. I saw only a few birds, small black-and-white ones that darted like terns above the island's spine. We could hear the dull thud of surf breaking on the windward side of the island, but the water in the cove was smooth and clear, and deeper than I'd expected.

I stripped to my swimming suit, tossing my shoes and T-shirt into the dinghy, and then Samantha and I dove over the side and swam in to shore. The beach was a broad sand crescent the same dark gray as the rock. Behind it was a level section of mixed sand and rock. The area was mostly in shadow now, but would be bright and hot when the sun rose a little higher. Nothing grew below the high-tide line, but above there were some gnarled shrubs and thorns and yellow grass growing in the rock fissures.

"I've seen lusher picnic sites," Samantha said.

"I like it. Remote, harsh, mysterious—a legendary place, Sam—this is where Odysseus was stranded for six years, bound in chains and sexually exploited by the siren Samantha."

She laughed. "Really? That nympho siren?"

"She used him cruelly."

"Good for her. How did he finally escape?"

"See that little cave entrance up there? That's where the terrible dragon lived, and maybe still lives. Odysseus tricked Samantha into entering the cave. The dragon ate her up, yum yum, and his belch blew Odysseus all the way to Ithaca."

"Dragons have such interesting names."

"This dragon had many names. One name was Arbaleste."

"Are you Odysseus in this dumb little epic?"

"No, I'm Homer."

"Blind Homer," she said.

Arbaleste ferried the others ashore in the dinghy, Petrie, Charles, and Antonia in the first run; then Cassy, Penny, and the supplies. Everything was unpacked and spread out on the sand. There was a big white linen tablecloth with an *A* monogrammed at each of the four corners, some blankets, two wicker baskets, and two ice coolers. There was cold chicken, cheese, prosciutto, crusty bread, pickles and olives, a pasta salad, and an almond cake for dessert. And there was wine, red and white, and plenty of German beer. We decided that it was much too early to eat. Time instead to hike and swim and drink. It was not too early to drink.

I put on my tennis shoes, pulled the cork on a bottle of wine, reinserted the cork, and walked off to explore the island. There was a rough sort of trail that tacked up to the ridge, made and used, I supposed, by the light tenders, who had to call periodically for maintenance and to replenish the fuel. A footpath led up to a scree slope which then brought me to a series of broad ledges that angled up toward the ridge. The cave I had seen— the dragon's lair—was waist-high and only a few feet deep. The climbing was easy. There were not many places where a fall might cause serious injury.

I was on a high ledge when I heard the rattle of falling stones, and turned. Antonia was a few yards behind me.

She smiled. "*Avanti*," she said.

She wore shorts and a sleeveless blouse over her bikini, and sandals that were not much good for climbing. Her smoky dark hair showed silver blurs where the sun struck it. She wore no makeup. Antonia's flawless skin, black eyebrows and long lashes, and full pink mouth were what makeup had been invented to counterfeit.

"Give me some of that wine."

"Not here," I said. "When we reach the top."

"Go, then."

She followed me up the angled ledge to a rubble-filled ravine, and we climbed that to the ridge and a sudden cool breeze. We could see the mainland from there, and Capri, both shadowy in the hazy distance. Below us, at the bottom of the reverse slope, surf foamed against the rock. The automated light was conical and about twenty feet high, mounted on a level area of the summit. The upper, lensed section turned slowly and silently, now and then blinking a faint orange in the sunlight. This was an important light. I did not doubt that there were many wrecks scattered over the outlying reef, some of them Greek and Roman, maybe Phoenician.

"Look," Antonia said.

I turned. Arbaleste was climbing one of the arch's pillars. The pitch was nearly vertical, and he carefully picked his way upward, pausing to select the right toehold, the right handhold, cool as ice, and I thought, there, the son of a bitch is an accomplished rock climber, too. Rock climber, sailor, gymnast, connoisseur, raconteur, lover, and he played Mozart on a white baby grand piano at three in the morning.

We were high enough so that Arbaleste and the others below were reduced to doll-size by perspective. Cassy and Samantha had risen from their beach towels and walked down to the shore. Their breasts were bare; they had removed their bikini tops for sunbathing. Penny joined them on the beach. Petrie and Charles watched

Arbaleste from the picnic site. Tom was smoking a cigar, and even at the distance I could see that his head was cocked in the characteristic Petrie *show me* way. The five of them, and Antonia and I, watched as Arbaleste approached the crux of the climb, the difficult transition from vertical to the horizontal span.

"Has he ever done this before?" I asked Antonia.

"Yes."

"What happens next? A handstand?"

"You'll see," she said.

Some of the small black-and-white birds darted around the upper section of the arch (did they have nests up there?), and others skimmed low along the shoreline. Replicas of the arch and the clinging man were reflected on the mirror-smooth water, and farther out the anchored sailboat cast its own detailed image.

"Anton," Antonia whispered.

Slowly, and without effort it appeared, Arbaleste pulled himself onto the horizontal span, rose to his feet, and casually walked to the center. He didn't strut, didn't posture, didn't glance toward those on shore for approval.

He lowered to his hands and knees and, without pause, lifted easily into a handstand. Antonia, her eyes wide, was smiling. She touched my arm as if to say, See, see what this man is? Arbaleste held his pose. It was dramatic, this solitary man posed like an inverted sculpture against the sky. No one down on the beach moved or made a sound. He would not fail. There was something about this Arbaleste that compelled people to surrender their trust. All of us knew that he was a cold, predatory man, and yet we all silently cheered his display of skill and risk. We were charmed. This was Arbaleste as he romantically viewed himself: the artist as criminal, the criminal as artist.

Then he changed the angle of his body, removed one hand from the rock, shifted his angle, and was left balanced on one hand. One hand, wrist, arm and shoulder. He held his line. There was no wavering. It was the same position I had seen when he'd done the handstand on the terrace wall, except that he held it longer now; he prolonged the difficulty. Great strength and balance were required, and courage. He knew the water below the arch was deep enough. But he knew, we all knew, that if you hit the water wrong after a sixty-foot fall, the impact can break bones, snap the spine, burst organs. It can kill you.

Antonia's breathing was shallow and fast. She seemed excited in a sexual way. All of the others below, Penny and Cassy, Samantha, Charles, even the cynical Petrie, remained frozen and silent. They believed in him and yet feared for him.

I expected it. He wavered. The clean, precise line of his body tilted, the center of his gravity changed. He lowered his free hand to the rock, but it was too late, he had lost control. He was going to fall. Samantha cried his name. Peninngton shouted something. But Antonia knew; she was not afraid.

Arbaleste's uncontrolled fall was swiftly converted into a perfectly executed dive. He tucked, and his downward motion was partly changed into forward rotation, and his body described an entire revolution and half of another before he came out of the tuck, straightened, and entered the water vertically and left behind a high, plumed splash. We all watched the spreading circle of seething white water. The water's surface smoothed and its reflections were restored. Arbaleste surfaced. He began swimming ashore. The others, even Petrie, were waiting when he waded up the beach.

"He's a man," Antonia said. "My God, he is a man."

"He's a jerk," I said.

She laughed. "You—you are just jealous."

THIRTY-THREE

The slope on the opposite side of the ridge was not very steep. We descended to a level rock slab some fifteen feet above the sea. The water below us seethed white, hissing, and surf exploded on the rocks and filled the air with a fine mist. The waves gliding down from the northeast were small, innocent-looking, but they turned concave when reaching shallow water, rose up and smashed into the stone barrier with startling violence. I tried to imagine what it would be like sitting in this place during a storm.

I uncorked the wine, took a drink, and passed the bottle to Antonia. She drank, wiped her mouth with the back of her hand, and grinned at me.

Antonia was a happy woman, simple, though not simple in a pejorative sense, not stupid. Here is the salty sea, here is the bright blue sky, here is the sunshine that warms my skin, here is the cool wine, here am I. She apprehended the world almost wholly through her senses. She lived at a physical level that had perhaps been lost to most through the hard demands of civilization. You paid for civilization by surrendering instinct and spontaneity. At heart, Antonia was a savage.

I said, "Why do you continue telling people that we're having an affair?"

"I want to make Anton jealous. But he's a stone."

"No, he isn't. And he does love you."

"Not enough."

"Well, it's a cruel game you're playing. Why did you pick me to provoke his jealousy?"

"Why not? You aren't so bad."

"I don't like it. I don't think you understand the possible consequences of your game. He could hurt you."

"Anton?" She smiled. "Never!"

"Or hurt me."

"Poor baby. Are you scared?"

"Is Anton faithful to you?"

"I'm sure of it."

"Then why make him jealous?"

"I want him to feel pain, show pain, so that I know I'm real to him."

"Real to yourself. Well, tell him that we aren't having an affair."

"All right. Now, would you like to kiss me?"

"Sure."

She returned my kisses in an expert but passionless way. We necked for a few minutes as though it was simply something you did on a picnic; it was without significance. And then we disengaged, sat up, and drank more wine.

"You're a good kisser, Antonia," I said.

"You, too."

"And you are a strange creature."

"Am I?" She was pleased.

She did not actively participate in Arbaleste's swindles. She deceived no one, except in a passive way, by her presence and by keeping Arbaleste's secrets. I supposed that she was legally culpable for the crimes. Antonia could be prosecuted, jailed, as an accomplice. I knew that she liked all of us. The judge, Petrie, Charles, Penny, me. Samantha and Cassy had become like her sisters. But her affection was not accompanied by concern. We were just minor actors in Antonia di Benedetto's personal drama. One day we would go, and other people would come along to like and admire her. Oddly, it was her crazy self-absorption that made her so attractive.

"You're dangerous," I said.

Again she was pleased. "Good. I like to be dangerous. What is life without danger? But I sometimes think that you are dangerous, too. You and your friends."

"Really? Why?"

"You are not what you seem."

"What do we seem?"

"Oh, very nice and ordinary and rather dull most of the time—money people. People who are always counting. People who must work hard to have fun. Am I having fun, am I having fun? Well, yes, perhaps you are having fun. But there is something else. Something—I don't know—something secretive and . . . wolfish."

I laughed. "And I thought you liked us."

"I *do* like you."

"Still . . . wolfish."

"Predatory." She laughed. "I mean you are not always honest."

"Are you and Anton always honest?"

"No."

"Well?"

"Well nothing."

"There are times when Anton himself appears rather wolfish."

"Anton is a fox," she said.

"I think we should go back now. I think that Anton, if he's ever going to be jealous, is jealous now."

We paused on the breezy ridge. Below, everyone was gathered at the picnic site except for Arbaleste, who stood apart. His feet were spread, his hands were on his hips, as he stared up at us. It was always difficult to intuit his thoughts, his mood; impossible at this distance. But I was annoyed by his stance and his continuing stare. I saw it as an attempt to intimidate. And so I stared down at Arbaleste as he, motionless, stared up at me and Antonia. Stalemate in an adolescent staring duel. Then I stepped close to Antonia, placed my left arm around her waist and raised my right fist palm-out with the index and little fingers extended. The sign of horns—cuckold!

"You shouldn't have done that," she said, but she laughed. "He can be a devil."

Descending is always more difficult than climbing. The grade looks steeper, your weight is usually on your heels rather than toes, and you tense a little with the exposure. We went down the rubble-filled ravine to a steep slab of rock, down a little farther to a ledge that traversed the slope at a gentle downward angle. Below was a talus field, fractured rocks, stone rubble. It was not a dangerous descent. The ledge was more than a yard wide most of the way, and at no point was the drop more than a dozen feet.

I assumed that Antonia was following a few paces behind me until I noticed that the others, not just Arbaleste, were staring upward. I turned just as she was lifting to a handstand. Her palms were flat on the rock, fingers curled over the ledge's rim, her head back as she looked down eight or ten feet to the pile of rocks below. Her form was good. She had practiced. Maybe Arbaleste had trained her. She appeared in perfect control when she lifted to the vertical. A little beyond the vertical, then. Her angle was wrong, and she tried to compensate with the strength of her arms and by flexing at the knees, altering her center of gravity. Was she imitating Arbaleste's fake loss of balance on the arch? I believed that she was going to save herself. Then I saw that she was losing strength and would be unable to restore balance. I hurried back along the ledge, but I was too slow, too late. Her arms buckled at the elbows, first the left, then the right, and she fell headfirst down to the rocks. She made a small, whimpering sound. (And that night I awakened hearing the sound of an arm bone snapping, and then the awful, sickening sound of her head striking a rock.) She had fallen straight down, half somersaulted forward after impact, and now lay on her back, feet pointing downslope. There was blood on her face and in her hair. She did not move.

"Antonia?"

I thought what you always think as I hurriedly looked for a place to quickly climb down: If only . . . If only I had been more watchful of her during the descent; if only I had reacted faster when I saw she was failing; if only she had not resisted the fall when it became certain, had gone all the way over and landed on her feet or buttocks—then she might have broken a leg, an ankle, but not her head, not her neck.

Arbaleste and the other men were running up the talus slope toward us. I reached Antonia and kneeled at her side. I could not tell if she was breathing. There was a terrible gash on her forehead at the hairline, and her neck appeared to have a lump on one side. Her neck was not crooked, not angled, there was just that fist-sized lump. I could not find a pulse.

Arbaleste was first to climb the talus slope. He halted, breathing deeply, and looked down at Antonia. "Don't touch her," he said. "Stop touching her."

She was still bleeding. Didn't that mean that her heart was still beating, she was still alive?

The others reached us, Penny first, followed by Petrie, and then Charles.

I got to my feet and backed away from the body. Samantha and Cassy remained down on the beach, their faces turned up toward us.

Petrie said something about radioing for an evacuation by helicopter. Arbaleste kneeled next to Antonia. He touched her bloody cheek, her bloody hair. He lifted an eyelid to see if the pupil reacted to light. He made a hissing sound. Arbaleste looked up at me. I could not read his long stare. There was no obvious hatred in it. No malice, no threat, but its peculiar quality and its duration worried me. I would have preferred open hatred.

Charles, who had been a nurse at a California prison, kneeled next to Arbaleste. He lifted Antonia's limp hand, searched the wrist for a pulse.

"I think . . ." Charles said.

Petrie was looking at me. I could not interpret his stare, either.

"I think I've got a pulse," Charles said.

Arbaleste bowed his head and closed his eyes.

"Yes . . ."

We didn't know what to do. We could not carry her down, not with her neck broken, not without splinting her broken arm, not without dressing her head wound. Petrie again suggested radioing for a helicopter, but he didn't move, and no one responded. We waited.

It was hot in the sunlight, hot among the heat-radiating rocks, hot there waiting for death. Below, Cassy was crying and Samantha was trying to comfort her. Beyond them the cool sea (flashed with semaphores of light.

"I think . . ." Charles said. But he was not certain. Her pulse was so weak, her respiration so slow.

"No," he said later. "I'm afraid . . ."

It took twenty minutes for Charles and Arbaleste to become absolutely certain that Antonia was dead. She'd made the transition, the passage, and now it was just a matter of the rest of us finishing out this day.

Arbaleste would not permit me to help carry her down the rocky slope to the beach. He, Petrie, Penny, and Charles descended with the body, moving slowly and gently, as if she were made of glass, as if she might actually be alive and still sensitive to pain.

They wrapped the body in the white linen tablecloth. There were flies. How was it possible that flies could appear so soon? Blood seeped through the shroud monogrammed with the letter *A*. They carried her to shore and placed her body in the dinghy. Arbaleste rowed her out to the yacht while Petrie and Pennington swam alongside, and the three of them, with some difficulty, got the body aboard and down into the cabin.

Samantha, Cassy, and I waited on the beach. Cassy, in a daze, looked for her bikini top. Charles had blood on his hands; he washed them with beer and dried them on a towel. We were silent as we waited for the dinghy to return. I felt that I was being accused. The others avoided my glance. Was I somehow responsible for Antonia's death? I mentally defended myself: she had joined me voluntarily, followed me. The climb was not difficult or dangerous. Anyway, she had not fallen during the climb or descent, but while foolishly trying to impress Arbaleste. We had shared a bottle of wine, and the alcohol had at least slightly affected her judgment or reflexes, but how could I be expected to foresee her stunt? Still, I hadn't acted quickly. There had been that instant's hesitation. If I had reacted immediately I might have been able to rush back along the ledge and . . . Perhaps I had been negligent. Once we had gone off together I became, in part, responsible for her safety. And if I was in part responsible for her life, then I was a priori in part responsible for her death.

We sailed near the wind on the voyage back, close-hauled, and the boat was steeply heeled most of the way. Petrie and Charles went below to secure Antonia's body, so that it would not be thrown from the berth. Arbaleste would not give up the tiller. Once, I turned and caught him looking at me. I thought he might have nodded a fraction, smiled a fraction, but I couldn't be sure I hadn't imagined it.

We arrived back in Castelnuovo at a little after five, sunburned and windblown and depressed. Petrie had radioed ahead, and the police and an ambulance were waiting for us at the marina.

THIRTY-FOUR

Arbaleste was permitted to ride in the ambulance with Antonia's body. The rest of us were questioned at the marina. The police were sympathetic. It was not necessary for us to accompany them to the municipal building for further interviews. There was not much to investigate: seven persons had witnessed an unfortunate accident. The poor woman. Signorina di Benedetto was beautiful, was she not, a resident of Castelnuovo for the last three summers, well known and well liked by the villagers. Tragic. What can be said? It was a tragedy. Her body would remain at the hospital morgue pending notification of family and instructions as to the arrangements. Things would have been more complicated had she not been an Italian national. The paperwork, the governmental meddling became intolerable when the victim was a foreigner. The police knew us; that is, they knew that we were the distinguished visitors occupying the clifftop mansions owned by the rich signore from Milano. But Antonia di Benedetto—what a sorrow!

Petrie told the senior police officer that some of us had arranged to temporarily leave Castelnuovo this weekend. He and the tall old gentleman had urgent business in the United States. Others wished to travel; a visit to France for one, a stay in Rome for another. The lease on the villa was good for another five weeks. It might be vacated for a period, but we all expected to return in August. The policeman saw no problem. We were free to do whatever we pleased. Life must go on. He, personally, was pleased that this tragic accident had not totally disrupted our holidays, and he was pleased that we would be returning. There were many who believed that this famous coast was most beautiful in August. Hot, yes, but doesn't one prefer heat at a seacoast resort? Many tourists would be arriving in August: Italians, Germans, English, Americans; there was always a festival atmosphere during the entire month.

We thanked the policemen, said good-bye, and went to the house. Judge Samuelson emerged from his room to greet us, and said that he felt much better after his solitary day of rest, but he still looked tired, and he took the news of Antonia's death hard.

No one was hungry despite not having eaten since early this morning, but we all badly wanted a drink. We closed the curtains against the penetrating late afternoon sun, made our drinks, and gathered in the big room. There was a blank space on the wall where the Degas forgery had hung; Arbaleste had taken it away last night.

Petrie said, "It's time to get out of town. Penny?"

"We're packed," Lord Warfield said.

"The judge and I are driving up to Naples in a few hours. Do you and Cassy want to ride along?"

"Yes. We can make connections to London from the Naples airport."

"Charles?"

The fair-skinned Charles had not acquired much of a suntan during the summer, but today he had burned to the color of a cooked lobster, and there was a scatter of tiny sun blisters on his forehead.

"I'm going to Antibes for a few weeks," Charles said. "I'll drive to Rome in the Ferrari and turn it in at the airport there. But I need money."

"I'll give you a few thousand."

"No, Tom. I want my share of the money."

"You'll have to wait a while. We all have to wait until a few legal matters are settled. The money is safe in Panama."

"You wouldn't cheat me, would you, Tom?"

"Sure I would. But not on this deal. You earned your share."

"And did your friends earn their shares? Karpe, McNally, and Cavaretta?"

"No, they didn't. But we all made a deal and we're stuck with it."

Charles nodded, but it was clear that he was unhappy. And when Charles became unhappy he immediately commenced scheming for a way to restore his happiness.

"Shaw?"

"I'll follow you up to Naples in my rental car, catch a flight from there. Maybe I can get a seat on your plane."

"Good. That son of a bitch Arbaleste is going to understand everything very soon, and none of us wants to be around then."

I said, "I'll stop off to see the rental agent. Give her money to pay off the servants, and tell her that the house will be vacated for a week or two, but that we'll be back."

"Samantha?" Petrie said.

"I'll ride up to Rome with Charles. I have friends there, and since I'm on this side of the Atlantic . . ."

"You'll hold back on your story for at least a few months, won't you?"

"The way I feel now, there won't be a story."

"Good. Kill the story and maybe we'll vote you a small percentage of the money. More than you'd get from selling the story, anyway."

"I don't know about that," Samantha said with a sly grin. "There might be a monster book in all this weirdness."

"Well, Christ," Petrie said. "I guess we did it." Tom had a weakness for proposing toasts, and now he started to lift his glass to offer a few words of self-congratulation, but then he remembered Antonia, and of course realized that this was not a time for victory laps.

"Let us," the judge said, "drink to the memory of that lovely girl. Antonia."

We drank, then dispersed to pack and prepare for "exfiltration." Samantha came to my garret to collect a few of her things.

"She's sort of sacred now that she's dead. Saint Antonia. Will anyone regard me as sacred after I die, Dan?"

"I will. I'll burn a candle."

She laughed, gave me a quick kiss on my cheek, went out of the room and down the hallway.

PART IV
Dancing

THIRTY-FIVE

We were like the Earp gang heading down to the O.K. Corral. Pier D was an isolated floating dock at the far end of Cotty's Marina, so narrow that we had to walk single file toward the *Catcher*'s berth. Petrie led the way, followed by McNally and Cavaretta, then Leroy Karpe, and I brought up the rear. Even at six in the morning the temperature was ninety degrees and the air so saturated with humidity that objects were blurred. I was soaked with sweat after a forty-yard walk.

Surly gulls sat on pier posts; cormorants, perched on buoys, dried their wings; and pelicans, looking broken and ruffled, as if they had fallen out of the sky, huddled along the shoreline. We saw no one. Cotty's was the county's low-end marina, and dock D was where Cotty put the bad boys.

This was my third day back in Florida. Martina had complained that she had twice awakened in the morning to find the Mackey brothers playing catch in front of the lighthouse. Each time they had grinned and muttered something about a debt owed them. She was more annoyed than frightened, but Tom and I had concluded that the intimidators must now be intimidated.

Catcher was berthed at the end of the pier. A dirty boat, with flaking chrome and tarnished bronze and peeling varnish. It smelled of fish and leaking fuel. The boat was low in the water; they probably had to pump the bilges twice a day.

Petrie boarded the boat and moved to the stern. McNally and Cavaretta joined him there by the fishing chairs. I climbed the ladder to the flying bridge. *Searcher* dipped beneath our weight. The brothers, if they were not still too drunk, would be aware of uninvited visitors. We were armed. Petrie was carrying a walking cane, ordinary except that there was an iron ferule at the tip instead of the rubber no-slip cup. Tom had a collection of bladed weapons at home—rapiers, foils, sabers, cutlasses, walking sticks and umbrellas with concealed swords—but this was a standard cane except for the steel tip. Tom was a fencer, and he would, if necessary, use the cane as a sword; a stiff "touch" to the solar plexus or groin would bloodlessly disable an aggressor. Both McNally and Cavaretta had blackjacks in their rear pockets. I had a tire iron that I'd taken from the car trunk. Leroy, who remained on the dock to repel possible Mackey reinforcements, had his face. Usually a man who has been badly beaten, nearly killed, loses heart for future fights. Not Leroy. He had his scary face and bad temper.

They came up out of the dark cabin like a couple of shaggy bears emerging from hibernation. Kyle carried a gaff with a wicked steel hook; Earl had the kind of club you use to bash a fish into oblivion. They blinked, scratched, coughed up phlegm, winced at the morning sunlight. Kyle was trying to figure things out. Earl waited for his brother to finish thinking before he learned if he would be permitted to go berserk.

"Good morning, boys," I said. They turned, looked up. I wanted them to know that there was also an enemy above.

Then a woman came up the ladder and moved across the deck to stand between them. She was in her thirties, thin, barefoot with toenails painted purple, and dried-out bleached-blonde hair that looked like packing excelsior. No one else emerged from the cabin. Maybe the Mackey brothers shared her as they shared pot and beer and trouble.

"Run along now, darling," McNally said.

The woman glanced first at Kyle, then Earl, then crossed the deck, stepped lightly to the pier, and hurried past Leroy and down toward shore.

There was a moment when I thought there was going to be a brawl. The brothers had size, a gaff, and a club, and they had their touchy pride. But they were looking at a lawyer they knew and a pair of ex-cops they had encountered before. I was above them clutching a tire iron. Leroy, on the dock, had his face. It might have been Leroy's face that ultimately stopped them.

"You remember me, don't you, guys?" Petrie said. He gestured with his cane. "I defended you in court on felonious assault charges a few years back. I miraculously got you probation. And how did you repay me? You didn't. You still owe me forty-five hundred dollars."

Kyle Mackey was astonished. "You come out here like this to collect money?"

"I might soon slap a lien on your boat," he said, "before it sinks or the statute of limitations runs out."

"You want our boat?"

"I want to tow it out to sea and sink it myself. Sink the stink, the fish blood and fish scales, the roaches and rodents, the barnacles and teredo worms—sink this abomination."

"Aw, Tom, come on," Kyle said. He was trying to determine if he should be amused.

Earl had angled his body so that he could watch me.

"Fuck this talk," I said. "Let's just bash out their—I almost said brains."

"What's wrong with *him?*" Kyle asked in an aggrieved tone.

"Don't ask Petrie," I said, "ask me, you two-hundred-kilo bag of shit."

Tom pointed his cane at Kyle. "You've been harassing his girl out at the lighthouse. You've made her anxious. That won't do, Kyle. Earl? No, Earl, bad boy, very bad."

"Kyle?" Earl said. *Can I club, please, Kyle?*

Both McNally and Cavaretta moved forward a couple of steps. Their right hands were behind their hips. The Mackeys might assume they were carrying guns.

"Let's kill them in self-defense," McNally said.

"Let's kill them," Cavaretta said, "while they unlawfully take flight to avoid prosecution."

"You two ain't cops no more," Earl said.

"You hear that?"

"He said we ain't cops no more."

"Earl said that?"

"He learned to talk since the last time we saw him."

"Look at that hook, look at that club. Let's kill them while they resist arrest."

"Kyle?" Earl said.

Kyle tossed his gaff over the side.

"Kyle?"

"Throw away the club," Kyle said.

"It ain't right," Earl said. "It ain't right people do this." He angrily threw his club into the water.

Leroy Karpe came aboard the boat and moved to the deck well. He was about six inches shorter and eighty pounds lighter than either of the brothers, and he had to tilt his head back to look at them. He stared first at Kyle, then Earl, as if memorizing their faces, and then he nodded, turned, and left the boat.

We followed Leroy single-file down the pier.

"Tom," Kyle called. "Tom? You ain't going to take away our boat now, are you, Tom?"

THIRTY-SIX

I met Martina for lunch that afternoon and told her that the Mackey brothers would not be bothering her anymore.

"Good," she said. "And is the mysterious business in Italy finally concluded?"

"*Fini*," I said, though I doubted that Arbaleste believed it finished.

"Then why don't you and Tom come out to the lighthouse for dinner tonight?"

"A vegetarian dinner?"

"Seafood, probably."

"I'll bring the wine."

"No, I have lots of wine. I found some bargains at the supermarket, one from South Dakota. Guess what's pictured on the label?"

"The faces on Mount Rushmore."

"How did you know?"

"I insist," I said. "I'll bring the wine."

I kept my twenty-five-foot sloop at the Bell Harbor marina, but I used a rowing skiff to go back and forth to the lighthouse. Petrie sat in the stern of the boat smoking a cigar while I pulled at the oars. It was late afternoon, still hot and bright, and I worked up a sweat rowing against the incoming tide. Petrie told me about his meeting with Chester Dalhart that afternoon.

"Yes," he said, "Chester rejected half of the items on my expense sheet. He used a red pencil. Slash, they would not pay for the Ferrari rental. Slash, no forged painting—was I mad? Slash, he would pay only half of the outrageous villa lease. It went on like that, slash, slash, slash. He referred to our contract, in which he reserved the right to reject unnecessary and exorbitant expenses."

"And you said?"

"Naturally I said, so sue me."

"And he said?"

"He said that he very probably would sue me."

"And you said?"

"I said, 'Chester, my dear friend and colleague, there is eleven and one-half million dollars sitting in my bank account—never mind where—and that money is drawing interest every day. It will continue to draw interest during the period of your spiteful litigation, which I can probably stretch out three years. Now, Chester, think about the publicity that your lawsuit will generate. Investors will be named, mocked, and reviled.'"

We were drawing close to the lighthouse now. Cerberus was running across the reef toward the stairway to the dock. He would bark savagely, ruff bristling, until we arrived, and then he would grovel.

"And Chester said?"

Tom took a last puff on his cigar, dropped it over the side, and said, "Chester fumed and fussed, but finally promised to consult with members of the consortium. They'll surely tell him to stuff the expense sheet and grab the money pronto-presto."

Martina's greeting was cold. She met us at the door, abruptly pivoted, and returned to the kitchen. There was a big red snapper—spear hole behind the gills—on the cutting board, along with three smaller fish. The red snapper looked familiar. His identity was confirmed by the presence of Raven's skull and bones displayed on the oak credenza in the living area. My little duffel, still wet, was on the floor nearby, next to Cerberus, who gave me a shamefaced grin of complicity.

Petrie glanced at me, then turned toward Martina. He spoke to her back. "Fresh fish," he said. "Nothing like it."

I said, "Let me know when it's time to fire up the grill, Martina."

"In the meantime," Petrie said, "I'll put the Pouilly-Fuissé in the refrigerator."

Martina, for all her altruism toward the animal kingdom, was a savage and effective undersea predator. She couldn't help it; she loved seafood. She explained the contradiction in the time-honored cop-out: She wasn't perfect; she was only human, after all. Anyway, she needed the protein since she didn't eat mammals.

There was a setup of liquor bottles, mix, a bowl of ice, and some sliced limes. I poured a Scotch and made two gin and tonics, left one of them on the kitchen bar, and carried the Scotch to Petrie.

"Oh, tanks," he said. He was enjoying this. "Tank you."

Martina was busy inside the kitchen partition, gutting

and fileting the fish, seasoning the filets, preparing a salad and vegetables. Petrie and I sat quietly. Raven's jawless skull watched us with a loopy, yokel grin.

"Hot," Petrie said.

"Hotter than Italy," I agreed.

"It's the humidity. The dew point."

"Late July. It's always like this late in July."

Tom began staring at the dog and making hostile, teeth-bared faces, which caused Cerberus to whine and drool.

I grilled the fish outside, and then we sat down to an excellent meal, but only Petrie seemed to enjoy the food and the atmosphere. He thrived amidst discord. Martina did not speak. She had not spoken since we had entered the house. It is difficult to maintain silence so long; it requires discipline and sacrifice, and a potent grievance.

After the meal, after the dishes had been cleared away and a final glass of wine poured, Petrie took over.

"Okay," he said to Martina, "enough of this low frequency persecution."

He got one of the stools from the kitchen counter, carried it out into the center of the living area, and set it down.

"Come," he said to me. "Sit."

I thought, why not? I'll play the dunce if he can find a way to reduce tension. I crossed over and sat on the stool.

"Martina, sit over there."

She looked at him.

"Sit."

"I'm not a dog," she said.

"I am so sorry. Please, make yourself comfortable on a chair or settee. You are the judge and jury. Dopey here is the defendant. And I . . . I am counsel for both the prosecution and defense. Marty?"

"This is absurd," she said, but she moved to the settee.

"There," Petrie said, pointing at Raven's skull, "is the accuser. The victim. Or is he the victim? We shall find out during this session of moot court. We may learn that Raven is the sinner and not the sinned-against."

Petrie was enjoying this tremendously. He was able to mock me and Martina and at the same time perform a little satire of himself and his profession.

"First," he said to Martina, "to save time and oratory, we shall have to agree to several stipulations. Agreed? Right. Your honoress is aware of many links in the long chain of events which ultimately deposited this ugly skull on your ugly credenza. Yes?"

"Skip the theatrics," she said. "Get on with it."

"Stipulation: You do not dispute the fact that I, Thomas Petrie, esquire, represented one Peter Falconer on several matters, including two rape charges, but more importantly, on the matter of his vast inheritance. And that I hired this fellow"—a careless wave of his hand—"to locate said Peter Falconer down in the Keys, where he was living a dissolute life, so that Peter might be apprised that his inheritance had passed through probate and was proceeding without dispute or hindrance. That, in fact, on his thirtieth birthday, days away, he would become filthy rich."

Martina assumed a formidable defensive posture, crossing her legs and arms and lowering her chin.

I said, "Can the defendant speak?"

"No. The defendant stands mute at present."

"Tom," Martina said. "This show is not half as amusing as you think. Will you get to the point? I want you both out of here in ten minutes."

Petrie's cell phone began chirruping. He removed it from his pocket, briefly opened the circuit, closed it, and slipped the phone back into his pocket.

"Stipulation: Falconer, his prep school roommate, Charles Sinclair, a Jamaican thug named Bully (both men associates of Raven Ahriman), two runaway teenaged girls, and a professional cameraman had been making a weird movie in a remote area of the Keys. Picture heat, isolation, drugs and alcohol, anarchistic sex. Things flew out of control."

"I know all this," Martina said.

"Sure you do. We're stipulating."

"Let's stipulate that we're not going to stipulate anymore."

Petrie approached me. He was the friendly defense attorney; I was his sympathetic witness.

"What do you remember about the night of September tenth, last year?"

I said, "It was stormy. A grade one hurricane—Lorraine—was in the Gulf, passing to the west. It was a nasty night, high surf, wind, rain."

"Did you receive a telephone call that night?"

"Yes."

"From whom?"

"You."

"What did I tell you?"

"You said that Raven Ahriman was in town looking for revenge, and that he had beaten Leroy Karpe nearly to death, and that he surely was coming after us, you and me. You thought he might come here, to the lighthouse, despite the storm."

"And what did you do?"

"Nothing. Martina and I went to bed."

"Did you tell Martina about Raven?"

"No. I didn't want her to worry."

"And in the morning?"

"I got up early. I let the dog out. I got a speargun and went outside to look around the reef."

"The speargun was your only weapon?"

"I had a knife, too."

"And what did you find out on the reef?"

"Raven was there."

"Was he armed?"

"He had a handgun."

"Wait," Martina said. "Wait, please. I don't want to hear the details. No blood, no agony, no dying. Please."

"We'll stipulate that Daniel killed Raven."

"In self-defense," I said. "And in defense of Martina."

Martina leaned forward and covered her eyes with a palm.

"And then?" Petrie asked.

"I took the body a couple miles out to sea and dumped it over the side."

"Why not call the cops?"

"I decided it was better for all of us to get rid of the corpse. It might have been the wrong decision."

"You weighted the body and sank it in one hundred feet of water. In that case, what are the skull and bones doing here?"

"Charles returned to Bell Harbor this spring. He thought he could blackmail us. He hired the Mackey brothers, and they found the remains."

"Still, how did the bones get here in this room?"

"We—you and I, Tom—located Charles at the Motel Sans Souci. He had the bones. We took them. You put them in my office safe. I didn't know what to do with them, so I took them here and wedged them into a crevice in the reef. It was intended to be just a temporary disposal."

"We may speculate here. Today, Martina, while diving for dinner, found the duffel."

"Evidently."

He turned to Martina. "Do you have any questions for the defendant?"

"You bastard," she said to me.

"That isn't a question," Petrie said.

"Why didn't you tell me all this?"

"The time never seemed right."

"You killed a man here, and you never found the right time to tell me?"

"I killed him in self-defense, and in defense of you."

"And you couldn't tell me?"

"I tried."

"Go away, both of you."

Petrie's cell phone was beeping again.

"I understand," she said, "that while you *might* have been forced to kill this man, you weren't forced to deceive and conceal. You killed him here, as I slept. I remember the day. We had breakfast a few minutes after you killed this man and buried his body at sea. And you never found the right time to tell me?"

Petrie irritably snatched the cell phone from his pocket, opened it, and extended the aerial. "What?" he said. He said, "This is a bad time." "When?" he said. "Shit." He looked at Martina. "Yes, Levi," he said.

"I'm sorry," I said to Martina. "You're right, of course. I should have told you immediately."

"Who?" Petrie said. "Keep them on it. No. No, for Christ's sake, don't call the sheriff or the SA. They'll find out soon enough."

"This is my home," Martina said. "This is where I can be me. And you killed a man while I was sleeping, and buried his body at sea while I was sleeping, and you didn't think I deserved to know?"

"Have they talked to the ticket agents?" Petrie asked. "Judge, listen, I don't care about your damned ethical considerations at the moment. No. That's right. Give me some time. Listen . . ."

"I'm guessing," I said to Martina, "that Tom is talking to the judge about Phil."

"All right," Petrie said. "Yeah. Just keep the lid on for a while. Levi? Levi, I'll be there in forty-five minutes."

He inserted the aerial, closed the phone, and returned it to his pocket. "Phil scooted," he said. "The judge went down to see him and found all of the lights on and Phil gone. The monkey was wearing the electronic monitoring device around its neck."

"Oh, Lord," Martina said wearily.

"Levi called in Mutt and Jeff. They found his car in a Miami airport parking lot. They're talking to ticket agents now, but they don't know yet where he's gone."

"He's gone to Italy," I said. "Castelnuovo."

Petrie cocked his head. "You think?"

"He knows a lot of what we've been doing, where we've been."

"I don't know."

"Foreign country, empty house, Arbaleste there. Maybe he wants to get even with Arbaleste. It's a place to run to, anyway."

"Long shot."

"Will you two please go away now?" Martina said. "Please."

"It was a terrific dinner, Martina," Petrie said. "Thanks so much." He turned to me. "Chop-chop. Row me ashore. My client just buzzed, and I've got to go to work."

His phone rang again. "Yes, Levi," Petrie said. "No kidding. All right. Keep them on it."

Martina got up and went to the door. Cerberus joined her there and leaned against her leg.

"Uncle Phil," Petrie said, "flew Alitalia to Rome this afternoon."

"I'll go," I said. "There's nothing keeping me around here."

Martina turned her face away when I tried to kiss her. She was miserable: her lover revealed to be a killer and sneak, her home defiled by violence, her dear uncle a killer and fugitive. Martina was not a fragile woman, but as I paused at the door I saw that she was trembling, and there was a dark something in her eyes that I had never seen before. She refused my offer to stay, refused comfort.

THIRTY-SEVEN

I hired a taxi at the Naples airport for the drive down to Castelnuovo. It was dark when we arrived at the house. I paid the driver, climbed over the locked back gate, and entered the yard. The swimming pool had recently been drained and cleaned, and now was slowly refilling. It was quiet except for the sound of flowing water and the faint music coming from Arbaleste's house. Lights glowed in some of the windows there, but our villa was dark. A small window leading into a pantry had been broken. I still had my keys.

I waited for my eyes to adjust to the darkness, then went in through the back door and down the hall to the big room. Enough moonlight came in through the front wall of glass to illuminate the central area and reveal the form sprawled out on a settee. He was snoring. There were a couple of glasses on the coffee table, a bucket of ice water, a half-full bottle of brandy, and a platter containing scraps of prosciutto, olives, and half a loaf of stale bread.

I switched on a table lamp. The light did not affect his sleep. His exhalations stank of brandy.

"Phil," I said. "Phil?"

He was sleeping in his clothes. His feet were bare—white, blue-veined feet that reminded me of Alice's feet poking out from beneath the tarp. He had dyed his sparse hair black and hadn't shaved for a few days. He had the labored, arrhythmic breathing of a passed-out drunk.

I slid open the glass door to let in some fresh air. Light spilled out onto the terrace of the villa next door, but the music had ceased. I went back inside.

"Phil," I said loudly. He stirred, gasped and choked for a moment, and then rolled over onto his side.

There was not much of a sea breeze tonight, just enough to cool the room a little and carry the muted thud and hiss of a hard surf rolling up on the beach below.

The mix of genuine and forged drawings and paintings was still hanging on the wall, surrounding the blank area where the Degas had been. I was surprised that Charles hadn't removed them. The Derain oil and the Daumier cartoon were valuable.

"Phil! Goddamn it, man, wake up!"

His puffy eyelids lifted and he stared blankly at me. Then, with an effort disproportionate to the simple task, he managed to sit up.

His voice was husky. "I dreamed someone was watching me."

"Someone was watching you. And a whole bunch of other people are looking for you."

He reached for the brandy bottle, but I beat him to it. "I need that," he said.

"How drunk are you?" I asked.

"Drunk. But not so bad now. I've been sleeping

for"—he glanced at his watch—"for about six hours. Jesus, I'm dying of thirst."

"I'll get you a Coke."

"A beer. Make it a beer."

I got two bottles of beer from the bar cooler. Phil drank half of his in a single draught.

"I fucked up again, didn't I?" he said.

"Oh, yes, you surely did."

"Will they take my house?"

"Your house is security for the bail bond. But maybe they'll let you keep it if you go back quick and on your own."

"I thought I could be a fugitive. But I can't, I'm too slow, too old, too dumb. God. I'm in hell. This is hell."

"Yeah, well . . ."

He finished his beer. "I want another one."

"After you clean up. You look and smell like a wino."

"Now I got a nanny who tells me what to do."

"Wino spelled w-h-i-n-o. Go take a shower and shave. Try to wash the dye out of your hair. Put on some clean clothes. Obey your nanny."

"Help me," he said. His face creased, seemed to compress, and I thought he was going to cry, but then the grimace turned into a sad, crooked grin, and he got up and walked toward the rear of the house.

I went outside. It had been a hot summer, there was a buildup of plankton, and the sea flashed here and there with bioluminescence. The surf, far below, looked like boiling green fire as it rolled in toward the beach. I looked in the direction Cassy had pointed on the night of the party, but I didn't find Cassiopeia or Camellopardalis or Cepheus—mythic names for unimaginable constellations.

Phil had cleaned up, shaved, washed most of the dye out of his sparse fringe of hair, and changed into slacks and a white shirt. He looked better, but the alcohol had done its damage; at his age, he might need weeks to recover from the binge. We sat together at the bar. He had another bottle of beer, though this one he sipped, pacing himself.

"No trouble at the airports, getting through security and passport control?"

"No trouble."

"I don't suppose you have a return ticket."

"But I do. From Rome to Atlanta to Miami. I figured buying a one-way ticket might make them suspicious."

"Going back will be tougher. You're probably in the computers now. We'll try it tomorrow."

"Whatever you say, Nanny."

"Has anyone next door seen you?"

"No, but I've seen him doing a fucking handstand on the terrace wall. A naked Tarzan."

"When?"

"This morning, early." He sipped his beer, ran a forefinger through the wet rings on the bar, then said, "A girl was here. A woman."

"When?"

"This morning. A couple hours after I saw Tarzan."

"What did she look like?"

"Pretty, nice smile, dark red hair. I got the feeling she knew who I was."

"She does know. She's a reporter, and was in Bell Harbor during the publicity about Alice. She saw your photos in the newspapers. Did she ask a lot of questions?"

"No."

"How long did she stay?"

"She went upstairs, came down with a little portable typewriter, and we had a drink. She's nice. I liked her."

"Did she say where she was going?"

"No. She said good-bye, good luck, and walked out the back door."

"All right. Do you think you can sleep now?"

"At ten thirty?"

"Can you? We want to get an early start in the morning."

"I can sleep if I have a few real drinks."

"Come on, Phil!"

"Two drinks now, and then a drink now and then tomorrow, to keep me from shaking to pieces and climbing the walls."

"I didn't know you had this problem."

"I've binged three times in my life. Four, now. A problem, maybe, but rare."

"Where have you been sleeping?"

"Here. I don't like being closed up in strange rooms."

"Will you keep it to two drinks?"

"I promise, Nanny."

I went up the three flights of stairs and down the attic hallway to Samantha's room. She had left a few things behind: a stained blouse, a pair of canvas espadrilles, a nearly empty bottle of suntan lotion. I found a little trash can full of shredded paper; notes, maybe, for her story.

I walked back down the hall to my garret. It was

even more cramped and stuffy than I recalled. I cranked open all of the windows, undressed to my shorts, and lay down on the narrow bed. Muscles in my legs twitched. It felt as though all the nerves were burning. General fatigue compounded by jet lag compounded by a low-grade fever.

THIRTY-EIGHT

I was awakened two hours later by music, played louder than earlier this evening, and voices. A man's voice, a woman's laughter. Arbaleste and Samantha. I went to the corner window. They were not in the triangle of terrace visible from my room. The music was a lush orchestral production with a hint of jazz, the sort of thing familiar from Hollywood musicals of the thirties and forties. Then Arbaleste and Samantha whirled into view. They danced well together. They glided, turning, to the end of the terrace, then along the front wall, and then they vanished. Sam was wearing the rose red dress and red pumps she had bought for the party, and her hair was up. Arbaleste was in his tux. Again they swooped into view. Samantha's pleated skirt ballooned, whirled. She laughed. They stared into each other's eyes. There was a hint of parody in their movements. Fred and Ginger. Fred and Cyd. Anton and Samantha. It surprised me that Samantha danced so well, particularly in that old ballroom style; I had always thought of her as a clumsy girl. They danced around the terrace and again passed out of sight. The music soon ceased, and they didn't reappear, though I heard their voices.

I quickly showered, dressed, and went down the stairs and through the glass doors. Arbaleste and Samantha sat at a table at the far end of the terrace. There was a white tablecloth, candles burning in a silver candelabrum, and two ice buckets mounted on metal tripods. An old phonograph was on a smaller table nearby. All of the other deck furniture had been removed to allow room for dancing. At first they didn't recognize me; I was in semidarkness and they sat in a bright spray of light. Then they both got up and walked to the end of the terrace.

"Dan, you're back," Samantha said.

I had never seen her happier or more beautiful; she was in love.

"I'm pleased to see you, Shaw," Arbaleste said. And he did sound pleased; and his smile looked genuine, not the usual polite reflex. "Come over, join us."

"No, thanks," I said.

"Please do."

"Yes, Dan, you must. Anton has some fabulous champagne."

"I'm not dressed for your elegant little party." I was wearing slacks, a polo shirt, and jogging shoes without socks.

"Nonsense," Arbaleste said. "We must talk, Shaw. I have to congratulate you on your coup. I really do insist that you come over and have a glass of wine."

"Yes, please," Samantha said. "Everything is all right now, honestly."

I crossed over to the other terrace. Samantha kissed my cheek; Arbaleste firmly shook my hand, and the three of us walked to the table. There was a spare chair, but no third champagne glass, and so Arbaleste went inside to get one.

"I didn't know you could dance like that, Sam."

"Did you ever ask me out dancing?"

"Well, you're both very good."

"Anton is good, I'm mostly faking."

She was still wearing the diamond ring on the third finger of her left hand.

I said, "Did you ever tell him that we weren't actually engaged?"

"It hasn't come up. I didn't think to mention it. I don't see that it matters now, do you?"

"Have you slept with him?"

Her gaze was defiant. "Yes. Last night, this morning, two hours ago. He's a wonderful lover."

I smiled. "He's probably taken lessons."

"Don't be mean," she said. "Don't spoil my night."

"I'm sorry. How did you two get together?"

"I was bold. I knocked on his door, that's how."

"How much did you tell him, Sam?"

"I didn't say much. He had already figured things out."

Arbaleste appeared with a crystal flute glass and another bottle of the "fabulous" Moët et Chandon wine. He removed a half empty bottle from one of the ice buckets and placed it on the table, then inserted the new bottle into the ice. He sat down.

"Do you dance, Shaw?"

"Not in that flamboyant ballroom style," I said. "I just shuffle."

He poured wine into the three glasses, lifted his, waited for us, then said, "*À votre santé!*"

"And to your health as well," I said.

We drank, and Arbaleste emptied the bottle into our glasses.

"And how are your comrades?" he asked. "Judge Samuelson, Thomas Petrie, and the fairy—Charles."

"All of us are considerably more prosperous than a week ago."

"As I am correspondingly less prosperous. You know, it isn't as though all of you were smart; I was blind."

"It's a good forgery."

"A magnificent forgery. I still can't believe it isn't a genuine Degas. I look at it for hours. The painting, the provenance—but I should have investigated it further."

"Oh, let's not talk about this," Samantha said. "Not tonight."

"And to think I was so gullible as to deposit eleven and one-half million dollars in your account."

"Anton, please."

"Let us dance," Arbaleste said, smiling at her. He lifted a 78 record from the stack, removed the jacket, and gently placed it on the turntable. Samantha stood up. Arbaleste made a small bow, took her right hand in his left, and placed his right hand on her waist. They paused a moment to determine the tempo, and then moved away. The music had a strong Latin beat. Samantha was slinky, Arbaleste was suave. I looked through the stack of 78 records: They were all from the big band era—Benny Goodman, Stan Kenton, Xavier Cugat, the Tommy and Jimmy Dorsey bands, Harry

James. I watched them dance around and around the terrace. Again, I sensed that though they enjoyed the dancing, they were engaged in a little parody, too. And again, Sam surprised me with her grace. There were a couple of lifts and, at the end, an elaborate dip. They returned to the table flushed and smiling.

Arbaleste removed a champagne bottle from the ice, pulled the cork, and filled our glasses.

"I've simply got to pee," Samantha said. She went into the house.

Arbaleste said, "I suppose we should discuss . . ."

"No need," I said. "Turnabout is fair play."

"Good. She's a lovely girl. Very American."

"She is, and you're an American citizen, aren't you?"

He smiled. "I expected that you had conducted an investigation."

"We didn't learn an awful lot. The Hudson Valley years, your time as an art student, the episode in Poland."

"Poland," he said, and he laughed. "I carved the face of the Virgin in the tree."

"We assumed that. Anyway, since we're all Americans here, you can omit the accent."

"But the accent isn't a pretension. I spoke languages other than English when I grew up. The accent is genuine."

"Then it's probably the only thing about you that is."

He laughed. I had never heard him laugh before tonight, or seen him grin; he had only smiled, calibrated smiles that he awarded or denied on a system of his own.

"You won't succeed in making me angry," he said.

"Then I'll stop trying."

"It might prove to have been a salutary experience, to be swindled as I've swindled others. I won't say I like it. But it makes me pause—perhaps it's time to consider quitting. I seem to have lost my touch."

I drank some of the wine. I didn't doubt that it was an excellent champagne, though it seemed a bit dry and sharp to my uncultivated taste.

"Tell me," he said, "who is the genius who forged the Degas?"

"You know I can't tell you that."

"I'm not interested in revenge. I'm interested in hiring the man."

"I thought you intended to quit?"

"One can always find employment for a forger as good as yours."

Samantha returned to the terrace, and Arbaleste quickly rose, smiled, and pulled out her chair.

"I had four eyes in the mirror," Sam said. "Too much wine?"

"Insufficient wine."

"I forgot," Sam said to me. "I saw Charles in town today. Is he with you?"

"You saw Charles?"

"I'm sure I did. He was going into a hotel."

"Charles," Arbaleste said, "begged me to sleep with him. He said he was desperately in love with me."

Sam laughed. "No!"

"Yes."

"What did you say?"

"I said that even if I were inclined toward

pederasty—which I'm not—I would not be attracted to him."

"And what did he say?"

"He wept."

"No!"

He held up his right hand with three fingers lifted. "On my honor." He noticed me looking at his salute, smiled, and said, "I was a Boy Scout when we lived in America."

"I'll bet you made a fine Boy Scout," Samantha said.

Her pinned-up hair was coming loose, her makeup was a bit smeared, and she seemed to be having difficulty in focusing her eyes. I felt very fond of her, and protective. She was two glasses of wine away from becoming obnoxious.

"I almost became an Eagle Scout," Arbaleste said. "I had nearly enough badges."

"But . . . ?"

"But my family returned to Europe."

"You would have made a superior Eagle Scout," Samantha said.

Arbaleste, normally a tense, guarded man, was relaxed tonight. He was cheerful. He was talkative. His face was not frozen, expressionless. His voice had more inflections and a gentler tone. He revealed some of the charm that others talked about but which I had seldom witnessed.

Samantha was—I tried to think of the right word—Sam was besotted by him, giddy with love and admiration. Her cheeks were flushed, her eyes shone. She was radiant from the wine and dancing and love.

I asked her if she had a cigarette; she didn't, but

Arbaleste removed a gold case from his inside jacket pocket, opened the lid, and offered it to me. I took one, and leaned forward to accept a light from his gold lighter. The tobacco was strong and faintly perfumed.

"I thought you didn't smoke," I said.

"I don't, but others do. Tell me: the man staying in your villa—he was one of the Florida investors?"

Sam would not meet my glance.

"I remember him. Karras. Has he come to Italy for revenge?

"No."

"I was concerned. Revenge is always a factor in my business. Pity about his wife. Is he a fugitive?"

"Until I can get him back to Florida."

Sam said, "I'm getting drunk, Anton. If we're going to dance again, it had better be soon."

"Now, then. The Tommy Dorsey orchestra?" He shuffled through the albums, found the record he wanted, and placed it on the turntable.

I asked, "How did you learn so soon that the Degas is a forgery?"

"Our friend Charles was kind enough to phone me from Rome and inform me."

"Did he gloat?"

"Oh, yes."

He switched on the old phonograph; the needle arm moved, lowered to the first grooves, and we heard the mellow strains of "Dancing in the Dark."

He took Samantha in his arms and they began to dance. It was a slow, romantic number, the reed instruments dominating, and after the introduction the vocalist—Frank Sinatra—commenced singing the lyrics.

His voice sounded thin; he had been a kid when the piece was recorded. It did not appear that Sam's dancing had been affected by alcohol. Perfectly synchronized, they slowly turned and glided around the terrace. When the number ended they returned to the table and remained standing while he selected another record, this one performed by the Duke Ellington orchestra.

"I really am glad you're here, Shaw," Arbaleste said.

"Me, too," Sam said.

They resumed dancing to a jazzy up-tempo version of "Poor Butterfly." Their steps were quick and intricate. One might assume they were professionals, until Sam made a false step and stumbled. They paused while she removed her pumps and tossed them aside. There was not a vocalist, but some of the words ran through my mind as they danced. They passed close by the table and whirled away. Arbaleste lifted her in the sort of move you saw in ballroom dancing and pair ice skating. Not much strength was required for the lift, her momentum helped, but you had to be strong to lower your partner gracefully and in step. They danced past the table again and along the front of the house and then out into the open terrace. Sam's skin flared. She smiled adoringly up at her lover. Another lift, ordinary at first, but something changed midway and Samantha was suddenly sprawled horizontally in the space beyond the terrace wall. For an instant she was frozen in time and space. There was a microsecond's pause while gravity changed her horizontal motion to the vertical. Her red dress, her red hair and tanned skin, illuminated by the terrace lights, stood out three-dimensionally against the blue-black sky. She was suspended in air, arms spread wide, and then she was filling, gone.

Arbaleste, at the far end of the terrace, smiled at me and held out his empty palms. See? No Samantha.

I was never able to recall Sam's expression, even though her face had been turned toward the terrace, toward Arbaleste, during that instant of suspension.

Arbaleste, smiling, waited for me.

She did not scream. Or, if she screamed, the sound was absorbed by the pounding of the surf and the music. Absorbed, or erased from memory by the shock.

Arbaleste walked a few paces, leaned down to pick up Sam's shoes, and casually tossed them over the wall.

Much later I recalled or imagined a scream, one that altered in pitch and volume as she fell. No doubt it was imagined.

Arbaleste appeared quietly delighted by his action, as if it were no more than a clever, harmless practical joke, and he expected me to share his mirth.

His right hand had been placed on her left hip. They were halfway through a turn. He had used her impetus, lifted her and pushed hard, straightened his arm in a sort of shotput motion, throwing her over the wall and into space.

Arbaleste waited for me. Not much time had passed, surely less than ten seconds, while I tried to comprehend, catch up with events.

It was like a flashlighted mental photograph, Sam suspended prone against the star-sprayed sky, arms flung out, red dress, red hair, bare feet, red lipsticked mouth, wide eyes, splayed fingers . . . I see her that way in my dreams. Then she was gone, falling eight hundred feet through the darkness to the rocky beach below. She must have screamed.

Arbaleste confidently waited. He looked slender in his tuxedo, but I knew how strong he was, and how fast.

"You didn't even mention her name," he said.

Samantha? No, of course he meant Antonia.

After a moment's silence, the phonograph had automatically begun replaying Ellington's upbeat version of "Poor Butterfly."

I picked up one of the ice buckets and pitched the melt water and ice shards over the terrace floor. I did the same with the other bucket. There were only a few dry patches on the marble now. Arbaleste was wearing dress shoes with leather soles and heels. My jogging shoes would provide better traction on a wet, ice-strewn marble surface.

Arbaleste waited patiently. He looked quizzical rather than worried. His confidence was not diminished, but he now realized that he actually knew very little about me—I might be more than a lazy, womanizing personal secretary.

I smashed a champagne bottle against the wall. It broke off short, but with a few jagged spikes of glass at the business end. I then picked up another bottle, poured out the contents, and began advancing. The broken bottle was in my left hand, the intact bottle in my right. I paused when we were about fifteen feet apart. He slipped his right hand into his jacket pocket. Whatever was in his pocket reinforced his confidence. The slippery marble deck didn't worry him. The two bottles didn't worry him. My size advantage didn't worry him. Arbaleste enjoyed danger. For him, a deadly fight was at least as sporting as risky handstands or diving sixty feet off a stone arch.

I took a couple more steps forward. He appeared casual, amused, but obviously he had been seized by a cold, an insane, rage. How else could he have slept with Samantha this afternoon, and tonight danced with her, made her happy, and then thrown her like a sack of trash over the cliff? He had tricked her, tricked me, and I felt an anger equal to his own. But I knew that I had to be cool, as he was cool; my rage had to be restrained.

"I really am so glad that you arrived here tonight," he said. "What luck. It wouldn't have been the same without you."

I moved forward a few more steps. He removed a stiletto from his jacket pocket, and the five-inch double-edged blade flashed open with a click. He backed into the protective V of the terrace's outside corner. I would have to go straight at him. Music still played.

"The poor butterfly," Arbaleste said.

I stepped forward a pace, then halted about five feet away from him. He held the knife at waist level, the blade angled slightly upward. No slashing; he was prepared, with short strokes, to drive the knife up into my groin, belly, or chest. He moved the blade from side to side. They teach you, in knife fighting, to keep the blade moving. You can quickly convert the lateral movement to forward thrusts.

"Samantha was a dizzy slut," Arbaleste said, "but sweet in a way. I liked her."

I moved a little closer but remained—I thought—outside striking range; but he took a quick forward step and thrust out the knife. I jumped back. It had been close. I had watched Tom Petrie work out with the foil, and Arbaleste's quick, bent-kneed step and thrust was a fencer's move. He had uncoiled with startling swiftness, recoiled.

I shifted to my left, next to the wall. He half turned to face me. Now he had less room in which to maneuver the knife; his right hand and arm were somewhat restricted by the wall. My changed angle revealed movement, a shadow. Phil had come out onto the next-door terrace.

Arbaleste started to slip sideways along the back wall, but I cut him off, backed him into the corner. He was sweating. We both were sweating. Sweat had soaked through my shirt and burned my eyes.

The knife flashed out as quickly as the strike of a snake. I retreated.

Christ, Phil, I thought, are you just going to stand there and watch me die?

I felt a warmth on my lower abdomen. No pain, just a spreading warmth. Arbaleste was encouraged by the blood. He eased away from the wall. I backed up.

I held the broken bottle in my left hand at about shoulder height, ready to jab his face with it; the other bottle I held cocked like a club. But this stance exposed my chest and belly. I backed away. I had learned how fast he was. Not just fast, but economically so, without hesitancy or waste motion, quick as a cobra. I retreated. I was close to the table now. I thought I might be able to dash through the open doors into the house and then . . . then what?

"Cut it out," Phil called. ("Cut it out," words and a tone that you might use to warn roughhousing boys.)

Arbaleste was disciplined. He was distracted for only an instant, swiftly recovered, but his timing was a fraction off, and then, as he lunged, his front foot slipped on the wet marble. He did not go down. He recovered quickly. I swung the bottle. The blow struck his forehead at the hairline, and he dropped the knife and staggered away to the open terrace. I hit him again with the bottle. He half turned, his knees buckled, and he fell hard to his knees and then pitched facedown on the marble.

"Jesus," Phil said as he came onto the terrace. "Jesus, he stabbed you."

I removed my shirt. It was a small cut, less than an inch wide, but I couldn't tell how deep. The point might have been stopped by a rib. There was a lot of blood but not much pain, just a burning sensation. I probed the wound with a fingertip, thought I felt a rib.

Phil was at my side now. "He stuck you," he said.

Arbaleste moved. He squirmed for a moment without coordination, like a half-crushed bug, and then managed to drag himself to a sitting position. There was a big lump on his forehead, and blood in his hair where I had hit him the second time.

Phil picked up the stiletto and studied it as if it were a rare artifact. He was drunk. There was blood only at the point.

Arbaleste was trying to rise to his feet. His legs weren't quite able to function.

The phonograph now started to replay "Poor Butterfly." Phil switched it off.

Arbaleste buried his face in his palms. "*J'ai mal à la tête.*"

"What did he say?" Phil asked.

"He's got a headache."

"*Aimeriez-vous aller danser?*"

"What's that?"

"He's asking someone if she wants to go dancing."

"His brains are scrambled."

I grabbed Arbaleste at his armpits and hauled him erect. He sagged, stumbled, but managed to bear most of his weight. I walked him over to the wall.

"Dan?" Phil said.

I pressed Arbaleste's upper body flat on the top of the wall. His head was beyond the rim, and he stared down into the black abyss. He struggled weakly. I waited until much of his strength was restored, waited a bit longer for him to become lucid enough to understand exactly what was going to happen. He began to fight desperately. He was a strong man, and I couldn't prolong the torture any further.

"My God!" Phil said. "Don't!"

My left hand tightly gripped his neck; I lowered my right hand to his crotch, lifted first, then pushed, and Arbaleste screamed all the way down the beach, to Samantha.

Phil and I stood together on the empty terrace. It did not seem finished; surely there was more, a continuance or complete comprehension. Phil, more than a little drunk, looked at me. What now? I felt swathed in a physical and emotional isolation. This strange, sleepwalker's state lasted for a few minutes, and then we crossed over to the other house.

"Pack your stuff, Phil," I said. "Don't forget your passport."

He went to the bar, poured some whiskey in a glass, returned, and gave me the glass.

"How's that cut?"

"I don't think it penetrated my abdomen. We'll know soon if it did."

"We've got to make a compress, tape it up." He crossed the big room and turned down the hallway.

I telephoned Petrie at his house. It was about six o'clock there. He answered on the third ring.

"Things have gone to hell," I said.

His voice was sleep-thickened. "Tell me."

"Phil's here."

"All right."

"We're going to run."

"Is that a good idea?"

"Arbaleste and Samantha are dead."

"I see."

"He threw her over the cliff."

"And you . . . ?"

"Yes. And so we need your help."

"Go on."

"If it works, if we're lucky, we'll be in Tunis in two or three days."

"Tunis. All right."

"I'll be out of touch. We'll either arrive in Tunis in a few days or we'll be in custody somewhere."

"Are you okay?"

"I think so. I've lost a little blood. Mostly I just feel very, very tired."

"That's normal after the adrenaline is used up. What's the political situation in Tunisia?"

"I have no idea."

"Well, if I can get a visa, if I can make the connections, I'll be there when you arrive or soon after."

"Thanks, Tom."

Phil, carrying a roll of tape, some gauze pads, and a pair of scissors, returned to the room.

"You want to talk to Phil?" I asked Petrie.

"No, I don't want to talk to that son of a bitch."

"All right."

"Luck, pal," he said, and he hung up the telephone.

I sipped the whiskey. My mind was starting to clear. "Phil," I said, "find some rags or towels, go next door, and mop up the blood. And I left my shirt there. Bring it back."

"First I'll patch up the cut."

"No, I'll do it. Leave that stuff. Just go and do what I said."

"I make a special point of obeying killers," he said, and he went through the glass doors and outside.

THIRTY-NINE

We had no difficulty stealing Arbaleste's yacht. Few marinas are well secured. It's easier to steal a boat than a car. There were no locked gates at Castelnuovo's marina, no night watchman, and I knew from our sail to the island that *Avanti* was not rigged with an alarm system. I also knew that the keys to the hatch padlocks and ignition were concealed in the cockpit drain. That made it even easier; we wouldn't have to break anything or jump the ignition.

You stroll out on the pier, a couple of yachtsmen getting an early start, go directly to the right berth, and board the boat. You are quiet, out of courtesy to people who might be sleeping on neighboring boats, but not stealthy. You start the engine, cast off the lines, and motor out of the harbor. When you are well offshore, you kill the engine, then set and raise the sails—three sails on *Avanti*, mainsail, staysail, and jib. Phil was a powerboat man, but he had done some sailing, enough to help out on deck.

It was two o'clock when we stole Arbaleste's yacht, a time when there is rarely activity at the yacht section of a marina, though the nearby commercial docks were busy with boats being prepared for the run out to the fishing grounds. Now, three miles offshore, the sea around us was dotted with red and green running lights, and bright masthead floods as the crews readied the nets.

The wind was blowing from the north-northwest at ten or twelve knots. Crisp breeze, moderate swells, a sky flecked with fish-scale clouds, cirrocumulus that could be the forerunners of a storm. We might encounter heavy weather tomorrow or the day after, but it wasn't a big concern. Properly handled, *Avanti* could ride out all but the most violent gales.

I looked back toward Castelnuovo and, scanning along the coast, saw the brightly lighted Arbaleste villa poised above the dark void. The broken bodies of Arbaleste and Samantha lay at the base of the cliff. Or maybe the surf had extended far enough to float them, drag them down the sloping beach and out to sea. I hoped so, but I knew that in time the sea often surrenders the bodies it has seized.

Karras made his way back along the tilted deck, looked down at me for a time, then sat across from me in the cockpit. I could just make out his features in the dim green compass light. He had rarely spoken since seeing me kill Arbaleste. He had obeyed my commands, followed me, accepted my actions without demanding explanations, and now he needed to talk.

"You didn't have to," he said.

Didn't have to kill Arbaleste.

"The man was finished, out. You didn't have to."

Didn't have to coldly murder Anton Arbaleste.

"Look, I know . . ."

I know I killed my wife, but that was different.

"You waited, Dan. You waited until he was fully conscious. You forced him to look down. You made him know. And then you did it. It was . . .

It was the coldest and hardest thing I've ever seen. It was murder.

"I know, by God, I know . . ."

Know that I killed my wife, but what you have done is so much worse . . .

There are categories: first-degree murder, second-degree, parricide, infanticide, serial murder, terror murder, political assassination, voluntary and involuntary manslaughter, justifiable homicide, vehicular homicide, state-sanctioned executions, mercy killing and killing in self-defense, and more, and every variety has been assigned a place in the meticulously graded moral and legal scale—the pedantry of violent death.

"Remember Samantha, Phil? The redhead you met at the house? He threw her over the wall."

I could not read his expression in the compass glow.

"They danced. He made her happy. And while they were dancing, he threw her over the cliff."

"Why?"

There was no single true explanation, no rational motive. I could tell Phil about the lovely Antonia, her fall on the island, and Arbaleste's conviction that I had been responsible for her death. He wanted revenge. And then Samantha turned up at his door. What better revenge than to kill Samantha—known to him as my fiancée—by throwing her over the cliff? Another fall, a long,

long fall. An eye for an eye, a woman for a woman. But that didn't fully explain it. That was the sort of thing you told juries, who demanded logic, or rather, who demanded the appearance of logic. Juries were motive-obsessed. But why men kill is far more complicated: why Phil had killed his wife, why Arbaleste had killed Samantha, why I had killed Arbaleste, while so many in identical or similar circumstances refused to kill.

"Maybe you were right to kill the son of a bitch," Phil said, but he wasn't sure.

"I'm going below for a rest," I said. "Keep the same compass bearing."

We were free of most of the fishing boat traffic now. The light at the island where Antonia had died was flashing on the horizon. We sailed at about six knots, and the water around *Avanti* hissed and foamed a phosphorescent green, the same green as the compass light.

"Even so . . ." Phil said.

Even so, it was the way you did it.

He didn't call me. The wind remained steady out of the north-northwest. I awakened at dawn. Horizontal bars of light streamed in through the row of portholes above the opposite berth. Loose objects rattled in the lockers. I lay in the starboard berth (the same one that had held Antonia's body during our return from the island), and tried to convince myself that I had chosen the correct course of action.

Phil was a fugitive. He had been indicted for murder, jumped bail, and fled the United States. It was likely that by now he had been traced to Italy, to Castelnuovo. The bodies of Arbaleste and Samantha would soon be discovered by beach walkers. But even if the surf and tide had taken them out to sea, Arbaleste was missing and we were sailing Arbaleste's stolen yacht. We could not enter an Italian port. The Italian peninsula was behind and above us; Sicily lay to the south and Sardinia to the west. France was not an option, nor Spain.

I left the berth, moved to the chart table, and shuffled through the drawers until I found a large-scale chart of the Tyrrhenian and central Mediterranean seas. I had selected Tunis as our destination because we needed an out-of-the-way port in a country where the law was flexible and bribery an acceptable way of doing business. And a place outside the European network of laws and communication. I spread the chart out and drew a straight pencil line from our estimated present position to the city of Tunis. It was roughly a two-hundred-mile sail, two days, maybe three, and there was no land between us and the port. *Avanti* was equipped with GPS; I could press a button at any time and satellite triangulation would give our position within a few meters.

I climbed the companionway ladder to the canted deck. Phil, pale and puffy-eyed, suffering from a force-twelve hangover, looked exhausted.

"You should have called me," I said.

He relinquished the tiller and moved to the other side of the cockpit.

"I was thinking about killing myself," he said. "It would be easy. Just slip over the side."

"Wait until we sight land, Phil. I'll need your help until then."

His smile was tight. "I live to serve."

Within a couple of hours the wind shifted a few degrees toward the north and began to blow harder. *Avanti* shuddered, gear straining, in the occasional twenty-five-knot gusts. Dark cumulus clouds were massing on the horizon.

"It's going to blow," Phil said.

"I'll reef the main and take down the jib. And then you get some sleep."

"Do you have some vague notion of where you're going?"

"Tunisia."

"Which is where?"

"North Africa."

"We're sailing to Africa?"

"It isn't that far. Two days, two and a half."

I went forward, put a reef in the mainsail, and then lowered and furled the jib. The boat was less well balanced then, and we lost a knot or two off our speed. I didn't like the look of the sky. You didn't need to switch on the marine radio to learn that it was going to storm. I wasn't familiar with these waters, these weather patterns, but I did know that for five thousand years ships had been going down in the Mediterranean. I returned to the cockpit.

"Tunisia," Phil said. "Then what?"

"Then, with a little luck, and with Petrie seeding the fields with money, we'll fly to some other place, and fly again to the States."

"I always told Martina you were a fuckup," he said.

"Go below, Phil."

"Wake me when it's time to inflate the raft," he said, and he went down into the cabin.

Avanti now and then surfed down the faces of the seven-foot seas. By early afternoon the sky was completely covered by cumulonimbus clouds, dense and dark, vertically developed, and the sea was a poisonous jade green. The wind continued to increase, and again shifted a few points toward the north.

By four o'clock the wind had increased further and shifted a few more degrees, and the seas were eight feet high with foamy, tumbling crests. The height of the seas was not a concern, though the swells were closer together than I liked. The plunge from crest to trough to crest was short and abrupt. There was not the long "fetch" you find in open Atlantic or Pacific waters. Rain mixed with the salt spray. Lightning arced from cloud to sea, and thunder often obliterated the sounds of wind and waves.

Phil came up on deck. He lost his balance, nearly went over the side, but managed to save himself by grabbing a shroud. He slipped down into the cockpit.

"Sleep?" I asked him.

"A little."

"Seasick?"

"A little."

He took the tiller while I went forward to tie another reef in the mainsail.

The weather progressively worsened. Toward night the wind reached a steady gale force, and some of the big waves began to turn concave along the faces. A little more wind and they might start breaking. Lateral lines of foam extended over the sea. The rain was steeply angled, almost horizontal in the gusts. Clouds as thick and black as oil smoke seethed and spit lightning. I altered course to reduce strain on the sails and gear.

"It's bad," Phil said.

He was scared. Even potential suicides can be terrified when the exact time and means of death aren't of their choosing.

"We'd better heave to," I said.

"Should have done it two hours ago."

It was a tricky and dangerous maneuver to come about, turn *Avanti*'s bows into the wind. Phil took the tiller, and I carefully made my way forward over the wet, steeply angled deck. I backed the staysail, set it in opposition to the double-reefed main, then returned to the cockpit and tautened the main from there. The pitching and rolling moderated. Motion and way were reduced as the contrarily set sails stalled the boat, steadied it. There was no risk now of *Avanti* surfing down the face of a breaking wave and broaching. She would, I expected, ride the waves like a cork.

We went below into the cabin. I secured the hatches; Phil lit an oil lamp that rocked in gimbels. Neither of us could eat. We each drank a little water and climbed into the berths.

The storm did not become any worse during the night. I managed to catnap. Every hour or two I went up on deck, looked around, and then, rain-soaked, chilled, returned to the cabin. Phil was worried, but I had great confidence in *Avanti*—she would find her way among the heaving seas.

By noon the next day the winds had abated and the cloud cover was beginning to break up, though the metallic gray-green swells remained confused, rising and subsiding all around. We saw a freighter on the horizon in midafternoon, another near dusk. The sky was fully clear by midnight, speckled by stars and frosted by moonlight. We saw far-off ships' lights several times during the small hours.

The next morning was clear and bright, with a steady wind out of the northeast, and we sailed all day at about six knots and logged one hundred and forty miles in a twenty-four-hour period. The wind died at sunset, and we used the engine to motor toward the coast. In the morning we could smell Africa, smell it before we saw it, and then the coast emerged yellow-ochre out of the heat haze.

Tunis had a big port. There were many tankers and freighters anchored in the harbor, and more tied up along the quays. Smoke, warehouses, big cranes, a dredging barge, water fouled by fuel and industrial wastes and city sewage, a dry heat that seared the lungs and dried the eyes. We anchored a hundred yards offshore, within view of the customs shed. There was not a Tunisian flag in the lockers, but I found an Italian tricolor and the red quarantine flag, and ran them up the mainmast. Phil and I rigged an awning above the cockpit. We sat in the shade, sipping water and waiting for the customs and immigration people, but no one came.

In the late afternoon we saw a kid, fourteen or fifteen, rowing a battered skiff directly toward us. He was one of those grinning, mischievous third-world kids who, for a fee, showed you around, changed money, arranged sexual liaisons, served as interpreter, attended to your needs and desires. His skiff banged against *Avanti*'s hull. He squinted up at us, grinning. "Hallo," he said. "You come with me, okay? Yes?"

"Yes," I said.

We closed and padlocked the hatches, got into the skiff, and allowed the kid to row us ashore. He then led us through a maze of streets and across a stone-paved plaza to a plain, mud-colored hotel. But it was cool and clean inside, nicely furnished in an austere African style, and there was a bar. The brat led us past a staring desk clerk, down a hall, across a courtyard restaurant, and into the bar. Tom Petrie, a cigar clenched between his teeth, drink in hand, sat hunched on a bar stool.

He looked at Phil. "Jackass," he said.

He looked at me. "That pretty yacht now belongs to the Tunisian Minister of Customs and Immigration."

He dug in a pocket, removed a wad of brightly colored currency, and gave it to the boy. "Beat it, Abdul."

"Beat it yourself, Jack," the boy said, and he turned and half ran from the barroom.

"Nice kid," Tom said. "I wish I had a son like that. Okay, what will you drink, gentlemen?"

Phil ordered a brandy; I asked for a bottle of beer. There was no air-conditioning in the bar, but it was dim and big ceiling fans churned up a breeze.

"I'm the fixer," Tom said. "I'm the cleaner-upper. I'm the guy you call when you have been overwhelmed by your own stupidity. It's a thankless task."

"Thanks, Tom," I said.

"Don't mention it."

PART V
Foxes

FORTY

It was a hot, rainy August; a hot, dry September; and in October a high-pressure system moved down from the north and cooled the Florida peninsula all the way to the Keys. Each year we waited for what the weather people called a "Canadian air mass."

Martina refused to see me. We encountered each other on the streets of Bell Harbor, at a restaurant or theater, but she refused to *see* me. She severed our unofficial engagement in a long, lucid, and very reasonable letter. I could not argue with her premise, just when she had decided to forgive me for killing a man not fifty yards from where she slept, disposing of the body at sea, and not *telling* her—just then, she had learned that I had killed yet *another* man in Italy, thrown him over a cliff. Her uncle Phil obviously had told her about that night on the terrace. He had also told her that I had been sleeping with Samantha during the summer. Sam, it seems, had mentioned our affair to Phil during their brief encounter.

"You scoundrel," Petrie said to me. "Wait until I tell Marty about Antonia."

"I didn't have an affair with Antonia."

"Sure you did."

"No."

"She told everyone you two were having a passionate affair."

"No," I said. Then, "Tom, do you think I have some responsibility for Antonia's death?"

"No, but Arbaleste thought you did, and it's his opinion that caused all the grief."

Phil was confined in the county jail pending trial. He gained weight on the carbohydrate-heavy diet, lost more hair, had trouble with his prostate, and complained to whoever would listen. He began espousing very conservative political views. Bond had been revoked, of course. Petrie was fighting to save Phil's home; he argued that his client had voluntarily surrendered to the authorities. The prosecutor in the case, Nestor Naranjo, demanded that bond—Phil's house and property—be forfeited. The judge would decide.

*   *   *

I frequently spoke by telephone with Signorina Polozzi, the real estate agent; and Castelnuovo's senior policeman, Captain Enrico Conforte. Conforte had many questions for me. I answered them as well as I could, telling the truth when truth was harmless, lying the rest of the time.

Conforte was baffled and suspicious. He suspected foul play. When, Mr. Shaw, did you last see the missing persons? He was trying to induce the federal police to enter the investigation, but so for they had resisted. No bodies, no evidence of a crime. However, they pointed out, Arbaleste's yacht had left the marina the night of the supposed crime. Wasn't it logical that the missing persons, Anton Arbaleste and Samantha Ridley, had departed on a summer cruise? (But the house had been abruptly abandoned, doors open and lights burning; surely . . .) The federal police, Conforte said, were sarcastic. They had no respect for small-town policemen. Yachts sailed all over the Mediterranean during the summer, from Athens to Gibraltar, from Sicily to Nice— wasn't it most likely that Arbaleste and the woman were now at sea or safely docked in some port? Conforte had to concede that it was possible. Still, he was suspicious—not so much of me, but of the situation as a whole. I volunteered to come to Italy and assist in his inquiries. He thanked me and declined my offer, which I would not have fulfilled in any case.

I phoned Signorina Polozzi to notify her that, unfortunately, we would be unable to extend our stay in the villa to the end of the lease. Business affairs did not permit it. I asked her to take charge of closing the house, settling any wage claims with tradesmen and servants, and arrange for any necessary cleaning or repairs. Was a thousand dollars enough? She thought that, including her fee, two thousand would be sufficient. I wired her the money.

Polozzi was a fluent gossip. It was all a scandal as well as a mystery. Imagine, Signore Arbaleste had taken a new mistress so soon after Antonia di Benedetto was so tragically killed. (Some now wondered if it really had been an accident.) No period of mourning for the gentleman, no sign of grief. This bold, shameless

Samantha woman—you are well rid of her, Mr. Shaw—cohabiting with the gentleman before the poor di Benedetto girl was cold in her grave.

"When did Samantha move in with him?" I asked.

"Two days before they vanished."

Sam had gone to Rome with Charles, and soon after returned. She was in love with Arbaleste. She couldn't stay away.

I said, "Captain Conforte now believes that they went cruising in Arbaleste's yacht."

"Some do believe that."

"What do you believe?"

"I don't say that *I* believe it, but there are those who say they committed suicide together. They would not be the first to leap off that cliff."

"But why would they commit suicide?"

"Because they murdered poor Antonia di Benedetto so that they could be together, and then were overcome by guilt and the fear of God."

"I was one of the persons at the island that day. We all saw the accident."

"I am only telling you what some people think."

"Well, I suppose that it is possible that it was a double suicide off the cliff, and the tide took their bodies out to sea. But it seems more likely that they sailed away on Arbaleste's yacht."

She reluctantly conceded that they might indeed be sailing. Or sunk to the bottom of the sea.

"Signorina Polozzi, one more thing. There are some paintings and drawings in the villa. Will you see that they are safe until they can be collected?"

"There are no paintings and drawings."

"Are you sure?"

"That nice young man, Charles, took them away."

"When was that?"

"On the same day that Arbaleste and the Samantha woman were missed. Charles stopped at my office that morning. He lived in the villa you rented, he was a guest, and so I didn't protest when he said he was going to collect his artwork. I gave him the key."

"You did right. The things belonged to him."

I asked her to phone me if she needed any more money to put the villa in good order, and suggested that she phone me—collect—if she received any information about the Mystery.

Captain Conforte began to believe that the yacht had been lost at sea. There had been a storm soon after they left Castelnuovo. The bodies had not been found, or, if they were found, they hadn't been identified. I was told by the captain that it was not unusual for human remains to wash ashore all along that coast, from Naples to Salerno and beyond. Millions of tourists came during the summers. Many were unfamiliar with the dangers of the sea; they were stupid and careless, and a few were suicidal. Swimmers drowned, boats capsized, sport divers perished, sailboarders went out too far and failed to return, there were treacherous rip currents along the coast, sudden squalls, lost yachts and fishing boats. So bodies washed up now and then, but some were impossible to identify after many days or even weeks of immersion. They were badly decomposed, naturally, mutilated by fish, no longer human in aspect or contour. Captain Conforte now believed that Anton Arbaleste and Samantha Ridley were gone forever.

*　　*　　*

I went into a coffee shop for a giant take-out Styrofoam cup of cappuccino, and saw Martina sitting at a table with her new boyfriend, Ellis Slocombe, a successful painter of portraits in the style of John Singer Sargent. The portraits, Charles would probably say, were forgeries in every aspect but signature. You didn't know you were rich and prominent along the Gulf Coast unless you had a Slocombe portrait or two hanging on your wall. Martina did not see me. She knew I was there, standing at the counter, but she did not see me. Slocombe nodded. I thought, Slocombe, I could kill you if I wanted to, buddy. It's what I do. But I spared his life, and left the coffee shop unseen by Martina.

*　　*　　*

In October I took the examinations for the Florida State Bar, along with eleven other applicants. We were a mixed and motley bunch, male and female, black and white, sane and insane, none of whom would inspire the citizenry with much faith in the justice system. I believed I had done well in the essay, very poorly in the question-and-answer section.

"I'm sure I failed," I told Petrie.

"Good," he said. "The republic is saved for at least one more year."

*   *   *

After months of conflict and threats of litigation, Petrie and Chester Dalhart finally came to an agreement on the dispute over expenses. The money was distributed. Charles, now in London, was wired his share. Leroy Karpe bought a used Beechcraft airplane for several hundred thousand dollars. McNally and Cavaretta closed their detective agency and retired to lives of tedium. Both bought new houses, new cars, and took up golf. The entire group, despite advocacy by Petrie and me, refused to vote a small percentage to Penny. ("He's already a lord, ain't he?") The judge made a contribution to his university's building fund. I didn't know what to do with my share of the money. A lot remained after taxes. I thought that maybe I would buy a yacht, one as fine as *Avanti,* but the idea didn't excite me. It seemed that all of us were bored and a little depressed. We missed Castelnuovo. We missed the adrenal high of deception, risk, and crime. We missed the action.

*   *   *

I received a holiday card from Penny and Cassy (Lord and Lady Warfield), informing me that they had married and were now honeymooning in Bermuda.

*   *   *

A new character appeared in Martina's Sunday cartoon strip, a disreputable red fox with pointy teeth and low morals. His name was Don. I was told that he bore a certain resemblance to me. "Don—Dan," people said, "Hah, hah, hah." There were many carnivores and omnivores in Martina's strip, but until Don you never suspected that they feasted on the herbivores and insecrivores. But Don was a psychotic killer, the terror of the swamp and woodlands, and he wanted to eat all the gentle rabbits, chipmunks, and songbirds. Don was a criminal. Don was worse than a criminal—he sympathized with the developers and polluters.

"Don's you, all right," Petrie said, "especially around the eyes." The judge didn't see a clear character resemblance, but he admitted that there was something suspicious about the name. Candace thought Don was cute. Nestor Naranjo, the SA's chief prosecutor, told me that he was preparing to prosecute Don for various crimes and misdemeanors, including serial murder.

I wrote a note to Martina, complaining of injustice, and declaring that if her libels didn't cease I would kill and eat her. Signed, Don. She didn't reply.

FORTY-ONE

I received notice of the results of my law examination in February. Candace presented me with the official-looking envelope. She had taken to wearing very long false fingernails, painted taupe, and they made it awkward for her to do things like type and handle mail.

"Open it," she said.

"Later, Candace."

I went into my office and tossed the letter on my desk. It glowed, it dominated the room. I was sure that I badly failed the exam, but that would not be indisputably true until I opened the envelope and read the contents. Until then, I had passed; I was licensed to practice law in the State of Florida.

Judge Samuelson came into my office at noon. He immediately saw the envelope.

"You haven't opened it?"

"I'm denying reality."

"You're postponing realization."

Levi had completely recovered from his fatigue, declared himself as fit as when he was fifty, and lately seemed to regard himself as a rather dashing figure, an international player. He now wore his white hair in a pompadour, down to his collar, and had grown a gunfighter's mustache.

"Lunch?" he asked.

"Sure."

We ate corned beef sandwiches and cole slaw at a backstreet delicatessen. Levi told me several stories which illustrated how ingeniously he had participated in the conning of Anton Arbaleste.

Late that afternoon Petrie phoned my office and asked—commanded—me to meet him at a waterfront bar called Neptune's. It was touristy, fake nautical, with hanging fishnets and rusty harpoons and salvaged boat paraphernalia. It was the kind of place where waitresses gave you bowls of free peanuts and asked you to throw the shells on the floor. That, apparently, contributed to the ambiance.

Petrie was sitting at a table that looked out over the harbor and lighthouse. A TV carrying one of the cable news networks was glowing from a shelf in the corner. Armored vehicles were rolling down a dusty street. Tom had a liter stein of dark beer; I ordered a tonic with lime.

"Have you been following Martina's cartoon strip?"

"No," I said.

"You lie."

"So what?"

"You've noticed that Don is reforming?"

"Never. Don will never reform."

"He caught a sweet little bunny and wouldn't eat him."

"He wasn't hungry. He was saving Dilly for another time."

"Don is being rehabilitated by a new character, Artemis, a lovely female fox with long eyelashes and demure ways. Artemis is taming and mellowing the brute, teaching him compassion. That vixen is pulling Don's teeth, buddy, and it ain't pretty to watch."

"Christ."

"She's publicly emasculating our Don."

"I can't believe we're discussing a cartoon strip."

"But we are, and I'll tell you why. Martina is signaling you that she's open to a reconciliation."

"Maybe I don't want to reconcile."

"Sure you do."

"Maybe I'll write her another Don letter."

"No, you'll see her."

"Will I? I guess I might."

Petrie grinned. "Don hasn't got a chance, the poor bastard. Once he lived wild and free, knowing the rapture of chase and capture, meat and blood, but it won't be long before he's choking down wheat germ and changing diapers."

"I've had enough of this conversation."

"Then let's pursue another topic. The envelope. Remove the envelope from your inside jacket pocket. Remove it, tear it open, read the contents."

"What envelope?"

"The one containing notice from the Florida bar."

"How do you know about that?"

"Everyone knows."

"I'm sure I failed the exam, Tom."

"You can take the examination again. Show some guts, man. What would Don do?"

"Don would . . ." I got out the envelope, tore it

open, removed the letter, and read it. "I passed," I said. "I'm a fucking lawyer."

"Oh, woe, the standards are so low, the expectations so high. Congratulations. Now you got to buy me dinner."

"Okay."

"But not in this fake joint. I've got reservations at another fake joint, Le Bistro. It'll cost you plenty. But maybe I'll consider allowing you to sit second chair at Phil's trial next summer.

"I'm green as the grass."

"I didn't say I would allow you to participate. But just to appear at that trial should—what? *What?*"

I followed his glance. The TV in the corner was displaying the forged Degas. It was a shock to see that painting again. It was even more beautiful than I remembered, a masterpiece, and it hardly mattered that it had been painted by a forger named Carescu. Obviously Charles had stolen it from Arbaleste's empty villa at the same time he had collected the other paintings and drawings.

". . . not long ago discovered at a flea market in New Orleans . . ." a British-accented voice was saying.

I thought, Charles will never get away with it; but then an interior voice insisted, Yes, he will.

". . . estimated market value of between fifteen and twenty million pounds . . ."

Then Charles appeared on the screen, dressed in a pinstriped black suit, a gray vest, a club tie, and a bogus Legion d'Honneur ribbon in his lapel. The effort to project sincerity aged him ten years. "I care nothing about the money," he said, "everything about having this splendid painting returned to the world."

The television switched to other news.

"We'll have to kill him some day," Petrie said.

Martina was waiting at a table in Le Bistro. The restaurant tried to recreate the atmosphere and menu (but not the moderate prices) of a neighborhood French bistro.

I saw that Martina was not expecting me. Petrie had tricked both of us, yet she did not protest when I sat down.

"I don't dine with vulpines," Petrie said, and he turned and left the room.

Martina did not lose her composure. She hated scenes, and was now probably calculating whether I would cause a nasty scene if she got up and left.

The waitress—dressed as a naughty French housemaid—brought us menus and took our drink orders. Martina wanted a glass of wine; I asked for soda water with a lemon twist. She shot me a quick glance.

"I'm on the wagon until summer," I said. "Quit smoking, too."

She did not pat my head.

"How's Cerberus?" I asked.

"He misses you."

"I'll go out to see him."

"No, you won't."

One side of the menu was in French, the other side in English.

"I passed the bar exam," I said.

"Did you?"

"You've been seeing Ellis Slocombe."

"It's really none of your business who I see."

"True. Do you think Don and Artemis will eventually

get together?"

"It isn't likely."

The waitress arrived with her pad and pencil and long legs.

"I'll have the *lapin*," I said. The rabbit.

I turned to see if Martina would smile. I was pretty sure that if she smiled, I would be saying hello to Cerberus tonight.

CPSIA information can be obtained at www.ICGtesting.com
Printed in the USA
BVOW05s0920160414

350832BV00002B/2/P